WALL STREET
TO
FRANCE

WALL STREET
TO
FRANCE

RIANNA SHAIKH

Archway Publishing books may be ordered through booksellers or by contacting:

Archway Publishing
1663 Liberty Drive
Bloomington, IN 47403
www.archwaypublishing.com
1-(888)-242-5904

Because of the dynamic nature of the Internet, any web addresses or links contained in this book may have changed since publication and may no longer be valid. The views expressed in this work are solely those of the author and do not necessarily reflect the views of the publisher, and the publisher hereby disclaims any responsibility for them.

Any people depicted in stock imagery provided by Thinkstock are models, and such images are being used for illustrative purposes only. Certain stock imagery © Thinkstock.

This is a work of fiction. All of the characters, names, incidents, organizations, and dialogue in this novel are either the products of the author's imagination or are used fictitiously.

ISBN: 978-1-4808-1047-1 (sc)
ISBN: 978-1-4808-1049-5 (hc)
ISBN: 978-1-4808-1048-8 (e)

Library of Congress Control Number: 2014920131

Print information available on the last page.

Archway Publishing rev. date: 6/15/2015

"The best things in life are free. The second best things are very, very expensive."

—Coco Chanel

1

BOOK CLUB FOR THE ELITE

It was Tuesday, and I, Sophie Becks, had been invited to my best friend's house for a book club. A book club, of all things! I had never been a big reader. When I was young, my dearest mother had all sorts of clubs and such, but I always thought that they were pedantic and boring. Middle-aged women in pearls and fancy attire, sipping the finest wine money could buy. Though, it didn't sound quite as bad now that I was an adult with a friend like Jan.

Jan was an exceptional woman married to a billionaire Dutchman with no time to spare for her. She was the classiest woman you could ever meet. I had long been curious to meet her extensive list of social friends, and now, here was my chance. I thought I could definitely learn a lot from Jan and her elite Long Island friends. Jan was in her forties, and I was in my twenties, and our friendship had been signed and sealed at Barneys. We were wonderful friends, and got along better than Bonnie and Clyde. Sometimes she also served as my part-time mother.

When she'd called to invite me, she had said, "Darling, please be kind to these ladies. Remember they went through their young and single stage years and years ago." Which meant that they'd had more flings than rings at my age.

"I will certainly try," I'd said with a smirk.

Now I was hoping I wouldn't regret going, as these were women who could kill you with a kind-sounding word, or their wedding rings. No, seriously.

I sped down route 25A, past the private police present in every town on the north shore. I could never understand the reason for driving a Ferrari or Bugatti around here, as you really needed to keep close to the speed limit. Otherwise, a very attractive police officer would pull you over and gladly ticket you; well, ticket your husband, as we all know they are the suckers forking over the money. I did drive very fast at times, but at other times, I drove like an old person…from Florida. Of course, with the last name "Becks," the police here knew me as well as the salespeople at Van Cleef & Arpels. My father's Maybach drove like a speedboat in shallow water, practically levitating across the surface, and frankly I didn't want to get caught driving it, by the police or the old man. It was the trend on Long Island for anyone over forty-nine to drive a sports car. Every well-to-do, middle-aged citizen felt they must own a Bentley, Aston Martin, or a mini something that cost a quarter million dollars. Excellent.

I dialed my father's office to make sure he was working, as he was passionate about his over-the-hill crisis toys.

His airheaded assistant, who showed way too much cleavage, answered, "Miss Becks, your dad is very busy right now. Shall I put you through to his phone?"

"No, thank you, I'll see him later."

The women at my father's law firm were treacherous. I didn't mind them, but whenever he worked late, I wondered why my mother didn't lose the plot. If he was my husband, I'd enroll his behind in the local church for some evening charity events.

As I passed many a brick mansion on the private roads of Muttontown, I was intrigued by the show of wealth. Jan van der Loo had private security at her great big golden gates, and I'm sure that Ker, her husband, had placed alarms not only on the house but also on her perfectly sculpted behind. Ker was a Wall Street tycoon with great ambition and a spotless character. That was extremely rare. It was like finding the world's best-cut diamond and then realizing it also had perfect clarity.

As I stopped the car at their lion-guarded gates, Jan's security guard smiled at me.

"Hello, Mr. Winters," I said.

"Miss Becks, hello!" He always paused and smiled as if we were long-lost friends. "You're here for the book club?"

"Yes, I'm here to read, you know, books, with friends," I said, smiling.

Me read? Maybe *Vogue* but not the old stuffy books I'm sure those ladies were reading.

"Well enjoy," he said, as he opened the gates like a magician. All that was missing was his command of "Open Sesame."

"Yes, I hope to, but I'll have a shot of brandy if I start to get ridiculously bored."

He laughed and shook his head; he was probably wondering how such a young, pleasant woman had gotten messed up with these old scandalous housewives.

Driving up the private road to Jan's mansion took a little under five minutes. The Georgian mansion was beauty and perfection itself, and as if that wasn't quite enough to blow your mind, it was also nestled prettily on the shores of the Long Island

Sound. It was quite a life. Then again, if you had the chance to meet Jan, you'd see that she was indeed the classic epitome of rare refinement, minus, of course, her occasional affairs to fill in the blank gaps left by her husband. Jan was very kindhearted, and her spirit shone through like diamonds from Van Cleef. She made all the other housewives look common.

I parked my car at the circular, pine-lined driveway, with "Van der Loo" engraved in the blue Bahia marble in front of the mansion. I walked up the few marbled steps to the walnut front door, where Jan stood in a houndstooth suit and a pair of Chanel pumps to match. She wore a strand of pearls and diamonds and Barbie-pink lipstick that set off her dark-blonde hair.

"Darling, you are so beautiful," she said, fixing my collar and dusting my Polo-crested blazer. "Okay, honey, now no profanity please, sip slowly, and no beating or yelling at anyone if they insult you."

I smiled, "Oh God, Jan, then why did you invite me? You know I can be a riot!"

Me a riot? Never. I was very well-mannered. As a child, I had not only an etiquette teacher, but a mother who behaved as if she was once a kidnapped princess, who had grown into a stiff, uptight queen in a foreign land. Maybe if she really was an old abducted queen, I could return her to her former land and free myself from her completely.

Jan led me through hand-painted hallways with polished marble floors, crystal chandeliers, and art, made by Picasso himself. We walked into a library, fit for the president and his afternoon teatime with his mistress.

"Good afternoon, ladies," Jan introduced me. "This is my dear best friend, Sophie Becks!"

"Hello, ladies," I said politely. I then seated myself on a dark-blue Victorian chair, and Jan's maid handed me an old, hand-painted, gold-dipped teacup filled with English tea leaves along with a saucer.

"Thank you," I said to the maid.

Laid on fine rose china were petite French cakes, along with fruit tarts and tea sandwiches. Looking around at the refinement around me, and the fanciest of ladies in suits and pearls, I thought to myself, *Dear God, what the heck have I gotten into? We were probably going to be reading* Oh Where Is My Daddy Now?

Then an older Botoxed beauty in her Chanel tweeds stood up and announced, to my great shock, "We are reading *Fifty Shades of Grey*. Have you read that yet, Sophie?"

"Holy crap," I said, coughing. My profanity sounded absurd coming from this very formal library of a tea party room, but I was taken aback. I had thought we'd be reading about the Dalai Lama or orphans in a third world country, or something of that sort. But I had heard that this book contained explicit sexual details, like, "Darling, tie me to the bedpost, and give it to me like Julio Iglesias." Good gracious.

"Yes, we are discussing *Fifty*," said one of the ladies, holding up her Royal Albert teacup and saucer. "By the way, I'm Isabella."

Yes, a refined afternoon tea party discussion of sadomasochism. Made perfect sense, I thought.

Isabella wore a silk shantung pink blouse with a necktie and trousers to match. Her smile was like one of the angels painted on the ceiling of Jan's library, except those angels actually smiled. Her face needed its own translator. Another lady, Roxy, was in her fifties, dressed very proper for her age, and seemed to be wearing all the pearls she had ever owned.

"Sophie, dear, do you care to deliver?" asked Isabella.

"Pardon, deliver what?" I asked.

I wished I would have gulped some brandy out of the crystal bottle in the foyer on my way in.

"Deliver your thoughts on the book," Isabella replied.

I looked over at Jan, and she flushed the color of her pink lipstick. She opened her eyes wide at me, as if to say, "Don't you dare say anything profane!"

Oh great, I thought. "It's quite simple," I said. "Any woman who desires a touch in such a way that it defiles her is turned on by this book."

"Oh my, that's exciting," said Isabella. "Go on, dear."

"See, it's our nature as women to want respect, but we also crave crossing sexual—"

"Oh, that's lovely!" shouted Jan, hoping to cut me off mid-stream.

"Please let her continue," the woman in pearls interrupted.

Jan cleared her throat, wanting to move on to the next woman with boring thoughts and no firsthand experiences on the topic.

"Shall you, Becky, tell us your thoughts?" asked Jan.

"No, Jan, dear, do let Sophie finish."

I looked over at Jan and smiled. I'd never read the book, but I'd heard about the effect it had on women.

Like a true storyteller, I continued, "Housewives crave not only a physical, but a mental sexual touch. As we all know, your husbands are no help with this because they're never around. I mean, for God's sake, yes, they are the Bentleys and Ferraris of your lives, but your sexual needs and desires have been repressed for too long. This is especially true for housewives married to

Wall Street brokers, and you are all married to Wall Street men."
I then devoured my tea, pretending to have said too much.

"Oh my, Sophie, thank you for your enlightened speech,"
said Jan.

"Go on," one of the women said. "We have been married for
ages, and yes, our husbands are never there. Why do you think
I can't smile? Sure, it's Botox, but I am so *ecstatically* unhappy."

Uh oh, I'm destined to be a home wrecker, I thought, *but forgive
me: I just don't believe in matrimony, and these ladies only serve to
prove my point.*

"The bottom line, ladies, is simple," I said. "Sex is very important for your well-being, but married men don't do all that
they must for us. They value their accounts more than their
wives."

"Sophie, that's what I'm talking about; it's our lives," said
Roxy or Rosy or whatever her name was.

"Anyway, ladies, I must leave. I have some very important
things to address, the first one is making sure I don't ever marry
a Wall Street man, and another is a very important meeting I
have in the city." And I excused myself.

Jan chased me down the hallway. "Sophie, where are you
going?"

"I have to leave, Jan. I'm sorry, but this is just not my
thing, and I've got an appointment with a stockbroker in the
morning."

"How ironic! Darling, you just slammed Wall Street
men, no?"

"I don't want to marry one, but I can make money like one.
Then I can live like every woman in that room. You look like a
million dollars. Sure, you're all unhappy, but who cares?" I kissed

her on both cheeks, and she hugged me tightly. I wondered why she wasn't upset with me for my honesty.

"Darling, please call me later," she said.

"Will do." I kissed her on both cheeks again, as I dearly loved my friend, my Van der Loo.

"And darling, welcome to Wall Street," she said, gleaming with light.

And loneliness, I thought. *And more Van Cleef than a celebrity on the red carpet. Those women are what I never, ever want to be*, I said to myself as I walked out of her $10 million mansion.

On my way out, I saw a young, hot, sweaty man trimming the hedges lining the property. As I emerged from the door, he stopped what he was doing and glanced over. Jan quickly opened the walnut door wider and smiled and waved.

"My goodness, you must be the gardener," I said, looking around. "You do such a stellar job keeping these gardens immaculate!"

"Thanks," he replied, as he ran a rough, masculine hand through his dark, wavy hair. He was dressed in a ripped, dirty, white tee, washed-out jeans, and some sort of construction boots, looking like a model covered in strategic fake dirt on a photo shoot; and his smile was brighter than a camera flash.

I stood there smiling as he returned to trimming the hedges. I turned to stare and smirk at Jan. "How inappropriate, Jan. You'd better get back to your *Fifty Shades*."

Who am I to judge? I thought to myself. *A woman's gotta keep herself happy and busy.*

I got into the Maybach, turned on and turned up the Sirius XM, and stopped at the gates.

"Leaving already?" the guard asked with a smile.

"Yes, it was way too stuffy, and there were no strippers. Well, except the gardener. Is he really a gardener?" I asked. "I'm very concerned, as I want to make sure that guy doesn't trim the wrong hedge ..."

The guard laughed. "Miss Becks, you are a breath of fresh sea breeze." And I'm sure he meant it.

"See you around, Mr. Winters."

Mr. Winters smiled, and I'm sure he needed it, if those ladies were what he dealt with all day long.

As I passed the guard gate, a black Rolls-Royce pulled in next to me, with the phantom husband himself, Ker. I had great respect for him, and he was a good contact for me on Wall Street.

"My favorite Miss Sophie. How are you, my dear?"

Sitting in the driver's seat of the Maybach, I felt fine, but somehow simply saying "fine" wouldn't be enough. "Ker, how can I ever thank you for the opportunity of a lifetime?"

He gave me a half smile and placed his hand on the outside of the window. His golden band glistened on his finger, and I saw the agony in his eyes.

"Well, a thank you will suffice, but more than that, it made Jan happy."

What a sad moment. Jan being happy, yes, that was good. But Ker making Jan happy, probably not. In fact he hadn't been able to make her happy for a long time.

"Well, you two are a pair in paradise," I said sarcastically, waving my arm to take in the surroundings, but he didn't pick up on it.

"Yes, we are that and even more, anything to make her happy," he said.

"Well, hurry on in, because the perfect, timely book is

being read in your polished library room, and those ladies are exceptional."

I was lovely, I know.

"Make me proud, Sophie, and be the best broker you can," he said. "Remember that money isn't the root of all evil; it's the beginning of many choices." He pulled down the long winding road as if he was tormented by being such a success.

Just then, the gorgeous gardener was leaving the house, as well, in a black BMW. He was like the lucky bee on the most prized flower, paid to do his job and then some. With a wave and a smile, he buzzed down the driveway and out of sight. I wanted to sit down there and then and write a novel on how sad a story it was, when a man worshipped money more than his wife, but crap, I had to focus on making my own first million. And not just as a Wall Street broker, but a female Wall Street broker.

My drive home was brisk, and I parked the car carefully, as if it had never been moved. I had dinner plans with my family that night, and a conference with two new brokers at Chance Duren's firm the next day. I was exhausted already. And the worst part was, I never even got to read *Fifty Shades*. In truth, my own love life was only one shade…nonexistent. Sad, but true.

But right now, my focus was dinner and bed. My father's driver would be driving me into the city very early in the morning.

2

WALL STREET OR BUST

I rested well, and I was up early, dressed in a pantsuit, no tie, and no thong. Today was strictly all business.

At 5:45 a.m., I greeted my father's driver at the front door. My brother, Rain, was also up early, leaving for Manhattan. We were strangely alike in our work style and ethics, though I think we were closer when we were children.

"Rain," I said with a nod.

"Sophie," he nodded back. "You look sharp."

I stepped into the Lincoln limo, a gift that my father had whipped up for me. After all, I was on my way to a life of wealth, starting off clean as a whistle. Success was an integral part of the Becks genetics. Forget marital bliss and harmony; it didn't exist with my parents or with anyone else I knew that had anything.

Having a driver and a limo already at my disposal, you'd wonder why I wanted to be a broker. Well, I'd seen the movies, my friend's husband made a zillion-billion by investing others' money into stocks, and everyone I met or knew was stinking rich. All with just a little downside: they were a tad unhappy, but they could buy the *B* out of Barneys on a Sunday.

An hour or so later, I arrived at the offices of Chance Duren, and there was nothing shabby here, except the wannabes that wore suits from a store. I sat in a waiting room where the wood was cured better than bacon. My leather chair wasn't cow, but alligator, and the secretary even looked partially animal. She had lips like Angelina Jolie, except the rest of the Jolie must have gotten lost in the plastic surgeon's office.

Sitting in the waiting room, I found myself surrounded by men of distinction. Some were handsome, others were hot, and a few looked like they were ancient. Having done my research on the web, I knew that the senior brokers at this firm were highly attractive and impressive, not only for their Patek watches, but their waves of enthusiasm. And my new boss, Chance Duren, himself? He looked like a mixture of George Clooney and Richard Gere. Oh holy crap, how would I ever be able to focus on my job when I was surrounded by such good looks, money, and manners. Never did that come together in one man. Never.

We were led into a high tech conference room fit for special agents, and when Mr. Clooney/Gere himself walked in, I sat upright in my chair and tried not to drool.

"Welcome to Chance Duren. I'm Chance, and this is my company."

That was a beautiful name, and it was almost impossible to focus on his speech. I had wondered why all these polished, high-powered men always seemed to be in some tabloid or another, announcing, "I never cheated on my wife." The men on Wall Street were as sexy as they were arrogant.

Back to his big speech. Yes, he was Chance Duren, blah, blah.

Then, a man with a perfectly tailored suit, silk pocket square, and spit-shined alligator shoes (the more you make, the funkier your accessories, I guess) stood up and addressed us, "I'm Jaxwe, and I'm the top producer at Chance Duren. I will be training you until you pass your Series 7. You'll cold call until you get ten qualified leads; no breaks, no fucking crap talk, and, oh," he turned to me, "I'm sorry, are you here for the secretary position?" What a jackass.

"Are you speaking to me, Jax-weee?" I asked.

Everyone laughed. If I made half as much as this guy did, forget the alligator shoes, I'd immediately change my name to something less annoying.

"Yes, you, you are in the wrong place," he said very annoyed.

"I'm sorry you feel that way," I said, standing up in my custom suit with my silk, ruffled shirt and Chloé pumps. "I'm here to become a stockbroker and not just any stockbroker; I'm here for your title." He smiled as if I'd tickled his ego. "I'm Sophie Becks."

I looked at Chance Duren, on the side of the room next to the window, and saw him smile. It was a powerful moment. I think it was right then and there that I realized my need to punish men for their cockiness and lack of respect for women in custom suits and Yurman pearls.

Damn you idiots, I thought. *And besides, I probably need to touch up my lipstick.*

After that awkward encounter, awkward for Jaxwe, that is, I went to the phones. Cold call Switzerland? Sure!

"Good morning, I'm Sophie Becks from Chance Duren," I said into the phone.

"On Wall Street," added Jaxwe, buzzing in my ear.

After I hung up, he lectured me. "Sophie, you are too fucking kind to these people. This is not a charity event; this is Wall Street," he said.

"I'm sorry. I didn't think I needed to be rude," I retorted.

"I need a cigarette," Jaxwe said petulantly rolling his eyes, and walked out the back exit to have a smoke.

The guy was an ass, and I was a lady. Ladies and asses didn't belong together on Wall Street. The phone buzzed and it was Mr. Duren calling me into his glass office.

"Yes, Mr. Duren?" I asked, as I entered his office.

"Just call me Duren, Becks. Please sit down."

I sat down in front of his beautiful mahogany desk, and he reiterated many of the things Jaxwe had said, but in a kinder, more constructive way.

"So let's recap a little," I said. "One, I'm too kind and polite."

"Yes," he responded.

"Two, stop with the 'thank you so kindly.'"

"Yes," he said. "That's for your boyfriend."

Yeah, right, I thought.

"And three," he said, "lose the convent girl, 'Oh, I'm so sorry you lost your dog' crap, get manly, get mad." He certainly mimicked me well, as if I were too girly and polite to cold call. "Think leads, big accounts, and your first million."

And that I did. Walking out of Duren's office, I now had my head on straight. I watched as Jaxwe sat there yelling at his clients, with his spit-polished shoe on the desk, drinking some rubbish in a bottle. You should have seen the ingredients; my mother would have thrown him in an orphanage if he were her son. And honestly, I didn't know if I wanted to be a bloody man or woman, all I knew is that the filth of those greedy, hungry lunatics made me want to be better than them.

"Sophie, Sophie, I'm speaking to you! Get me some water and a cup of coffee," yelled Jaxwe.

I walked over to my desk and picked up the phone. I looked at the unsanitary, disgusting telephone receiver in my hands and put it to my ear. I fiddled slowly with the numbers. It was a bloody asylum. Jaxwe got out of his chair and pressed the button to disconnect my call.

"I told you I need coffee," he yelled five inches from my face, as if I was in Russia and getting paid to eat his kielbasa.

Then I had an epiphany. I couldn't do this, at least not like this. Sure, I was polite, I was raised that way, until of course, you pushed your finger on my ego one time too many. Yes, I needed this career, but not for the price of losing my mind. Crap, he was getting bitch-slapped pronto. For Pete's sake, the guy was not even a polished diamond; he was cubic zirconium, which I didn't have much respect for.

"Listen to me, you son of a bitch, don't you *ever* bloody speak to me like I'm your bitch, okay? You want frigging coffee? It's over there. You want water? It's over there, so politely help yourself."

Every single broker in the room stood up and applauded, and honestly I thought this would be where I got fired. But not on Wall Street; instead, this was my turning point. And guess what? Jaxwe was my bitch after that day.

My first day of training had been so brutal that I fell asleep in the back of the limo on my way home. Once home in Long Island, my father's driver, who was such a gentleman, walked me to my door, the price of success.

"Darling, how was your first day on Wall Street?" asked my father when I walked through the front door. "They didn't eat you alive, did they?"

"Not quite. It was like working in your office with high-paid lawyers who have more ego than I do shoes, etcetera."

He smiled, and put his jacket and keys in the foyer. I watched him as he made his way into the hallway and into his own personal asylum.

I knew that I could be brutal, but honestly I was a lady trying to make it on Wall Street, and I was thirsty for my very own success. I never wanted to be a housemaid or a designer or even a doctor, spending my entire life in a classroom, then working my way to being a specialist, only to make a few hundred thousand a year, with all that risk. I thought about being a lawyer, but since my father was already renowned in that field of gold, I couldn't possibly live up to his standards. So, I needed to make real money on my own. And after all these Wall Street wives I dined with, I felt privileged to get a front-row ticket to highly materialistic madness, with Bentleys and private invites to Bergdorf Goodman.

When I was born, the delivering doctor told my mother that I was going to fly with the elite and achieve beyond my wildest dreams. He surely forgot to tell my dear mommy the other part, that it would be the *crazy* elite. I was crazy to even think of diving into these waters, but the truth was, I was ready. It sort of reminded me of an interview that Chelsea Handler once did with Russell Brand.

"Russell, I heard you're a sex addict. What do you have to say about that?" she asked.

Russell responded, "It's bloody fun."

Yes, it wasn't so simple to desire diving in with the sharks, but I had it on my "to do" list.

"Miss Sophie, can I take your jacket?" asked Hannah, my housekeeper, who I hoped would never find the right man or, for that sake, any man, that might take her away from us.

"Please take my bag and my phone, Hannah, and bring some tea?" I said. I'd be lost without her empathy, her sympathy, and her services as my psychologist.

Interestingly, my first day of my new Wall Street career had been quite daunting and intimidating. It had been anything but simple, and truth was, I may have hung out with Jan and her Wall Street money much too much.

Early the next morning, I had a rebuttals meeting. I thought it'd be as easy as leisurely shopping at Barneys, but it turned out to be anything but easy. It was more like a one-of-a-kind sample sale at Hermes in Paris. I realized quickly that I needed to drop the manners and grasp the steel balls on my desk.

Duren called me into his office again. I was now officially one of the guys. No, he didn't circumcise me; he liberated me.

I would cold call for ten hours, get leads, and then study for three hours from my Series 7 book. I felt like a nun in a convent. When you were told, "You must start from the bottom up," that was not crap. No joke, if this was the bottom, I certainly couldn't wait to get to the top.

It was torture, but I didn't mind. I would get home at 11:15 p.m., and get up at 4:00 a.m., but I did it smiling. I'd never really smiled like this before, even though I was making no money and spent all my time studying, even while eating. I really had to thank my grandparents for the trust fund. At least I had the luxury of living in a wealthy home, and had a housekeeper who made me meals. However, my relationship with my parents was troubling. I was maybe a little emotionally challenged because of them.

The Series 7 book was big as my head, and at times I swore I needed someone to translate it all for me. It was like learning

Danish and French at the same time. I loved French. *Bonjour. Comment ça va?* Yes, exactly, but Danish, darling? I really wasn't interested in it. I read the chapters at least a million times. I had the greatest difficulty in the sections on math, options, and bonds. My anxiety levels rose until I began suffering from anxiety attacks. Anxiety, caffeine jitters, pressure to succeed, anything else? Surely, there weren't any frogs I was currently interested in, let alone a prince. Maybe a king would suffice? By the time I'd be done with becoming a stockbroker, my good manners and hard won refinement would surely have left me, and what was the use of a lady who didn't have those? But the pressure was on. I was finally becoming someone; someone who was blazing her own fine path; someone whom my mother wasn't taking a liking to.

I felt sorry for my mother. She watched me and saw how tiring my days were, and she truly thought I was forever lost to her and her image of what a daughter should grow up to be. I spent most of my time locked in a room, and the other half traveling back and forth into Manhattan. Maybe so, but at least I looked well put together. There's nothing worse than a woman working in an office and wearing party outfits. Seriously, what were those ladies thinking? Sexy and professional was like wearing a priest collar and a thong. Very unorthodox, and very unholy. My God, one's attire was everything. I was always well dressed at work, in suits with monogrammed collared shirts; appropriate all the time, around the clock. I definitely didn't have a multitude of custom suits and $20,000 watches, but I never looked as if I needed a blank check either, like some of the other folks.

On Thursdays, it was custom for the office to go to a close-by bar and have drinks together. I didn't want to go, but I tagged along because it was a custom and being present was important. I sat there listening to all of their problems: wife problems, girlfriend issues, work gossip, and mistress dilemmas. I was like the father confessor of the group. One time, as the bar band played some lost-love song, I decided that if I didn't become a successful broker, I would definitely become a psychologist.

Slowly, my male characteristics became emboldened. My newfound aggression wasn't from the new profession, but from the disappointment of my early life that had led me to feel so cornered and empty. I needed a great career in order to fill the inadequacies I'd felt my entire life. I didn't believe in marriage, *ever*; more so, after working on Wall Street and listening to all those men weep unhappily about their dilemmas. I was already messed up about relationships before I even got here, and now I was beginning to think that all men were not just dogs, but schizophrenic dogs. Seriously, they needed a different woman for each one of their moods.

Now I hung around men all day, and not only did I understand them, but I became one of them. Hours upon hours, I dialed and dialed and dialed. I pitched from here to England, to Australia, and China. I spoke to CEOs of major companies, business owners, and presidents of all sorts of businesses. My broker-dealer had meetings that injected great sales tactics and enthusiasm into every one of us. After all, enthusiasm sold! Truthfully, if you couldn't cold call, you should just quit. You either had it or you didn't. My new best line was, "I don't give a crap if your mother died; leave it all at the door." I vowed to say some more rosaries when I got time, which didn't look like anytime soon.

My first few months passed quickly, and soon I needed to

take my Series 7 exam. Jeez Louise, I was mentally exhausted from the pages of technical math, options, bonds, and so on. On my mirror I had taped pictures of everything to inspire me, from Bentleys to my dream house in the Hamptons on the ocean. A picture of Mother Mary was positioned right next to the expensive cars. I didn't know how I had become so materialistic and yet prayed so much; it didn't really make sense. But being twenty-four, I guess it didn't have to make sense yet. I just knew that I would be the one who would get ahead in life, and be the woman in the Aston Martin, wearing those big Dior shades.

3

POLO ANYONE?

Yet another day and another meeting. If anyone had told me that becoming a broker would mean rubbing elbows with high society, I would have gotten myself a whole new wardrobe; along with other things, of course. Today I was to meet Duren and my colleagues at his polo mansion in Mill Neck, where well-mannered, overconfident men in their best attire were never on their best behavior. It sounded intriguing to me, like a scene from *The Great Gatsby*. I loved Mill Neck, and Mill Neck and polo were like David Beckham and "Nacho" Figueras playing in the same arena, very rare.

Brokers at our firm were characters straight out of the film *Wall Street*. I simply had to learn how to adjust to this sort of life, and today was a trial run. Not bad this early in my career, sitting on Duren's expansive backyard deck, with some of the highest-paid men on Wall Street, sipping Long Island wine, and watching the sport of kings. My days of cold-calling anywhere and everywhere in Europe had been exhausting. Imagine that! Who knew that speaking to men day in and day out could make you so darn tired.

Sitting on the floor of my closet, I couldn't figure out what to wear. In seconds, I was slipping into a pair of skinny Valentino trousers, paired with a silk shirt and my lilac Jimmy Choos. Time was of the essence; I had to make this look work and get my face on in a matter of minutes, and when in doubt, stick to what you know.

I also knew that the polo event would turn into me listening to a few brokers babble about the prostitutes they had screwed the night before, while their poor wives were at home, drinking themselves into a stupor and watching *The Real Housewives of Beverly Hills*. If it were me, I'd wire my husband's money to another bank, change the codes on the gate, and invite my boy toy over, but that was just me.

Waltzing out of our Long Island chateau, I grabbed the keys to my father's Jag. The man had great taste, what could I say? And maybe even too much money to put in a bank in Switzerland. I knew nothing of Swiss bank accounts, but I loved Swiss chocolates. Swiss men, however, no comment. Not much experience on that side of the globe, which was fine with me. I liked my men smart, local, and with some class and brains. Add in a polo match, or simply being sweaty, sexy, and riding a horse, and it made me want you even more.

At the gates to Duren's mansion, I drove slowly down a very long tree-lined driveway, with shiny cars parked all the way to the mansion. This was clearly the boss's playground. Nice. As I closed the door to the Jag, I looked at the men smoking cigars on the marbled steps, posed like pretty boys waiting for anything in a skirt. I smiled. Thank God I wasn't wearing a skirt.

Within seconds, Duren walked into the foyer in a pink, buttoned Polo shirt, orange khakis with a belt that most men couldn't pull off, Gucci aviators, and Gucci loafers. Someone save me! This man gave me hot flashes at the young age of twenty-four.

"Hello, Duren," I said, shaking his hand.

"Sophie Becks, welcome to my polo mansion," he said.

"Polo mansion, not too shabby," I exclaimed.

He smiled, and it was like a handwritten note on Crane & Co. stationery. By the way, what the hell was a polo mansion anyway? I knew about having multiple mansions, but to make one exclusively for polo? Jeez! Thank goodness I wasn't married. I needed to Google Duren. He took extravagance to new levels.

"Hey, Becks, you couldn't get an appointment to a spa with the rest of the girls?" Jaxwe asked.

Jaxwe: annoying, decently dressed, sometimes at least, white teeth, dark-brown hair, freckles, and the highest-paid broker at Chance Duren. He was still bloody annoying, and for all the money he made, he was disappointing in the looks department. *And how sweet*, I thought sarcastically, *he actually cared about me going to a spa*.

"No, Jaxwe, you need it more than I," I responded.

All the guys laughed, but really they were worried. I was the first lady in their world of steel balls. Must be hard and lonely, those balls of steel.

Duren led us through his bachelor quarters, except he wasn't a bachelor. He was actually married. His wife was probably a beautiful eighteen-year-old that didn't even know how to use a bidet. As I walked the halls and admired the marble, which was the finest marble in all of Europe, I was shocked that anyone could make this much money legitimately. The place was very contemporary, and there was nothing feminine about it. The furniture in the rooms looked like children who had lost their mommies. The mansion was so cold and masculine, and had an enormous theater on the ground floor. Men did love their theaters.

We took an elevator to the third level, because for some reason, stockbrokers didn't walk and smoke at the same time. It was either one or the other. I didn't know if that was an occupational impairment from the ten cups of caffeine they drank per day, or simply that they couldn't be bothered to take the trouble to climb stairs. They also used profanity like I drank sparkling water, and their every thought was filled with ways to make millions doing nothing but getting their anger out on a poor old filthy rich guy in London or Switzerland. Yes, this was my kind of business.

Indeed, I was a lady, but rumor had it that one couldn't be a lady and make a quarter million a month. Jaxwe had said that I needed to, "Man up, dog." Whatever that meant. I'd need to call up P. Diddy for that, except I didn't know him. Yet.

We got out of the elevator, and Duren led us to a balcony overlooking the polo grounds. In my home we overlooked fields of trees and flowers, but on this side of the rocks, it was quite a bit more opulent.

"So, Becks, what can I get you?" Duren asked.

"Sparkling water, please." Everyone drank wine and I drank sparkling water. Typical.

Then bad boy Duren stood up and gave a toast. "A toast to all my brokers, and to Becks for making your first million. I haven't yet seen a woman make it; let's hope you have what it takes."

Let's hope? I would show this rich ass what I could do. Heck, I was a bloody Becks for crying out loud.

Duren walked to the edge of the stone balcony to watch the

polo match begin. I wanted to stomp him like a divot, but the truth was that I needed his training and discipline.

"Becks, why do you torment yourself like this?" asked Philippe. Philippe was a new broker, and what a sight he was. His look was very preppy, and he had blond hair, green eyes, and more poise than any woman. His idea of success was equivalent to Maseratis, Ferraris, and things that boys liked, but he had more morals than most men on Wall Street.

I was at a loss as to how to answer him, but just then Duren walked over.

"Enjoying the game?" he asked me.

"Yes, I live for polo. I used to play," I said, surprising him.

I couldn't quite understand the need for the polo match here, as the brokers were too involved with their cigars, wine, and the waitresses, who were fortunately clothed, as they brought out desserts from La Bonne Boulangerie. I must have been the only one sober and not dropping f-bombs like we were at war. And to make it worse, I was on a diet.

"Good, you should enjoy," Duren said. He then made his way to a group of men, laughing loudly and puffing the air with their cigars.

"I don't really understand Duren," I said to Philippe.

"There's not much to understand. He's very lonely for a man in his position," Philippe replied.

A half hour passed, and still no one was paying attention to the game. I focused on it; these guys were hotter than a day in August.

"Sophie, are you enjoying the game or the men?" Duren asked after making his way back over to me.

"It's hard to say," I replied. "I'm a fan of nice things."

"Then why don't I introduce you to the best players money can buy?"

"Sure," I nodded.

He led me to the back stairs and through floor-to-ceiling French doors. I was a woman with exquisite taste, so sure I wanted to meet his polo crew.

As we walked through the mansion, I noticed photographs on the walls from his vacations around the globe. I must have been lagging behind, because the next thing I noticed, he was grabbing me and slowly pulling me toward him. Our eyes met, and my heart beat out of my chest.

"I'm so sorry, I was…" I stuttered.

"It's okay, there's a lot to see," Duren whispered with a smile. His mouth wasn't on mine, he was simply speaking; but it felt like he had just entered my being. He was not just a handsome face with exquisite taste in things. He was refined, and though he ran a Wall Street playground, he seemed whole and grounded; he was never flirty with the young, plastic girls that appeared everywhere in his upscale social scene.

As we approached the field, I stood beside him, and I looked up to see the other brokers, stuck together like scales of a fish, in deep conversation. The polo players were dismounting from their horses, greeting Duren as if he were the prince of Saudi Arabia. I shook hands with them all, and, as luck would have it, one of the players was Chaz, who I'd known from my old polo club in Muttontown.

"Sophie Becks, so pleased to meet your acquaintance again," Chaz said.

"Yes, same here," I responded with a smile.

"You know each other?" asked Duren.

"Yes, we played polo together years ago," I replied. "Except now he's a pro, and I'm, well, not a pro." But I was still in love with polo.

Chaz was just another Long Island guy that didn't care to make something big out of his life, similar to my other brother, Robin.

"Good game," I said to Chaz. "I see you've improved quite a bit."

"Yes, I'm all in now; it's my whole life. Well, see you around, Sophie, and, Mr. Duren, thank you for the game." Duren nodded. He was *the man*. I wasn't sure what type of man, but he was *the* man.

I stepped on the divots, glad that my heels weren't sinking into the grass. Duren watched and smiled, sipping his red wine.

"I have no life," I said smiling.

"Not true. At least, that's not what I heard," Duren said.

"I beg your pardon? Spill, young man," I said cheekily. I spoke to him as if I'd known him forever.

"Well, Ker only had good things to say about you. He said that you and his wife were best friends."

"We are. I think that's why I landed in your territory," I replied.

Suddenly, Duren became silent, as his eyes glared at something behind me. I turned around to see a lady of equal parts great beauty and great rage storming towards us. Their eyes locked, and he looked furious to see her.

"Chance, honey, is it possible I can have a moment with you?" She was clearly pissed off, and the words spit out of her mouth like snakebites.

"Not now. Can't you see I'm in the middle of a brokers' conference. I'll see you at home later."

"Conference? This is a conference? I can't believe you and your stupid…" she said, pointing at me.

"Enough," he responded, cutting her off.

She stood there with her Hermès bag and Manolo shoes and stared at me rudely.

In my head, I thought, *If you are gonna look at me like I stole your husband, at least get the new Hermès. That one is from a collection two years ago.*

"This is Sophie Becks; she's one of the brokers at my company."

"Then hello and good-bye. I'll see you at home," she said, storming off through the mansion.

Oh please, I thought, *just go home to your other mansion, and your housekeepers, and your pool guy.*

"Wow, what great communication skills! If this is what a Wall Street marriage looks like, I'd rather shop at Barneys all day."

"Sorry about that. I just can't understand my wife sometimes; she's too much."

"You're not the only one. Men don't understand anything about a woman, but the body parts." I smiled.

He smiled and then laughed. Grabbing a golf ball that had been lying on the field, he held it up at eye level.

"When you see this, what do you think?" he asked.

I began laughing, simply because I'd always thought that golf balls were like a man's balls.

"What kind of question is that?" I asked him with a smile.

"Your mind's in the gutter, Becks. Take it out of the gutter, and answer the question." He had become serious all of a sudden. I couldn't understand him for the life of me.

I tried again, "Well, I see the damage it can do if you throw it fast enough."

His face lit up as if pleasantly surprised that I was not just a pretty face. "Not bad." He replied. "In fact it's the same concept."

"Meaning?"

"Meaning that in this business, with a little ambition, you can get further than most," Duren stated as matter-of-fact.

"Hmm, interesting that you would say that."

"I've been successful at what I do because I'm smart about it. I'm good at it too, naturally," Duren continued.

"And you are not as committed to your wife as you are to work," I added. Duren was struck by my obvious statement.

He cleared his throat, paused, and continued, "And looking at you, I see a strong work ethic beneath your demure demeanor." He glanced back at the house and squinted, as the sun began to fade in the distance. "You can be a success at this if you truly want it. But, you can never have this kind of success and be happily married."

In movies about Wall Street, the bosses always had so much less than Duren, but were far cockier. Duren was the opposite of the norm; I don't think he was fazed by anything, surely not by his wife. It goes to show you that money couldn't save a marriage, or make you love a woman as much you loved your work. None of these men cared for their wives as much as they did for success. If only women were more like them. But then, what would that world look like?

From behind me, I heard Jaxwe's voice as he approached, "What's the conversation about, boss?"

"Jaxwe, it looks like we may have a winner on board," Duren said. "I estimate that she'll get to your level in less than six months." He handed me the golf ball and walked away from us. "Meet me in the library in ten minutes everyone," he announced loudly, so everyone could hear him.

Holding the little golf ball in my hand and watching him disappear into the house, I felt lost; lost in the mind of Duren. Who was he really? I was seeing him more clearly now, from a much deeper angle.

"He's married, Becks, and Wall Street isn't the place to find fucking love," Jaxwe commented, watching me carefully.

I looked at Jaxwe. I didn't know how he had become the best broker here, but I knew that I was about to make his success look minuscule.

"Jaxwe, get a therapist," I said dismissively, as I walked into the library to meet the other brokers. I glanced behind me once, and saw Jaxwe studying my behind. *He should be studying other parts of me*, I thought, *because only time will tell who will fail and be replaced.* I was not going to let anyone or anything get the best of me.

In the enormous library, filled with books that I'd never seen before, or cared to see, all of the brokers sat in leather chairs. Duren's hands were in his pockets, and he pretended not to see me walk in.

"Shall we begin?" he asked us. Surely this was more civilized than most meetings on Wall Street.

After a few points of business, Duren was about to ask a question when my phone buzzed with a text from Jan, and I replied, "I'm busy."

She responded, "With your imaginary man?"

I laughed, and Duren looked over at me.

"Becks, do you care to share?"

"My apologies. Someone texted me and I needed to respond."

"I can see that. When we were on the polo fields and my wife walked up, what did I say to her?"

This was another side of Duren, the coldhearted side.

"You said you were busy and you'd see her later, correct?" I said.

"Correct."

I didn't want to interrupt his high, but it wasn't my fault that he was so bloody obsessed with work and money and had a disaster of a marriage. I smiled and tried not to laugh my ass off.

"Why is that funny?" he asked.

"I don't wish to respond further."

He was clearly intrigued, and the other brokers obviously thought I belonged working at a bakery or a florist. But I thought it was all baloney and so damn funny.

"Go on, Becks," he said.

"No, I'll pass really."

"Go on, let's hear it," he insisted, his anger growing in intensity.

Everyone was silent, and I walked to the front of the library, as boldly as I could. Yes, I was sexist, and I hated men and their half-morals. Did they really want to hear about it?

"Okay, where would you like me to begin, Mr. Duren?"

"Why did you think the conversation with my wife was so funny?"

I stood there beside him, poised and calm, and stared into his captivating blue-green eyes.

"I think you are funny, smart, sort of hot…sort of," I began.

Everyone oohed and whistled.

"I think that men like you are too obsessed with money

and accounts," I continued, "and your own crap; it's like a new cologne I'm smelling." I fidgeted a bit.

"Then why become one of us?" he asked. Did he really want to know?

"Well," I responded. "I was born with overachievement in my DNA, and with all of my boyfriends, the next one was always better than the last. And, my mother thinks that I'll never amount to more than a shopaholic who marries some billionaire that I have to screw once a week to get a nice bank account."

Duren let out a real, deep laugh. It was probably the only real laugh he'd had in years, practically orgasmic.

"And one more thing, if I may add," I said, staring at my Jimmy Choos and pacing the front of the room with my hands tucked into the pockets of my silk trousers. "I want to beat your brokers at their own game, and make them look like kindergarteners. That's really why I'm here, to be so stinking good at this; to be the one woman that's truly made it." I must have been drunk on sparkling water. Was that even possible?

Duren was beside himself that I could not only speak my mind without editing my thoughts, but also look into his pretty eyes and let him taste my fury. He cleared his throat, and half smiled with a serious look in his eyes.

"Then let's see what you're made of. Okay, end of meeting," he said challengingly.

Duren looked at me as I followed the rest of the brokers out. I didn't know how to make any sense of what had just happened, but it felt empowering. Now I had to really prove myself, and I would do it or die trying.

4

LAVENDER VICTORIAN BATH

It was Saturday morning, and my drapes were still closed, though I could hear the sound of the rain pouring heavily on the doors of my bedroom balcony.

My eldest brother, Rain, "the great success" of the family, had a lovely, tranquil apartment in Manhattan, which he could escape to whenever he pleased. He made millions of dollars a year selling something my father was not pleased with. Bully for him, I was not impressed. I guess that's one of the things I had in common with my father. No matter what one achieves, they could've done better. Good enough is never enough.

The loud sounds of Chopin echoed throughout my bedroom, as my alarm sounded. *Good choice of alarm*, I thought to myself. *I'll never tire of that beauty.* As I turned off my heavenly alarm, I sighed, *I wish I were that talented.*

Looking around the room, I spotted my things scattered everywhere across my bedroom and floor; my Dolce pumps were by the door, my Valentino red dress was draped over the sofa, and my Chanel earrings askew on my night table. Now where was the button I pressed when I needed my housekeeper? Ah, life in Brookville.

Today I really needed to sit in the study in my home and study for a bazzilion hours.

Did I need to finish college to do this all over the right way? It was torture. I mean, couldn't they just sell a Series 7 at Barneys? I'd always hated those books that made you smart, and tests, and such. And surprise, I didn't graduate from Yale. To be truthful, I never had hopes that high.

I lay in bed a while longer, lazily lost in the beautiful painting on the wall, covered in my downy white comforter pulled up to my shoulders. Resignedly, I reached over and grabbed my book off the night table and opened it, yawning as if I hadn't just slept for ten hours straight. By the time I turned to the page on options, I needed something fried or dipped in milk chocolate. I swear, I'd better read this book fast, or I was clearly going to be fat by the time I was done with it.

There was a knock on the door, and Hannah, our fabulous and much-needed housekeeper, brought up my breakfast.

"Wake up, Sophie," she said, cheerily. "My dear, how do you read in the dark, like that? Wouldn't it be easier at a table?"

I tried very hard to roll out of bed, wearing just my tee shirt and shorts, with my glasses on, and my hair tossed like a salad. I slipped into my monogrammed, velvety loafers and opened the door to my balcony. There were always birds outside my window. Poor birds, they were probably tired of me by now. But I was lucky to have the birds visit me at times, God knows that no one else did.

I sat out on the balcony at my bistro table and had breakfast looking at my cell phone. So many texts, and I didn't even have a personal life. It was all business. Business! Gosh, I had lost all desire to date at all at this point. I mean, it's not like anyone was interested in me either right now. I was too private a person to be the delight of men, who were too into themselves and their wealth. Men, to me, were like caged gorillas, and I was never a fan of the zoo, so gorillas weren't in my plan. I ran great distances to be alone, and I certainly didn't want to end up like Duren's wife and all the others. Though, in truth, his wife was stunning; long legged, fit, she probably did Pilates all day. But let's be real, her diet also likely consisted entirely of plain greens and grilled salmon. Yuck.

I believed that I was destined to be a lonely success story. No love, no marriage, no friends except for Jan, well Jan had many different personalities, so maybe that counts for a few friends in one. Eating my poached eggs and sipping on tea with natural calorie-free sugar, I tossed my scone to the birds. My god, I love toasted things with butter, but after Duren's polo match, and the desserts from Boulangerie, I figured I'd better start eating healthier.

Halfway through breakfast, Rain joined me; my overachieving, very good looking big brother, with a little black book the size of the Series 7.

"Rain, Rain, Rain," I sang annoyingly. "Why the hell would your mother call you that, dude? I mean you could have been Tom, or Randy, or something normal," I smiled, teasing him.

"Well why did she call you Sophie? You don't look like a Sophia Loren, not that there's anyone around to notice," he retorted.

"That would be very hurtful, if only I had feelings," I replied sardonically.

I sipped on my chamomile tea as Rain sipped from his mug of Starbucks coffee, gazing outward to the many acres at the back of our home. It was lonely living on five acres of land with no company. My parents were almost always gone, or to be more precise, my mother was always gone. She had a life of her own that couldn't be traced, even by the FBI, but she had a list of friends that were categorized as the "must know" of the world. Traveling the globe, living the life of the Rockefellers, and sadly, my parents were terribly, unhappily married. My father was like most men, sadly incapable of any real communication with my mother. He could make a brief call or leave a profane voice message, my mother always complained, but that was it. Now, I imagined, after many years of marriage, it is what it is.

Not only was I surrounded by land, I was surrounded by neighbors I never knew. From a great distance you could just make out my neighbor screaming to her nanny or helper, or maybe it was her pool guy; in this neighborhood, pool guys start work very early. I would always laugh, and promise myself never to become like those ladies. All that I saw, most of the time, were cars, that's why I am so darn good at identifying cars. My neighbor around the corner drove a Ferrari. He always smiled and waved as he went by. I see he finally got with the celebrity shades program, his next step would probably be a hair transplant.

"So what's on your agenda today, Soph?" asked Rain.

"I've been trying to study and get this done with, you know." No, Rain couldn't know a darn thing.

"Hire a tutor! That's what every other not-so-smart person does..."

"Well, you'd know a lot about that type, Rain, after all you've had so many of them!"

My brother took his newspaper and bopped me on the head

with it. I grabbed my remaining poached egg and dropped it on his white pants.

"What self-respecting man wears white pants?" I teased him, jumping up and running out of my room.

It was on! Rain chased me down the stairs, out the back French doors, and into the garden and onto the tennis court. We were like kids, except grown ones.

"Sophie, you are so crap!" he yelled.

"I know you are, but what am I?" I exclaimed, as I ran fast, zig-zagging across the court. I was out of practice and I needed to catch my breath.

Hannah dusted the mats on the balcony, as she watched us.

"You little children, should I change your diapers?" she called out, laughing. Hannah was always so very thoughtful and appropriate. But diapers?

"Please do, Hannah! Sophie will surely need one when I'm done," Rain retorted.

I ran down the hill and into some goddam, bloody friggin' hole. My foot was stuck in a rabbit's hole. Holy crap.

I fell flat on my belly with my hands and face buried in the mud. My face was filthy, my glasses were cracked, and above all, the bathrobe that I stole from my father's bath, was now in ruins. Rain, my idiot of a brother, just stood there, looking at me. His hands ran through his dark brown hair, and as I looked up, all I could see was his watch glittering in the morning sun.

"Rain, do something," I cried out.

"You look like a pig in mud," he taunted jokingly. I grunted.

Hannah came running and I began to yell hysterically, "Rain, this is the appropriate time to show some bloody manners, get me up now!" But, true to form, my brother simply chose that time to check his emails.

Then, out of nowhere, and I mean nowhere, a man ran over to me and helped me up, as my stupid brother just stood there laughing. This strange man, simply lifted me up, carried me up the hill, and sat me on my mother's very expensive English trellis chair.

"Are you okay, miss?" the man asked.

"Am I - I don't know, my foots are broken," I whispered.

He struggled to conceal a laugh, as he grabbed my feet.

"Your foots look okay," he whispered.

"Oh good, 'cause I'm going to kill my brother," I replied.

As Hannah brought out an ice bucket and towels, you'd think Rain would finally show some sympathy, but no, never. Typical man.

"Soph," Rain began. "You are in good hands. I'm going to get going to Manhattan. Thomas, here, will look after you." And just like that, Rain was gone. What a sweetheart of a brother!

As dear Thomas wiped my feet clean and iced them, I suddenly felt embarrassed. My glasses were clean now, and I could see clearly that he was as handsome as any prince in a fairly tale. He was definitely no frog. Well, at least not yet. Often in the real world, they start out as princes and then they turn on you. First you think, oh my god, a bloody good man, and then, well you know what happens.

I was a mess, caked in mud and dirt, and wearing a filthy bathrobe and slippers. I had lived in this house forever, how come I didn't know this Thomas person? Was he the gardener? The pool guy? The dog walker? Oh, wait, we don't have dogs.

"Miss Sophie, will you be able to make it to your room?" a voice brought me back to earth.

"What? Did you say something, Hannah?" I asked. "I must have hit my head, as I'm clearly hearing things. Hannah, could you please take me to my room."

Hannah laughed and grabbed my hand. "Let's go, Miss Sophie."

OMG. What a moment! I was smitten, or maybe it was just a concussion. But as Hannah walked me to the back door, I looked back and waved. And Thomas waved back, smiling.

Hannah was a lifesaver, she drew me a bath with salts and lavender. For, in truth, a bath without lavender, was like summer without a Maserati.

I stepped into my Victorian bath, throwing the robe to the floor. As the water poured into my bath, the soap bubbles expanded and filled the tub. I loved bubble baths in old Victorian tubs. As I washed my hair and my face clean of all the gritty dirt that was everywhere, I swore to myself that Rain was going to get paid back, big time.

Dipping my head under the water, I could hear my phone ring and ring. I couldn't imagine who would be calling me now.

"For heaven's sake, I'm trying to bathe," I yelled. Surely no one heard me, but today clearly wasn't a cherry one for me.

After the fourth ring, I jumped out of my bath, white bubbles covering every body part.

"Hey Becks, it's Duren." An awkward silence ensued.

Finally, I responded, "Hello Duren, how are you?"

"Very well, how's the studying?"

Oh that's right! I was suppose to be studying until my brain cells all fried. Gosh, the things I must endure to become a Wall Street top producer.

"The truth is, I'm so impossibly tired from that bloody book, can't I just buy my 7?"

"Miss Becks," he said, trying hard to not laugh. "I'm afraid one must work hard to achieve success."

"Okay, thank you, Dalai Lama," I retorted. "That's pretty straight forward words of wisdom. Yes, I'll get on it as soon as I have completed my bubble bath." That is if no one else bothers me. Heck, it's hard to focus when there's so much going on.

"Well, if you need anything, just call, stay well."

Stay well? Is it my mind, or was that just weird. Like in, 'Sophie ...I need you darling.'

Getting back into my bath with the bubbles and warm smell of lavender, I knew I couldn't think of him in such an explicit way. Sexiness will get you anything and anywhere, but on Wall Street it will get you slammed with a lawsuit. I closed my eyes and began thinking more clearly. I breathed in deeply and felt more calm and collected. And then, the thought of my new hero came wandering through my mind. I would be lying if I said I wasn't thinking of Thomas. Tho-mas. Sigh.

Glancing at my Rolex, I realized it was time to suck it up and get back to studying. I needed to pass the exam and focus on the road to being better than Jaxwe, and as successfully forthright as Duren.

"Sophie?" Hannah peeked her head though the door of the bathroom.

"What now, Hannah?"

"Did I disturb you? It's your lunch, it's ready."

"What's for lunch and who made it?"

WALL STREET TO FRANCE

"It appears that Lona did, and it's grilled lamb, thumbelina carrots, glazed, I suppose, with salad of spinach and some spring things in there, plus…"

"Say no more, I'll die of hunger and grief if you do."

Hannah smiled and walked to my bedroom where I had papers, computers, and clothing everywhere. Hell, you'd think that I was living out of a suitcase.

"Sophie, do you suppose I can clean this mess up?"

Do I? I thought. "No thanks, and please don't have anyone bother me today, I have to study like mad."

"Alright. Have a good day, and your tea is in the teapot."

"Thank you, Hannah. Please close the door behind you."

Quickly washing my hair, I wrapped myself in another robe, and walked to my bedroom. In the corner of the room, I had a French antique table with two English arm chairs. Sitting alone with the tray and utensils, I ate lunch in the silence of the day. Thank goodness it was quiet. Lamb wasn't really my thing, but Lona had executed it very well. The spinach was raw and crunchy, the way I dislike it the most, but it wasn't as bad as having to pass a Series 7.

Everyone's expectations of me weighed heavily and, as time would have it, I wasn't getting any younger. I was soon to be twenty-five, isn't that almost half of my life gone? Yeesh!

Munching on my English platter of elegance, my palette felt exhausted by Lona's sad meals. For crying out loud, if I don't become successful as a stockbroker, I'll have to learn to cook, or even worse, find a husband. Sad. I pushed my plate aside, walked over to my secretarial green hand-painted desk, moved the woven back chair, sat down, and placed my Olivier glasses on. I so dreaded this book, the size of my family's brain. Nevertheless, a girl must keep on moving, and in this case, keep turning the pages of the book detailing the most successful career I'd ever dreamed of.

After an hour of my head engulfed in options with a capital "O," there was a knock at the door.

"Come in," I called out. "Mother, it's been a while."

"Dear Sophie, you look terrible. Must you refuse to take care of yourself, your hair, anything? Please do something." Yes, that was my mother. A very pleasant creature…when she's asleep. Could anything ever be right in her eyes? No, not ever.

"Anyways, mother, I'm studying for my Series 7, so please, I beg you, no more sarcasm."

"Sarcasm? Darling, this is serious, you are a young lady looking like an old hag from a bad film I'd seen years ago."

Sitting there, I contemplated all sorts of things that I couldn't dare to say to her. Luckily, I had other things to think about. Today I had met a man whom I had not known about previously, who was simply gorgeous, and seemed to have good moral character. That last bit was important to my family. What did I need? I needed someone to bring lust back into my life. God, if I kept this up, I'd be sixty years old and in the book club with Jan, reading *50 Shades of Grey*, and hoping that some professor would spank me in my Agent Provocateur.

"Anyways, darling, congrats on your, your, whatever it is you are doing."

"Yes, mother, my, my whatever it is I'm doing is called becoming a stockbroker."

"Oh, like those scandalous movies with the gorgeous men and bad behavior?"

"Yes, that's exactly what I need," I replied, "gorgeous men

around me in custom suits with shoes that cost more than my handbag."

"Do remember your morals and good breeding, darling, you are a lady and always, always remember that."

Breeding? What was I, a horse? Mummy dearest walked out of the room dressed like she was the queen of the land, and I? I was the lowly maid waiting for promotion to lady in waiting, or something like that.

Ugh, back to studying. It was so tiring, but soon many hours had passed when I'd fallen asleep at 2:00 am. It was a bitter, restless night.

5

MAKING ACQUAINTANCE

And Sunday was just as restless. I tried hard to study, but my thoughts kept returning to the mysterious Thomas.

By Monday, as morning dawned, so did the beginnings of a plan to get to know more about this man, even though I knew that the last thing I needed now was a man messing up my head; obviously, it was already messed up enough. I couldn't think clearly; all I thought about were stocks, bonds, and Thomas. I wished that Thomas was the one grading my 7. I'd pass with honors if a fling happened afterwards, but if the fling came first, though, he'd fail me. I always messed it up after three dates. I didn't do commitment or *forever* very well. Maybe I was scared, or had been dropped as a baby, but I shared the same genetic makeup as a man in that department.

Hannah walked into the kitchen. I knew I was simply a disaster to look at, but at least I had ambition.

"Hello, Miss Sophie, how are you today?" she asked.

I had hoped that Hannah hadn't discussed my little moment with Thomas to anyone, especially Rain. Rain was still on my crap list, and that was normal for him. He was always busy with one of his high-end fashion models. Sure they were beautiful, but did they have a brain cell to share among them?

I watched Hannah smiling as she handwashed the dishes. She always poached both my eggs perfectly at the same time. Well, she'd better get it right if she wanted to continue her employment here. Totally kidding! I loved Hannah; she was all around wonderful.

I hadn't seen Rain all day yesterday, and I was relieved.

"Miss Sophie, I see your friend," said Hannah, nodding out the window.

I placed my teacup on the pale-white, marble kitchen counter, and I peeked through the French glass pane to see Thomas carrying a box across the tennis court. My stomach spun in circles as I looked at him, with those guns of steel and buns that belonged to a model at Chippendales. I could barely take my eyes off of him. His crew of workers were not too bad either, but they couldn't hold a candle to him. He was pretty in a very masculine sort of way. He wore ripped jeans, a t-shirt with a blue hoodie, and those bad-boy boots, which, normally, I wasn't particularly a fan of. His hair was gelled up to the sky, and sure, it was a bit longer than most men, but his highlights were better than a blond right out of Fekkai. I didn't know Long Island could look this good scruffy.

Hannah stood up and walked behind me, peering closely at me without an invite. But forget the invite, she seemed to like what she saw too.

"Miss Sophie, are you staring at Mr. Thomas?" she said with a hint of a smile.

Looking away, I was embarrassed that I could be caught staring at a man with arms like that carrying a box of heavy things. Shame on me! And shame on Hannah.

"Oh, not even. I'm looking at the tennis court. I never realized all the money that my father has spent on this house."

What the heck was I to say? Something like: *I love the red roses in bloom alongside the tennis court? I didn't know that we had vine hedges around the tennis court? Or, I've been thinking I should take up tennis?*

"How kind of you to say such good things of your father, but I know you like what you see." And she pointed to the guns of steel.

God, this was *awkward*, but yes, I liked it all right. I turned away, holding the empty blue and white rose teacup like a new pair of designer shoes. I walked away slowly, pretending to hum the song that played on our intercom.

"Miss Sophie, the teacup?"

I looked at her, lost. I clearly couldn't think straight. Hannah gently grabbed the cup from my hands.

Well, now I felt stupid and filled with awkward things, like feelings. No, I didn't just say that. Oh my gosh, I must be suffering from the aftermath of hitting my head on the dirt floor. Scientifically, does that make sense?

I strolled down the hallway, which was plastered in the most delicate of flowers and moldings, towards the piano room, and took my phone out of my robe. I closed the door behind me and dialed Jan.

"Hello," said Jan's housekeeper.

"Hi, Jacqueline, it's Sophie. Is Jan available?" I said, filled with anxiety.

"Oh, darling, she's in the salon getting her nails done. Is this urgent?"

I thought, *Hell yes!* But, of course, I had to behave like a lady, composed and poised, so I replied, "Yes, it's quite urgent, I think."

"Okay, hold on, and I'll get her."

"Sophie, are you alive?" Jan asked.

"Really? Can a dead person talk?" I said laughing.

"In all honesty, that isn't funny."

"Jan, I think I have a concussion! Is it possible to hurt your head on dirt?" I asked, playing with keys on the piano, lost in fear and engulfed in anxiety. Feelings were really not my thing.

"Darling, if you have met a man, please let him not be married. I'm in the middle of a crisis here, and if you are in the same position, we will both surely drown."

"Huh, what? A married man? I'm not that kind of woman. A man is bad enough. Married man? No way am I doing that." I exhaled. Jan always calmed me down, and I figured she was older and wiser. At least, she knew men like she knew diamond rings. And cars. And refined everything.

"What crisis are you swimming through?" I asked her.

I sat there for almost an hour listening to her babble about emotions. Some were very intense and very misplaced, another reason that commitment seemed like Mars to me. I was going to need a shot of sparkling water and extra lemon. *Someone spike my water, please*, I thought.

After I hung up the phone, I tried to entertain myself by sitting at the piano and playing "Chopsticks." I didn't like to play the piano much. When I was younger, my mother thought I was going to be a pianist. My parents had a piano tutor come over at least five times per week. But music gave me peace; I listened to Beethoven, Mozart, and Bach profusely every day. I considered it musical meditation. It brought back memories of my life as a teenager.

"Hello, Sophie," a male voice appeared in the room.

I stood up, frantic and anxious. I should never again judge medicated women; I was beginning to think I needed something to calm me down. And what the polo, holy crap, it was "Sir" Thomas himself, here in my piano room.

"I knocked and no one answered, and I didn't know where to leave this," he said, holding a box.

"Didn't you see Hannah in the kitchen?" I asked, still unsure what was happening here. I wondered why Hannah would let him in, when I was looking as if I needed a blank check to get my ass together.

I took the box from him, and tossed my hair, acting as if I were in a business suit.

"Thank you, Thomas!"

As he walked away, he looked into my dark eyes and asked softly, "How's your foots?"

"My foots are working fine, thank you."

He smiled and walked away.

Blank mind and racing heart. I must be crazy...

I walked down the corridor, past my mother's perfect silk draperies on every window, and into the kitchen. I was pissed off as hell.

"Hannah, Hannah!" I called, and, of course, Hannah was nowhere to be seen.

I was fuming now, and it was already after nine in the morning.

"Crap, I have a meeting today with Duren," I whispered to myself.

I ran up the flight of stairs and called my driver. I then jumped into my large bedroom suite of a bathroom. I had thirty-five minutes to look like a million dollars. Doable.

At ten, my doorbell rang. I slipped my Polo blazer on and painted my lips peach. I brushed my brown wavy locks, and down the staircase I went.

"Hannah, I'll see you this evening, and by the way, thank you for sending Thomas into the piano room, so very thoughtful," I called out sarcastically.

"See you, Miss Sophie, and he insisted that he see you."

As I walked to the car, I locked eyes with Thomas, who waved. I was so nervous that I pretended to not really care. At this point, I figured that before my parents had left for Europe they had hired Thomas to do some things around our little mansion of a home. So my heart may as well go back to beating normally if this guy was only a handyman.

I stepped into the car and looked at my phone. My brother Robin, who had been away in Rome, had sent me a text. Truth be told, Robin was having major woman issues. He was six feet tall, with dark, curly hair and green eyes. He was very athletic and brilliant, but when it came to women, he was stupid as any man, high powered and all. He'd gone to the hardest-to-get-into schools on Long Island; luckily for him, Dad knew just about everyone.

I called him. "Robin, I totally miss you," I said.

"Sophie, what's going on over there? I really can't wait to get back!"

I paused. "Get back? What happened? Where's Dana?" Dana was his supposed girlfriend, soon to be fiancée. He had moved to Rome to follow her as she followed her dreams, and probably a billionaire oil driller. The girl had character, looks to kill, and a body like goodness on crack. My brother was a saint that looked like a football player. He was a genius when it came to his career, but he was not as driven as Rain.

"Well, um, Sophie, don't tell Mom and Dad, but we broke up."

"What the heck! Did that bitch break your heart?" I screamed at the top of my lungs. I was mad, at him and her. What bothered me most was that he was broken. The guy had been so in love that he'd left a well-paying position to follow his heart to Rome. Who did that? I'd go to Rome to visit St. Peter's Basilica or maybe the Sistine Chapel, but not to follow love. Well, maybe if he were out the ordinary, but I was getting ahead of myself. Remember, Thomas was just a handyman in tight jeans.

"No big deal. We can chat when you're back, which is?" I asked.

"Late tonight, at JFK," he said with no apparent emotion. "And, Sophie, don't tell Rain."

"I love you, kid," I said, and then I hung up.

My fairy godmother had just sent an affirmation that love was the equivalent of walking into a rose garden and searching for the most amazing bud, and then, after much searching, you picked the one your heart desired. You finally thought you got perfection, yay, hurray! But then boom, it was dead. I looked out the window, feeling incredibly sad, and I was never really sad.

As my driver pulled up to Wall Street, I powdered my face and glossed my peach lips.

"Right here is fine, thank you," I said.

He smiled, and in a strong Russian accent, said, "Have a very nice day!"

"You too."

The guard in the lobby greeted me. He looked exhausted from it all. His look to me seemed to say, "What the hell are you thinking being here?"

I reassured myself that I was one of those heartless bitches on Wall Street. I belonged here.

I placed my alligator Hermès on my desk, looked up at my fellow brokers, and said, "Good morning, bitches, time to kick ass!" Surely, I meant it to be a joke.

They all laughed and came over to my desk. But before I could do anything else, my dear Mr. Duren came over, looking fine in his black-and-blue pin-striped suit with suspenders and a pair of glasses I was sure he didn't need to see clearly.

"Sophie, you're late. In my office," said Duren.

The guys in great suits and watches that cost as much as a mortgage pretended to be too cool for phone time and watched as I walked behind Duren. I noticed how Duren's hair glistened, shiny dark blond. He was sexy and yet very coldhearted at times.

As I walked by them, the morons in the room mouthed, "Ooooh, someone's gonna get spanked."

"Whatever, guys," I responded.

Duren and I immediately went into his glass office, with a breathtaking view of Manhattan. My gosh, I sure hoped that I could have one of these sometime in this life.

"You were late, and you better have a good explanation," Duren said, as if this was news to me.

"Well, Mr. Duren," I began slowly, but matter-of-factly. "We had a robbery at our home this morning." Oh my God, what had happened to me? I actually lied to my boss.

"A robbery? I'm sorry. Is everyone okay?"

Okay? I thought. *We are all bloody fine; I just lost my mind.* I had to stop myself from laughing, so I thought of the worst thing that could happen to me: losing my walk-in closet.

The man was sympathetic, and for the first time I realized that he wasn't just an inartistic bastard who bathed in hundred-dollar bills and Dom Pèrignon. He had feelings. It was good to know that my lie brought out his emotional side.

I left his office and headed to the conference room for a production meeting, which in English meant handing out trophies to the top-producing brokers/maniacs at our firm; trophies I was sure that they put on the shelf next to their trophy wives. A trophy was exactly what I needed now. Well, after that robbery incident.

I went into the conference room with all the leading men in attendance, including those who took their jobs much too seriously.

"Donate some money to charity, Jaxwe," someone screamed out to him.

"Good morning, boys, Sophie," Duren said. Yes, I was the only lady in there. Wicked.

6

FIRST IMPRESSIONS LAST

Duren's speech was anything but demure, it was as arrogant as expected. I thought to myself, *We know you have more money than anyone…blah, blah. Ah, where's your lonely wife again?*

Okay, maybe I was just hungry. An hour into this stockbrokers' production meeting, and I was famished. For Pete's sake, I had had a cup of tea and poached eggs for breakfast, and now this meeting was cutting into my lunch at Cipriani. That was a no-no.

And, I was so very bored. I wasn't a stockbroker yet, but I'd already seen it all; the $5 million mansions with housekeepers, a sports car for every part of your personality, the wives' shoe closets, and the invisible, sexy mistresses. Gosh, spare me the crap. Working on Wall Street meant a life of luxury and play. On Wall Street there was a saying that all the boys adapted to quickly: "You work hard, you play hard." Well guess what? There was far more playing than dialing.

"Jaxwe, you have kicked ass this year! Who makes $159k in a month? Who the hell does that? I know: Jaxwe!" Duren was yelling Jaxwe's name like he was in bed with the guy. I wondered what Duren would give me if I opened a big account. Maybe his polo mansion with "Nacho" Figueras as my personal polo pro. Jeez, I needed to hurry up and make it big already.

Then to make this meeting even better, or worse, Jaxwe gave a speech. "Just think, Sophie Becks, top producer, in your dreams," Jaxwe laughed. So did everyone else.

I looked at my Cartier and smiled, interrupting his golden moment. "You have two months to feel like a supermodel, Jaxwe, 'cause I'm still gonna kick your ass."

Everyone looked around at me, shocked. *Yes, I'm just getting warmed up, big girls.* This business was bringing out the mad bitch in me. I wanted to shred that bastard to pieces and say, "What the hell? Fuck you, fuck your mama, and fuck this." Okay, not really; the f-word wasn't my thing.

Duren wrapped up the meeting, and I left the room. I went back to my desk and cold-called like someone on crack and coffee. Yes, we knew Jaxwe was talented and full of liquid gold. These men must have taken a class on cockiness. Yes, Cockiness 101, because this much cockiness simply wasn't an inborn trait. Heck, I was talented just to be the only woman in the room. Couldn't I get a trophy for that? Maybe the keys to one of his half-million-dollar custom wheels would suffice. Most of the time at work, I felt like a man. I wanted to be in their world, but I wanted to do it wearing pencil skirts and Prada Mary Janes.

Duren came over to my desk and whispered, "I must say you are getting pissed off, very good. You're taking your Series 7 next Thursday, right?"

"Of course," I said, smiling. While I fiddled with my pearl earrings, I thought, *Gosh, I am so flushed with anger right now. Flushed down a bidet! No, a toilet.* I was mad at Duren. It was like he knew all my trigger points.

"Sophie, are you okay?" It was another broker, Jarred, who inquired as he squeezed my hand.

"Good. Just f'ing lovely!"

Jarred was always very polished, dressed in a custom European suit, gold-brushed Cartier watch, a tie that he probably killed someone to get, good color from an island somewhere, and a little black book from Poland. Though he was black, all his women were Polish, just like his mom.

After that production meeting, I had to cold call for five hours straight. So I sat at my desk, and thought, *You really need to get on track and work for that Bentley, girl!* And one, two, three, I switched gears and made one of my brokers freaking rich.

It was the last call of the day that was the best.

"Can I speak to Mr. Dinaway?" I asked over the phone.

"Who is calling?" said a woman in a proper British accent.

"Sophie Becks, from New York City."

"What's this about, Miss Becks?"

"It's about humanity itself, and it's urgent!"

Of course I was full of BS, but if it worked right, you could get a long way on that. I got him on the line, and he chatted me up like a new found friend hoping for more, much more.

"Mr. Dinaway, I look forward to sending you info on our company and having my senior broker reach out to you later today," I said casually.

"Sophie, dear, anything for you."

"Cheers!" I said and then hung up my telephone.

I stood up from my cheap, black, ugly, spinning, merry-go-round chair, as if my behind didn't need some comfort after working alongside all these men, and crowed, "And that's how it's done, fellas!"

The guys looked at me, and were blown away like Venetian glass. One hundred leads in five hours. Even Jaxwe of Wall Street couldn't pull that off.

I put on my gold-buttoned, crested blazer and grabbed my Prada handbag. I saw Duren watching me through the glass walls of his office. There was no need for communication as I walked out of the office and lobby to the elevator. I pressed the down button on the elevator and went out to the first floor, through security. Voilà! I was in my limo. Well, it was Rain's, but I figured that after our last encounter, he was going to suffer where it hurt most, in his pocket.

I felt like a hotshot, high on caffeine; maybe too much caffeine. Luckily, the traffic on the Long Island Expressway wasn't too bad today. At 7:00 p.m. sharp, my limo spun into my driveway. The gates were open, which rarely happened unless my dad was having his lawyer friends over for poker night or some ridiculous meeting for all his hotshot junior lawyers. Whenever I saw them, I ran the other way.

As I rolled my window down, I saw Thomas rewiring the cameras at the front of the house. What the heck, 7:00 p.m. and still at work? He must not have a lady in his life.

"Sophie, hello," said Thomas.

"Hi, working late?" I replied.

"Yes, it's what I do best."

I rolled my window back up. I felt like inviting him in, not just into my kitchen, but into my heart. There was something about him. He had class about him. Even though I didn't know him, I felt so much for him. He wasn't a charity case, I could tell, but if he was, I'd get involved.

I tipped Vlad, the driver, as he opened my door and walked

me to my front door. Vlad handed me his card, and as I took it, I looked up to see Thomas staring at me.

"It's just a business card," I said to Thomas with a smile. Why on earth did I have to make that known to him? I didn't know.

Thomas climbed down a ladder and walked toward me. "It'd better be just business, as Rain asked me to keep an eye on you."

Protective and handsome, it felt like a good pairing, like cheese and grapes, or caviar and wine. I stared into his big, bright eyes, and my world flickered like the last light left on in the universe. What the hell? Earth to Sophie Becks.

With greasy hands, he sent Vlad back to his limo and opened the door for me. I must have totally forgot how to use my hands.

"Good night," he said.

I leaned on the door as it closed behind me. Could this be real? I wasn't totally heartless, but I was very scared of being like all those other women, alone and betrayed. I had made a point to myself to never be anyone's wife or mistress. Walking into the kitchen, I took a bottle of wine, maybe Rain's, from the refrigerator.

I poured myself a glass, and was about to take the first sip, just as someone screamed, "Sophie, don't!"

"What the—?" I exclaimed. "Rain, what's your problem?"

He grabbed the bottle and my glass out of my hands. "You are not drinking my wine." And he threw a tantrum as he left the kitchen.

"My goodness, it's only a little bottle of Screaming Eagle Cabernet. What is it, over two grand per bottle? You can afford it," I muttered. That boy needed a real woman.

Well, the wine thing didn't work out, so I brewed a cup of Darjeeling instead, steeped to perfection. I grabbed my mother's teacup, the finest you could buy, and poured myself tea, a little milk, and something organic. I then proceeded to the pantry, crossing my fingers that there would be something puffy and drizzled with dark chocolate.

"Dear God, please send me something pastry," I said as I opened the pantry.

There were biscuits from Belgium, Cadbury chocolates from London, and rusk, which was Indian. I grabbed the rusk, partially because I liked the exoticness of India, but also because it was a highly dip-able treat.

I sat there alone in the dim lights and ate my rusk, dipping it first into my tea. It wasn't from La Bonne Boulangerie, but it would work.

As luck would have it, Hannah soon walked into the room. "Can I fix you a meal, Miss Sophie?" She was so kind, if only all mothers were like her.

"No, I'm already full from tea and rusk, but thank you," I said. She was pleasant, and I was lonely. I didn't have many friends. I had Jan, but she was so much older than I was. Sometimes I just wanted a friend that was my age, not much of a party girl, not alcoholic, not the type that dressed like a prostitute, perhaps a professional. And my free time would never involve an elite Muttontown book club. See, that was why my friendship list was *très peu*.

"How was work today?" asked Hannah.

"Okay, though I'm very tired."

Hannah poured me some more tea. Even though I knew she was paid to be there, it was so much better than being alone. I sat on a fabric chair, sipping tea, and felt so tired I could have fallen asleep right there.

"Miss Sophie, do you need to lie down?"

"No, I'm fine, thanks."

I blankly scrolled through my phone and noticed a voice mail from Robin from earlier. I must have been too busy when it came in, and figured I'd just listen to it later. I pressed the play button and heard my brother's sad voice.

"Hey Soph, I'm at the airport." The background noise sounded busy and bustling. "Leave the door open, OK? I'll be there around 4:00 a.m. via town car. See you soon."

I deleted the message, thinking that I should have asked him to pick me up something at the Vatican. A holy rosary! If I had, my brother would have probably laughed and hung up on me.

I was too tired to walk up the staircase, so I headed down the corridor to the guest bedroom, which was at least five sizes bigger than my bedroom. As I slipped into that fluffy down bed, with goose pillows and all, I thought about how my mother would kill me if she saw me now. Shoes on her fine carpet, me on her imported down bed, maybe from Goose Land itself.

I looked up at the crystal chandelier hanging from the coffered ceiling and yelled for Hannah. She came in a jiffy, but I was too tired to talk. I signed to her with my hands to take my shoes and pants off.

"Miss Sophie, no bath?"

"No, I'm too tired," I mumbled. "So many meetings and calling."

And as she tucked me into bed, I couldn't say any more. I was talking for a living now, and I surely needed to learn another way to communicate.

"Poor goose!" I exclaimed to Hannah, sleepily.

"Good night, Miss Sophie."

"Bonsoir," I replied.

I felt as if I was in Paris at the Louvre. Oil paintings hung precisely on every wall. Then, in my fatigue, I realized where I had acquired such passion for the finery in life. My dearest mother knew true refinement far better than motherhood. I yawned, tossed the pillow over my head, and snored like a bear in hibernation. I was resting in opulence.

7
To Google or Not …

I slept like a princess in the wilderness of the down bed and comforter in the guest suite, but all night I had nightmares of Peter Rabbit and Aunt Jemima. Hmmm…what would dream interpreters say about me? Well, all I knew is that I would never sleep on down again. I felt as if I were sleeping on thousands of geese that had been martyred just so we could cover ourselves with their feathers.

Nevertheless, I was only about a week away from my 7 exam, and I needed to focus on being a success and not a mess. Truth be told, I was beginning to feel anxious and panicky. Not good. I think I needed to be on a wine therapy program. Drink wine and seek therapy. Though whenever I thought of my Series 7, all that came to mind was stress, anxiety, panic, and an extreme fear of failure. I was beginning to feel like a mess and more than a little psycho. But let's keep that to ourselves, shall we? I knew quite a lot about life, but I didn't know how to relax. However, if the pea brains I met every day could do it, so could I. Heck, if dumbass Jaxwe could be a Wall Street tycoon, I could own the moon. Well, we'll see how far that analogy got me.

I awoke in the middle of the night, and headed up to my

bedroom, my glasses sitting crookedly on my face. As I walked up the stairs, I looked like I'd gone bunny hopping all night. I walked into my bathroom, and reached above the hand-painted pedestal sink to open my medicine cabinet, helping myself to a caffeine pill. Why sleep? At this point, I was desperate and a caffeine pill could only help.

The not-so-funny part was that I ended up staring at one page for over an hour, or so it felt. Certainly, the caffeine pill had kicked in and slowed my ability to study. I wasn't the brightest star in this family to start with.

Suddenly, Hannah burst into my room, panicked and closing the door behind her. "Miss Sophie, we have a problem. I was up going to the bathroom and saw a strange dark car coming through the gate. Oh my God, who would that be? We are in great danger."

Great danger? Really, she does make such a big deal out of things. Whoever it was, maybe I could kidnap him and make him tutor me, I mused to myself.

"Hannah, it's 4:00 a.m.," I scolded. "Okay, okay." I sat up in my bed and fixed my glasses. I put on a pair of shorts lying next to the bed, inside out, and stood up. And then I promptly sat back down. "My gosh, never again will I take another pill."

"What did you take?"

"A water pill. No, not water, a caffeine pill."

You should have seen the look on her face, it was like "Honey, I Shrunk the Kids" or something. As we both tried to communicate with each other, I realized I wasn't getting anywhere, so I headed to the French doors to my balcony.

"You're going the wrong way!" Hannah screeched. "Apparently that water pill or whatever pill altered your thinking."

"I got this, Hannah." I said reassuringly. Confidently, I opened the door to my room, and the front door beeped as it opened.

"Sophie, you can't go out there! It's too dangerous!" Hannah pulled my hands back and closed the door. She then grabbed my phone and dialed Thomas.

I stood at the door wondering if I'd taken a caffeine pill or if, instead, I'd taken something hallucinatory, as this was now getting surreal. Were we really in any danger?

"Mr. Thomas, it's Hannah," she said into the phone. "We have a problem."

"Is Sophie all right? Did you call 911?" Thomas's voice was loud enough that I could hear it through the phone. I was now laughing so hard at the absurdity of this situation, that I was rolling on the floor. This pill had kicked in like nobody's business.

Hannah shushed me. "Please get a hold of yourself. Miss Sophie. This is an emergency." She sounded like a principal scolding a student.

"No, I didn't call them, I called you. You're closer," Hannah said urgently over the phone.

"What's going on?" Thomas asked.

"Please, some stranger is trying to enter our home," Hannah cried.

"I'll be right there," he said and then hung up.

There were cameras all around this place that he seemed to have been wiring forever. Shouldn't he have seen this burglar? I couldn't think straight. Obviously my brain took pure caffeine in the worst way possible. Now I began to feel like those brokers, head pounding, heart racing, high on an empty brain.

As I sat there laughing, the doorknob to my bedroom turned,

and Hannah grabbed one of my four-inch heels. "Stand back," she screamed, and as the door opened, she threw the high heel and hit poor Robin on the forehead.

"What the heck was that for?" he asked.

"Oh my good God, Mr. Robin, I'm so sorry!" Hannah ran to him and hugged him. "I'll go get you a cold pack."

As she left, Robin helped me get up from the floor and then sat down on the bed. "What the hell is going on?" he asked.

"It's a long story, but I totally forgot to mention to Hannah that you were coming. You look handsome, by the way," I said, giving him a hug.

As we sat there on the bed talking, Hannah brought a cold pack and placed it on Robin's head.

"Thanks, Hannah!" he said.

Then the front door opened again. I peeked out my window and saw two Jeeps full of men in the driveway. "OMG, we forgot to stop Thomas!"

"Oh!" Hannah ran to the door, where Thomas was standing in a long-sleeve Henley with sweatpants. It took a while for Hannah to communicate the proper information to him.

"Can I see Sophie?" he asked.

She stuttered, "Y-yes."

I wondered why he wanted to see me and why he had asked about me. I stood on the mezzanine, overlooking the grand foyer and crystal chandelier hanging twenty feet up.

"Hey, Thomas, all good?" I called down. What a pitiful moment. Romeo and Juliet had better moments. "Thanks for coming."

"It's not a problem. If you need me, call me."

I smiled and blushed. I couldn't believe that I was feeling the burn of his sensational eyes and awkward stare.

Robin stood by my door laughing, and whispered, "I love you, Thomas." I knew he had never imagined that I ever could fall for anyone. Maybe fall off the bed or something, but never in love.

"Thanks for looking out for my girl here, who is very single, by the way," Robin said.

"Hey, Robin, Welcome back. What a surprise." Then he looked at me and said, "So Sophie is single. That's good to know." I was fuming with embarrassment.

Thomas smiled, and he and Robin spoke briefly before Thomas left.

"Wow, Sophie, you are certainly digging our Mr. Thomas!" Robin said.

"Stop it. Let's get some sleep. I'm so tired, and I'm going to have to spend most of my nights awake and studying."

I went to my bed to try and get some sleep, but Robin wanted to catch up on everything that had happened on his travels. He crawled up onto the bed next to me, and proceeded to chatter like a kid at a slumber party. We used to do that a lot when we were kids. Sometimes we talked all night and never fell asleep until the morning. I loved both my brothers, but Robin was my absolute favorite. He had many issues with my parents, as he was always a radical kid with many differing views on things that were important to my father.

He was quite different from Rain, who was a horrible womanizer, with a penthouse on Central Park. I had no idea what was going on in Rain's life, nor could I care. Maybe he never cared much about me either. He seemed to have selective everything, selective emotions, hearing, and onward. Suffice to say, he only showed emotions with drop-dead gorgeous women with Ivy League educations, and not his own family. Some of the women he was involved with were even married. However, his work ethics were legendary, his achievements were astounding, and his bank account was like that of an Arabian oil driller. Maybe that was why women loved him.

I felt safe lying next to Robin. He always took care of me. He was content with his level of success. He was well off, but he had no need of skyline penthouses and a harem of Bentleys. Robin wanted the one thing that he didn't have, a woman to love him for him. He wanted old-school, mama-and-papa love, unconditionally. Well, *bonne chance, monsieur!* I hadn't seen that yet. Sure, our parents were still together, but I was sure our Hamptons home wasn't just for weekend vacations. My mother ran there often to get time away from us kids and my dear father. Maybe more to get away from him than us. My father could get a bit too intellectual, and he was so boringly level-headed. I couldn't imagine him being anything but logical. Sometimes I felt as if I didn't know enough to hold long conversations with him. He was austere and exceedingly smart, and I wondered if he didn't have a double life like one of those Bond guys.

My phone rang at ten in the morning, and I tried to find it with my eyes closed. After smacking Robin's head a few times, I found it.

"Darling, how's everything?" the person on the other end said.

"Who is this?" I replied groggily.

"It's your mother!"

How on earth did I forget the sound of my mother's voice? Lord, I would never be able to live down this moment.

"Oh, Mother," I said, sitting up in bed as if I was about to get scolded. I hit Robin on the back and shook his arm, but to no avail.

"Is everything all right?" she asked.

"Yes, clearly everything is lovely, like…ouch!" Robin had pinched me hard.

"Ouch? What's ouch?" my mother asked.

"Ouch, meaning great."

"Okay… how was your exam?"

"I'm taking it next week."

"Great, make us proud, darling. Your dad and I are going to be home on Sunday."

"Nice, see you then."

I was eager to hang up, but then she asked, "One more thing, how's Rain?"

"He's as rare as rain in winter!" I said sarcastically.

"My God, he's just like your dad. Another Becks man, working all the time."

Wow, I thought, *what a happy marriage; together for the family, together for our name's sake, together but not happily ever after.* In my family, we'd break our legs and arms before we screwed up anything associated with our last name. Seriously. That was my dad's anthem. I remember him always saying, "Our family's name is very important. Don't screw it up, children."

"Good-bye, my darling. Say hello to Hannah," my mother said.

I said good-bye, hung up the phone, and turned to Robin.

67

"Don't pinch me again. And what the heck are you going to do at home now that love has bitten you to rags?"

"I am going to get me a career and a penthouse and maybe a Ferrari," Robin replied. "I'll change my last name and just cruise on by." Robin was funny, but often in a sad way. The poor guy was lost.

"That's pitiful. You sound like Rain," I blurted out. I stood up and walked into my bathroom.

A few moments later, Hannah knocked on the bedroom door and called, "Miss Sophie, your morning tea."

Robin opened the door and said in an English accent, "Miss Hannah, the princess is busy scrubbing her ass, so I'll take the tea."

"You are so stupid," I called out from the bathroom. "My tea, please?" I said as I walked back into the room. I took the cup from Hannah. "Anyhow, I've got lots to do. I have to finish up my practice exams and check in with Duren. Thankfully, he's given me a few days off to study. So, Robin, I suggest you clean up your act and get with the Becks protocol, 'cause as I remember, our father thinks nothing of you, young man." And then I sipped on my long-brewed tea with lemon and honey cubes. It was to die for, especially after the fiasco of the caffeine pill.

"I don't know what I'll do," Robin replied. "All I know is that I have a lot of my own money, so I'll be fine, Soph."

"Your hardworking money or Gramp's trust-fund money?" I retorted.

Now Robin was back home and, like magic, he had a clean slate. My parents were going to lose their minds when they found out. Jeez Thelma and Louise, Robin was only twenty-nine. He had plenty of time to fix his life, and on the bright side, no phony bimbo to call his own. Yup, leave that one for Rain. My good fairy godmother had better turn Robin's sad love story around in less than three days, before my parents came home, as my dad would have his derrière toasted. Robin didn't even have a law degree to fall back on. Terrible in my father's eyes. The Becks household was about to get turbulent.

And Rain, well, he was going to love this. Robin and Rain were never best pals growing up. My dad had always wanted Rain to be a lawyer, but he owned his own small, but very successful securities company on Wall Street. Even so, Rain was the best thing to happen financially to our family. Robin, on the other hand, should have become a monk and moved to Tibet, writing twice a year, as my father never really understood him at all.

But enough of the Debbie Downer issues. Robin and I were going to cook dinner together as a welcome home. I didn't have any recipes, but fear not, I could Google like a pro. We decided to make grilled salmon and a green mesclun salad with some healthy flax oil and vinegar dressing.

As we began cooking, the fish on the grill began smoking up the backyard, Hannah panicked.

"Hannah, darling, we are flame broiling the salmon," I said.

"Well, whatever you're doing," she replied, "the fire department just called, checking in."

"Oh, okay. Robin, this crap is burning, you dumbass. Turn it."

"Sophie, you can't cook to save your life," he said, turning the fish.

We reluctantly finished grilling, and dinner was served à la carte. I sat with my fancy utensils and china with grilled salmon on my plate and salad. I couldn't really eat the salmon; it was burnt to a crisp. So instead, we toasted our sparkling water and sat there staring at the stars.

"So what's going on with your exam?" Robin asked me.

"Ah, studying and such. I have no life except for my job and this house." Maybe that was too much info, but heck, no one ever asked me any questions. "I have no social life. All I need is a Series 7 license, and then voilà, I'll be on my own, living it up."

"What do you call this then?" he asked, gesturing to their expensive home and lavish grounds.

"Just a warm-up, dude."

He grabbed and hugged me while laughing. As we both ate our green salad with vinaigrette, the back door opened. I could see the shadow of a male.

"Whoa, am I fuckin' seeing things, or are you back, Robin?" It was Rain, killing the moment, as usual.

"Hey, what's going on, big brother?" Robin asked, as Rain pulled up a chair and placed his polished Testoni shoes on the table.

Fixing his tie, Rain stared at Robin. Maliciously, he asked, "What's wrong? Your dreams of being married to that white trash didn't turn out well?"

I almost choked. I stood up, cleared my throat, and pointed my fork at Rain. Then all hell broke loose.

"Don't you talk about her like that, you ass. You've never had any respect for women, ever!" Robin yelled. Then he took his plate inside.

"Is it mandatory that you always, always treat him like you are so much better than him?" I asked Rain. Rain really did always have to kill any good moment.

"He's a failure, Soph. He's a fucking failure, and you know it." He towered over me and pointed his index finger at me.

"How dare you, you pig! You have no respect for anyone. He's right, you are an ass."

As I turned to walk away, he grabbed my arm and pulled me back. Robin came out of the kitchen in a rage.

"Don't you dare grab her like that. Didn't anyone teach you how to treat your sister? It's bad enough you can't treat your woman well," screamed Robin.

As Rain got ready to hit Robin, I couldn't believe that this was my family, my brothers. Robin yanked on Rain's collar, tearing the shirt as the gold buttons fell to the floor.

I put my plate down on the glass table and walked away. What was I to do? I didn't want to speak to anyone at that point. I went to my room, shut the door, and blocked it all out. I didn't have time for BS. I had an exam in a week that my life depended on.

Sure, it was normal for brothers to fight. But as far as Rain was concerned, we were all impoverished and could never measure up to him. He was that successful. With one successful sibling, it didn't matter if you graduated Yale; if you weren't like him, you were the sour grape in the bunch. I didn't want to be a grape or sour. Closing the door to my balcony, I began a few practice tests on options over and over and over.

8

BOOKWORM

Thursday morning came, and it was rainy and stormy. Wind rustled through the trees, and I stood in the kitchen thinking about what happened with Rain and Robin, and how I felt I was taking sides, which, of course, I was. Robin was the better brother, and Rain was the idiot who acted like a cold-blooded bully, with no emotions, and certainly no value for family. Good work ethic minus any other ethics. I sat down to let my tea leaves brew, as I poured some milk into my delicate English teacup. What a proper lady my mother was, everything in this home reflected her opulent taste and my father's blood and sweat. I didn't know at what point they had become so wealthy, but ever since my brothers and I were little, my father was always busy working.

I opened my laptop to check on Duren's e-mails. He sent at least two every day. Suddenly, the kitchen door flew open, and Rain walked in. He stood behind me breathing his thoughts at me, or so it felt. I pretended to be busy with my e-mails.

"I'm sorry, Soph. I am certainly not your best friend right now, but I'm still your bro—"

"My brother?" I exclaimed. "How can that be? You never care about me or Robin!"

I sipped my tea and closed my computer. I felt defeated after seeing the long list of things Duren suggested I do to prepare. Yes, read *The Art of War*, right after I strangled my brother for his lack of both emotional availability and the ability to understand he was being a dick with a bow tie.

I looked out at the gardens as the wind pushed around the almost-faded roses and the trees' orange leaves. It reminded me of how Rain treated me.

"I feel very unsure of how this conversation will go, but please understand, Soph, that it's just that I don't know exactly how to deal with him, that's all. He's such a screw-up. For God's sake, he's the opposite of me and *you*."

This is where I should sit down and pretend to be in detached calmness and at one with myself, but I was no Buddha.

"Well that's a great confession for a priest!" I screamed. "Maybe you should follow our parents and go to church and confess to Father Dickin!"

"He's not Father Dickin, he's Father Deakon," Rain replied calmly.

"What do you know? When was the last time you even went to church?" Silence hit us like a rock.

"Soph, what's your problem? Why do you always take sides with someone who stupidly screws up his life, for what, for love?" Rain asked.

"One day, you'll do something even more stupid than find love, and then you'll understand Robin." I said. I wasn't even sure what I meant, but what I did know is that Rain could never understand someone like Robin.

I left the room and walked down the hallway, trying to escape how I really felt about all of it. I opened the door to my father's pristine study and grabbed the key to his Porsche.

As I drove down the driveway, I heard Robin call out to me, "Living recklessly, I see!"

"Good morning, Robin. Your idiotic brother is once again cooking up breakfast for you. It must be revenge for fiddling his teenage girlfriend," I yelled back. When they were boys, Robin always stole Rain's girls, so that could explain some of the competitive blood between them.

I waved as I continued down the long driveway, passed through the gates, and flew down the back road as if I owned it. I rolled the windows down and looked at all the mansions in my neighborhood. It was old money, but it was the Beverly Hills of Long Island. It made you wonder if you lived next to Oprah; you'd never know.

I turned up the music in the Porsche. I was listening to Tarkan, some Arabic channel, maybe Turkish. Arabic music was anything but subtle.

I accidentally opened the glove compartment, and a paper flew out. There was probably information I didn't want to know on that paper. There were far too many secrets in this family. I crammed the paper back inside and slammed the compartment shut.

Speeding down 25A, my phone rang. I scrambled to answer it, but the number was unknown. I guessed it would probably be the landscaper or Duren.

"Hello, Sophie Becks speaking."

"Hey, Sophie, how are you?"

"Hi, who is this?"

"It's Thomas."

I grinned. What the heck was my problem? I hadn't the slightest clue. Then I saw bright police lights in my mirror.

"Gotta go. About to get a speeding ticket." I hung up and pulled over.

This big dude-looking police officer walked up to my car, and my heart raced. I didn't even know how many miles per hour I was going. Have you ever heard of someone going to jail for showing off? I thought, *Lord, save me*, as I made the sign of the cross.

"Sophie, what the hell is wrong with you? You are endangering yourself, young lady!" the officer scolded.

"Dude, really, is that the best you can do?" I grinned. I sighed in relief as I realized it was Joshy, Robin's best friend when they were kids.

"So how's Robin doing? It's been forever since I saw him. He's married, right?"

"Ah, nope, no girl. No wife, no kids, heck, not even a dog to call Benny."

Joshy laughed. He was all right looking, nothing to make him worth putting into a novel, though.

"Soph, you are a riot," he said as he touched my hand.

"Anyway, it was great seeing you, Joshy. Say hello to your dogs for me." I sped off back toward home. I looked into my rearview mirror, and he was texting. I was sure he was texting Robin. Either that, or one of his dogs ran away and his pet sitter was calling him to alarm him. See, he was a freak when it came to his dogs. Have you ever gone into a high-end department store and seen someone pushing a stroller with a dog in it? That was Joshy. Sad.

My phone rang again. "Hi, Sophie, it's Mr. Duren's new assistant, Beth. I'm calling to inform you that your Series 7 is scheduled for Wednesday."

"Unbelievable, a day earlier?"

"Is that going to be okay?" asked Beth. Her manners clearly weren't going to last long when she met with the other stockbrokers.

"Thank you, Beth. Now if you don't mind, I'm going to get back to my studies."

"Yes, Miss Becks, and good luck."

Yes, right, good luck. I needed to surround myself with Buddhas for the next week, sipping on serendipity tea from Tibetan mountains. God, how impossible this was!

I got out of my father's car and walked back toward the house, hoping that everyone would have gone their separate ways for the day, maybe for the week. Well, a year would be just fine for Rain, as I really couldn't care to see him for a while.

I tiptoed up the spiral back staircase to my bedroom, and then my phone rang, again.

"What was your problem? Getting pulled over by a cop?" Robin asked me.

"Really, can you believe Joshy is now a cop?" I said laughing. That wasn't polite, but really! "Please, for the law's sake, Joshy isn't a *real* cop; the guy is obviously just bored and wanted to say hi. Besides I'm very busy." I hung up. I knew Robin was pissed off that I wasn't responding rationally. Whatever.

In my bedroom, I undressed, slipped into a big T-shirt, and got under my puffy, non-down comforter. I closed my drapes via remote, pulled the covers over my head, rolled onto my stomach,

---

and slept for hours. Yes, my Series 7 was happening and it was coming early.

The loud sound of beeping awakened me, and I sat up feeling terribly scared. I was crumbled, petrified, very tired, and maybe more emotional than ever.

"Darling, it's your mother."

"Are you okay?"

"Yes and no," she exclaimed.

"What's the matter? Is Dad all right?"

"Yes, he's okay, but he's had a bit of an accident. I'm afraid we won't be home on Sunday."

"What type of accident?"

She hesitated and said, "I'll call later."

She hung up with no good-byes and no "I love you." There were never "I love yous," but this obviously wasn't good. I wondered what had happened. Could this day feel like fallen skies even more? It felt as if clouds were passing over me, each one darker than the last.

I was in such despair and panic when I remembered to call back Thomas.

"Hello, my dear Sophie," he said.

"Hi, how are you?"

"I'm great, sitting out east, hanging at the vineyard. Looking at the grapes."

"What vineyard?"

"My parents own a vineyard in Mattituck. Let's have dinner here tonight," he said.

"I don't know ... Well, I could use the company."

"Well, I'll pick you up at 7:09."

"7:09? Exactly? Not 7:08 or 7:10?" I said laughing.

"Nope. At precisely 7:09."

"Ok, yes, I'll expect you then," I said, smiling as if the moon had lit my heart.

How romantic. I didn't like romantic. But I, Sophie Becks, had temporarily forgotten the dark clouds scurrying over me. I was elated, overjoyed, ecstatic. After all the drama, there had better be some peace and all.

9

VINEYARDS

After hanging up the phone, I felt like Cinderella right before the ball, except she hadn't been invited and didn't have my walk-in closet. But nevertheless, the prince fell in love with her simply because she was adorned in natural beauty. Well, so I always thought.

As I walked into my closet, I turned the chandelier lights on, and sat on the pink velvet-tufted Louis VI armchair. I looked around, as I took my velvet loafers off and put my tired feet on my glass footstool. In another person's house, this closet could have been a living room or maybe a formal dining room.

My mind was racing, and I couldn't stay still in the chair. I started pacing the room, trying to figure out how I could be so discontent when everything in my life was straight out of a storybook tale. Sure, all the pieces were coming together in my life, but I felt so torn, like an important piece of paper that had been dropped into the wastebasket. I was really beginning to worry about my increasing train of negative thoughts. I grabbed my iPhone and looked through the dates, hoping I'd pass my 7 without having to take it eleven times or so. Then I checked my e-mails.

I went through my dress racks and decided I must be so utterly boring, as I had black dresses in every style and silhouette: lace, silk, with bows and frills, and more frills. I'm very particular that everything has to fit my voluptuous figure to perfection. The not-so-funny part was that I had two or three pairs of shoes in very bright colors, but I barely wore brightly-colored blouses or dresses.

I did wear bright-pink lipstick, though, to liven up my pout. You'd think I'd have a husband already with such amazing lips. Nah. I may be a man's temporary dream but not permanent wife material, as I could bankrupt a man in twenty-four hours. Anyway, I doubted that anyone could want me for such a long time as forever. And I felt the same, forever seemed too darn long and wintery. That explained why I loved Wall Street brokers, and never became a vet or a doctor, or something normal.

After forty-five minutes had passed, I grabbed a black, fitted, satin dress and held it up against me, staring at myself from all angles. I mean *all* angles. I was my very own Joan Rivers. I was highly critical of myself and didn't need anyone else to mouth how awkward blue and pink could be. I had a strong fashion sense, thanks to mommy dearest.

I glanced behind me and saw Rain standing by the door. I sighed deeply. *What now?* He just stared at me as if he was about to tell me my non-existent dog died.

"Soph," he began, "I know the last day or two haven't been the best, and I haven't always been the best brother..."

"And what? What now?" I exclaimed.

"Well, Dad isn't well, and I'm going to fly to England to see him."

I tried to remain cold, as my anger towards Rain had still not subsided. "You should let Robin go instead, as he's much more thoughtful and caring."

I couldn't bare my soul to him, so what the heck. There was a hole in me that couldn't be filled at that moment. I put my dress down and walked away, slamming the door to the closet behind me. That meant kiss my derrière. I walked into my bathroom and closed the door. As I stood alone, staring at my clear reflection in the mirror, I thought, *What a mess!* And on top of this, I had a date in less than two and a half hours. I broke down into silent tears. Of course I was worried about my father. I knew that something terrible must have happened.

I started a bubble bath in my Victorian tub, filling it almost to the brim. I needed to relax. Closing the 24-karat tap, I dropped my robe to the floor, and sank into an ecstasy of lavender bubbles with the scent of roses. Obviously I was lost in what I didn't know; what was the urgency of Rain leaving to England? My father's private jet would take Rain's lunatic self over the pond. God ever forbid that Rain had to travel with the rest of the world, like a commoner! He might not make it. I just wasn't feeling any empathy at all toward Rain these days.

As my mind worked its way through so many different thoughts and emotions, I lost complete track of time. An abrupt knock on the door had me jump out of the bath and throw on my robe.

"Miss Sophie, Mr. Rain has left, and Mr. Thomas said he's on his way."

"No way, Hannah! I'm so not ready."

I ran into my closet and only God knows how quickly I was ready. I slipped on stilettos and brushed my hair back, painted my lips peach, and sprayed myself lightly with something exotic.

"Is this a fruit? Smell me, Hannah?"

"Miss Sophie, you smell romantic. Maybe you've found love?"

"Good gracious, Hannah, that's TMI!"

"What's TMI?"

"Too much info," I replied with sarcasm. "Where's Robin?"

Before she could answer, I ran down the spiral staircase with a smile that I'd never had before. The doorbell chimed, and I stood at the door trying hard not to look so darn desperate to see him, but in truth, I was. I opened the door, and Thomas looked like a model from an ad I'd seen in a magazine.

"Hey, you, you look like one of those Real Housewives."

"I could be many things, but a real housewife, never." That's one way to break silence.

"Are you always this funny, Sophie Becks?" he replied, as we walked out the door.

Thomas opened the passenger door to his million-dollar-looking sports car. He has a million-dollar sports car? I sat there staring at him as he made his way to the driver's seat. I hadn't even noticed the yellow flower on his dashboard until he handed it to me. "For you, my princess!" he said.

"Oh God, please, Thomas, I'm far from that."

"I know," he quietly responded.

As we headed down the driveway, Robin sped through the opened gates in my dad's Porsche and almost crashed right into us. Thomas slammed on the brake and grabbed my hand. Robin rolled his window down and said, "Hey, man, what's going on?"

"Good evening, Robin. I'm taking your sister to dinner."

I was lost in the feeling of Thomas's hand holding mine; my heart beat like a bear running through the wilderness. Crap, was it supposed to beat this fast?

"Soph, all good?" asked Robin, eyeing Thomas's hand in mine.

"Yes, all good!" I replied.

"Well, have fun, and remember, don't fall in love. That crap just f's you up!"

We laughed, but Robin was dead serious. And if you doubted it, you could see it in Robin's face; he was already f'ed up.

Vineyards were beautiful and sophisticated in Long Island, but I wasn't a big drinker. Sure I liked a glass of wine now and then, and mostly imported water from France; but that was as fancy as I could get without getting too drunk.

"Do you drink wine?" Thomas asked.

"On occasion. I'm a shopaholic, mostly, not a wine drinker."

"I see you have exquisite taste and all. Certainly your entire family has that flare of elegance."

"Yes, is that what it's called, a flare of elegance? Not bad. Are you sure you're not a writer?"

"Nah, I'm a few things, but not a writer."

A few minutes later, we pulled into a vineyard that his family clearly owned. Their last name was plastered on the sign and on some of the bottles that my dad drank at dinners.

"You own this place? I thought you were into security and that sort of thing?"

"I am, but my parents had this when they were way younger. I think your dad and mine used to come out here a lot before my parents bought the place."

I paused as I realized that this was my dad's best friend's son.

"Uh oh," I murmured.

"What's wrong, Soph?"

I stared out the window and thought, *What am I doing? What will my parents think?* This wasn't just a random preppy business-man, or a sexy handyman; this guy was from a very reputable, ridiculously wealthy family. And he sure didn't feel like a playboy, the kind I usually ran into on Wall Street. If I screwed this up, I may be homeless. My dad didn't have just anyone for friends; he had only the upper crust. I suddenly wanted a shot of something.

Thomas opened my car door, and I stood up, holding my vintage yellow clutch that matched the flower he had given to me.

"This is just the first date I've had in two years, you know. For grape's sake, I am probably a nun by now," I said laughing.

Thomas held my hand and kissed it gently. I bit my lips as, honestly, he was so hot. And I could feel the heat rising within me. Well, it was August, you know.

"Well, Miss Sophie Becks, I'll try to be a gentleman," he reassured me with a smile.

I looked into his eyes and saw all sorts of things. I followed him through many rooms filled with things for making wines. The air was filled with the aroma of wine, and all the hallways were whitewashed, like the walls in France. This place looked antiquated and was sure to have quite a history.

Grapevines hung over a field protected with a glass roof and walls, and in the middle were bistro tables. A lit candle floated on water in a bowl filled with rose petals, in the middle of a table. Rows and rows of grapevines grew over the house, all in all, not too shabby!

"So this is a vineyard?" I asked.

"Really?" Thomas said, laughing. "Well, it's definitely not a high-end department store."

We smiled and stared at each other.

"Madam, wine," a man in a tuxedo said, as he handed me a glass of red wine.

As he walked away, I looked at Thomas and asked, "Is this how it's done, you know, wining and dining a lady?"

He stepped closer to me while looking into my eyes and kissed me on the forehead. He pulled my chair out like a gentleman. "A man knows how to treat a lady like a lady."

In that moment, I simply couldn't think of any horrible, sexist things about men. I felt like a lady for a short while, and it felt wonderful. I sipped my wine. God knows I don't really drink, but I was sure that a few sips couldn't hurt. Maybe I would think clearer after the wine, as this guy seemed to be shutting out all my good-thinking bulbs. Did I have that many to start with anyway?

The sound of a violinist enhanced the wine experience even more. I recognized the tune as a Vivaldi. "You have impressed me, sir," I said.

"Then I'm doing my job. I was told you never get impressed at all."

"Are you a player, Thomas?"

He almost choked on his red wine and stinky cheese. "Not really, but I'm not good with relationships either, a little FYI."

"Sounds like I found a good match." No, he wasn't a player, he was just the pimp of the vineyards.

The waiter brought out the first course, many different cheeses.

"I hope you like it; it's raw cheese from my mother's kitchen."

"Your mother makes stinky cheese? My goodness. My mother makes my father bankrupt."

I cut the cheeses and placed some on his plate. "It's delightful," I said. "Not bad for stinky cheese."

"Stinky cheese is my specialty, along with wine, of course," Thomas responded.

The waiter next bought out something that smelled absolutely delish. I wasn't that hungry after the globe of cheese that he brought earlier, but the second course was roasted goose, Jesus.

We talked and laughed; usually you would do only one or the other, but we truly enjoyed each other's company and were quite attracted to one another.

After hours of tasting the delicacies, I'd had enough, and he pulled my chair out for me.

"Thank you, Thomas."

"No, it was an amazing date, Sophie. Thank you," he whispered to me.

Our walk to the car was quiet. The air was clear, and the sounds of crickets were overpowering. I leaned on the door, staring at him. He held my hands in his, and a million words appeared in his eyes, though none out of his mouth. It was magic, but in my head, I knew I was screwed.

"When will I see you again?" he asked.

"I have my Series 7 next week, so I'm on lockdown for a few days."

"Well, when you are done, I'd like to lock you down."

"Really? Lock me down? I'm Sophie Becks; that's so impossible."

And right then, he pulled me to him and kissed me on the lips, soft and deep. My brain played the violin, the cello, the drums, and an electric guitar. I ran a hand through his soft and slightly curly hair. It was then that I realized that I needed to go

WALL STREET TO FRANCE

home and run on the treadmill. It wasn't the wine, or the goose, or the cheese; it was that he was a woman's man. He opened the car door, and as I sat down, he knelt down in front of me, staring into my eyes.

"It was a wonderful starry night, and your kindness was, well, kind," I said, unsure what was about to happen now. He moved closer, and our lips spoke a language that I could have learned if I'd had the time.

As he drove me home, he said nothing further. He just held my hand in the silence. It was 12:45 a.m. when I got home. He walked me to the door, and kissed me softly goodnight. As he walked back to his car and got in, he looked at me through his open car window.

"I'll see you soon, Sophie Becks!" he called out.

"Yes, *bonne nuit*. I'm tired, and your wine was good," I replied.

"Yes, *bonne nuit*."

When I turned back to the door, Robin had opened it and was standing in the door frame, smiling. "Hmm, Sophie, you speak French now? Were the grapes that foreign?"

"Shut up," I said.

Robin waved to Thomas. "*Bonne nuit, Monsieur Thomas*. I suggest you get yourself a French tutor, as my Sophie is speaking French now."

Thomas rolled with laughter as he drove off.

I smacked Robin's head with my clutch and then ran up the stairs and locked the door behind me. I lay in bed thinking of nothing but Thomas until I almost fell asleep.

Robin suddenly knocked on the door. "Soph, do you want me to sing you a Thomas lullaby? 'Cause I know you're not sleeping."

"Okay, go for it," I yelled through the door.

"Lullaby, please don't sigh, Thomas will make you some red wine … Lela … Lala … Lah …"

Yup, it went on and creaking on. I grabbed my earplugs. The song, and his singing, were horrid.

10

THE FIRST LADY OF BROOKVILLE

My date the other night had gone quite well, I supposed. Truthfully, I didn't date a lot, so frankly I didn't know how it was supposed to end. To say the least, Thomas was a gentleman.

It was Sunday, and my parents and Rain had landed successfully at Republic Airport this morning, in their private jet. I was on the back veranda eating my wheat-free morning oats, with organic milk and raisins. It was good, but I really couldn't focus on it, as the breakfast had taken a backseat to thoughts of Thomas.

"Mother, Father," I greeted them, kissing them on both cheeks. "It's so good that you are back." And with that, Rain, Robin, and I sat very quietly as Hannah brought out their breakfast tray.

"Dad, how are you feeling?" I asked.

"I'm fine, and how were things around here?" he deflected.

"Things were quiet," I responded.

"Robin, I see choosing love didn't work out for you?" my father said. "Son, it rarely does; that's why a career ..." He cleared his throat. "Well, a successful career like Rain's is more worth-while. Love is a mere fantasy with an awful lot of downtime, especially when that woman decides to leave you."

At this point, I began coughing, and almost choked on the bloody wheat-free oatmeal crap.

"Dad, isn't that a bit harsh and cold?" I politely stated, but oh my goodness, that didn't sit well, hell to the no.

"Sophie, when you find a very successful man that loves you for your heart, call me. Love is all bullshit!" my dad said.

"I beg to differ, Jack!" My mom interjected, teary eyed. "Why would you tell our children that? Have I not given you love and my life?"

My dad looked at her, paused, stood up, and cleared his throat. "Vivian, love is never enough. Look at your house, your second house in the Hamptons, your cars, your filthy rich list of friends. Is that love? If I gave you only love and none of this, we would not be sitting here with these children." And like a lawyer making his closing arguments, he walked out of the room after his pimp speech. I sat there with my oats. I didn't even know why I was trying to be all gluten-free; this crap sucked enough. But now, my mother and father came home with a whole shopping list of issues.

It's hard for me to admit, but I felt bad for my mother. Yes, he left out her mini cottage of a walk-in closet and her million-dollar shoe collection. And yes, my mother is the First Lady of Hermès; she had a nanny, driver, gardeners, and housekeepers. Must I go on? And to make it all worse, she didn't make cheese, like Thomas's mom. But she was my mother.

My mother stood up, in a very dignified way, and said calmly,

"I'm going to be at my Hamptons home for the week, if you need to reach me."

No problem, Mother, I thought. *Just leave Hannah, here. She's all we need.*

"Robin, see to it you get yourself acquainted with a six-figure job by the end of the month, or your dad will probably disown you," she concluded, as she left the room. There it is, that explains why I'm this messed up.

"So much for unconditional love," I murmured. I pushed my oats aside and left the veranda to go to my room to study, so I could be a top producer on Wall Street. Quite possibly, a miserable, highly successful female stockbroker. Hopefully.

As I studied, I could hear the chaos of my mom and dad arguing down the hall; the slamming of doors and the profanity. I never thought that my parents could be this off-balance. I sat up on my bed with my glasses on, my hair in braids, and wearing a plaid tunic and black trousers; I looked Amish.

It got quiet, and I tiptoed to my door to hear if they were still fighting. But as I put my ear against the wood, the door slammed open on my head.

"Jeez, Robin, can't you knock?" I cried out.

"Something is not right with them. Someone's screwing someone else!"

"Duh, genius. For someone who graduated from the Ivy League, you sure are slow. Are you smoking pot, dude?"

"Stop it, Soph. Ever since I moved back, I've needed something to focus on, but this is a mess," he sighed.

"Mom is probably getting romantic with a heart surgeon, as we all know Dad is emotionally unavailable."

I always thought I was way off for not being an overachiever like Rain, but maybe I was being a little hard on myself here. I had my exam in three days. This certainly wasn't going to help, and for God's sake, I was no psychologist; but I might need one if I continued living here. In our perfect chateau of a home, it was dreadful how dysfunctional my family was.

Hannah knocked on the door, which was still open. "I don't want to pry, Miss Sophie, but this has never happened before, and I've worked here for years," said Hannah in a panic. "I'm very worried about your mother and father."

"Okay, Hannah, try to relax. Try closing your door and imagining that you are in Barcelona, where there are many churches." Apparently, churches were a good idea. Hannah went back to her room, and from time to time she'd text me.

My phone buzzed again, this time with a text from Thomas, "Hi princess, dinner?"

WTF? Dinner again? I texted back, "No thanks."

A question mark followed.

"I'm studying," I replied.

He sent me a smile emoticon.

I wanted to make this quick and painless for him. His family was normal, wealthy, and always in the local newspaper. These were good things. Mine was complex.

Robin left the house, and I was, at last, all alone and listening as my mother threatened to leave my father. Her clothes were already in the designer suitcases and down the stairs. I watched as Hannah helped her to the car where her driver awaited. And without further ado, my mother left.

It was more than enough to bear my parents' normal escapades, but now a separation? My father was probably just sitting in his study and looking around at all the things that had been thrown. I walked down to the reading room, and peeked through the cathedral windows, until I couldn't see her car anymore. Then I closed the drapery and looked around to see books everywhere. No one read much, but books were on my mother's list of important collections in a proper life. I hoped a second husband wasn't next on the list.

I turned around to find my father standing at the doorway. He breathed a sigh of relief, which annoyed and confused me.

"Dad, what was all that?" I asked him.

He took his merry time to console me. In fact, I couldn't imagine my parents ever consoling me. They were brilliant in raising me to be in the front row with the elite, but they never showed emotions, not when I was young and not now.

"You should sit for this, Sophie."

I sat down, not only unhappy at what was occurring, but also worried for my father. Though he was a high-powered attorney, he could well be homeless if he didn't play his cards right, as my mother was a tigress. She was all woman, and you'd better believe that if she ever truly left him, she'd take his therapist too!

"Your mother and I need some time apart right now. That's the best I can do."

Involuntarily, tears welled in my eyes. I couldn't believe that after forty years of marriage there was still a possibility of divorce.

"I'm not stupid," I said. "Was this really a trip around the globe, or was it a 'Honey, let's just quit; the kids are old enough now' trip?"

Fuming, Dad stood up as if there was something else on his mind that he couldn't talk about. "This cannot be discussed further," he announced. He fixed his polo shirt and his gold-toned ring, which had changed colors from years of use, and walked out of the reading room with such put-on dignity that the only thing missing was a Hermès silk scarf around his neck.

Men! I swore I wasn't ever falling in love and getting married. And Thomas, well that was something else yet again. That lane was now officially closed off for me. Clearly, men like my dad were going to play hardball at work and lowball at home when it came to their own balls.

11
LUCKY TO BE ME

I was relieved that the day was finally here. I had made it through all the insanity, and a lot would be determined if I were to pass my Series 7 this morning. Not only would I become a Wall Street broker, but I would have a great shot at becoming the bloody overachiever that was in my DNA.

At breakfast, Hannah looked after me as if I were her very own daughter. She cooked my oats for a half hour on slow with organic milk and raisins. I became aware of why people often get very attached to their housekeepers. Sometimes they are closer to you than your own family.

"Breakfast, Miss Sophie," said Hannah, placing my bowl on the table with a plate underneath it and silverware on the side.

"My mom bought this cutlery in Barcelona," I said.

"Yes, it's very Barcelona," she replied.

Robin walked into the kitchen and sat down next to me, and Hannah attended to him as well.

"Your steel oats and banana, Mr. Robin."

"Yes, good morning to you, beautiful Hannah," Robin said, a little too gleefully. I suddenly felt nauseous. "It seems our parents are getting a divorce, ladies, as Dad had a bit of a fling with his assistant," Robin said aloud.

I was devastated. Hannah dropped a teacup and saucer onto the floor, smashing them to a thousand pieces in a second.

"Hannah, my mom would have deducted that out of your thousands," Robin said, laughing. "I know this is a shock, but it was only a matter of time, really."

"No, Robin, this can't happen," I said. "It shouldn't."

I was very angry at my dad for having a double life, especially since my mother was such a sophisticated, attractive woman. Sure, cheat all you like, but dammit, my mother had enough style and refinement to bring any mistress to shame. Who could be better than Mom? No one. Surely whomever Dad was with just wants his money.

Without thinking, I scooped big spoonfuls of oats and added heaps of brown sugar to my bowl. *Who cares if I get fat?* I thought. *There's no justice in this world.*

"Miss Sophie, brown sugar isn't part of your diet," Hannah said, alarmed.

"Yes, Soph, step away from the sugar," Robin mumbled.

I was dressed in my best attire: silk blouse with Peter Pan collar and a blue Polo blazer, both custom fit, and my Dolce pumps with fine pearl earrings encircled in diamonds. I needed to get out of here.

"My car will be here soon. I'll see you later," I said.

I was miserable and emotionally drained. If it wasn't my brothers acting like little girls, it was my mom and dad acting like impudent teenagers. It was all too bizarre and heartrending.

I waved to Robin as I left. He grabbed one of my hands and held up my chin with the other. "Make me proud, Sophie!"

"Get yourself a life!"

My mind, during the ride to the city, was everything but calm and peaceful, so I requested classical music. The driver played a piano concerto, and my mind played along with the tune as my fingers would on a piano. My mind was always tamed with keys and strings. Today I had a new driver. I hadn't seen him before, but I was in no mood to be social.

"Are you Rain's sister, Madam?" the driver asked.

"Yes," I responded, and gave a small smile. The old man smiled back, and I looked at him in the reflection of the front mirror. "Why do you ask, sir?"

He paused and responded, "His girlfriend always asks about you, but he wasn't sure you'd like her."

Wow, that's convenient! I thought. "His girlfriend?" I asked, incredulous. I couldn't believe that my brother, the player, had a *girlfriend!*

The limo pulled up to the front of my building on Fifth Avenue, and I tipped the old guy and smiled. "Please don't mention that we spoke of Rain, all right?"

"I won't, kind lady. Don't worry," he replied.

I walked to the elevator, fixed my hair in the mirror, and dusted my crested blazer. I had to remind myself that I wasn't here for a bloody date; I was here for the most important exam of my career.

By 10:30 a.m., I was taking my Series 7 exam, and at that point, it didn't matter much if my father was a screw up, if my mom was too high maintenance, or if my brothers were elite businessmen or monks. I was going to become a success, no matter what.

After a few hours, I was a free woman, and my career's

destiny was in the hands of the fates. But as I stepped into my private car, I was overwhelmed with texts and calls. The only call I answered was Thomas.

"My dear Sophie Becks, how did it go?"

"Well, I guess it went well. I'll find out soon."

"Well, if they all know what's good for them, they'll get ready to worship the ground you walk on. You'll be running that place in your smart little skirt and heels, in no time," Thomas said and paused.

"Thank you, Thomas." I bit my lip, as my mind flashed back to when he held my hand and kissed me.

"So, dinner tonight?" he asked.

"Hmm, you waited a week for me, right?"

"I did."

"Then dinner it is," I said, smiling.

"See you at 7:09 p.m."

I hung up, laughing silently to myself.

"Miss Becks, back to your Long Island home?" the driver inquired.

"Yes, sir, it's my only home right now."

I leaned my head on my hands and looked out the window, thinking so many things. On one hand, I was so relieved and on cloud nine for being finished with the exam. I already felt accomplished in so many ways. I was finding my way on a career path I was good at, finally closer to becoming that Wall Street broker I had always wanted to be. But on the other hand, I had my crazy, dysfunctional family and all that was going on right now. I sighed deeply.

While lost in my thoughts, my phone rang. It was Jan.

"My God, Jan, you've been MIA lately. Where on earth have you been?" I said.

"Sophie, darling, congratulations!" she cried into the phone.

Jeez, did I miss something? "The results aren't in yet, are they?" I asked, confused.

"Yes, Ker called. You passed, darling!"

Ker lived, breathed, and probably wouldn't mind dying, on Wall Street, as he was, unfortunately, much more passionate about his life as a stockbroker than his marriage. However, Jan wasn't a typical woman who needed a lot of emotional sustenance. She loved him, but she knew he was a top-level broker on Wall Street, and therefore she'd have to settle by suffering with having all that money could buy. So, unlike most women who bitched about their wealthy, overachiever husbands not being available, she said 'to heck with it. After all, someone had to work to pay for her extravagant lifestyle. I admired her, not for her wealth or her billionaire stockbroker husband, but for her attitude. She knew what she was in for, and she accepted it without complaining.

By passing my Series 7, I was finally in the door. I realized that I was less experienced than most of the brokers, but I wanted this more than they did, and I was going to kick Jaxwe, and any other broker at my firm, into second place behind me.

"Dinner tonight?" asked Jan.

"I can't. I'm having dinner with Thomas!"

"Sophie, my darling, are you already giving up your singlehood?"

"No, no, and *no*! Never happening!"

Sure, we laughed it off, but the truth was I was looking

forward to seeing him. Maybe he could be my boy toy, if nothing else.

The car pulled into the driveway, and I saw Robin standing out front with the biggest bunch of red balloons I'd ever seen.

"Congrats, Sophie!" he screamed.

"Oh, Robin!" I jumped on him, dropping my bag and everything else on the ground. "Oh no, my Hermès!" I looked on the ground by his feet.

"I love you, little sister," he laughed, and spun me around like when we were kids.

"Okay, this is where you put me down," I said.

"My little sister is going to become just like her big brother, successful, cranky, and far too important to answer her damn phone, very soon!"

"Oh, Robin!" I smacked him on the head. I loved the kid. He made my parents spend hundreds of thousands on Ivy League schools that most people can't even get into, and here he was, jobless today. But he was at peace with himself, that was the main thing.

We walked into the house, and I stood in the foyer, feeling the emptiest I had ever felt for this overly successful family. Looking at the framed pictures on the walls, I couldn't even cry, nor did I really want to. You only become who you want to be but once, and this was my time.

Hannah came over, and hugged and congratulated me. In her hands was my favorite carrot shake, the one that my mother made when I used to be close to her; when I was little, and we didn't have so much to accomplish all the time that we forgot family time and *love*. I looked at Hannah and wondered, *Where is my mother?* On one of the most important days of my life, the housekeeper, not my mother, greeted me with such warmth. Thank goodness that Robin and I were in harmony, though.

Hannah was in her mid-thirties or so, and wasn't married yet. She was very beautiful and voluptuous, had the brownest eyes you'd ever seen, and the golden brown complexion of a Spanish goddess. I saw her glance at Robin in a different way than she usually did. *Did she just smile at him? As in, "Aww, what an amazingly sweet man Robin is."*

"I'm so tired, Hannah. I'm just going to go up for a bit and lie down. Thomas is picking me up at seven."

"Thomas," Robin exclaimed. "Wow, you must really dig him."

"Oui, I dig him," I replied.

I stepped out of my four-inch designer heels and ran up the spiral staircase to the second floor. As I looked down from the balcony, Robin let go of the bunch of red balloons, and they floated to the top of the staircase like out of a scene of a movie.

"I do love you, Robin Becks!" I called down to him. "You are the best part of coming home. You are the best part of this insane, freaking family." I yawned as I went into my room and hopped into bed. And asleep I went.

12

YACHT ME OR NOT

"Sophie, wake up!" called Hannah. "It's six o'clock and your date will be here soon."

"I'm exhausted, Hannah. Can you get me a dress from my closet with some shoes, pleeease!" Standing over me, looking at me like I was a lunatic, she was still divine.

"Okay," she said, prancing into my 2,500-square-foot closet. If I didn't have that closet, I'd have no choice but to get married. Because if I couldn't love my things, I'd have to love someone else. I know it's stupid, but it's also practical.

Hannah was a godsend. I got out of bed and took my pants off.

"I can't believe I slept in my silk pants. My dry cleaner would be like, 'Oh no! You don't sleep in silk, Sophie,'" I said, laughing.

"You'll be fine, Soph," Robin said, as he walked into my room laughing. "You'll make your first millions soon, and then sleep around with some idiot womanizer, and he'll buy you the whole of Henri Bend-something,"

"You're an idiot, Robin, and besides, I'm not into playboys." Not yet at least. "Aren't I going out with a nice family-oriented guy this evening?"

"Yes, one who drives a Maserati and owns a vineyard," he countered.

"Really, Robin, do you want me to go out with a priest?"

"Chances are, if you did, he would be a fine-ass priest in a hundred-thousand-dollar sports car."

I walked into my bath and closed the door, laughing. "Don't worry, dear brother. I ain't getting married. You and I will live together until I'm ninety, at least."

Weird as that would be, he didn't respond. I opened the door a little, and peeked through to see Robin sitting on my bed, looking at the photograph of the three Becks siblings on my nightstand. Robin was funny, but deep within, he had a lot of grief in his heart. When we were little, Robin, Rain, and I were close, but we were oceans apart as adults.

My bath began to overflow, so I took my monogrammed towels and spread them all over the marbled floors to soak up the water. I stepped into the tub, and soaked for a few minutes without anyone bothering me. It wasn't long before a knock on the door shattered the silence. I was covered in bubbles up to my chin, and the warm scent of lavender wafted through the room.

"Come in," I called.

"Are you dressed? It's me." It was Rain. I wasn't dressed, but I was covered with bubbles, head to toe. When we were children, we would all bathe together in the old Victorian tub at our grandmother's house in Newport, naked. Eww!

"You can come in. I'm covered."

"I wanted to congratulate you on your success," he continued.

"On my success. Thank you, Rain."

There was a world of silence between us these days. I couldn't imagine speaking with him for much longer. I still wasn't over our fight the other night, but there's an old adage - "Blood is thicker than water."

"Listen," he sputtered haltingly. That was unusual for him. "I was wondering…just wondering, if you and I and Robin could have dinner at my penthouse next week?"

He had a way of taking me from insane hatred to a smile, just like that.

"Do you have a fever? Or a secret? Are you dying of some horrible disease?" I queried.

"No secrets. I think that this mom-and-dad thing has been hard for all of us, and it's time we, well, stuck together. I hope you can forgive me for being such an ass."

I was touched, and though I couldn't believe it, a tear slowly rolled down my cheek. I looked away from him and washed my face in bubbles, hoping he hadn't seen it. Seriously, I needed to toughen the heck up here. I was going to be a Wall Street broker soon. I couldn't afford feelings. Emotions were for women, and in this business, I was no woman. Yes, I was still technically a woman, my breasts were proof of that, but I was running from my emotional side. Surely it would catch up to me at some point, like in all the novels I've read. It would undoubtedly catch up with me at exactly the wrong time.

"I'll let you finish your bath," Rain said, as he reached for the door.

"Thank you, Rain," I replied, and he left.

I got out of the bath and put on a white Egyptian-cotton robe. I thanked my lucky stars that Robin, Hannah, and Rain had all left my room and gone elsewhere. I'd had enough of emotional moments for one day.

As I was drying off, I got a text from Thomas; he was outside, and he was early and wanted to know if he could come in. Oh great. We weren't even an item yet; we were still just fondling each other's minds.

I got a second text seconds later, "Never mind. Your brother let me in."

"Great," I responded.

I slipped on the pink dress and pink shoes that Hannah had picked out for me. She had also chosen my black Hermès bag. I was surprised that Hannah hadn't found my pink Dior saddlebag, though maybe she thought it was too much pink. I brushed my hair, powdered my face, and put on a little mascara and mild fragrance, not the killer perfume that most women splash on. And yes, I put on my famous pink lips, courtesy of Dior. Not bad for five minutes. I really didn't want to let my brothers bother Thomas too much. But it was too late, because as I hurried down the stairs I saw Thomas joking around with the two stooges.

"Hi, Thomas, I see you've met both my brothers."

"Yes, and you look beautiful."

We looked at each other and smiled, and I suddenly felt hot and musty, like I was in a desert.

"Yes, we were warning Thomas about you," Robin said.

"Oh, thanks!" I said.

Rain looked at me and smiled. "Take good care of her," he said to Thomas. I wondered what had happened to Rain. He stared at me while sipping red wine. "By the way, Thomas, this is the best wine I have ever had." Rain was such a wine lover; he had a very refined palette.

"I'll send a case over to your penthouse," Thomas said.

"That would be great," Rain replied. "Maybe drop it off yourself, and I could show you around."

"Nice," Thomas replied, as he shook their hands and escorted me out the door.

Robin stood in the doorway next to Rain, and mumbled, almost out of earshot, "Every time I see him, he's driving a new sports car. He'd better not break her heart."

"He won't," Rain responded. "She'll break his heart once she starts working 24-7. That girl is made for Wall Street. She'll have to choose money over love, every time. Just watch." Robin was often confused by Rain, but he had a valid point. Love and money, paired with great success, didn't often work out harmoniously.

As I got into Thomas's car, I looked through the open window and was pleased to see my two brothers still talking without slamming each other into the wall. Thomas rolled the window up and stared at me with lust in his eyes.

"So, where are we off to?" I asked him.

"Surprise," he said. Then he handed me a bag and started driving. "For you."

"You don't have to get me anything. You know that, right?" I opened it, smiling, but also thinking that I was in no position to fall in love with this man.

"I know, but you'll need this."

I opened the bag excitedly. "Earphones, perfect." Every broker needed a good pair of earphones!

I leaned over to kiss his cheek, and his lips locked on mine. A flame engulfed us, as our lips melted into each other's. Not quite, but that sounded intense, right?

I pulled away. "My God, you're driving! Keep your eyes on the road!"

That short kiss was soft and passionate, and though our eyes stayed on the road from here on in, I could feel our hearts beating. It was so sensual and felt so right, at least for tonight. He placed his hand on mine, as he drove even faster and switched lanes like a maniac.

"Are you trying to kill me?" I asked him.

"Nope. Is my driving scaring you?"

I laughed.

"I thought so," he said smiling.

We pulled into a parking space near Cold Spring Harbor. I could have been about to fall into the water and I wouldn't have known it, because I was lost in his big hands and deep green eyes. His eyes were like the rarest of David Yurman's gems.

He opened my door and held my hand, as we stepped onto a yacht. "It's just you and me and Captain Batton," he said.

I was nervous; that kiss, a yacht, the moon and stars sitting all the way up in the sky, as the wind tickled the trees, it was intoxicating. We walked down a few steps to the dock. The boat was like a little house on the water. Soft music was playing, and a candlelit dinner had been prepared by a chef with a French accent. *Très cliché*, I thought. Thomas sat me down and ordered sparkling water with lemon for me, because I told him I wasn't in the mood for wine. He asked for a glass of red wine for himself, and I poured it for him, slowly.

"So, tell me, Sophie, are you dating anyone else?" he began.

"Not at the moment." I replied. "Why do you ask?"

He took the bottle from my hand and placed it onto the glass table. He took a sip from his wine, lost in his thoughts, "I don't want to play games with anyone."

I was intrigued by his abruptness. He clearly wasn't looking for a one-night fling, either. But I was not in any position to get caught up now, especially with my father's best friend's son. What a question to ask a woman on a second date!

"I think that I'm going to be extremely busy with my career, now that I can begin it in earnest," I said. "And I never have been able to have a serious relationship with anyone."

Thomas gave me a serious look, and then glanced away.

"Yes," he agreed. "I'm too busy with my business to settle down now anyway."

Hadn't he heard that I was the last one anyone would want to settle down with? The chef entered the dining deck at just the right time, and served us dinner. We sat down and had the most amazing dinner, without further discussion.

"No stinky cheese this time?" I asked.

"No, do you need some, with red wine?"

"Not tonight, my palette is very content," I purred.

One thing led to another, and soon his arms were around me, and my hands made their way to the back of his head. I was flaming with desire, the kind that submerges you completely into depths that cannot be fathomed.

"You are an exceptional woman, and I do want to get to know you better," he said.

"Better? Are you sure? I'm pretty complicated," I said.

He pulled me closer to him, and we almost breathed the same breath. I didn't know how ready I was to just lie there beside anyone. It wasn't about my career; it was about my reluctance for real intimacy with anyone. He held my hands and softly kissed my palms, staring into my eyes. Feeling lost in the moment, we gazed at each other without moving.

Taking my hand, Thomas dimmed the lights and led me down the stairs into the formal living room.

"Do you like it?" he asked.

I nodded, "Impressive."

It was just us, no one else; nothing but soft lights and soft music. Now I knew why wealthy men cheated; it was easy, safe, and quite costly. All you needed was a yacht and a private French chef. Thomas poured himself wine, while I sat on the leather sofa, admiring the exquisite paintings on the walls; only I would notice paintings on a yacht. Thomas sat down next to me and took my hands in his. Abruptly, he glanced away from me.

"What's the matter?" I asked.

"Nothing," he said, standing up and looking out at the water. I got up and gazed at him, as he softly placed his hands on my face. "I do want you, but not like this," he whispered.

I didn't know what to think, but in truth, I felt relieved. He excited me, but I didn't want to get so carried away that I lost my head. I needed to stay in control, but I sensed that that ship had already sailed. Thomas was in control here. We lay on the sofa, staring at the ceiling, me curled in his arms. The closeness we now shared was on a level that I had never experienced before; more than a friendship, but less than lovers.

"There's a reason I'm not coming on to you," he said. "It's because of your father."

"Well gee, that's a relief. I was thinking I wasn't good-looking enough for the likes of you," I said, sipping on my tea.

"Sophie, you are one of those girls that either you want to just sleep with or fully commit to, and I'm not ready for you to act as if I don't exist."

"Yes, I agree that we shouldn't do the dirty and then act like we aren't important to each other."

Our lips touched, and I couldn't help but want him. I think

I must be crazy. Tell me I can't have something, and that's the very moment I want it.

As we began our return to the harbor, I felt we were on the same page. This guy was afraid of commitment, and I wasn't the girl that either slept around or the one that cared. And commitment issues? Darling, I'm writing the book on how to avoid commitment.

I stepped out of the cabin and into the bow of the yacht as Thomas held my hands. It was chilly out, so he placed his warm and manly sweater around me. Instantly, my telephone rang, and I grabbed it from my bag to see ten missed calls. I called home.

"Soph, are you okay?" asked Robin.

"Yes, I'm okay." I walked a short distance away from Thomas.

"What is he doing to you to keep you out there so late?"

"Don't be a dad, okay? I'll be back soon."

I suddenly needed space from everyone and everything, and I longed to get into my own big bed, and sleep alone. Looking out at the dark waves and taking in the scent of the ocean was therapeutic, yet I knew that Thomas was watching me. I shivered as I held his sweater tighter over my shoulders and sighed. Thomas came over to me and held me from behind.

"What's the matter, Sophie?" he whispered in my ear. "You're shivering. Let's go inside, OK?"

We walked inside and I sat down on the soft leather sofa in the formal living room, while Thomas fetched me a cup of tea.

"It's not the fancy stuff you drink at home," he said. "But this should do the trick."

"You're so silly, Thomas. This is organic ginger and pear. I don't drink this fancy at home."

The tea leaves were in a little linen satchel dipped into boiling water in a white teacup. I sipped it slowly, and he put a warm woolen blanket around me. It was sweet the way he cared for my wellbeing. Was it normal to be like this? He was caring and kind, and I wasn't used to being treated with such gentleness. Sure, I'd always had people take care of me, but because I paid them, not because they genuinely liked me. Wall Street men certainly didn't treat you like this, maybe that's why I didn't normally date them. They were lions; Thomas was a mouse.

The captain came over the intercom to tell us that we were back in the harbor. I looked over at Thomas and yawned. I was exhausted both emotionally and physically. We exited the boat and walked down the ramp and into Thomas's Maserati, where I buckled my belt as he spoke to the captain. They seemed to know each other well.

On the way home, the radio was turned off, and we were quiet. Even though there was no verbal conversation going on, the emotional exchange between us screamed a million different things.

"So, Thomas," I broke the silence. "Where do you live?"

"Mill Neck."

"Oh, it's beautiful there. My boss has a polo mansion in Mill Neck."

"I bought a home on the lake there a year ago. A polo mansion, huh? Nice! He must be one of those high rollers with ten mistresses and a gin and tonic in both hands at all times," he quipped.

What was I to say? I smiled.

We pulled into my driveway, and I had to wait to be buzzed in. I never remembered the codes for anything.

"So, I guess I'll see you soon, Sophie Becks."

"Thank you for a beautiful night, Thomas. You are quite the gentleman."

He leaned over, and we shared a kiss that, at once, made me realize that all the passion I'd once had for him I'd left at sea. I walked up the steps to the grand old front door, and then looked back and waved. He waited until I got inside. *Oh Thomas,* I sighed to myself. *You are polite, kind, and far too gentle for me.*

I took off my shoes and stepped quietly to the staircase. As I was walking to my room, my dad was busy in the living room with his laptop.

"You're home, I see," he said.

"Yes, Father, I'm home." I was shocked that he was home and up so late at night; well, so early in the morning.

"Good night, Sophie."

"Night-night."

I only had a few hours to sleep before my car service came to get me. I washed my face, threw on my nightgown, turned my phone on silent, and closed my eyes.

13

LIGHTS, CAMERA, ACTION!

The next morning, my alarm buzzer went off forever, until Hannah hurried into my room and shook me. "Sophie... Sophie..."

Today was my very first day as a stockbroker, and I'd had my first suit custom-made by European tailors. It had been delivered and paid for, the stamp of success.

Somehow, I had to shrug this love thing aside. I figured I could always fall in love at thirty or forty. I didn't have to worry about it too much right now. Thomas was a good man, but falling in love was worse than dabbling in the stock market and losing all your money. I wished love were more like *Vogue*, a perfect presentation, with posed, photoshopped photographs. Instead, you got heartache and men dressed to perfection, but with no bloody clue how to make you happy, or you them.

My early morning routine continued, as I washed my face with milk, brushed my teeth with Marvis, and brushed my hair with my Fekkai products. I soaked in a lavender-and-rose bath, while I sipped a cup of loose tea and listened to some therapeutic Bach. After my long soak, I lathered my skin in L'Occitane, simply heaven on your skin. God knows I needed it. Here I was, on top of my game and making myself astoundingly happy.

"Miss Sophie, your oats," Hannah said, as she dropped my breakfast off. She was definitely due for either a raise or a promotion, I couldn't decide. Nevertheless, I played my Bach loudly as I soaked and saw that my oats were thick and gooey, yuck.

"I'm not hungry, Hannah. Thank you anyway," I said. By now she'd gotten used to my anyway-the-wind-blew moods, and it amused her.

A few more minutes of soaking led to panic. *What time was it?* My driver would be picking me up shortly. I wiped my skin, slipped into my lingerie, and pulled my trousers up my petite body. I was stunned to look this badass Wall Street. This was a pivotal point in my life, and hopefully, my career would soon take off like Tom Cruise and that blonde from that aviation movie.

Hannah opened the front door for me with a smile, and fixed my pintuck, colored shirt with gold, monogrammed buttons.

"You look like a million dollars, Miss Sophie."

I smiled back at her. That was supposed to be my mother's line, but my mother was probably having a masseur lather her aches and pain away, more or less the memory of being a mother at all.

I stepped into my limo and was off to Wall Street, this time as a real broker. No big deal, right? I already felt like a million bucks, times a hundred. When the car pulled up to the building, I felt as if I'd never really seen it before. Looking at all the men in suits with polished shoes and briefcases, I knew one thing for sure, apart from how hot they looked…I was born to do this.

I walked into the office and everyone stood up and applauded. Duren handed me a key.

"What's this for?" I asked.

"It's a teaser for what lies ahead of you. You must focus," he said intently.

"Focus, that's going to be hard if you keep inviting me to polo," I replied.

He smiled, and it warmed my heart. Well, not exactly, but let's just say this man had charm to spare.

"It's the key to my Hamptons beach house," Duren responded. "Feel free to use it as a weekend getaway."

I was taken aback, but happy. I could feel it; I had arrived. I was nervous to begin, but on Wall Street if you didn't have some anxiety, you didn't have a heartbeat. I was ready for the opening of my accounts; ready to kick ass and all. Surely, brokers were all insane, but insane was also quite normal on Wall Street. Just as normal as a shopaholic who buys a thousand pairs of shoes, silently consoling herself that she needed just one more pair. Yup, sounded familiar.

Well, this was where I gave my acceptance speech. Jaxwe stood in the corner looking impressed but doubtful that I would ever really pose a threat to him. Well, wasn't he in for a big surprise! Duren's underage-looking assistant gave me a glass of sparkly with lemon.

I cleared my throat, raised my glass, and toasted, "To the men and boys among us. You don't stand a chance." There was cynical, yet nervous laughter in the room. "And thank you, Duren," I continued, "for giving me the chance to make millions of dollars. I look forward to being your best female broker, hell, the best broker, period. In fact, I'll be the best you've ever had." There was a silence. "The best you've ever had," sounded sexual, and I could be the best he'd ever had, if he weren't my boss and wasn't married to a giraffe supermodel with legs and no decorum.

Duren shook my hand, and I knew this was the beginning of a blissful career. I didn't understand why he'd taken me in under his wing so much. Yes, he was super gorgeous, but he was always ethical.

"Make me proud, Sophie. And now, everyone get back to opening accounts," he said.

A senior broker would soon be appointed for my training, and in approximately twenty minutes, I'd know which idiot drew the short stick. Let's see which hotshot got the pleasure of training me.

At 10:05, Duren sent me to Jaxwe Jocks.

"What the heck?" I asked him. "Jaxwe is a cocky son of a… you know."

I tried to count backward from ten, but it was no use. All the relaxation breathing techniques didn't seem to work either. Hell, I even looked at my $10,000 Cartier, courtesy of my emotionless father, to no avail. I was having a panic attack.

"Composure and enthusiasm," Duren said firmly. "And Jaxwe has had more success in his career than any other broker in this firm."

I was livid. Talk about setting me up with the one guy I'd grown to compulsively hate! Looking behind me, I could see Jaxwe standing at the glass door, posing in his custom suit with a new tie, smiling as if he'd lost his emotional virginity.

"I look forward to you making me even richer with your forty new accounts." Jaxwe smiled with enthusiasm. Idiot. I'd probably get all forty accounts in one month; that's how pissed I was.

"Right on, let's get to work. Enough of your bragging," I retorted.

Jaxwe stared at me, and I was annoyed at how he smiled

and twirled his eyes up and down at me. Then I noticed Duren smirk at me. Idiot number two, except this one was super hot and talented.

It was 12:00 noon, and I was on the phone with Mr. Jabari from Switzerland. At first, he told me that he was broke, so I'd empathized with him. It was funny what a little empathy could do for clients on Wall Street. By the end of the call, he was opening an account with $200,000. Nice start.

"Yes, not bad for a new broker," said Jaxwe, who'd been listening on a second line. He nodded at me.

"Tea break," I said.

Jaxwe went over to the other brokers, and they all sat around talking and laughing. I sat alone in the conference room, sipping my tea and scrolling through my iPhone.

Jaxwe entered the conference room and said, "I've got a client that I can't close. Mr. Kumar. Neither can the other guys. *If* you close him, you get whatever you want from any of us."

"Rest assured I don't want your small miniscule hot dogs," I replied, without even looking up from my phone. His eyebrows lifted like a chick with bad Botox. "Don't worry," I continued. "After my cup of English breakfast, I'll show you boys a thing or two."

"Sure you will, Sophie Becks," Jaxwe said flippantly, as he exited the room, checking out the body of an air-headed assistant in desperate need of a more professionally appropriate wardrobe.

I'm not going to lie; I was a little intimidated, but I wanted to be better than him, so I had to be fearless. Another broker, Randy, approached me as I left the conference room, and soon I was no longer intimidated; I was aggravated.

"Rumor has it, your daddy dearest defends brokers like us," he said smarmily.

"Really, Randy, what's that got to do with the fact that your tie is more awkward than your assistant?" The guy made $250k last month. If I had made that much money, I'd look pristine, as pristine as a brand new Bentley just off the boat from Great Britain.

I turned toward him and pointed my finger at his uneven green eyes. "You couldn't afford my dad!"

I knew what I was up against. Bullies, all of them. I took my cheap, germy commercial phone and dialed the client who wanted diddly-squat to do with these jerks. I looked over at Jaxwe, muted the call, and waited for him to pick up the other phone.

"If I get this account, what do I get?" I asked him.

"Well, um, what do you want?" he responded, as if I couldn't really do this.

"Your Patek," I replied quickly.

"This watch was from my first paycheck," he said indignantly, holding his wrist up in the air. "It's worth ten times more than your bullshit Cartier."

"Listen, Jaxwe, do you want this new account with Mr. Kumar, or not? Worried I'll be able to do what you losers couldn't?"

"Fine, you'll never be able to open this account anyway. So, yes, if you do, by some fucking miracle, you can have it." Really! A miracle, the bastard!

I was connected to Mr. Kumar in five seconds.

"Mr. Kumar, Sophie Becks."

"Sophie dear, how can I assist you?"

"I'm a broker from the Wall Street firm of Chance Duren. How are you this lovely morning?"

"Dear, I have a broker already, and I'm happy with him."

"Well, that's a line I've never heard before. Let me ask you, Mr. Kumar, are you happy with your wife?"

He paused and laughed. I turned his card over and saw that his net worth was $10 million. I didn't give a crap if I had to import belly dancers from Arabia to dance on his desk, I was getting this account.

Brokers surrounded me, and Jaxwe placed his Italian leather shoes on his desk and kept his eyes on me. Sure, I was about to pee my pants, but I distracted myself by looking at my shoes. Blue velvet bow, a gold square buckle, and blue alligator leather. Not bad for $995.

"Have you ever met a man happy with his wife?" Mr. Kumar asked.

I thought, *Wow, this is my kind of man.* "Mr. Kumar, I have met many men in my life, and they were happier with their mistresses than their wives. That's like comparing me to your other broker, isn't it?"

He laughed and then said, "Don't call me Mr. Kumar; call me Hritik."

"Very well, Hritik. I have an idea about this stock that has a very promising track record." I went into detail about a stock I looked up on my screen, and what did you know, I had an audience.

"How much do you think is enough to make me smile?" Hritik asked.

"Hritik, I cannot guarantee you that the stock's not going to go down, but I can guarantee you that I'll work harder than your wife to make sure you always have a smile on your face when you get your statements."

Duren walked over to me and handed me a note that said "250k."

"That sounds like my kind of woman. What do you suggest?"

"Hritik, you seem like the kind of man that likes to go all or none, so I think a quarter million would be a good start for a portfolio made for a new beginning."

"Consider it done."

What the hell! I screamed in silence as Duren high-fived me before walking back to his office.

"Excellent. I'll email you all the instructions," I said.

"Yes, Sophie, keep me smiling," Hritik replied.

"I will, Hritik. In time, I will."

I hung up and walked over to Jaxwe, who was now lost in a grand dilemma.

"The watch?" I insisted, with my hand palm side up, reached out toward him.

"This is a hundred-thousand-dollar watch, Sophie."

Like I cared. I wouldn't care if it cost the same as a Maserati. Maybe I'd give it to Robin for his thirty-second birthday.

"Stop being a little bitch, Jaxwe. Hand it over," I said with more passion than Hansel or Gretel looking for bread in the forest.

"Today is your first day; that's impossible," he whined.

"Hmm, you may have a point, but is it valid?"

I had four brokers standing around me in awe, but Jaxwe? Nope. No offense, but men like Jaxwe often can't seem to handle it when they come across a woman who may, in fact, be even more talented than they are. Getting that Patek was a glorious moment for me. I put it on my other wrist and smiled. Sure, I should have felt guilty, but I was loving the moment, super loving it.

Duren was getting turned on as well, watching the steam I was blowing off his top brokers' royal asses. He called me on my business line to come into his office. As I knocked on his glass door, I could tell he was happy to see me.

"Come on in, Becks. You're not gambling in my office, are you?"

"No, sir, I'm just setting things right."

He smiled and handed me a bottle of sparkling water. I took it and sat down.

"Good job, so far. You opened three accounts today and raised over half a million dollars. You are definitely a natural," he said with a smile.

"Only thirty-seven more accounts to go. Just imagine, by the time I'm done I'll have a whole collection of men's watches."

He laughed.

"But why stick me with Jaxwe? He is to me what wives are to husbands; two balls and a chain around my neck."

"I'll tell you what, Becks. If you open ten accounts by Monday, you can forget needing to get the rest of the accounts," Duren said.

"What, are you serious?"

"Yes."

I contemplated how I could do this without breaking any fingernails, but then I asked myself, *When Amelia started flying airplanes around the world, did she doubt herself?* Never. In fact, she left the old man behind.

"Okay," I said as I stood up from Mr. Duren's custom leather, tufted chair and smiled at him. I liked him, simply because he truly believed in me. That was something hard to come by in my life. He was good-looking with a capital G, but he was as kind as kind could be.

I left his office amped up like a crack addict. I paced up and down the floor with my phone, pitching my rebuttals and making new ones.

In my first week as a broker, I was determined to break all records. I was a woman in a man's world, but these idiots only had testosterone and no brains, manners, or good judgment. Surely, by the end of the week, I would be passing down my skirts to some of these brokers; I was more man than their daddies.

I had not just arrived, but I had been born to be a broker, and as the first female broker at Chance Duren's, I was about to knock the argyle socks out of these brokers' alligator loafers.

14

FOUFOU MEN

It was a week later, on a Friday night, and I opted for dinner at home with Rain and Robin. I didn't know what had happened to my wayward parents. It made sense that, between my mother's lifestyle, my father's work, and their business marriage, they were rarely to be seen. Hannah decided that she would try making us something Barcelonese, whatever that was, and I would try it, after my bubble bath of course.

It was 8:39 p.m., and I was soaking in my heavenly bath, sipping on a piña colada that Robin had made. Robin was now officially retired, living off my parents, and becoming a wonderful homemaker. After Mom had left, a week ago, over my father's remorseful confession, Robin had taken over the care of us and our home. He'd become so good at it that he was up at five in the morning to send Rain off with a freshly brewed cappuccino. It was good to finally see them being civil to each other. Wasn't that how we were raised?

After my bath had lost its vibrancy of lavender and bubbles, Hannah knocked on the door and called out, "Miss Sophie, can I come in?"

"Yes, Hannah, please do." What could possibly be so serious that she'd interrupt my bath right now?

"I forgot to mention that this box arrived from Mr. Thomas."

"What is it?"

"I couldn't say. I'll put it on the vanity. I must get back to the kitchen, or I'll burn the fideuà."

"Huh, fue-what?" I asked.

As I wiped my wet hands, I wondered what Thomas could possibly attempt to do to make me more attracted to him. The present was in a red velvet box with beautiful silk purple ribbons and a little gold charm engraved with my name. Who did that?

I hadn't returned Thomas's call in days. It wasn't that I wasn't interested. The guy was finer than the wine from his vineyards. But with me, "fine" meant that I could move on very quickly. I wasn't ready for all this love nonsense. It didn't make any sense to me to fall in l-o-v-e. Maybe it was because love wasn't a sales call or a pair of high-end designer shoes from Milan.

I gently placed the box back down on the marble countertop, grabbed my towel, and wiped my body dry, thinking of Thomas: his eyes, his eyelashes, his eyebrows, the fine watch he wore as if it were a part of his body. Fine, I say.

I sat upright on my bed with my drink in hand. The smell of exotic food from Barcelona, Hannah's heritage, perfumed the house. I'd never had Barcelonese food before. God knows my mother wouldn't know what to do with all of that flavor.

Opening the red box, I felt an empty emotion wrapped in butterflies in my stomach. Why was I so nervous about what he had sent me? I couldn't bear to think what it was. I took a quick look inside, and glimpsed a presentation of utmost elegance: the item was wrapped in light-purple silk tied in a soft bow flowing down the edges, sort of like the bows that my nanny used to tie my hair with when I was little.

Inside was a gold necklace, with a heart pendant with a diamond in the middle. I took a deep breath and felt the urge to place it back in the box as if I'd never seen it, but I couldn't simply put it back in the box. I held it, thinking of him and wondering if I was really missing something, something meaningful. I turned the pendant around, and read the inscription: "Give me a chance" on the back. Give me a what? This was magic, magic at the worst possible time. So many feelings flowed through me, but I couldn't give in, as I wasn't ready to get trapped in a web of lust or love. As I carefully placed the gold heart back in the box, I knew that I had some decisions to make. But not here, not now.

I threw on some comfortable linen pants and a lilac silk blouse. I brushed my hair loose and slipped on my velvet loafers. I then waltzed into my bath to powder my face and gloss my lips nude. I'd totally forgotten the lit scented candles on my vanity, so I blew them out and headed downstairs. As I descended the staircase, I held firmly onto the railing, as my mind was filled with a storm of emotions that I'd tried so hard to pretend didn't exist.

I walked into the kitchen, which smelled delish. The French doors were open, and the moon lit the back veranda beautifully. On the bistro tables, candles floated in containers with petals of some type of purple flower. The table setting was lovely, with toile placemats and silver cutlery. The glasses were placed next to the blue napkins inscribed with the letter *B* for Becks. I suddenly missed my mother. Sure, she wasn't the best, but her not being here felt wrong, like wearing the wrong hat at a polo match.

On the table were bottles of wine from Thomas's vineyard,

and though I really wanted to call him, I couldn't. The last thing I needed was a lover that couldn't let me go when I needed breaks, which happened often enough!

Hannah came out with a tray filled with food of all sorts.

"What is all this?" I asked.

"In my country this is what we call fideuà, zarzuela, and calçots!"

I looked at her and had no idea what the hell she was talking about, but I gave her a hug. And then I saw Robin walking out of the kitchen with a case of sangria, and I smiled. He looked happy to be a male domestic.

"Dude, what the heck happened to you?" I asked him worriedly.

"Soph, I love you," Robin said with a smile. He kissed my forehead and hugged me. It felt just like when we were kids and getting in trouble.

Then Rain walked out of the house with a glass of wine in hand, and the guy was dressed way too formally, even for me. Robin looked liked his assistant and I his mule. Rain was always polished, even at a non-event. Rain and Robin hugged, and I was pleased to see a bit of unity between them.

As Hannah gave us a rundown on her meal, my phone buzzed; it was Thomas. I declined the call and placed the phone on the table. Robin, Rain, Hannah, and I all sat down to the music and food of Barcelona. It was very peaceful.

Rain gave a toast, and it was clear that he'd already had too many glasses to drink, "To you all, Robin, Sophie, and Hannah! Hannah, your food is just delicious, as always, and this wine is even better! And with that, thank you, Thomas, for new friendships and new relations."

What the heck? Did I hear that right? Thomas, huh? I looked behind me, and by the steps to the kitchen stood, yes, Thomas. He made his way over to my brothers, shaking hands and all that boy stuff they do with their hands. *Just kiss the freaking guy already*, I thought.

I looked over at him as he stared back at me, grinning his gorgeous jaw. Did I say gorgeous? Focus, I must focus.

"Hey, Thomas, how have you been?" I politely asked.

"I don't know. How have you been, Sophie?"

"Busy with work, very busy." I looked away as my brothers watched us from a distance. It felt as if the Great Wall of China was standing behind Thomas. "Thanks for the..."

"Don't worry about it," he said, clearly pissed.

Rain came over and handed Thomas a plate. It really didn't matter what kind of plate. It meant that he was staying for dinner, and my hair was tangled in knots. I wondered if I looked hot or just like a hot mess.

We all sat there in the warmth of the night, eating and drinking the finest Long Island wine. The starry sky had nothing on Thomas, as his eyes were like green crystals sparkling across the table. I could barely eat. I sipped on sparkling water with lemons. Heck, I hoped, at least, the lemons were from Barcelona.

Everyone was quiet at the table, until, like the sound of crickets chirping, my phone rang. It was Thomas. He hung up and walked into the kitchen. I got up politely and followed behind him. He was pacing in the kitchen as he ran his hands through his dark locks. He didn't know I was standing right behind him.

"Thomas, I'm so sorry."

He turned around, angry. I couldn't explain why I hadn't called him back.

"You ignored my calls for a week, Sophie."

"Yes, I'm sorry, I was busy."

"I know you were," he said with such kindness that I couldn't be mad at him for showing up tonight. "I tried calling to tell you that Rain invited me tonight. And that I wanted to see you."

I looked away, thinking of everything that had led me to this moment: my parents and my observations of the futility and heartbreak of romantic relationships. I was twenty-four years old and running from anything with a heart. I was beyond savable.

"Sophie?"

"Yes?" I said.

"I've missed you." He kissed my hands and looked into my eyes. I felt as hot as a fifty-year-old with menopause.

I walked closer to him and placed my hands on his face, and our lips met, like no other meeting before. A flame of desire had emerged, and it was more passionate than shopping for a new pair of shoes on payday. I was enveloped in his web, at least for right now. I held his hands, and he kissed me, and I couldn't bear to walk away from him.

Robin walked into the kitchen and cleared his throat to warn me of his presence. "I'll just be a minute," he said, dropping some glasses in the sink. I took a few steps back from Thomas, and looked away.

After Robin left, Hannah came in and handed me my cell. "It's Jan," she said.

"I'm in the middle of something, Hannah. Please have her call back."

"She said it's serious, and insisted you take it."

I glanced at Thomas, and he nodded. I held the iPhone to my ear, and asked, "Jan, are you okay?"

"Can you come over right now? I need you."

Jan was a strong woman; she was never a mess. Well, apparently, tonight she was.

"I'll be there in a few," I told her and hung up. I turned back to Thomas. "I'm sorry, but I have to leave. Jan needs me, and she's my best friend. I'll call you tomorrow."

"It's late. I can take you," he replied.

"It's fine. I can drive."

"I don't mind," he said.

He didn't want me out alone at night. I'd never felt so protected. Within minutes, we were in his car, one I hadn't seen before. To say the least, he had many toys. This one was a moonlight-blue Ferrari.

"Do you own a car dealership?" I asked, as we stopped at a light.

He paused and rubbed his chin. "No, but my brother does." He stared into my eyes and pulled me closer, chin to chin, trying to kiss me, I'm sure.

I pulled away smiling, and pointed to the light, "The light's green."

"I know," he said, gazing at me as if he hadn't seen me in weeks.

He drove like a racecar driver, and though he wasn't a bad boy, he certainly looked like one. Not that bad boys were my thing. I was Sophie Becks; I appreciated men of distinction.

After a few minutes of silence, he changed the music to something romantic, one of those songs that are the backdrop to Parisian love stories, like in the movies. It hit me hard, as his right hand made its way to mine.

"Down this road," I said, pointing out Jan's driveway. After three minutes, we reached the grand black gates. Sure, she wasn't a celebrity, but her life reflected such divine elegance.

I rolled the window down. "Good evening, Mr. Winters. I'm here to see Jan."

"Hey, Sophie, new car? New boyfriend?"

I laughed, looking at Thomas, but Mr. Winters was serious.

"Yes, new everything," I responded.

He smiled, as the big gates came apart. I rolled the window up, and Thomas seemed lost in his thoughts.

He finally asked, "Soph, are you seeing someone else?"

"No, I don't believe in relationships."

"Are you sleeping with someone?" he asked seriously. Talk about an odd question, and an even odder moment.

"How should I answer that, Thomas?"

His green eyes glared into my flesh. "I don't want to be chasing you around if some Wall Street idiot has already laid claim to you."

Though I felt flattered by his jealousy, I didn't have time for this high school behavior. He continued up to the mansion's circular driveway, and admired the house and grounds.

"Your friend in the mafia?" he asked.

"No, you idiot. Her husband's old money," I responded, pretending to be slightly insulted.

Jan was at the front entrance in a robe. Her long, blonde hair was tangled in more knots than mine, and she looked as if she'd been crying for days.

"Thank you, and I'm sorry," I said.

"Sorry about what exactly, Sophie?" he inquired.

"Sorry about...well...just sorry."

"Good night, Sophie," he replied.

I leaned over and gently kissed his pink lips, and it was simply the softest kiss we'd ever shared. I opened the door and walked over to Jan, who hugged me as if there would be no tomorrow.

"Sophie, darling, who is that?" she asked.

"Oh, just someone, you know."

"No, I don't know," she countered.

Thomas rolled the window down and said, "I must say, your home is very impressive."

"Thank you. My husband's a Wall Street something."

Thomas smiled, "Well, that's a big something."

She smiled and waved, as Thomas drove off.

"My husband's a very-big-asshole something," she said once Thomas was out of sight.

"How do you really feel, Jan? Like hello, you're supposed to be astoundingly happy, right?" I had a smile on my face that was priceless, given that I really never smiled. I was terrified of getting those laugh lines, duh!

"Oh my God, Sophie, are you in love?" Jan asked.

I blushed. *It doesn't mean anything*, I thought.

"You never blush like that!" Jan exclaimed.

"Please, let's focus on you right now. I'm here for you."

We walked into her foyer, which was fit for a queen and her servants. There were crystal chandeliers from Europe, and silk-striped draperies from ceiling to floor. For Pete's sake, the only thing missing was Ker's face in mosaic on the wall.

"Jan, what's wrong?" I was worried like mad about her.

Though we were best friends, we generally spoke more on the telephone than in person, especially since I'd become a hotshot broker. I kid you not: I'm now too bloody busy for even a private sale at Barneys.

She led me to her bedroom and closed the door. Her bedroom was elegant, with a twist of French country. The walls were washed in something bumpy and shiny, and the moldings were ancient but intricate. Her glorious four-poster bed looked as if it had come from Caesar's bedroom. It was a shame there wasn't anything Roman about her sex life, well with Ker at least.

I looked up at the ceiling. It was as if Michelangelo had painted it himself. There were hand-painted angels in 24 carat gold-leaf on the ceiling, and I wondered to myself, *what a way to kill the mood? How unholy was my mind,* I mused. I was there for her issues, but my goodness, I had never seen anything like this.

"Sit down," Jan said, as she patted the bed.

"I would much rather sit in your velvet wing chair."

"Why?"

"I don't want to mess up that bed by sitting on it with my ratty pants."

"Who goddamn cares? It's not like I'm going to be living here for long," she blurted in anguish, crying like a child.

I was never going to cry like that. Unless, of course I made the fatal error of meeting a man who had the key to my heart. How unlikely.

"Okay, I'll sit down," I said. I dusted my behind and sat on her silk duvet cover; it was floral from the eighteenth century, with Jan and Ker's initials embroidered in silk. Though really, I'm sure this bed only served one purpose, to sleep in.

Ker had more money than any Wall Street tycoon. But he had very little time for romancing his gorgeous trophy wife. You'd think that with that much money, he'd pay someone to rearrange his ridiculous schedule so he could keep up with the gardeners and playboys that kept his mansion pristine, and his wife sane.

"I have done some terrible things, Sophie, that have finally come to light," Jan said. "And I can't fix it."

I sat there, lost, and at the same time, in great awe of Jan. What was she missing? Passion, yes. She wanted a man to take her in her flower garden and show her how to till the soil. Ker was only into making millions and playing polo with the assistants, the ones I saw everyday who wore short skirts, ten-inch heels, and red lipstick. So, as opposed to re-baptizing their marriage, men often took a bite of the forbidden fruit.

I had to pull Jan together. When she was in her groove, she never cried. Crying to her was unnecessary hysterics, but now she was bawling in her bedroom like a child, as I held her, trying to comfort her.

"Ker doesn't want me back, and the hell with him," she said.

Jan was a sophisticated woman who drove a Rolls and wore pearls from Neiman. She had maids and butlers and everything but a bloody therapist.

"It's going to be okay, I promise," I said cradling her. I didn't know if it would be okay. I didn't know if it was the gardener that she'd miss, or her millions tied up in a prenup. This was all too scary for me. I was already scared before I had opened my chapter on men, but now I was outright disturbed.

"Hey, I'll go get you something to drink. Have you eaten?" I asked, as I wiped her tears with my hand.

"I haven't eaten, but I'm fine."

"No you're not. I'm going to get you something to eat. Your house assistant needs to be fired for neglecting you."

I didn't know what I was trying to prove; me in a kitchen was like a fish climbing a tree. Her home was impossibly complicated. I went left, then right, another right, and where the heck was I? I saw a strange man in a suit, smoking a cigarette like he belonged there. Who was this strange man in my friend's house? I was freaking out.

"Do I know you?" he asked.

"No, probably not." I replied abruptly. "Though, where's the kitchen?" I asked.

"You're that Becks girl?"

Yes, lovely, "that Becks girl," what a great first impression.

He shook my hand. "I know your father; I'm one of his clients. Nice to meet you." Then he pointed me in the direction of food.

"Say, what's going on with Jan and Ker?" I asked. I needed to know how exactly we got into this mess.

"Well, all I know is that they had a very explosive argument, he slammed her against the wall in front of everyone, and then left. I doubt they'll work this one out."

"Well, no offense, but what does he expect when he's never around? Anyway, a pleasure to have met you, and all that."

He stared at me like I was an escaped lunatic straight from the asylum, and I went to the kitchen. The refrigerator had clear doors, and all the food was marked with dates and ingredients. I wondered who lived like this. I supposed, only Jan.

I heated up something marked "organic pumpkin soup" and toasted a slice of multi-grain bread, and then walked back to Jan's room with a tray . Oddly, there was not one person left in the house to talk to; maybe her staff had all been fired.

I must say I was worried about Jan's mental condition. She was very gentle by nature, and if someone else had had to label all her food with ingredients and such, how would she ever survive a divorce?

"Here you go, dear. Soup and toast, with a cup of chamomile to ease your nerves," I said.

I could tell she felt better after a few minutes, and I felt better knowing that I had some humanity left in me. Jan grabbed my hand and kissed it, like my mother used to when she had feelings.

"How are things on your end?" she asked me.

"Lovely," I responded.

"And that new guy of yours? Did you do the dirty yet?"

"No!" I shook my head.

"Well, you look happy, that's all."

"I'm fine, busy with work. You know, Wall Street."

"I know. But don't end up like this, Sophie. Filthy rich and stinkin' unhappy. Darling, there is more to life than chasing Bentleys and diamonds in designer heels."

I looked at her. I'd never thought she was unhappy, until now. I was sad for her. And the Bentley… darn, Jan, why kill my dreams?

"On a better note, I said. "We should get away. Right away. How about the Hamptons?" I asked.

She thought about it, staring out her grand French doors, lost in the moment, and wishing that a trip away could simply erase all her pain.

"I could definitely use time away," she replied.

"We've got to find you some happiness out there, and champagne. I hope the two go together," I smiled. I hugged her, and she reciprocated with all the love that I never could feel from my mother.

I stood up and made my way to the doors, lost in my own

dilemma. I didn't know why I had such mixed emotions about relationships and marriages, and all that bitter stuff. Couldn't anyone be bloody happy anymore?

"So what should I pack?"

"Maybe something scandalous. Not your grandma panties, surely."

"Only you, Sophie. Do you think that's why my marriage stinks? He didn't find me sexy and scandalous anymore."

I wondered how to answer her, as the last thing she needed was more fuel for that killer flame. "Well, I can't say. Men are not like other humans; they're like stocks, volatile as hell."

"Darling, you are such a classic. I hope your future husband isn't too successful to sleep with you."

"A husband? *My* husband. I don't know about men. Sure, I went on dates, but marriage? That's complex. Me, married and being domestic? No, I'm far better off where I am."

"That's what I used to say until I met Ker. I fell madly in love with him, and though he's never around, I…"

"Please," I interrupted her. "He's a great provider, not a great lover. That explains why you left your thongs in the garden."

"Sophie, you are so cruel, but it's true."

As I helped her pack some lingerie, I grinned. It was ridiculous to have a conversation like this with her in the bedroom of the man that once was her everything.

"I do know one thing," I said.

She placed a few bralettes into her lingerie silk bag and looked at me, "What?"

"Before I get married, I want to have all my fantasies fulfilled, as marriage looks far less appealing than a custom library with books and mementoes from around the globe."

I laughed and looked at my Patek, realizing how late it had become.

"My driver will take you home, my darling," Jan said.

15

French in the Hamptons

The next morning, Hannah graciously helped me pack. She must have been sent to me by angels. She was better than any assistant. She was always on time, cooked fine, brewed immaculate tea, and spoke English as if she were from Oxford, well sort of. Sometimes I thought life would be sweeter if half the people I dealt with were foreigners who spoke no English at all, hence communicating with them would be stellar. It would only be a yes or no.

"I'm not going to the beach," I said. "Please burn that bikini, Hannah."

"You are going with Miss Jan. She doesn't like clothes too much."

"So I'm supposed to dress indecent?" I asked, laughing.

"No, just a little bit less like a librarian." She gave half a smile.

"Okay, sounds good. I'll try to not be so Wall Street."

I worked with sexist pigs all day, and I was a very conservative dresser, unlike most of the women at work. I never could understand how men were to take you seriously if you dressed in a revealing way. Work was the one place I really didn't do sexy. Outside of work, my style was more preppy than anything else.

My lack of sexy style was okay, because if I ever had a husband he would probably be a priest. I didn't think priests were allowed to have wives, though, unless they were from the Middle East or something. I'd heard weird stories where men of certain cultures were allowed to marry and have four wives or so. Why not? As long as the woman could marry four husbands. Let's be fair, now. But four husbands! I couldn't even imagine one.

Well, after last night with Jan, I didn't envision marriage bells and doves flying over Oheka Castle. I felt that too many people in marriages were unhappy alcoholics, and convenient sex with Mr. Forbidden was the new skinny cocktail. So to heck with it all. I wouldn't do love; not now, not ever.

"Remind me to send a card to Thomas, Hannah," I said.

"It's his birthday?"

"No, it's going to say: 'I'm becoming a nun. Please move on.'"

She rolled her eyes as she packed my vintage suitcase with a grin on her face, but you could tell she thought I was a complete goner.

"You need this vacation," she said.

I nodded, as I busily texted Jaxwe. He was so mad that Duren said I didn't have to open forty accounts that he was losing his mind over it. He was constantly texting me outside of the office as if we were buddies. Seriously, that was a bit freakishly stalkerish.

I texted, "Tell it all to your psychologist, and please no more texting."

I was becoming one of them, heartless, arrogant, and everything I wasn't supposed to be as a lady. Well, I'd realized that I take after my mother. My mom hadn't even reached out to me since that epiphany, nor had I seen my father. I'd called his office but to no avail.

I was tired of everyone these days. It was too much crap to sort through. It was bad enough I was going to be twenty-five soon with no diamond in sight. Well, at least Robin was happy with his discontent and lack of success in his love life. As Robin reasoned, "If it hasn't happened for me, then it's not for me."

I often looked at him and thought, *Whatever works, buddy*, but I was happy he wasn't as messed up as others I dealt with.

My packing was done, and I was very eager to get going. I thought about how lucky I was to have a boss like Duren. I liked his father-like qualities that my own dad didn't have. That is awkward to say, especially since Duren was so darn sexy. But, as they say, honesty was purely getting out the junk in your soul, even though it wouldn't necessarily free you.

"Thank you, Hannah." I looked at her with a smile. "I can't imagine you not being here."

"This job is my life," she replied. "You are all my family, Miss Sophie."

"Oh, you are such a good lady," I said, and gave her a hug.

"Your mother 's driver will be here shortly to collect a few of her things, and I have to finish packing it in boxes," she said.

I felt disappointed that my mother was closer to Hannah than to us. I couldn't have even imagined this chapter in our lives, but my mother had separated herself from all of us. All she cared about now, were her things.

"What things does she need?" I asked in a rage. I was livid with a capital *L*.

"Um, her clothing, her books, some kitchen stuff, and her teas."

Her teas? What would I drink? My God, not the teas!

"Okay, then you must attend to mommy dearest," I said sarcastically.

As Hannah left, my phone rang.

"Hello?"

"Becks, it's Duren."

"Thank you for the keys to your Hamptons house, Duren. I was in dire need of a few days away."

"It's not a problem. I'm going to have one of my housekeepers at the house for you, and my son, Cooper, will be out there if you need anything."

"Really you don't have to, and I can't say..."

"Don't, Becks; it's all good. Oh, and congratulations again on your big account with Jabari. He sent over half a mil."

Jabari ... I couldn't remember a thing, except that I was needing and taking vacations as if I'd been on Wall Street for years.

"No way," I said.

"Yes way. You are meant for this business. Go clear your head, and when you get back, you're on your own. No more accounts for Jaxwe."

What the hell and oh my God! I loved this man; it was so weird how love fit itself into kind gestures. I sighed with relief. I was climbing this ladder very quickly. Maybe it was hereditary to be good at business and incompetent emotionally.

As I ran down the stairs, I noticed Robin at the door staring outside at Hannah. He seemed to be taken by her. I crept up behind him. Was he interested in Hannah? Oh Almighty, this could not be.

"Robin!"

"Sophie, what the hell?"

"Yes, that's what I was thinking. Stop ogling Hannah."

"What, Hannah? Oh no, I was wondering about Dad."

Dad was talking to the driver, and he was *pissed off*. Robin and I cleared out from the doorway as he stormed through. He threw his keys to his bad-boy sports car on the sofa and yelled at us, "Who the hell does your mother think she is?"

I turned around and laughed silently. I always suspected my mother was my father's boss and he just didn't know it yet. Ha. Obviously she was calling all the shots.

"I tried to make this work, but in all honesty, your mother is so completely incompetent when it comes to love and honor to anyone." My dad had tears in his eyes. I'd never seen that before. "So, children, I am going to file for a divorce."

I was speechless. A divorce! And Jan's limo was already waiting for me outside.

"No troubles, Dad. I'm sure you'll work it out," I said patting him on the arm.

From the assistant he had an affair with, to his millions wrapped up overseas. It was no biggie.

"I can't save you all from your own flaws," he said. "Heck, you want to make tons of money on Wall Street. You have my DNA, but lack of emotions, that's all your mother."

Words couldn't find their way to my vocals. Truth was, I loved a good rebuttal, but not today. My father was hurt, and as much as he was heartless, he had passion for success.

Silently, I closed the doors to our Brookville home, wondering where and when I started defrosting my heart. As I got in the limo, I put on my Bvlgaris and acted as if I was happy. Rule number one on Wall Street was that you always acted *as if.* A top broker I once met taught me that as I sat in his pimp conference room and stared at him as if he were the reigning new Wall Street lord. But he was an ass with impeccable taste, money to burn, and mistresses supplied by a high-priced madam in Manhattan. Oops, I think I've said too much!

So act as if you're so bloody happy, even if your wife left you for the plumber. Act as if the next call could and will change your life. Yup, every stockbroker is a bloody actor in an exceptionally-tailored suit. Some needed serious psychiatric evaluation, though. Brokerage firms really needed to add on that service. I was all of the above.

"Darling, you look pale. What's the matter?" asked Jan.

"Nothing, I'm just ready to have the time of my life."

Jan looked amazing for a broken woman; in fact, broken women often looked better than happy ones. The happy ones were overweight and in sweats. The broken ones were in five-inch heels and tight dresses, and had hair like a Barbie doll and lips like Dior. I liked broken any day. I smiled as I studied Jan; she was the image of perfect beauty.

"You're wearing your wedding ring," I said.

She gave me a smile that only she could pull off, and said, "Yes, I am. It's a beautiful ring, isn't it?"

"No comment," I said and meant it.

She looked as if she knew what she had, and how it could be the way it was before. However crazy it was, it was still her marriage.

Over an hour or so later, Jan leaned forward toward the driver. "Mr. Shenta, can you pull over at Southampton village?"

"Yes, Mrs. Jan."

We got out of the limo and walked through a few boutiques.

"I am not feeling that shopaholic today," I said. "Maybe we can eat?"

"Yes, darling," she said as we walked into a very Tuscan restaurant. We sat down, and it was therapy time. Better get a shot of something.

"I'll have a skinny martini," I said to the waitress.

"Sorry, we don't have skinny anything!"

"Okay, I'll stick to sparkly with lemon."

"Sparkly?" the waitress inquired.

"What is this stupid town? Who doesn't know sparkly?" I said, while looking at Jan.

"Darling, not everyone is fancy like you." Jan smiled.

"Yes, sparkling water with lemon," I responded to the waitress.

Jan laughed. "I can so see you with your own butler and chef when you marry that vineyard."

I started coughing. "I could have choked; don't say that again. His name is Thomas, not vineyard."

"I hope his grapes are bigger," Jan said laughing.

"Oh my goodness! Really, his grapes?" Okay I was laughing. But grapes? "Better not be champagne grapes," I retorted.

The waitress brought Jan her glass of red wine and my sparkly, and we were good as gone.

"So, how's Ker?" I asked.

"He threatened to leave me last night, so I told him I'd leave."

She wore these very black Jackie O. sunglasses. If she teared up, I'd never know.

"He wasn't there to begin with, so don't worry that you've lost him," I said.

"Yes, I've made a family that he wasn't a part of, only his bank account was. Now I have to face the music, two teenagers later." She had two glasses of red wine, and then the sunglasses came off. The tears followed. I held her hands, and we looked like we were dating.

"Sophie, don't; they're looking at us like we're lesbians," Jan whispered.

We both sat there, sipping our drinks and eating organic greens over grilled octopus.

After two long happy hours with ourselves, the driver pulled up and opened the door. As we were leaving, the waitress asked, "Are you celebrities?"

"Nah, just really screwed up," I answered. She smiled, and I walked to the limo.

Our ride to the Hamptons had been tiring. I was exhausted emotionally, and Jan was drunk. Yes, already. This was going to be a hell of a trip. I hoped Duren had lots to drink at his house.

The driver pulled up to Duren's gated home and pressed the call button as he looked into the security camera. It was like I had arrived at James Bond's beach mansion. The tree-lined driveway led down to the oceanfront mansion.

If this was my potential future, I was definitely going to become the female Hugh Hefner. Forget the wedding, just mail me the silver bells from Tiffany. There was something about Wall Street; it could make you obsessed with money and power. Most of the men I'd met had chosen money and power over their wives and their happy picket-fence families. It was a natural high with a great lay.

We got out of the limo, and Jan took her oversized shades

off and said, "Where the hell am I? Is this grape boy's house? My gosh, I didn't know grapes could make you live like this."

I laughed so hysterically that I could have peed myself. "No, it's my boss's summer home."

"You have two men! I thought my life was a mystery, but, darling…"

"No, I have no men. Please sober up, and then we'll talk. I don't have conversations with drunk folks. Yes, especially women. It's like they say, 'Don't pitch the bitch.' Same concept."

I pressed ten buttons on the front keypad, but no response. I couldn't remember the codes. Like hello, I didn't graduate from Yale; my brain could only do so much. I called Duren.

"Where the hell is Helene?" Duren asked.

"Helene, who?"

"The housekeeper, she is supposed to be there."

"I'll find her. Go back to your calls. I'll figure it out or climb through a window."

"Don't hurt yourself!" he said. He cared, how thoughtful.

"I'll try," I said.

"Yes, do that." A brief moment passed. I didn't even catch that he'd hung up.

Within minutes, as Jan and I were sitting on the steps, a car drove into the driveway. A young man hopped out and shook my hand.

"You must be Sophie Becks?"

I was bewildered. What the heck! Who was this?

"Yes, I'm Sophie," I replied.

"I'm Cooper, Chance's son."

"Oh! Thank you for coming," I said gratefully.

"No problem. Helene is on her way, but I'll open the doors for you."

He plugged in the code, and he was on his way. For having a father like his, Cooper was dressed as shabbily as a beach bum in Montauk.

Jan took her bags in, and I was eager to see his home. I opened the French doors to the deck, and was instantly enamored of sheer, silk drapes billowing in the air from the cool ocean breeze. Duren's style was very Wall Street and manly. Multicolored marble ran all through the house with Roman-style marble pillars. The ceilings were high and coffered in wood.

My God, I thought instantly, *this wasn't his home, it was his shag pad.* I was sure of it. I thought the polo mansion was mind-blowing, but this took the cake.

I showed Jan to the kitchen, in order to sober her up a bit. There were more Sub-Zeros in here than a chef's kitchen. The room was done in dark wood and marble, and there was a big *D* for Duren in the middle of the marble floor. The artwork on the walls looked as if they belonged to the Met in the city.

I opened the fridge and pulled out a bottle of common sparkling water. There were freshly cut lemons in a glass jar with "Sophie" written on a white label on the front. How thoughtful, but I wondered if Mr. Duren was buttering me up for something. Why was he so good to me?

Then a lady, Helene, I assumed, came into the kitchen.

"*Bonjour, mademoiselle, comment ça va?*" asked Helene.

"*Je vais bien,*" I replied. What the heck, French? Come on, Duren, you sure know how to mess my mind up, I thought.

"*Je m'appelle Helene.*"

"*Je m'appelle Sophie.*"

I took French when I was little, and I loved French men, but come on, a French housekeeper? I really wanted to kick Duren's rear.

"I need rest," Jan said. "You are both speaking French, and we're in the Hamptons, not Paris."

"Sorry, darling," I responded. *"Parlez-vous anglais?"* I asked Helene.

"Oui."

"Good!" I exclaimed as if I'd just come up from the ocean for air.

With directions in English from Helene, we walked to our rooms. I jumped into bed, exhausted from the drama of my new career, to my life in Brookville, to Jan's life in Muttontown, to our French-speaking housekeeper in the Hamptons. Jan came into my room in a pink robe with her initials in purple. I rolled over to face her and started laughing.

"What's the matter, darling?" she asked sitting down in a big chair in the corner of the room.

"I have a question that I really wish you'd answer," I said.

"I've got a very bad headache, but I'll try."

"Why the hell do you, and everyone with lots of money, need to monogram everything?"

"Very simple," she said, with her hair in a bun and her pale legs resting on a tier of pillows, "See, sometimes we get so darn drunk, we forget who we are. The monogrammed things remind us."

What a moment it was. I laughed and then pulled the soft goose down comforter over me, turned over, and fell asleep. I slept for a few hours, and then I awoke to the French housekeeper talking to someone unseen.

I'd had it with French. When I was a kid, I had a French tutor, Madame Marie. God, I hoped she'd moved back to Quebec or Paris, as she'd made me hate French.

I looked over at Jan, who'd fallen asleep in the corner armchair. We were both tired out of our minds.

"*Le dinner est servi!*" Helene called into my room.

"What the hell is she saying?" Jan asked me.

"Dinner is served."

"Oh, lovely, I'm starved."

Jan got up, pulled her hair into a better bun, and went to her room to change. I lay in bed looking at my phone and the many texts I'd received: Robin, Rain, Thomas, and Duren.

"How's it going, Becks?" Duren had texted.

I responded, "*Très Français!*"

He sent me a smiley.

I couldn't complain; I was living a dream, albeit a very French one with no handsome men to look at, well, at the moment.

16

PLAYBOYS ARE IN

Dinner was beautiful. The food wasn't French, but it was quite filling. I sat on the back porch looking at the wealthy, lonely old men who waved as they sailed by. I was very much a beach girl, just not the public beaches, though. I lived for privacy. Well, I guess it was good that I tried my best to achieve more than others did. It was my gift to myself to make up for my lack of personal relationships.

I stared at Jan as she ate her meal in great silence. At some point, I thought that she was counting how many times she chewed each bite of food. She was too sophisticated to do boring; it must have been the wine earlier. The sun was setting, and I thought it would be lovely to walk on the sand and feel the breeze blow through my curly locks.

"You're lost in the ocean," Jan said. "Wanna go for a walk?"

I listened and breathed in the ocean scent, and then I stood up and walked across the paved patio flooring and down the wooden stairs that led to the ocean.

"Let's go," I yelled out.

And Jan followed. She wore linen pants with a blouse with gold buttons down the front. Her hair was the healthiest I'd ever seen: long and blonde, maybe bottled, but who cared? Whatever made a woman happy. Her eyes were as blue as the ocean, and she had the height of a supermodel, so beautiful inside and out. Okay, she was conflicted about her marriage, but who wasn't?

I never fully understood our friendship with the large age difference, but there was just something about her I loved; not the money that made her live like royalty, but her laughter, her joy, and above all else, her devotion to being genuine, with me at least. She had that joie de vivre.

We walked on the sand, with no words, just the sound of the waves trying to steal my feet. We looked at the homes on the ocean; each mansion seemed bigger than the next.

"What do I do when I get back to Muttontown?" Jan asked abruptly.

"Ask me something else, can you? I fear that anyway you look at it, it's going to be war with you and Ker."

She took a deep breath and responded, "Sophie, never marry unless you know that love is the only thing between you, promise me."

I stopped and held her arm. She was taller than I, and I looked up at her.

"Why the hell are you ruining my vacation with all this marriage-warning nonsense?" I continued walking, and she stood there mad; not mad at me, mad at her man. Heck, no one was interested in marrying someone as messed up as I was. That was called excess baggage and far too complicated. I had seen everyone I knew fail with love, so I had to be terribly stupid to believe that God would send me a soul mate to love.

"I know I should seek therapy for my lack of desire for a man to love me or marry me," I said.

"Darling, you have been bitten not by your own experiences, but by those of everyone around you."

I felt the bliss of sand between my polished toes and the scent of salt water, as seagulls fought for the fish that washed ashore. It was a feeding frenzy; why couldn't they be more civilized?

"Yes, everyone," I said. "I don't have anything that feminine in my psyche. In my heart, I'm like a man."

She laughed so loudly that I paused from saying anything further. She put her arms around me and kissed my cheek. "You are like my very own daughter, you know."

"Yes, your adopted daughter. The one from a bad home."

We had walked way past Duren's home, and it was getting darker out. The sun had already gone down, and the clouds were a palette of orange and red. It was a masterpiece of God's refinement; no painter could do that to a canvas, except maybe Monet or that guy who painted *The Starry Night*, yes, Van Gogh. Think how much wine he had to drink to envision that!

We turned back, and were nearing Duren's home, when I noticed a very handsome, Arabian-looking man in a white shirt with a crooked bowtie. He was sitting on the steps of a Mediterranean villa, and speaking something foreign on his telephone.

It was like *Sex in the City*, but in the Hamptons, and I was Carrie. Beside him stood a mysterious man in a black suit, maybe late forties, with a beard. All I heard was *huck* and *irakmin*, which sounded very Middle Eastern.

I locked eyes with the man in the crooked bow tie, and I felt a shiver. All the hair on my body stood up on end. His eyes were like those of a lion, with so much depth in them, and so many shades of green and yellow glistening like the colors of sunset. His skin was golden, like the sand from the Sahara, and his lashes were long and his lips were dry, maybe from the heat of summer. He could have used some lip balm. *Take mine,* I thought.

As I walked past him, I didn't see any women in bikinis. Usually men like that had a harem of them sunbathing. I felt all hot and shivery, something I had never experienced.

"Hello," he called out.

I looked back over my shoulder, and he walked toward us. Jan looked confused, as my attention was very clearly taken by him. She saw me blush like a sixteen-year-old with a crush on a college man.

"Hi," I said, as he took my hand and kissed it gently. "I'm Sophie, Sophie Becks."

"Hello, I'm Zur," he replied.

Oh my good self, could this be my awakening into the depths of love and lust? His accent captivated me. His face was like that of a king of Egypt; his features dark and striking like lightning. We couldn't take our eyes off each other. It was as if words were not from our world, our very presence conveyed so much more. I licked my lips, as my gosh, my heart was racing. Our eyes were engulfed in heat.

Jan grabbed my hand and said to Zur, "And I'm her friend Jan. Listen, Sophie Becks is very complicated. Good night." And she led me away from my knight in shining armor.

"What the heck!" I said.

"I'll see you again, complicated Becks," said Zur.

I turned slightly as my bodyguard, Jan, held my arm strongly.

"You sure know how to mess up my mojo," I whispered.

"Darling, here you were talking about love being baloney,

153

and then we pass by this Zar, or whatever, and you can't think straight."

"It was Zur, not Zar." I know I should have been listening to her, but I couldn't think. Once we got back to Duren's, I sat on the back steps and slapped myself.

"Gosh, what was that? It was so intense."

"Oh, Sophie. Now I'm going to have to worry about you," she replied, bewildered.

Thank God her phone rang. I really didn't want to hear this from her. She was forty-three with men issues. I was almost twenty-five, had no life, and was just making it big on Wall Street. By the time I found a man, if I found a suitable man, I would probably be nearly ninety, with nothing but droopy everything.

Helene came out and handed me a glass of sparkling water and lemon.

"*Helene, je voudrais du vin,*" I said softly, hoping I was asking her to bring me wine and not Clorox.

"*Oui, mademoiselle,*" said Helene.

"Well, look on the bright side, Jan. That French tutor did a good job, after all. I speak French to the French and scream in English at Americans. Let's toast to happiness and to foreign men with exotic accents, shall we?"

As we toasted, my phone rang. Jan looked at the caller ID, held it up to me, and said, "Oh, you forgot grape boy. Not nice, Sophie."

Jan answered the phone, "Hello, Sophie Becks's phone, how can I assist?"

"Hi, I'm looking for Sophie," I could hear Thomas say.

"Who may this be?" asked Jan, as I laughed my ass off.

"It's Thomas."

"Oh, darling, it's Thomas," Jan said, as I grabbed the phone and tried desperately to mute it, as I was laughing out of control.

"Hey, how are you?" I responded, when I finally steadied myself.

"Good, how's your vacay?" he asked. Oh, how'd he know? I didn't remember telling him.

"Good. Having fun. Lots of it."

"Nice! When can I see you?"

"When I get back."

"Yes, that's right. I forgot you don't like being chased."

I smiled, but it wasn't really true, as clearly, I now wanted to be chased by Zur.

"Well, I'll see you when you get back to Brookville," he said. "And Sophie?"

"Yes, Thomas?"

"Be safe."

I held the phone a while longer after he'd hung up. I couldn't explain it, but here was this amazing man with a great upbringing and manners, and I was running the opposite way. Maybe I wasn't ready for his goodness…and grapes.

Jan looked at me and smiled, "Let's go in, shall we? It's getting dark, and bugs are trying to eat me."

After we came back inside, we watched Helene's favorite French movie, *The Intouchables*. Luckily, there were subtitles, as we clearly wouldn't have understood half the movie otherwise. We ate French cheeses and baguettes with olives and sipped wine that complemented the cheeses. God forbid the cheese and wine weren't paired to perfection. Jan would have fired Helene.

As the movie neared its middle, the buzzer at the gate

buzzed. Duren had a sophisticated system, and the camera feed popped up onto the television we were watching. It showed a man at the gates in a sports car. I looked closer and recognized the mysterious man from the beach.

"*Oh mon Dieu, qui est-ce?*" asked Helene in a panic. "Who is it?" she repeated in English.

"It's a good-looking man in a sports car. Don't panic, Helene, Sophie can handle this," said Jan looking at me.

"No problem," I said as I pressed a button. The gates opened, but then I panicked. I was dressed in a nightgown, looking like someone out of *Little House on the Prairie*.

He drove up the driveway like an slick ad for a foreign car. I watched him on the television, yearning to know him better, to touch him, and speak whatever language it was he was speaking.

The doorbell rang, and Jan snapped her fingers at me. "Sophie, composure. I've never seen you this way."

Pacing the floor, I asked, "What do I do?"

"Put on your darn big-girl panties, and deal with it," she replied.

I didn't even smile in response, as I normally would. I walked to the door and opened it, forgetting I was in my silk nightgown.

"Hi, Miss Complicated, how are you?" Zur asked.

"I heard you speaking in another language before, I wasn't sure whether you were fluent in English," I remarked.

"I speak Arabic, Swahili, Urdu, and Turkish. English certainly isn't a problem."

"Oh, good," I said.

"Want to talk outside where there isn't anyone to listen?" he asked with a smile. I looked behind me and saw Helene and Jan staring at us.

"I'm in my nightgown."

"That's a nice nightdress. It is nighttime, no?"

I thought he was funny. I walked out to his car and sat in the front seat, in my nightgown. For the first time, I did not know what kind of car I was in, and somehow it didn't matter.

"I would love to get to know you," he said. I smiled, as my heart was overjoyed.

"I'm just here on a vacation. This isn't my house; it belongs to my boss." I looked out the window and then into his light-green eyes with hues of sunlight. I felt shy, and could feel my blush, and he smiled at me, staring.

"Don't stare! It's not polite," I said.

"I can't help it. You are the most beautiful woman I have ever seen."

"That's questionable," I replied, smiling.

We spoke for an hour, smiling and flirting. He asked if I was married, and when I said no, he sighed with relief. This had to be the guy for me, as clearly any other man would have driven away by now, speeding for his life. Heck, I was Sophie Becks, every man's nightmare. Seriously.

"Where are you from?" I asked.

"Now that's a complicated question. I'm from a lot of places."

"Hmm, that's not a straight answer."

He looked over at me and smiled, swiping his hair back with his big hands. I should have known he was more complicated than even my screwed-up emotions.

"I'm visiting from Dubai."

"Wow, that's a far distance, and cultures apart."

"Yes, I'm sure," he responded.

"Are you married? Just wondering."

"Just wondering, Sophie? No, I was never that lucky to find a woman who wanted me and not my money or my name." I was speechless. Who was he really? And did I really want to know? "Will you have dinner with me tomorrow night?" he asked nonchalantly.

"I'll check my schedule," I replied. "I have a few conference calls to make in the evening, but I don't know why not."

"I'll see you at seven?"

"Sure," I said smiling.

As I got out of his car, he smiled and stared at me in a deep way, as if he could read my mind.

"Sophie. Don't wear your nightdress for dinner, okay?"

"Yes, surely," I laughed. And he drove off dangerously fast down the lit driveway and into the night. I stood at the steps by the door until I couldn't see him anymore. Jan came to the door and stood beside me.

"I can tell by that look that you may have finally found a man that burns your flame," she said knowingly.

"Yes, I can't explain this, and I won't even try. I just feel something with him, and I don't like feeling anything."

I yawned and walked inside the mansion. I noticed Helene closing the windows and doors as the sea breeze blew through the foyer and into the formal sitting room. I walked up the staircase looking at the twenty-foot ceiling lit by the most beautiful crystal chandelier I'd ever seen. Jan stood at the bottom of the staircase checking her iPhone.

"Would you like some tea?" she asked me.

"What kind?"

"Chamomile with lavender leaves."

"Great, that sounds very refined, indeed," I said smiling.

I loved Jan, she was fit for royalty. Though, I did hope her husband picked her up soon. There was only so much bloody refinement a person could take.

17

Horses Are a Girl's Best Friend

The next morning began drearily. I woke up to Jan yelling from the balcony of her bedroom in the west wing of the mansion, which was far away from mine. I took the remote from the dark pine chest next to my bed, and opened the blackout drapes. I could barely open my eyes, so I grabbed my shades and put them on. I'm sure I must have looked like a rock star gone bad. But was there such a thing as a rock star gone good?

It was bright out, despite being very cloudy, and my mind revisited the memory of Zur; the beach, his eyes, his skin. My iPhone rang, and I grabbed it.

"Holy crap, FaceTime!" I yelled.

It was Duren. Awkward. I quickly brushed my hair, wiped my face, and then pressed answer.

"Becks, how's it going?" he asked.

"Just lovely, Duren."

"I just wanted to congratulate you on your newest big account, your second huge account this week!"

"Yay!" I said applauding myself. "How full of myself am I?"

For starters, women didn't open accounts. They didn't work in a man's world making a person's *yearly* salary in a month, wearing a pencil skirt and pintuck blouse, in four-inch Dolce stilettos with reading glasses on. As if I ever read anything but a man's mind. Now *that* was a reason to be full of yourself.

"I want to thank you again for letting me stay at your beach house. I'm loving it here."

Duren smiled, "Are you there with your boyfriend?"

"No, no, I don't have a love life. I'm all business." *Yes, no love,* I thought. *Just passion getting ready to blow my panties off.* I smiled.

"Good, because I need you 120 percent."

"Right, I'm already there," I said. And with that, Jan came bolting into my room.

"Gotta go," I said. "And by the way, why do you have a French housekeeper?"

"My wife is French."

"Your wife has impeccable taste."

"She must. Why do you think I work so freaking hard?" I smiled as a sentence like that deserved a smirk. "Okay, see you Wednesday, and drive responsibly."

Jan stared at me in great despair, and I hung up like there was no tomorrow.

"What now?" I asked.

"Ker is on his way."

I felt so many things when she said that, but more than ever, I felt that it was important that she fix her marriage for the sake of her lifestyle. And for mine! Hello, with Jan around, I always had to be on my best behavior. For crying out loud, this wasn't a seminary for *nuns*! My thoughts immediately returned to Zur.

Jan could not live like a normal woman. She needed

extravagance and pearls handpicked from the ocean. She couldn't live on a budget or ever be impoverished. She would be like a mermaid on land, and that never ended well. So, I was happy Ker wanted to try to work it out with her. After all, Jan had worked her fine backside off to live like that.

"I'm going to go pack my things. I hope I haven't turned your trip upside down, darling," she said, looking frail.

"Of course not. Do you need help?" I replied.

"No, Sophie sweets, I'm fine," she said, as she walked back to her room.

I pulled the down comforter over my head and closed the drapery with the remote. I needed more sleep, but I also needed to be of comfort to Jan, like a good girl. I dragged myself out of the comfort and warmth of my bed and headed to Jan's room.

"*Bonjour, Mademoiselle Sophie,*" said Helene, as I passed her in the hallway.

"*Bonjour Helene,*" I replied.

"Jan, darling," I said as I walked into her room. She was sitting on her bed looking forlorn, as if someone had just stolen her Versace gown. "What's the matter?" I asked.

"I don't know. What is the right thing for me to do?"

"Well, let's see..." I said, sitting down. "Hmm, do you love him?"

"Yes."

"Do you want to work this out?"

"Yes and no."

"Do you love the life you live?"

"Oh, heck yes." She smiled. Now I was talking her language.

"Do you love your Rolls?" I asked.

"Yes."

"Do you love having a butler?"

"Yes."

"Do you absolutely love your closet, the size of my entire house?"

"Sophie!" she responded.

"Yes or no?"

"Yes, of course I do."

"Well, then you and your husband are a match made, if not in heaven, then somewhere else; somewhere where high society runs through the fields of gold. Voilà, I've saved a marriage!"

She smiled and looked at me like I was a freak. "You are crazy, Sophie Becks! Now I know why you fit in so well on Wall Street with those lunatics."

"It's a gift," I said with a shrug, and smiled.

We walked down the spiral staircase with Jan's designer bag and matching suitcase. She looked gloriously beautiful in her pintuck skirt and jacket with a vintage pearl necklace. Her face was simply powdered, with red lips shined glossier than a Chanel lipstick ad. I held her suitcase as the gate buzzed. Helene rushed to meet us at the door just as Ker drove up the driveway.

"I'll call you when I get home. Do answer, darling" Jan said, raising her perfectly manicured eyebrows at me.

Ker stepped out of his dark-blue Rolls-Royce, wearing plaid shorts, a pink polo with golf shoes, and his signature Patek watch. He looked sort of like a not-so-hot George Clooney. It was amazing how money could make any man attractive.

"Sophie, how are you, dear?" Ker asked.

"Not bad, staying out of trouble," I replied.

He smiled, and I could see his crooked left front tooth. I

wondered what a woman like Jan saw in him. Sure he had charm and money, but was that really enough?

"Darling," Ker said, hugging Jan and kissing her cheeks as if he'd lost her for months.

She hugged him back and placed her Bvlgari shades on while looking at me. She kissed me on both cheeks, and I hugged her tightly.

"Do the right thing, regardless. I wouldn't want a random twenty-two-year-old to just waltz in and take everything you've suffered for," I whispered to her, as Ker took her suitcase to the car. Let's face it: men moved on much faster than women. They didn't grieve the same way if you left them; they went out and slept with prostitutes or young, airheaded bimbos right away!

I stood in the dark-cherry doorway and waved. Somehow, I knew that they'd work their issues out. Ker would, wisely, be afraid of her in a divorce. What Wall Street idiot, who was worth millions, would want a divorce? After that, your damn life was over, because your wife could make you homeless; and she would.

On the other hand, Jan was the First Lady of Long Island, a classic beauty with a taste of extreme luxury, and let's not forget she lived for charity events and her not-so-shabby book club.

As I walked back into the house, Helene had prepared a small spread of breakfast for me, and I was so pleased with her.

"Breakfast, Miss Sophie?"

"It smells divine," I said. *"Merci."*

"Oui, Mademoiselle. You are most welcome."

She handed me a blue English plate with poached eggs and salmon with spinach. Then she handed me a big brown box wrapped in a red bow.

"What's this?" I asked. *"Qui est-ce?"*

She responded, "A man left you the box."

"Oh," I replied, surprised.

I opened the box quicker than anything else. It was a lace nightgown. I couldn't stop laughing. It was beautiful, but what a weird gesture. At the bottom of the box was another smaller box. As I held it in my hand, Helene opened the kitchen ceiling-to-floor windows. I opened the box, and it was filled with rose petals. I took the petals out and found a note. I opened it.

"His phone number! Oh my gosh, how crazy." I looked up at Helene and she smiled.

I grabbed my iPhone and dialed his number. I couldn't stop smiling. My God, I was smitten like a mad person. Even if this guy was stalking me, I wouldn't mind. But, one thing was for sure, I couldn't wait for dinner.

"Hello," he said, answering the phone.

"Hi, it's Sophie."

"Hi, how are you?" Zur asked.

"I'm okay," I replied. "Thank you for that nightgown. What a weird gift." He laughed. "I was wondering if you wanted me to wear it later for dinner," I teased.

"No, that would be too much for me."

"Ooh," I said.

"What are you doing today?" he asked.

"I'm headed out. I'm thinking about doing a little horseback riding, and then there are some boutiques I must visit in Southampton. What are you and your entourage doing?" I asked.

"I'm playing polo at a friend's house."

"Polo, how impressive. That's one of my hobbies."

"What is?"

"Watching a man play polo."

"Yes, I'm sure." I could hear him smile through the phone.

"Well, I've got to go. There's another call coming through. See you later?"

"Be good, Sophie!"

"I will certainly try to be, Zur."

I wondered, for a moment, what kind of game I was playing. Then I dialed Duren's office, and his stupid assistant put my call through to the conference room.

"Becks, all good?" Duren asked.

"Yes, thank you. I was wondering if you have a car I can drive?"

"Yes, in the garage, you can drive my Aston. The keys are in the desk in the kitchen, top drawer!"

"Thank you, boss!"

"Having fun?"

"Yes, lots of fun. I'm headed down to the barn now for a trail ride."

"Call Cooper if you need anything."

"Will do. *Merci beaucoup*. Thank you."

An hour or so later, I had bathed and was ready to leave. I walked into the garage, and there I stood, living any woman's, or man's, dream; a beautiful, finely tuned Aston Martin. Yes, it was borrowed, but not bad for a trial.

I had never thought twice about being a broker. The one thing that sold me was the money that could be made, and the life that only a few could achieve. Sure, it was a dog-eat-dog world, but what the heck, we were all barking to become that stockbroker that made a quarter million dollars in a month.

Duren's Aston Martin looked like the immaculate conception of the car world. It was perfection. At this point, I wasn't content with just one car; I wanted the whole collection of cars that I'd driven in the past few weeks.

I drove down the driveway, and as I got to the gate, I saw a black Bentley parked to the side with lights blinking. As I neared the car, the black-tinted windows went down, and there he was, my knight in shining armor, Zur. I pretended to be nonchalant about our happenstance meeting, but actually, I was on cloud nine.

"Hey," I called out.

"Nice car," he replied.

"Yes, yours isn't too shabby either. Waiting for someone at the crossroads?"

"Nope, I found her already," he said, smiling at me.

"See you later?" I replied.

"Indeed."

I felt as if I was about to bungee jump from a plane. The feeling of being near him did something to me that was far more than magic; it was beginning to feel like an addiction. The desire to see him at every stop sign had me smiling. At the equestrian center in East Hampton, I pulled up and parked, or should I say, tried to park. I could barely parallel park, and I considered my license a gift from the person that passed me in my driving test. One of the perks of my family's last name, maybe the only one.

I walked into the barn and saw one of my past trainers.

"Hey, Stef!" I called.

"Sophie, what's going on? You're out here this summer? Oh my God!" She hugged me, and it felt good that someone was happy to see me.

"How are you?" I asked.

"Staying cool, wrapping up the summer. You?"

"Enjoying the heat of August." I smiled. Yes, I was enjoying the heat of Zur.

"You can use this horse, Ginger; she's all tacked."

"Thanks, Stef."

I put on my helmet and velvet riding gloves and jumped up on the horse. I always put my hands on the horse's back, speaking to it as if the horse was one of my adopted children.

"Hi, Ginger baby, all good?"

Ginger was white with streaks of brown and brown hooves. Her mane looked better than most women's hair.

Horses had always been one of my passions. I wished that when I was younger I'd had the courage that I had now; I could have been a great equestrian. I'd always wanted to compete in the Hampton Classic, but I'd never made it there. Maybe that was why I was so taken with horses and men that played polo.

On the trail, it was dusty and hot, but Ginger didn't mind. Someone came galloping up behind me, and I commanded Ginger to the side as this idiot passed.

"Sophie!" called out a strange voice.

"Oh holy crap, Robbie! My God, I was just thinking, *What asshole would gallop up behind someone like that*," I said laughing.

"Yes, what an a-hole," he repeated. "Stef told me you were here, and I hadn't seen you in years."

"I've been so crazy busy, and you know, life gets complicated, and you run to the hills," I said truthfully.

"That's cool. Want company?" he asked. I didn't, but I didn't want to be rude.

"Sure, but let's not gallop."

He laughed. "Out of practice, eh?"

"Big time, dude!"

The trail was long, and the horses walked slower than summer leaving and fall creeping in. The forest was green with life, and the cicadas were sounding their shrill mating sounds. I only hoped one thing. No, not that Robbie would stop talking, but that the mosquitoes and bugs, and all of nature's lovely creatures, would stay the hell away from me.

"So how're your parents?" he asked.

"Hmm, let's see," I murmured. "Older and still unavailable!"

"You are still the same sarcastic girl you were when you were ten."

"That's what they say," I replied.

"How are the boys, Rain and Robin?"

"Robin has returned from chasing love in Rome. And Rain, he is a very successful idiot selling securities on Wall Street."

"No way!"

"Why, you thought he would be a priest?"

"Nah, but wow, that's cool," Robbie said.

Robbie's dad worked for my dad many years ago as his driver. We were good kids, not too cocky. That was one of our mommy dearest's rules: "Be polite to everyone and anyone who did work for us." Everyone was someone, whether it was the garbage man, the hunky landscaper who wore only girl's fitted shirts, or Hannah who cleaned up after us, as clearly our mother wouldn't.

But that rule didn't seem to apply to Wall Street. Nope, those bastards would eat you alive like a worm thrown into the lake at fishing season. Thank God, I wasn't a worm.

"Where do you work?" he asked.

"Guess."

"You're like a fashion something or other."

I laughed like nobody's business. "Uh, no. I'm a Wall Street stockbroker."

"No freaking way! You?"

Yes, me! That was how far I'd come to being the ruthless woman I was today, except for the few emotions I felt here and there.

"Sophie, you are…Nah, I can't believe it."

I looked at my Patek; it was four o'clock, "Wow, I never imagined this trail was so long."

"Yes, if you continue, you'll hit the ocean in less than five minutes," Robbie replied.

"How cool would that be? Okay, so I'm going to speed this up." I placed my heel to Ginger and tightened my reins. We cantered to the ocean, Hamptons style.

I didn't know which was best: the view, the sea breeze, or me on a horse like a pro. I jumped off Ginger and walked to the ocean sand, where I took off my helmet, gloves, and leather boots. I put my bare feet in the sand as I sat and watched the waves.

"You still like the beach, I see," Robbie said.

"Yes, there's a stillness that becomes a bigger part of you when you sit staring at the waves."

In the middle of my stillness, my phone buzzed in the back pocket of my fitted riding pants. It was an unknown number, but I picked up.

"Hello, Sophie Becks," I said.

"Hey, it's Zur. Don't you love the view?"

"What, are you here?" I asked, standing up and looking around me as if I'd lost the plot.

"Just kidding," he said.

"Oh." I was relieved, but still wanted to be sure. Funnily

enough, there was a black car with tinted windows up the driveway part of the beach, to the right.

"Where are you? I want to see you," I said, urging him to show himself.

"I'm not there. I'm at my friend's."

"Yes, well, okay, I'll see you later," I said.

"Are you alone right now?" he asked.

"Not quite." I walked away from Robbie a bit.

"Be good, baby."

"Really? Be good?" I said, smiling as he teased me.

"Yes, I tell that to everyone."

"Do you call everyone 'baby' too?"

He laughed, and I shrugged it off. I walked back to the horse and noticed that the car now had its lights on. Somehow, I knew that Zur had someone watching from that car. Maybe the driver was too stupid to know his lights were on.

"Robbie, let's go," I said to him, as I mounted my horse.

We cantered back to the barn, and I practiced my posting.

"Not bad," Robbie said.

I smiled, as I slowed down Ginger and patted her, and Stef took her away. I hugged Robbie and Stef and walked to my car. It was now almost 5:00 p.m.; I was running late and I was exhausted. Not to mention, I had forgotten all about lunch!

I got in the Aston Martin, and drove home as if I was starring in *Fast and Furious*. Nothing else came close to the feeling of driving like this.

"Oh bother, not a cop!" I yelled, as I looked into the rearview mirror. I was on North Sea Road, for crying out loud. "How many lights does he need to pull me over? Gracious," I murmured.

"Officer, how are you?" I said, when he approached my window.

"Can I see your license and registration?"

"My what?"

"Registration."

"What exactly is that?" I replied innocently.

He started laughing. "Whose car is this?" he asked, as he looked at my license.

"It belongs to my boss, Chance Duren. Okay, let me check the glove compartment." I opened it, and voilà, there it was!

The officer looked at it with a smile.

"What now?" I asked.

"Mr. Duren's a good man. You must be more than an employee, if he let you drive this car."

"More, as in a girlfriend, or maybe a secret lover? Is that what you're implying, Officer? I'm a stockbroker at Chance Duren's firm."

"Oh, I've never met a female stockbroker," he said, dumbfounded.

Yes, the cliché that every woman sleeps with her boss to get a higher position. If you were an attractive woman, why work, right? I was livid.

"Do you know Mr. Duren?" I asked.

"Yes, who doesn't?"

"Well, let's get him on the phone, shall we?"

"You-you don't have to," he said, stuttering. He handed me back my things, registration and all. "Well, Miss Becks, I hope you drive the speed limit here on in."

"Thank you for your time, Officer."

"Drive safely," he said, as he got back into his car.

I sat there confused about what he said, that he thought I must be more than an employee. Yes, here I was driving Duren's car, a $200,000 Aston, staying at his beach mansion, worth maybe $4.5 million, and I was a brand new stockbroker at his firm. Hmm…Was I missing something? Duren was in his forties. He was attractive and had a lot of class for a man. But, somehow, I didn't see him as a potential "man in my life."

I drove past Tate's, not even wanting to get a gluten-free ginger cookie; now I knew I must have issues. I pressed the button to the grand gates, and Helene opened them for me. I was already in some sort of dream and didn't even know it, and then came Zur, from God knows where. Surely, that man next to him on the beach was a bodyguard. I was playing way beyond my normal playing field.

I went up the stairs into my room, and shut the door behind me; I couldn't deal with Helene and speaking French right now. I dropped my clothing piece by piece to the floor and walked naked into the huge bath. Chandeliers hung from the ceiling, and pillars of marble flanked both sides of the sunken tub.

Turning the gold tap on, I peeked through the windows and had a glimpse through the trees of a distant house to the side of Duren's, one of his neighbors. Then I turned my attention to the bath, retrieving the bubble bath gel out of the dark wood vanity. I poured it into my bath, slipped my feet in, and submerged into an ecstasy of bubbles. I turned on Mozart on the CD player, as I soaked. It was calming, which was good, as clearly I needed to relax my mind; it was hopping all around like a wild rabbit.

At 6:30 p.m., I forced myself out of the bubbles, washed my hair with the handheld ancient showerhead, rinsed my body, and exited the bath.

18

Where Art Thou, Zur?

"Mademoiselle Sophie, there's something in the mail for you," Helene called through the bathroom door.

"Come on in," I said.

She dropped off the package and left. I dried my wet hands, as water dripped from my hair and ran down my neck. I smiled as I knew the package could only be from one person - Zur. I unwrapped the brown box, waded through the tons of lilac tissue paper, and found a knee-length black dress, with lace sleeves and a red velvet belt with a golden button.

I held it up to me and looked at myself in the mirror. Where had this man been my whole life? I'd never had a man dress me before. Sure, I could afford a thousand dresses, but this was, by far, the nicest dress I'd ever had. I searched through my things, hoping I'd brought my best lingerie. Oh God! I'd told Hannah I didn't do sexy, but I really needed sexy tonight. Like, hello!

After a few minutes of flat-ironing my hair, I put on mascara and some foundation, to add a little sunshine to my skin. I glossed my lips with Dior and put on my pearl earrings, the ones my mother had given to me on my twenty-first birthday. Yes, even when love wasn't present, there were always pearls.

I slipped on my Chanel shoes, black patent platforms, and grabbed my Hermès Kelly bag. It was elegant and practical, fitting only what I needed - a makeup brush, lipstick, powder, eye-shadow palette, and my telephone. I sat on the floral Victorian settee in the bathroom, debating if I needed anything else. I was ready, and couldn't remember feeling that nervous before. Luckily, the dress fit my every curve, almost as if it were made for me. Just like him, I thought.

At 6:58 p.m., I descended the stairs. Helene came and assisted me, adjusting my dress and hair here and there, as if I were in a fashion show.

"You look *magnifique*, Mademoiselle Sophie."

"*Merci beaucoup!*"

As I checked my phone, and saw a missed called from Thomas, the gate suddenly buzzed.

"Not good," I said to Helene, as I showed her my phone.

"Another *monsieur*?" She smiled. Little did she know I had one for every car in the garage.

I opened the front door, and standing in front of his black Bentley was my glorious knight. He was like a masterpiece at the Metropolitan Museum of Art; not only rare, but priceless. *He'd better not turn into a nightmare*, I thought. You know how most frogs didn't really turn into a prince once you kissed them. Jeez, pretty much once a frog always a frog. But Zur wasn't a frog; he was well packaged, and I wanted him.

He held my hand, as I walked to the steps, and kissed me on both cheeks.

"You look amazing," he said.

"Thank you," I said with a smile.

Sitting in his Bentley gave me goose bumps. I didn't even

know why, but it felt special. Maybe it was because he was such a mystery, and a sexy one at that! I'd definitely lost my composure around him. He was so different than all the men I'd dated before. It certainly wasn't just the money. It was something more.

"So tell me, where are we going?" I asked.

"Where would you like to go, baby?" he replied.

"I'm your baby now?" I laughed.

He smiled, and we drove and listened to Arabian music, which I liked better than most music. I stared at him, as he glanced over into my eyes and touched my face. I bit my lip, in dire need of his touch.

He stopped at a stoplight and reached over to me, and our lips met like two lovers that had longed for each other their whole lives. His lips were soft and passionate. Up close, his eyes were strong, fierce, and intriguing, like the depths of the ocean. We stopped kissing and sat there for a moment, lost in each other's eyes. Then, as the light turned green, we leaned back into our respective seats, and Zur drove on. I'd never had a kiss that had been tattooed onto my mind quite like that. Sure I'd had kisses, but they were all sad shells compared to his. I looked out the window and saw a restaurant on the ocean that looked like a cottage. It was dark blue with green shutters, and I smiled, as it wasn't what I had expected.

As we pulled up to the restaurant, a man dressed in a suit and bowtie opened my car door. We walked down a paved path to a small, polished, very British room. Everything was covered in paisley and patterned roses, sort of like my mom's taste in decor. Hope she wasn't there! The staff were dressed in green and red, like something out of a Nanny McPhee movie. Suddenly, I needed a shot of something to forget my own old nanny. Looking around, I hoped that Zur was a lawyer or even a doctor, and not some Mafia dude with triple passports.

The man in the suit and bowtie led us to the back of the cottage, through an archway with iron gates and a garden with vines and fountains. Where the hell was I, Alice's courtyard? Zur held my hand as if he'd never let it go. *Forget dinner; just take me here and now,* I thought. But, I was a lady, well sometimes. He smelled of Calvin Klein and Davidoff, and all around me it smelled like roses in bloom with a splash of sea breeze. It was very sensual. I felt flushed with desire.

At the back of this odd, but beautiful place, was a blue-and-white tent on the beach. It was much more graceful than a circus tent, secluded and well designed. In the tent was a beautifully lit table, surrounded by gorgeous tapestry and vases of roses and candles. It was beautiful and very romantic, and then I suddenly flashed on Thomas and his vineyard. Thank goodness there was no violinist present.

The man in the bowtie came and opened up the other side of the tent, and I gazed at the ocean as Zur looked at me. I took my Chanels off and placed my toes in the sand.

"I wish you'd told me we were going to the beach. I wouldn't have gotten so dolled up."

"You look insatiably beautiful," he purred.

I smiled and looked away. Gracious, a girl had to blush from all of this. I was intrigued by him.

The waiter brought over our first course of Beluga caviar and some sort of tiny crackers, along with champagne and gold spoons.

"I'll have sparkling water with lemon, please," I told the waiter.

"No champagne?" Zur asked.

"No, I'm not a big drinker." He looked relieved.

I took my gold spoon and scooped a little of the caviar onto a cracker. As I took a bite, I murmured, "It's delish."

Zur sipped his champagne, and said, "Your eyes tell quite the tale."

"Do they?" I exclaimed.

His phone rang, and he answered it, excusing himself and walking out of the tent. I never understood the need for working at the dinner table, though maybe it was his wife, or girlfriend, or mistress. Or just his dog walker. Re-entering the tent, he paused and took in the sensuality of the scene. His eyes pierced me so deeply I thought I'd been dropped into the ocean.

He put his phone down, and said, "Sorry, it was urgent."

"How long are you here for?" I asked.

"A few more days, then I will be leaving for Dubai, and then to visit my brother. And you, my baby?" he asked, holding my hand and giving me a kiss.

"I'm leaving on Tuesday to go back to Brookville."

"That's on Long Island?"

"Yes, it is."

The funny thing was that the words didn't mean that much. Instead, we stared at each other, and our eyes did all the real talking. Our main course was served: duck confit with mango salad. It was like dining in Manhattan on the shores of the Hamptons.

Zur asked the waiters to leave, and we sat there, lost in candlelight with the sounds of the waves.

"Dinner is lovely, thank you," I said.

"You've barely eaten anything," he said, staring at me with

those lustful eyes. "Tell me, Sophie, what brings you out to the Hamptons?"

"Just taking a vacation from my stressful life." I smiled, lost in the waves, the sound of the sea air, and the scent of someone I desired.

"What do you do?" he asked.

"I'm a stockbroker on Wall Street."

"Are you serious?" he said, his eyebrows raising in an inquisitive, yet sexy way.

"Yes, of course," I replied.

"That's a tough profession for a woman, no?"

"You don't think a woman can make it big on Wall Street, is that it?"

"Well, no, no offense, but women often don't do very well on Wall Street."

"How exactly should I take that?" I replied directly.

"No, it's not you personally I'm talking about, but that's just the way it has been," Zur explained.

"I get that, but I think I'm a natural with what I do."

"You look like a natural," he said admiringly.

"What do you do for a living?" I pried. It was my turn to delve into his life.

"That's quite complicated to answer," he replied.

"Well, that's better than a lie, I guess," I said, annoyed. I knew that there was something mysterious about him, but I couldn't even guess what it would be.

He cleared his throat and swept his hands through his thick hair. He looked very stressed. What profession would make a man so uptight? The ones that aren't that honest, I supposed. He picked up his glass and took a sip of his champagne.

"Do you like working on Wall Street with all those men?" he changed the subject back to me. *Hell yes*, I thought.

"I'm not there for the men; I'm there to do what I do best."

"What's that, exactly?" His eyes searched for more answers.

"Make them look like pikers!" I exclaimed.

He smiled at me, and then my phone rang. A night without my phone ringing was like a night with no darkness. Rare, very rare. I checked the caller ID and it was Thomas. I placed my phone back down without hesitation.

"Your boyfriend?" Zur asked casually.

"No, I don't have one. Just someone I've dated from time to time."

The August breeze was a mixture of summer and fall, and as Zur contemplated my last statement, I walked out of the tent to the waves to disperse the awkwardness.

"Why don't we walk along the sand," Zur said. "I see that you'd like to."

I loved the feel of my feet on the sand with his hand in mine. The stars were twinkling, and the waves made music as they rolled and crashed. Zur walked beside me with passion welling in his eyes. As we got a fair distance away from the tent, he pulled me to him and kissed my cheeks softly. He put his arms around me, and I felt the heat of his face close to mine, as his lips brushed me with a sinful desire. We kissed again as if our mouths were one. His hands caressed my bare arms, and I wanted more; more of him touching me.

Zur took his hands from my arms, clasped my hands in his, and said, "Baby, let's not."

"Let's not what?" I asked. He looked into my eyes and kissed my cheek again. Then he took his blazer off and placed it around me.

"You look cold," he said.

He sat on the sand, taking my hands and pulling me down to sit on his lap. If I'd known this would be our date, I would have worn shorts and flip-flops. Okay, not flip-flops, as I don't own any, and yes, I probably would never have worn shorts on a date with Zur either.

He held me with such gentleness that I felt odd and frail in his arms. We looked at the waves as I rested on his chest. I began shivering as we again stared into each other's eyes. He touched my lips with his finger and then ran his hand across my cheek. He put his hands around the back of my head and pulled my lips to his. Our eyes couldn't get enough of each other, but soon, it was getting late, and it was time to leave. There was a path leading from where we were on the sand to the car. He helped me up and walked with me, hand in hand.

"I left my shoes and bag in the tent," I said.

"They will bring them."

He called someone at the restaurant, and told them in Arabic to bring my things to me at the car. As he opened the car door, I tried to dust as much sand off my feet and dress as I could.

"Baby, don't worry about it. I'll have it cleaned," he said.

But I insisted, as he stood there watching me dust myself off.

"Are you done?" he asked.

"Almost, I think I've got sand everywhere."

"You can have a bath when you get home, no?" he said. *Gee, thanks, I hadn't thought of that!*

"Here's your bag and your shoes," the waiter said, as if he knew Zur well.

"Your very sexy shoes," Zur said, kissing my cheeks, as he handed me my shoes and purse.

We got into the Bentley, and he drove slowly home, listening to Tarkan's "*Sevdanin Son Vurusi*."

"What's he saying?" I asked Zur.

"He's saying that…he is falling in love with a woman he doesn't know."

"Hmmm, how nice," I said, smiling. That wasn't really the song, was it?

He turned the song up a little louder and spoke the words to me. I was taken, smitten, drowning in delirium, whatever you want to call it - I was done for. Minutes passed, and he placed his hand on mine and brought my hand to his lips.

My phone began ringing, and as I took it out of my purse, I saw that it was Thomas again. Great. I glanced over to see Zur staring at me.

"You need to keep looking at the road, no?" I said.

"Your boyfriend is calling, no?"

"No."

"Then who's bothering you, baby?" he said, nodding at the phone.

I pulled my hair back into a bun. I did that when I got stressed. Zur slowed the car down even more, staring at me. I felt as if I was two-timing him. Why did I feel so guilty?

Five more minutes of crazy awkwardness ensued, until Zur pulled onto the private road to Duren's mansion. The gates opened automatically for us, and he drove in at top speed, coming to an abrupt stop in front of the front steps. I could tell that he wasn't happy at all; it was only our first date, and it had been so intense. Silence was our new companion. He licked his lips and looked over to me.

"I'll think of you tonight," Zur said.

That was so terribly sweet. I was a bit confused, since he also seemed annoyed. I smiled, and then he took my hand and placed it on his heart and kissed it. Middle Eastern men were very sexy and very nuts. But let's just forget the nuts part and focus on the sexy, shall we? After all, baklava had nuts, but everyone loved it, no?

"Go get some sleep, baby; you're tired," he said.

"Good night, Zur." I leaned over to him, and we kissed with more passion than before. It was fireworks. I really wanted to invite him in, but I didn't believe in giving myself up on our first meeting.

I waltzed out the Bentley as gracefully as I could, with a grin on my face and sand on my ass. What a night! He made every other man out there look pathetic and sad. I had been waiting for him my whole life, I just simply never knew it.

Helene opened the front door, yawned, and closed it behind me.

"*Bonsoir, Mademoiselle Sophie.*"

I was half asleep as well, yawning as I went up the stairs.

Helene looked at me from behind, and said, "*Sable,*" as she pointed to my derriere.

"*Oui,*" I answered, even though I had no idea what she'd said. *Oui* was always universal. Maybe she was pointing to the sand on my behind?

I took off my dress, slipped on my new nightgown, and hopped into bed. I couldn't even wash my face or brush my teeth, I was too tired. Snuggled under the goose down, my mind raced, thinking of dinner and Zur. Soon, I would go back to my normal life of Robin, Rain, my parents, and my workload of wealthy, demanding clients.

It was late, but I took out my iPhone and dialed my mother. *Ring…Ring…*

"Hello," she answered.

"Mother, it's Sophie. Are you okay?"

"Yes, I'm okay, dear. Are you?"

"Yes, not too shabby."

"Good, though shabby isn't an appropriate feeling."

I thought, *Really, Mother? That's the best you can do?*

"I'm almost asleep, Sophie. Can we talk tomorrow?"

"Sure," I said and hung up.

It wasn't like I'd called to discuss my love life with her. This guy was from Dubai. That statement alone would have erased me from the Becks retirement and/or trust fund, even after twenty-five years of being a Becks. What a disappointment she always was. There was never any emotion whatsoever, but as long as your manners were intact, you were okay in her book.

"Damn! Damn! Damn!" I yelled. "Someone save me from this screwed-up family!"

Then my phone rang. It was a FaceTime from Zur. I fixed my hair a little and pressed the button to answer.

"Hello, Sophie. Everything okay?" he asked.

He was lying in bed, shirtless. Why the heck did he have to look that good? Naked, with arms like a bodybuilder, and skin coloring of the most golden, sun-kissed tan. I tried to act nonchalant.

"Yes. How are you?" I replied.

"I'm getting ready for bed."

"Duh," I said, smiling.

He laughed. "I just wanted to say good night."

"Yes, good night, Zur."

"I'll see you tomorrow?" he asked.

"Sure."

"Night, baby."

"Night-night."

I shut my phone off and went to bed. I left my French doors open, so I could listen to the waves crash onto the beach, just as the waves of change slowly crashed into my life, moment by moment.

19

LOVE IS BLINDNESS

Monday morning, I woke up early to walk on the beach and get a workout in. I decided to walk in the opposite direction of Zur's place, as I definitely didn't need him to see me dressed so plain and simple. For Pete's sake, I was wearing my workout pants with an old t-shirt and a pair of sneakers.

The ocean always seemed calmest in the morning, as the clouds were soft and the sun was still waking from its sleep. I walked slowly along the beach and took in every moment. Feeling relaxed, I took my phone out of my sports bra and turned it back on. I was shocked to see that Robin had left me, not one, but nineteen messages. I dialed his number in panic.

"Robin, what's the matter?"

"Sophie, where've you been? I've called you so many times."

"I'm sorry, I had my phone turned off."

"Thomas also tried calling you, and well, you can deal with that on your own time," Robin said in such a curious manner, I didn't know how to respond.

"I, uh, don't know about that one," I said.

"Sounds like you and Rain have a lot in common," Robin

replied, sounding like a jerk. Rain was cold and hot, hot and cold with his lovers. Was I like that with Thomas?

"Well, is everything okay?" I said. "How's Dad?"

"He's fine. He's having a chat with Mom in his study. Sounds like they're trying to work things out, whatever. Nothing's wrong here, it was just that I couldn't reach you so I grew concerned."

"Well," I said, ignoring the parent-like worry in his voice. "I'm working out right now and have a few conference calls to make. We'll chat soon?"

"Yes. When are you coming home?"

"I don't know, in a day or so," I said, smiling.

"You must be having a blast, eh? But with whom? Is Jan still with you?"

"Let's not do this, Robin, okay? Chat later?"

"Okay."

I was eager to hang up and move on from Thomasville and my hovering brother. I made my way back to Duren's house and dialed the office for a conference call. The call lasted forty-five minutes, and Jaxwe was on the line, listening and trying to understand what it was about me that drove him psychotic. The forty accounts I once needed, were down to twenty in just two weeks.

"Not bad for a newcomer, Becks," said Duren.

"Well, can I look forward to my big commission checks in September?" I asked.

"Yes, I'll have Breezy send you the numbers. All good at the house?"

"Yes, it's been stellar!"

"We are going to have a brokers' event in two weeks. Looking forward to seeing you on Monday, Sophie. By the way, the Jabari account is up 20 percent. Are you keeping an eye on it?"

I'm keeping an eye on your hot neighbor. Too bad he isn't an account, I thought.

"Sophie, are you there?"

"Yes, yes, everything has an eye on it."

"Good, we'll talk soon."

After hanging up, I walked over to Helene, who was making breakfast. It was all vegetables, like hello, can I have real food? I ate and then walked into the garden to make a quick call to Thomas. While dialing, I broke into a cold sweat, unsure what to say.

"Hello, Sophie," he answered.

"Thomas, I see you called."

"Yes, look, are you just not interested in me?" I was baffled, but that was certainly direct.

"I've got a lot going on," I said, "and I don't know what I want." *Except Zur*, I thought.

"Can't you just be honest with me?" screamed Thomas.

"Honest about what?"

"Our relationship!"

I was conflicted. If I hadn't met Zur, I would have gone back to Thomas without a doubt, a question, or even an exclamation.

"I need time," I replied carefully. "I know what happened between us, but I'm just unsure what I want right now."

"Okay, I guess that's fair." And just like that, he hung up.

"Can't I catch a friggin' break around here?" I yelled.

I stood up and looked around, and there, in a black t-shirt and black linen pants, was Zur with a bunch of tulips in his hand. Helene must have opened the gates for him. I wondered how long he'd been standing there and what exactly he'd overheard. Darn it!

"Hey, Zur, how are you?" I asked.

He kissed both my cheeks and handed me the tulips. "I'm going to pretend I didn't hear that call, baby."

"Well, you obviously did."

"I just wanted to say hello," he said, and bit his lip.

I was angry. *How about calling me ahead of time instead of shocking me and yourself with how I can look without makeup and proper clothing?* I thought. I couldn't pretend I was happy with him.

"Want to talk?" he asked.

"No, I'm fine." I said coldly. See how frosty I could get? "I get tense and unreachable when I get myself in situations that I'm not ready for," I blurted out. But Zur's expression changed.

"Are you committed to him?" Zur asked, looking at the waves on the beach.

"I'm not. That's why he's mad."

Zur turned back toward me, reached out, and embraced me. It felt awkward. I don't think he was a very emotional person, but I could tell he was trying really hard to be comforting.

"It's going to be okay," he said, while holding me.

I was swept up in an tidal wave of emotion for him. Zur gave me comfort. What did you know, a man could actually offer me comfort?

"Early dinner at my house?" he asked.

"Yes," I replied, as he softly kissed my neck, further awakening my desire for him. "And tonight it's going to be just me and you. No cell phone."

This guy had no idea who I really was, and I didn't know who he was either. The odd thing was that neither of us cared. I was a salesperson, and I could and would sell ice to Eskimos! Now what did I sell to this man from Dubai? Nothing. He already had everything, including *moi*.

He left, and I looked at the tulips wrapped in a colorful fabric with ribbons around the stems. Tonight, he might bring me a few stars from the night sky; he was that into me.

At lunchtime, I soaked in the sunken marble bath, reading *The Art of War*. It was quite interesting, but I couldn't concentrate. I simply couldn't think at all. I wanted to study the art of Zur. *It's time to read about love*, I thought. Yes, my brain was definitely now severely compromised.

Jan sent me a text: "Where the hell are you, darling?"

Whenever Jan cursed, I was in awe. It sounded all wrong coming out of her mouth.

"In the bath," I responded.

"Oh, alone?"

"Yes."

"Did you sleep with Mr. Tall, Dark, and Sexy yet?"

"LOL, no!"

"Good. Please don't complicate your life. Everyone around you is filled to the brim with issues, and those overpaid Long Island therapists don't do crap!"

I sent her a smiley and threw my phone onto some towels on the bathroom floor.

The late afternoon was quiet here, with no one to bother me. I loved it, and I wanted to explore Duren's twelve-thousand-square-foot mansion. I found it quite intriguing that there were no portraits of his wife or son. If I had a husband like him, I would be pregnant every other year. But I didn't, and I didn't even believe in marriage. Marriage was worse than stiletto heels.

At least with stilettos, you could put them back on your shelf when they caused you pain, and never wear them again.

I looked around at the walls of the bathroom, which were adorned with oil masterpieces of women from the baroque era. They were surely worth thousands. I stepped out of the bath, dried myself with the body dryer, and slipped on my damask robe. I followed the long, striped hallway and made a right turn. There was a door on the corner, and I was eager to see what the ocean view would be like from the second floor. I turned the golden knob with a *D* on it, and smiled as I recalled my conversation with Jan about wealthy folk loving their monograms.

The door led me to a dark, rusty iron stairwell. I paused, and looked around the coffered ceiling for cameras. With none in sight, I clutched the railing and climbed up in my red velvet loafers. As I reached the top, there was a wall of French doors, from one end of the room to the other. I opened one of the doors, and went outside onto the deck, blown to pieces by how beautifully the ocean glistened with the sun's reflection.

There was a telescope out there, that spun in just about any direction. I looked through it, and then remembered Zur's home next door. I adjusted the telescope to the left, and could see Zur's back veranda. He was sitting on an armchair wearing nothing but swim trunks. There were two men beside him; one seemed to be the very same guy that had retrieved my bag and shoes on the beach last night, and the other was very slim and tall and wore a black blazer and polished black shoes. He had a head full of black, shiny hair, and his eyebrows were perfectly manicured.

I turned the telescope away, as I really wasn't comfortable spying on him, and focused instead on the ocean sand. I enjoyed looking at the older women walking briskly along the beach, trying to lose that last five pounds, or maybe just work out their loneliness. If you lived like this seven days a week, I would imagine that you could possibly get used to just being alone with your dog or the housekeeper.

I moved the telescope back to Zur briefly, and saw that he was now sitting next to the infinity pool. It looked as if he was giving the men orders, and then a lady with an apron brought him a drink with a wedge of lemon on top. I immediately wished that the telescope had come with a microphone, so I'd know what he was saying.

Zur stood up and went inside, and then my phone rang.

"Hello," I answered.

"Hey, baby, how are you?"

"I'm fine."

"Listen, something came up, and I can't see you tonight." It felt as if I'd been hit in the head with a big steel ball.

"Not a problem," I said, trying to mask my heartache. Yes, heartache, from just a few kisses with the man.

"You sure?" he asked.

"Yes. I'll speak to you soon," I said, and hung up.

I was disappointed. I didn't know why he cancelled our evening, but he did. I headed down the stairs and back into my bedroom, feeling quite anguished. *So this must be how Thomas feels,* I thought to myself. I sat on the end of the bed and wondered a million things. I was feeling things I couldn't explain. I threw my iPhone on the floor.

"He played me," I mumbled to myself.

Why would he cancel on me? Was it my call to Thomas? Maybe it was the cultural differences. After all, he was from a country where women wore Pucci scarves. I didn't even have a head scarf at all! Maybe a Hermès one, but that was for my neck. I heard a knock on my bedroom door.

"Helene, is that you?" I called through the door.

"No," an unknown male voice replied. I was nervous as I walked to the door. By the time I opened it, I was convinced it was an intruder.

"Oh my God, you scared me!" I exclaimed. It was Cooper. "How are you?"

"I'm sorry I scared you. My father insisted that I check on you, and there was no dial tone all morning at the house."

"Dial tone, huh? I spoke to your father this morning. Does he have amnesia?" Cooper laughed. "That wasn't polite. I'm sorry," I said.

"Have you eaten lunch yet?" he asked.

"No, at least not yet. I can just make myself something from the kitchen," I said smiling.

"Sure, and I can help," he said, returning my smile.

Cooper was twenty-three, tall, and fit. His hair was long and very curly, and he had eyes like his dad.

As we walked down to the kitchen together, Cooper asked, "So how do you like Wall Street?"

"I think it's the best place I've ever been. You live out here?"

"Nah, just June to August," he said nonchalantly.

"Cool. Do you know the neighbors?"

"Oh, which ones?"

"Anyone?"

"Well, the lady to the right, she's a little frumps. No loud music, no racing down the private road, or she'll have someone ticket you." He laughed. "And there's that billionaire guy from the Middle East on the other side."

"What's he like?" I said nonchalantly.

"I guess he's okay. I don't really know him. His family is very rigid, and private, and he rolls with security. Who does that in the Hamptons?"

Cooper sipped on a glass of red wine from his dad's collection. I took a glass of water, and we toasted.

"Here's to you, Sophie, and to your dreams of being like my father. Toasts and smiles," cute Cooper cheered.

"So what's your story?" I asked Cooper.

"I don't wanna be like you Wall Street brokers. I like life easy-squeasy, dig? I don't need all of this, like my mom." I started laughing, though it wasn't really funny.

"Why are you laughing?"

"I get it," I replied enigmatically.

"Well, I gotta go. Maybe if you are free later, you can visit me in Montauk."

"Thanks, Cooper," I said, "maybe I will."

For the next hour, I kept myself busy with my iPad, looking at stocks go up and down and scanning through my e-mails. I even put an ad on Craigslist for a new assistant: "Male assistant needed for Wall Street stockbroker. Must drive a sports car and be very tall, muscular, handsome, and hot. Experience not necessary!" In the span of five minutes and fifteen seconds, I had ten responses. Some were okay, a few were appropriate, and two were way indecent; it was an interesting mix.

By about three o'clock, I was fully aware that my knight in shining armor had ridden away. I looked up at the sky, and watched the clouds meander across. That's when I knew I would probably be fifty years old and making millions, but alone. Yes, my best friend would be my housekeeper. Sad, so very sad. But there was still hope. At least I'd undoubtedly own a mansion with a walk-in closet that had velvet shelves for my shoes. My garage would have Bentleys in every color, and my assistant would look like a Chippendale dancer. It was looking good already.

I sat on the back deck reading my emails, sipping on lemon water, and eating carrot sticks.

"*Helene, je voudrais du vin, s'il vous plaît,*" I requested.

"*Oui, Mademoiselle.*" She went to fetch the wine.

"My gosh, I need a French tutor," I said aloud. No one heard. I was alone and sad.

Helene returned with the wine, and I took a sip. I didn't like it. Gosh, that explained a lot, especially the future of Thomas and I.

At 4:00 p.m., I got dressed in shorts, pink pumps, a silk blouse, a Hermès scarf for my hair, and my Prada sunglasses. I dressed my au natural lips with pink gloss, and I headed out. I took the Aston. If I met the devil this evening, I'd be ready!

20

Stop, in the Name of Love

"That will be $1,198," said the salesperson at Calypso St. Barth on Jobs Lane. I handed her my Black Amex and looked at the necklaces in the glass case.

"Oh, I'll have that purple necklace with the matching heirloom bracelet too."

"The bracelet alone is $450," she warned.

"I wouldn't care if it was a thousand dollars; I'll have it and the necklace," I said. I didn't work my ass off for nothing. The salesperson was polite and smiled, even though I was a cranky pig.

I walked the streets of Southampton, admiring everything; the beautiful ladies sitting on porches in their wicker chairs, the storekeepers fixing the displays in their windows, and the children eating their organic ice creams. And let's not forget the husbands of the wives shopping. I felt sorry for them. Men didn't get enough credit sometimes, well the ones that deserved it, that is. And, surely I didn't normally glorify men. Hell, I generally needed a lot of therapy and alcohol to say good things about men at all.

I placed my four shopping bags into the trunk, got in the car, and headed to Cooper's house in Montauk. As much money as I'd just spent, I had no friends or acquaintances to do anything with. Yes, I know, very sad. But, in visiting Cooper I would also be doing something kind for Duren, so out of my respect for Duren I went out to Montauk. Stopping at Tate's Bake Shop, I got Cooper a basket of the best things to eat.

As I pulled up at Cooper's around 6:30 p.m., I admired his small, white Victorian house with navy-blue shutters and white wraparound porch, right on the ocean. I parked the Aston, and noticed a beautiful, raven-haired girl sitting on an antique bench on the porch.

"Hello, I'm looking for Cooper," I said.

"Yes? And you are?" she asked sternly.

"Sophie Becks."

Smiling, she walked over to me and shook my hand, "Nice to meet you. Follow me."

The place was very nautical, with whitewashed furniture meant to look torn up and pictures of sailboats everywhere. Every room had ceiling-to-floor windows.

As the girl opened the back door, the view to the ocean was breathtaking. Copper was out riding the rough, pounding waves. The girl pointed over to him, and I snapped a picture with my iPhone for Duren.

"His dad must be proud that he's such a beach boy," I said smiling.

"Between us, his dad expects way too much from him, and his mom thinks everyone should always be filthy rich and be so 'upper crust.'" She made air quotes with her fingers.

This girl was clearly sweet, but troubled by something.

"You know," I replied. "That's fair to say, but sometimes in life, your parents will want more for you than just simple happiness." I didn't care what she thought of me, but I did care that she understood what she was getting into by getting involved with a Duren. Things around here would never be simple.

She looked into my eyes, seeking an answer, "You seem to know a lot."

I smiled, but in truth, I wasn't sure what to say about that. I often wondered if I knew anything at all about relationships.

She was probably some girl whom Cooper had fallen for who wasn't deemed wealthy or successful enough for his parents. Duren was an overachiever, and his wife wore the badge of trophy well.

Cooper came out of the waves and walked up to me, wiping his hands. "Hey, Becks, good you came."

"Hey, Cooper, I brought you something." I handed him the goodies from Tate's.

"I love Tate's! Thank you. Cool! I didn't know you were this down to earth." He smiled.

"What did you think, I have 'stockbroker attitude'?"

"Totally."

"Nah, only when I'm trying to open accounts."

"You've met my girlfriend, Radha?"

Radha was a kind girl and seemed to be passionate about Cooper, but she was the type of woman that wanted to be a homemaker. I supposed I had to admire that, because where I came from the women would much rather be out five hours a day getting their nails, and other things, done.

"Dinner is served," Radha said with a smile.

I smiled too; I was impressed. We sat at a traditional dinner table, wooden with simple white plates and regular forks and knives. It was simple, but you sure could feel at home there.

I watched Cooper lean over to kiss her, and I knew that when love was real, it was real. And when it was fake, well… that's when you went shopping.

I picked through my food, as I'd seemed to have lost my appetite since breakfast. It was braised chicken and vegetables with whole-grain bread; a very healthy, motherly meal, the kind Hannah would make.

"This is delish. Thank you, Radha," I said.

My phone rang, and I excused myself and looked at it. It was Zur. I put it back down and pretended that it didn't matter. As we continued with dinner, it rang again.

"Aren't you going to get it?" said Cooper.

"No, it's fine," I replied casually.

After dinner, Radha served tea with dessert.

"This is well-brewed tea. What is it?"

"It's chai with orange tea leaves, ginger, and milk," Radha said. I loved it, but unfortunately I drowned it with some raw sugar.

At about 8:30 p.m., I knew I had to leave soon, as I was not a very good night driver. I kissed them good night, turned my GPS on, and drove off with music blasting. I tried to keep to the speed limit this time, because I didn't need to be pulled over again.

Forty-five minutes later, I knew where I was, and I drove slowly down North Sea Road through Southampton and onto the private road leading to Duren's. As I pulled up to the stop sign, there was Zur's car waiting with blinking lights. His window went down, and I pulled over to his car.

"Hi," he said.

"Hi, what's wrong?" I asked.

"I knew you were out, so I wanted to wait for you."

I didn't smile at all. "You're waiting for me at a stop sign. Does that seem normal to you?"

"You don't know who I am," he said.

I was speechless. "Who the hell are you then? Tell me."

"Baby, why are you cursing?"

"I'm not your baby, okay? And FYI, you cancelled on me last minute tonight; nobody does that."

He was speechless, and I knew then that he was nothing out of the ordinary.

"Have a good night," I said as I drove off.

I buzzed the gate and got no response. I buzzed again. Nothing. I pressed it at least ten more times, but Helene wasn't answering. Zur pulled up behind me and got out. Someone else drove his car back out of the driveway. That's weird, I hadn't even realized there was someone else in his car. He opened my passenger door and sat down, looking at me as if he had something to say.

"I'm sorry about tonight," he said. He held my hand and tried to kiss it.

"Where is Helene?" I muttered.

"Come over to my house."

I looked into his eyes and couldn't say a word. I opened my door and got out of the car, wanting more than ever to run from Zur before it was too late. He also got out, slammed the door, and walked over to me. I pressed the bloody call button over and over, to no avail.

Zur put his hands around me and held me to him. "I'm not going to walk away. I want you," he whispered softly.

His lips reached out to mine, and though my brain wanted to

WALL STREET TO FRANCE

shut this thing down, my lips willingly reciprocated his passion. I was Juliet to his Romeo. I just hoped our story ended better than theirs. My mind raced, and our eyes undressed each other right there. He lifted me up, opened the door to the Aston, and put me in the passenger seat. He momentarily unlocked his lips from mine and drove us to his home.

A house away, he pressed the call button, spoke to a man in Arabic, and drove down his cobblestone driveway. In front of his home were two black Range Rovers with dark tinted windows, a yellow Lamborghini, and a black Bentley.

Zur got out of the car and opened my car door, holding my hand as he walked me to the circular wooden brown door and through a courtyard with shrubs of all sorts. He called out to the housekeeper and asked me what I wanted to drink.

"Let me guess, sparkling water?" he said.

"Yes," I said, looking at the pool. Stone pillars with vines surrounded a square pool with green water and gold mosaics at the bottom.

Zur sat on a green chair and lit a cigar. We looked at each other.

Mia brought him a crystal bottle of scotch with tumblers. He poured some in a glass and took it in one hand, his cigar in the other. He looked like something out of *Scarface*. What was he about to say that he needed so much crap to smoke and drink?

I stood up and walked to the other side of the pool. His eyes felt like laser beams, and I could feel him look me up and down, smoking his cigar.

"If I am to give this a shot, there are going to be consequences, like my job, my family, and so forth," Zur began.

I looked at him. Give this a shot? What exactly were we giving a shot?

"I have had more than a few women in my life, and I've had no luck with love so far, therefore, I live my life guarded." He paused, smoked, puffed, and exhaled.

Somebody save me. This was way too intense, though I wanted him now, more than I had before, and no matter what he said.

"When I first saw you," he said, "I didn't know what it was about you, but I couldn't deny that I wanted you, more than I can say."

"Zur, don't," I begged. "Let's not talk about it right…"

"We have to. Here is the situation. If I'm going to be with you, I can't discuss my work, my family situation, and so on, and I don't think you would like that." What the hell was he smoking?

"Well, for starters," I replied angrily. "I'm happy you're being honest, at least about the part that you can't, or won't, be open with me. Am I going to be your mistress? Your prostitute? Who exactly do you think I am?" I yelled. He looked away. "I don't want to complicate my already messed-up life, and yours seems complicated as hell. I am going to go, okay? And let's just pretend we never met."

I walked away through the stone pillars and across the beautiful cobblestone floors. As I was about to open the wooden archway doors, he grabbed my hands and leaned me against the wall.

"Don't go. I'm really trying here," he said with desperation.

It felt as if we were never meant to meet, but Cupid shot us with his love-dipped arrows, and then this insatiable need to feel and breathe each other had taken over.

"You are from wherever you're from," I began. "I'm obviously not as complicated as you, and I don't—"

He interrupted me by putting his lips on mine. I was conflicted, because as much as I wanted to solve our earthly issues, I also wanted to be in his arms for as long as I could be.

He lifted me in his arms, and took me through the courtyard, up the cobblestone stairs, up a back staircase, through whitewashed wood hallways, and into a candlelit bedroom. He placed me on a bed of rose petals, locked the door, and took his European leather loafers off. I couldn't stop laughing. I held my head up, wondering if I were in some mythic love story. He was the hottest long-haired, golden-complexioned, full-bodied, complex human being I'd ever met, and I was lying on his bed.

I looked up and watched as the large, oval, dark iron chandelier dimmed, and went out. The ceiling were open black beams, in an almost Gothic style. I lay there as he made his way down my body; kissing me on my forehead, my nose, and my lips, as he undressed me, one item at a time. He peeled my panties off and kissed me slowly and deeply. I was in heaven on earth. Our lips never left each other, and I wished that this moment would never end.

I woke up at midnight, with Zur asleep next to me. I threw on his shirt and my shorts quietly. I didn't need more clothing than that. I grabbed my shoes and tiptoed to the door.

"Baby, where are you going?" he asked sleepily.

I sighed loudly, as if I couldn't stay. Gosh, if I did, I'd need a Paxil to deal with all of the new feelings rolling around in me.

"I have to go," I said, biting my lip.

"Why?" Zur sat up in bed, fully awake. "I just made love to you like I've never made love to any other woman."

I understood, but this was what I did. Hello, rule number one: have an intimate encounter, leave as soon as possible afterwards.

"I have to," I said. "And you're leaving tomorrow, aren't you?"

"Yes. When are you leaving?"

"Tomorrow. My brother's driver is getting me," I replied. Right, and I was guest-hosting the Oprah show too.

"You're wearing my shirt, baby," he said laughing.

"Helene will bring it to you tomorrow." I didn't even smile.

Zur's phone rang, and he looked at the number. "I have to get this," he said. He walked out to the balcony off his bedroom.

I sat down on his bed with my head in my hands, wondering what I had done to myself. How would I be okay again? *I'm so stupid*, I said to myself. He had a secretive life, traveled the world, and had two bodyguards. And here I was, just another Wall Street jackass.

After two minutes of not understanding anything he was saying on the phone, I walked out of the room and down the stairs. I made it through the courtyard, and when I stopped to put my Chanel pumps on, I caught a glimpse of myself in a gorgeous gilt-framed mirror. It was an amazing vision: me in his white linen shirt and my plaid shorts and pink Chanel pumps.

As I opened the door to go outside, I saw the bodyguard with the black blazer at the front door, smoking a cigarette. I waved and I could have peed myself. He waved back as he spoke into his earplug. I'd watched espionage movies before, so I knew how these people communicated.

When I was about to get into the Aston, the man in the blazer walked over to me.

"Good evening, I'm Syed. You are Miss Becks?" he asked.

"Yes, I am."

"Nice to meet you."

I looked at him, and honestly I wanted to cry. I was worlds apart from Zur, not oceans but *worlds* apart. I got into my borrowed Aston and drove off. Zur wasn't anywhere in sight. I was sure he was on the phone with one of his other women in Paris or Rome or Dubai.

I welcomed the fact that I had real feelings for someone. This was a place I'd never been before. *How did I get here?* I thought, as I drove into Duren's driveway.

The gates were open now, thank heavens, and I stood in the driveway for a half hour trying to gather myself. I finally stepped up the marble front steps and opened the door. I took my shoes off, headed upstairs, got into bed, pulled the covers over me, and fell asleep.

21

SAILING AND CHAMPAGNE

Tuesday had come so quickly, and I invited Robin to come out and get me. Things had gotten better between him and Rain, and voilà, Robin was going to drive Rain's new Bugatti Veyron to get me. Forget borrowing the Bugatti; it was a miracle that they were able to simply be brothers again.

As I packed my things into my vintage suitcase and Gucci duffel bag, I heard a knock on the door. I looked at my Patek, and thought, *Damn, that Bugatti is no joke. Fast and freakin' furious.*

"Come on in, Robin," I called, but when I looked around, I saw Zur.

"Helene let me in. Her French is spotless," he said smiling. More or less, *he* was spotless, standing there with his aviator shades and a cap on, in linen pants and a polo shirt with gold buttons.

I looked away and took my hair out of its bun. I hoped those shades were blackout, as I was not looking my best.

"Leaving without seeing me?" he asked.

"I didn't think you wanted to see me." I looked at him.

"Why would you think that?"

"Your speech last night was awkward," I said, as I placed my perfectly folded silk blouses in a garment bag.

"It's not awkward when you're being honest; it is complicated."

"Is it complicated, or are *you* complicated?" My phone buzzed with a text, but I ignored it.

"I'm not the guys you deal with normally," he said so bloody nonchalantly. I was tired of hearing that.

"Who do you think I deal with normally?" I asked. "Yes, I know: someone who doesn't need security with him 24-7, someone who doesn't pretend to be genuine, someone who knows how to be loyal. So what kind of person does that make you? I know for sure you're not a lawyer or a doctor."

Okay, maybe I had said too much. There was no need for him to utter any words now. He looked away, and I'm sure he was pacing in his mind, thinking about what he should do.

He said, "I'm supposed to leave this afternoon for Dubai. I don't know when I'll see you again. But I need you to know that I want to see you again. Last night was one of the most defining sexual moments of my life."

I held my laughter in. That line was very similar to something I'd heard one of the brokers pitch to a chick at a very upscale bar in Manhattan.

But in the midst of Zur's short but powerful sentence, I felt it was best to stay silent. My heart sank to the bottom of the deep blue sea, from the *Titanic* to the shores of what never was. I felt him more deeply than I had ever felt another. This was more than a sexual encounter; it was an attraction of the soul. Call me insane, but I was falling for this man, this very gorgeous, mysterious man. I looked away, staring beyond the land and sand to the distant ocean, wondering how someone could just walk into your life and change it in the blink of an eye.

"Baby, I'm speaking to you," he said, holding my chin up and making me stare into his captivating lion eyes.

"I can hear you," I replied.

"What time is your brother getting you?"

I checked my phone and saw that the text was from Robin: "Something came up. Can I get you later? P.S. - Mom and Dad are having dinner at home tonight."

He probably wanted more time to drive around in that exceptional car. And maybe, just maybe, provide a thrill to the married women in Old Brookville. Those women loved men like Robin.

"Later, he just texted me," I told Zur. "Listen, I am not quite myself. I'm—"

"Shh," he said. "We will work it out, naturally."

He put his arms around me in such a protective way. I'd never felt so reassured before.

"I need you to know that I will be back. I'm not sure when, but I will be back after I've settled some things in Dubai," he said.

I wrapped my arms around his neck, and our eyes locked. I put my fingers on his lips, teasing him, and he placed his lips on mine. He kissed me softly, over and over again. A kiss had never felt like this, not ever.

"Let's go sailing," he said. "I've arranged for us to spend some time alone before we leave."

"When do you have in mind?"

"Now."

He lifted me up and placed me at the bottom of the dark-cherry bed with pillow-top softness. We lay next to each other and looked at the ceiling, which sounds pitiful, but it was magical, profoundly sensual. We looked at each other and he held my hands. He kissed my palms and pulled me closer to him. I simply lay there against his chest.

"Sophie, tell me something?"

"What is it?"

"Where do you want to end up if you were to get married?"

I stood up as fast as a rabbit realizing it was about to be eaten. "Um, I've never thought about that much."

He grabbed my arm and knelt on the floor. Looking up toward me, he asked "Did I ask you something wrong?"

Wrong? Wow, that was bizarre. "No, I'm just not yet there in my life. At all."

He changed topics. "Okay, get ready and meet me downstairs, 'kay?" He put his cap on and stumbled to the door without any more words.

I felt a lot for him, but marriage? Honey, you'd have to get me drunk and take away a great part of my reasoning ability before I got there. No, I was not discussing marriage; that was a whole new chapter of my life that I slammed shut a while ago.

In my head, I was getting ready to ditch Zur once he flew back to Dubai. No, I wasn't quite that cold, but the things that were happening in my life right now never usually ended with diamond eternity bands. God, I was so like Rain.

I got myself dressed, somewhere between dainty and sophisticated, for sailing. I wore my polka-dot skinnies with my black ruffled silk blouse. I left my hair long and a bit wavy with a matching silk scarf that I always tied to my neck loosely. I finished the look with my Tory Burch gold-buckled low wedges, brown Prada bag, and humongous Prada sunglasses.

I painted my lips in Dior and illuminated my skin with a golden bronzer.

"Wait, I'm missing something. My phone," I said to myself aloud.

I went down the spiral stairs and out the ceiling-to-floor oak doors. Zur stood there looking as if he'd been slapped with a little of his own medicine.

He opened the door to his Bentley and said, "You smell like a runway model."

I smiled sarcastically, as that wasn't exactly a compliment, was it? I sat, and he grabbed his phone out of his pocket and put it into his glove compartment, locking it.

"Your phone turned off?" he asked.

"Why? Are you going to kidnap me?" I asked, smiling.

"No, baby, I'm not."

He started driving toward the harbor, and I rolled my tinted window down. The radio was playing a song from long ago, when I was sixteen and starting going bonkers on my parents. Yes, "Sailing" by Christopher Cross. It was soft and so appropriate, but it was for freaking lovers; lost ones that lived sophisticated lifestyles with housekeepers, door openers, drivers, and Bentleys.

I knew that, until now, Zur had put up a wall to keep women on the outside. But that wall was blowing open, cement pieces falling one at a time. I shivered.

"When are you going back to work?" he asked.

"Tomorrow morning, early as early."

I opened my email inbox on my phone, and as he talked, I tried to look through the responses to my advert for a personal assistant. I sure had quite a few interesting responses.

Zur grabbed my phone and turned it off, "Not now, please." I sighed, and he just held my hand.

This relationship was getting way too intense too quickly. We sat in silence for a few moments, and my mind was lost in the inevitable fight against reason: why I feel the way I do about Zur, about how he was not like Thomas at all, with his complex life, the distance, cultural crap, and his bodyguards, and most of all, if I was willing to let my heart and desire take me to places I wasn't sure I wanted to go.

I didn't want to be a celebrity, and I didn't need an entourage. Heck, Hannah was good enough for me; she cooked my meals, cleaned my laundry, and took care of me when I was exhausted. I never understood people that needed a bodyguard. Well, except in *The Bodyguard*. I'd take Kevin Costner any day. He was fierce but gentle, never could a woman normally get that lucky!

Zur pulled up to the harbor that led to the ocean, and the combination of the man and the vast blueness of the ocean made me realize that I would follow him wherever he took me. As I attempted to temper my feelings a bit, Zur opened the door to the Bentley, and took my hand. We walked along the dock to a small boat that looked like something out of a Tom Cruise movie. I should have been terrified, but I felt safe in Zur's arms. This little dinky boat with a huge engine sped fast. I was expecting sailing, though, and this wasn't it.

Zur held me in his arms as the wind blew my hair, despite the head scarf. He breathed softly into my hair, and caressed my face, well, my cheeks and chin, as my Prada shades covered up the rest. Thank God for those. As I looked in front of us, I was blown away by the beauty of the sailboat up ahead. It was blue with striped sails, and the sky above looked beautiful; it was as if he'd had this moment painted just for me.

As the bodyguard pulled the small boat closer to the sailboat, Zur stepped off and lifted me out and onto the sailboat. He waved to the bodyguard and said something to him in Arabic. Don't ask me what any of it meant, but it sounded quite sexy.

We watched as a few sailors adjusted the sails and the boat went further out into the deep blue sea. Zur took my hand and led me down the stairs to a private living room. We sat down, and he served us drinks from the bar.

"Sparkling water with lemon for you."

I took off my head scarf, and my hair was everywhere, all puffy and tangled. I was cold, as well, so Zur grabbed a soft throw and placed it around me.

"Thank you," I said, admiring him as he sipped on some wine. I spotted the bottle, and yes, irony at its finest. It was from Laslay Vineyards, otherwise known as Thomas's parents' winery.

"This is good wine," he said.

"Hmm, looks like it," I said, deep in thought. I was thinking about my date at the vineyards with Thomas. I smiled. I was being torn in too many directions at once.

"You know, this vineyard is on Long Island," Zur said.

"Yes, I'm sure it is."

Zur and I were two people who felt electric near each other, but in my mind, I didn't think he was actually coming back from Dubai. It would be too good to be true, and as my father always said to me as a little girl, "If it sounds too good to be true, Sophie, then maybe it is too good." The thought kept playing in my head, and I was distant.

Zur put down his glass and looked at me. "What's wrong?"

It was two thirty, and I could see through a window that it was a sunny, though a bit cloudy, day.

"Nothing," I replied. "I'm listening to you. What time are you heading to Dubai?"

"At eight."

"We have a few hours then, do we?"

I put my glass down and made my way to his lips. He opened his mouth and passionately kissed me, putting his hands inside my shirt. His mouth made its way to my neck, and I reached under his t-shirt and felt his chest like a blind person. My eyes were closed as I felt him, part by part, piece by piece. My lips devoured him as he kicked the door shut. He took off my silk blouse, threw it aside, and touched and teased me in places I never thought I had any sensation. We opened our eyes and stared at each other, as our lips spoke a million emotions with one touch.

"Baby, I am falling in love with you," he whispered, as he held me closer and tighter.

I froze. I could open accounts on Wall Street, and yell at Jaxwe like a servant, when in reality he made millions. But when it came to my emotions, I was stunted. Sure, take off my bra and my silk Agent Provocateur lingerie, but don't you dare touch my cold heart. But was my heart still cold, with Zur?

My silk panties were flung to the floor, and Zur stood there looking at me, naked in front of him. I leaned over to him, breathing the same breath.

"Why are you staring at me?" I murmured. He didn't respond, but I knew I was becoming the Zur whisperer. I felt his urges, his thoughts, his everything. Our two souls were becoming one. Zur and I shared moments of pleasure that money could never buy.

"I want you Zur," I called to him, and he placed his soul into me. We were inside each other's very being, and our love was not lust. It was love. This was love.

"Baby, I'm going to make you mine for the rest of my life," he whispered.

"Okay," I said, begging for more of him, his love, whatever; it was all mine for that moment.

An hour passed, and I lay beside him. He held me there, no words, bare, not even the silk sheets between us; nothing but ourselves, the way we were born. I was exhausted. This new thing I'd immersed myself in—love, sex, and everything in between—was very tiring, and for once, Zur was out of words.

He got up, put his boxers on, and grabbed a glass of wine. He sat on the fabric sofa next to the bed, looking lost, and staring off in the distance. I tried to see what he was staring at, but I couldn't see it. I looked away, as I could clearly feel his distance. This thing between us had dropped out of the sky without an invite. It was scary. We were both in trouble now, as love had landed where no man had ever gone before: my heart.

My phone rang, and I got up to answer it. It was Robin. I wrapped myself in white sheets and started to walk up the stairs.

"Baby, don't go up like that; there are men upstairs."

I told Robin I would call him right back.

"Who was that?" Robin pried.

"It's a long story."

"Yes, I'm sure, but Thomas is on his way out there."

"What?" I exclaimed.

"Just kidding," he said laughing.

Zur got a call as well, as I finished up talking to Robin. I hung up my phone, and when Zur was done, he came over and said, "Baby, I have to leave, but come over here."

I sat there wrapped in white sheets, like I was wearing an Indian sari.

"I have a lot of business in the Middle East, and I travel a lot. I can't say exactly when I'll be back, but I will."

"Shh," I said. "It was fun and passionate, Zur. But I don't need broken promises, and to me, all promises are meant to be broken."

"Why do you have to say that, baby, huh? Tell me."

"You have your life; I have mine. I'm not going to wait for you, and you're not going to wait for me." I got up, and he grabbed my hand.

"What's the matter with you?" he asked. "Did you just want pleasure, without emotion, without love?"

"Don't ask me that, okay?"

I turned the doorknob into the bathroom and locked the door behind me. I turned the hot shower on and stepped in, as tears flowed down my face. "Wrecking Ball" was playing through the stupid intercom system on the sailboat. Funny, it felt like I'd been hit with a big steel ball, and I needed some vodka to recover. How convenient, that I was in the shower crying my eyes away.

"Open the door, baby, please." Zur knocked insistently on the door, but I continued my cry in solitude.

I didn't realize that I'd been in the shower for so long, so I toweled off and opened the door. I didn't want to talk anymore. I simply put all of my clothes back on and walked up the stairs to where his bodyguards, yes two of them, were waiting in a speedboat to take us ashore.

Zur sat at the front of the speedboat, next to the captain, and staring out at the horizon. I sat at the back, thinking of how I was mad about him, mad as a crazy person in a mental asylum. Love could do that to people. I turned the opposite way as he looked around at me. He ran his hands through his hair; I noticed he did that when he got stressed.

We arrived at the harbor, and Zur climbed up onto the dock and reached his hand out to mine. We walked to the Bentley in complete silence; no serenity, just an intense quiet. Our ride back to Southampton was anything but pleasant, as I wasn't good with love or good-byes. This chapter in my life would be called "How I Screwed Myself Royally," and I'm sure women all over Long Island would get it.

When Zur didn't speak, you knew things were intense. We were five minutes away from Duren's place and there were still no words, in English, Arabic, Urdu, Swahili, Greek, or bloody French. Nothing.

He stopped at the gates and said, "I'm going to drop you here, so I don't have to watch you leave."

"Sure, and do have a safe trip. I wish you well."

He looked at me with anguish, and said, "I'll see you soon, baby."

I got out of the Bentley, and he drove off like a man running from his ex-wife. I stood at the gates, empty-handed and empty-hearted; so completely empty, as my life went from cloud nine, back to cloud one.

21

MY BUGATTI OR YOURS

It was seven o'clock, and I was ready to wish Helene *bonne chance* and much happiness. She poured me some tea and gave me crème brûlée. It was like Paris in Long Island!

"*Merci, Helene,*" I said, as she gave me my tea with a few blocks of raw sugar. She smiled at me so blissfully. I would definitely need a Helene in my life someday, when I was settled and, you know, married.

My tea was glorious, and the back view from Duren's house was *très magnifique*. The sun was setting, and the waves never ceased to do what they do. It was funny that humans weren't the same. I sipped on my tea and thought of Zur, our passion, our smiles, our time on the boat, and how displeased I was to not have that experience every day of my life. The man was mystifying, for sure, and our romps in silk sheets were lustful, but also filled with hints of togetherness.

For a while, it could possibly suffice, but I didn't know about forever. You see, no one had ever been worth forever before. But in a crazy way, when I lay beside him, I knew that if I were lucky enough to be by his side every day, it could grow to forever. I wasn't sure if even he knew what forever was. Regardless, he was on his way out, back to his normal life. And me? I needed to get back to work on Wall Street, kick ass, make my millions, and stay sane and sober. It sounded like a lot to do.

Helene let me know that Robin had arrived, and I placed my tea down and ran to the door as if I needed him here yesterday. I sprinted down the stairs, and he swept me off my feet and twirled me around.

"I've missed you!" Robin yelled. Then I saw the Bugatti.

"Holy crap!" I cried. It was a masterpiece of metal, dark blue with wheels like a bodybuilder, carved to its finest. And talk about horsepower! But no technical stuff; I didn't really do tech. "That is my kind of car, dude!" I said.

"My God, it's a wicked car. I've gotten pulled over three times since yesterday."

"Let me guess: Cooper?" I said with a smile.

"Cooper and associates!" he said laughing.

Helene brought my things, and Robin packed the car. Then, like magic, the black Bentley drove up. Zur rolled his window down, and I found myself grinning like a kid on Christmas.

"Baby, this must be your brother," he said.

I did the introductions, "Yes, Zur, Robin; Robin, Zur."

"And who are you?" Robin asked.

"Zur, you idiot," I said.

"I know, but who, precisely, is Zur?" asked Robin with an annoying smile.

I smacked him.

Zur smiled and shook Robin's hand. "I'm Zur. It's nice to meet someone who belongs to my baby's family."

"Yup, this baby moves very quickly," Robin said sarcastically, as he hugged me.

"That's a nice Bugatti, yours?"

"For the moment. It belongs to our brother. I'm taking it for a spin, hoping to get me some attention."

I was so embarrassed. What had happened to Robin?

Zur took out a bag and handed it to me. "Open it when you are alone, good?"

"Good," I replied.

He stared into my eyes with the depth of the ocean. Robin stood back, watching us, and looking as if his mind had just been blown. I held Zur's hands as he kissed mine, placed his left hand on my cheek, and said, "Be good, baby."

"I'm always good."

After getting into his car, Zur looked into my eyes again and blew me a kiss.

"Good to meet you, Robin; I hope to see you again," he said. And like the wind, my Zur was gone.

I stood there watching his Bentley disappear, forgetting all about Robin's presence.

"Soph, what the hell happened?" Robin said, bringing me back to the moment.

"I wish I knew, but it all happened so quickly."

I could have walked into Bergdorf and known what damage I was doing quicker than I could figure this one out. Here and now I was lost.

"Well, I see you're into playboys now," Robin said. "Just try to not sleep with more than you can handle, okay."

"Thomas, you mean Thomas? WTF, he's not my boyfriend."

"No, he's not, but it wasn't that long ago that you were kissing him in the kitchen, remember? Well, he is waiting for you to get back home, and now you've got two on board; one of them is our dad's best friend's son. Okay, just a reminder, though you work on Wall Street, you're still a lady."

I was infuriated as I got into the driver's seat and made Robin get into the passenger seat. I drove off listening to Vivaldi in a goddamn Bugatti, but as I turned off of the private road, and proceeded to the stop sign, I saw Zur's Bentley. He flashed his lights at me, and I smiled. I didn't know if Robin was pissed that I'd moved on so quickly or upset that the idea of him and Thomas being in-laws was now out of sight.

In about an hour, I pulled up to our home, and in truth, I hadn't missed it at all. I walked in with Robin carrying my bags, and to the left in the study stood my parents.

"Hello, Darling, you look well," my mother said.

"Hi, Mother, how are you?" I kissed my parents on both cheeks, not ready to discuss their marriage plans yet.

"How was your trip to the Hamptons?" she asked.

"It was fabulous and relaxing," I replied. Honestly, I couldn't care less about what was going on with my parents; I had gotten so used to my alone time. "I'm going to go wash up and head to bed. I'm exhausted."

My mother and my father, looking better than how I'd last seen them, both said good night. As I raced up the stairs, Duren called. I spoke to him for a brief minute and then hung up. I'd thank him properly tomorrow. Right now, I was eager to go to my room and open that bag from Zur.

Once in my bedroom, I stripped off my clothes, washed my face with SK-II, and headed to bed. Sitting on my bed, I opened the bag and pulled out a box. Inside the box was a ring, a black ring with a diamond in the middle. What did that signify? Surely it wasn't an engagement ring, but I placed it on my finger and smiled. I knew that Zur had to be coming back.

I opened my balcony door and walked outside in my robe, missing Zur, wanting him there. Having him in my life gave it meaning. I wouldn't just be about making all this money, I'd have someone to look forward to at the end of each day.

I went back to bed and worked a bit, sending emails and calling possible assistants. I had a deadline, I had to get an assistant before the morning, and I was determined to find one. In fact, I was going to get a good-looking, muscular hottie. Heck, I needed to piss Jaxwe off. After about an hour and a half, I hired someone after a Skype interview.

Relieved, I went downstairs to get myself a cup of chamomile tea. I was hoping for a cup of tea without the collision of any family members, but as luck would have it, my mother walked in and sat down. She was the epitome of great elegance in her striped silk pajamas.

"Darling, I know that I'm not always there, but I am very proud of you," she said.

I placed my teacup down and looked over at her, speechless. "Why, Mother, why now?"

"Does it matter?" asked my father, who walked in and stood next to me.

"A lot has happened recently, but we are always going to be a family, no matter what," she said.

"How wonderful. I'm going to head to bed," I said, annoyed. "This is just not my cup of tea. I can't deal with this crap; happy one day, torn another, happy families again, or not. Heck, Mom, you're not happy here with Dad, just admit it."

My parents stood there lost for words, as they should be.

I was supposed to be a dainty lady in pink ruffles with proper etiquette, but I wasn't.

"I work with men all day," I said. "I have a best friend who's forty-three, isn't happy in her marriage, and is only staying because she likes her lifestyle. I don't like pretentious, and that's what you both are." I stormed out of the kitchen.

Somehow, I had changed. I wasn't going to hold everything in and pretend, just because I was a Becks. I was going to let them have it all the way to my million-dollar bloody career.

It was late, but I called Zur and got an answering machine. The thought of him was torturous. I couldn't sleep, and I became anxious. This certainly wasn't what I wanted, but here I was engulfed in feelings for another, another that was millions of miles away by now, with his own life that had nothing to do with me. I wanted to call Jan, but I didn't need the, "Sophie, darling, what the bloody hell now?" speech.

I walked over to Robin's room, in need of company and a little empathy. I never knocked at Robin's door, so why would I start now? I opened the door and walked right in to see Hannah and Robin locking lips.

"Oh God, I'll come back," I said, covering my eyes. How awkward! It was like two worlds colliding and it just felt wrong. Didn't Robin realize that Hannah was more than just the housekeeper to me? She was like the mother I'd never had. She took care of me. What would happen if it all went wrong? Couldn't they find sleeping buddies at the organic grocery store or maybe a yoga class? Oh God, I needed therapy, a psychologist, something.

I stood at the door, yelling, "What the hell is wrong with you both? Were you that lonely while I was gone?"

Robin grabbed me and pulled me into the room. "Shut up, Sophie."

"Miss Sophie, I'm so sorry," cried Hannah.

"No one knows, okay?" Robin said.

"No, it's not okay. What did you do?"

"The same thing you did in the Hamptons."

Hannah stormed out of the room.

"You better hope she doesn't go back to Barcelona," I said. "Dude, who's going to take care of me?"

"You're a grown-up now!"

"Yes, I know, but why can't you think with your brain, and not with "little Robin?" I yelled, gesturing to his pants.

"You're such a hypocrite. What about Zur?"

"I can't seem to get him out of my mind. I'm a lost lunatic, okay?" I broke down into tears. Robin came over to me and held me.

"What is it?" he asked, worried. I was usually always composed.

"He lives in Dubai."

"What the hell! He's an Arab?" asked Robin. I laughed as I cried. "That's worse than me doing Hannah," Robin exclaimed.

He held me, and I sat on his bed with my head against his chest. I needed some love. Thank God Robin had been born with a heart.

"It's going to be okay, baby," he said, laughing.

I smacked him, laughing right back.

"Wait until our family hears about this one," Robin said.

"This family never runs out of issues, not ever."

"What are you going to do about Hannah?" I asked.

"I'll think about it in the a.m."

That night, I slept next to Robin. I needed comfort, and it was good to have a brother that understood that. It was good to have Robin around all the time. Heck, that was a good brother for you. I guess it didn't matter if he screwed the housekeeper.

22

WALL STREET DOESN'T SLEEP

On Wednesday morning, I was up at 4:55 a.m., getting ready for work. Normally, every morning on Wall Street was a natural high for me, but this morning, my mind was otherwise occupied with thoughts of Zur. I looked at myself in the mirror, hoping I could somehow snap myself out of it. Duren believed in me; that was probably the only reason I had gotten hired. I had fire in my belly, so to speak.

I slipped on my polished black Diors with the gold clasps. Surprisingly, Hannah was up already. With a knock on my room door, she came in with a golden-wired tray holding my morning tea and gluten-free steel-cut oats with organic raisins and blueberries. As I ate my breakfast, she smiled at me and handed me my ring, the black band with the diamond.

"I can't wear that to work, everyone will think I'm ditched," I said.

"It's hitched, Miss Sophie."

"In my book, hitched inevitably equals ditched," I said, smiling with my mouth filled with oats. "Thank you for all your help, Hannah."

"You are most welcome."

I grabbed my hairbrush, which had the nicest looking bristles I'd ever seen. It was a brush fit for a princess, but this princess has since turned into a masculine salesperson. I did my makeup for work, simple but demure. I put on pearl earrings with a strand of the finest pearls for my neck, compliments of my dad's hard-earned money. I grabbed my Hermès Birkin packed with all of my work things, and was out the door.

On my way out, I found the driver Mr. Wheathly. "What a name, poor thing, wheat and Wheathly are so darn close," I said to Robin.

"You are too much," Robin replied, rolling his eyes.

Sitting in the back of the limo, I rolled my window down and sent kisses to my Robin. He waved back, and then my driver and I were on our way to get my new assistant, Tanner Tibick. He lived in Oyster Bay, which was on our way into the city. We pulled into a private drive, rang the bell, and out came this hunk of a chunk, Mr. Golden Boy, Tanner.

"Hello, I'm Tanner. How are you, Miss Becks?"

"I'm, um, feeling very hot in this suit," I said, and cleared my throat.

Mr. Wheathly opened the door of the limo, and smiled at me. "Oh no," I whispered to him.

Have you ever wondered why all of those top brokers sleep with their assistants? Well, it's because they all look like Tanner, except female. I actually forgot Zur for the entire one-hour drive to Manhattan.

We got out on Wall Street, as Mr. Wheathly opened the door.

"Do have a pleasant day, Miss Becks."

"Oh, Mr. Wheathly," I whispered, smiling, "look around you: this is exactly where I belong. Pleasant is an understatement!"

I didn't look back, but I looked to the side and saw Tanner holding my Hermès Birkin with pride. The doorman looked at us, and said, "Welcome back, Miss Becks!" *Yes, I have arrived,* I thought, *and I will kick any and all asses I come across in custom-made, European-tailored suits.*

As I entered the office, Duren saw me through his glass-walled office, and called me in. I walked in and was elated to finally get my first check.

"Duren, I'm so thankful for the Hamptons vacation, and your hospitality."

He smiled. "Helene loved you. She said you were very kind for a Wall Street girl."

I smiled, staring at Duren as he sat back in his leather tufted library chair. As he looked back at me, I felt awkward for a moment; I had just remembered what that odd cop in the Hamptons had said about my "relationship" with Duren.

"By the way, I met a cop in the Hamptons, and he was really odd," I said. "I was driving the Aston, and he thought I was a, you know, um, a girlfriend of yours."

Duren wasn't a bad-looking guy, and he was very polished, but was I interested? No, not currently.

"Becks, I've shown you kindness. Should there be a question mark to it? Yes, perhaps, but maybe you are like the daughter I never had." He looked at the family photo that sat on his desk and turned it to show it to me: tall, skinny, beautiful, yoga-bodied wife with his son, Cooper, a beautiful family.

"My son won't ever become half of the broker I am. It's a shame," Duren said ruefully. "Cooper likes surfing and drinking beers out east; no taste for refinement or the finer things in life, like his mother."

I remembered Cooper and my conversation with Radha. "He has a very nice girlfriend, though!" I said.

"I don't know..." he trailed off, deep in thought.

What a disappointment he must be to him. I thought of my own parents and how they expected all of us to be Yale and Harvard graduates, and look at the three of us. All a mess, well, in our own ways. Sure, Rain and I were overachievers, but Robin was hopeless. He had no desire to achieve, content to stay bundled in his parents' blankets.

"Don't you see?" Duren asked me. "I believe in you, and watching you achieve makes me happy."

I felt happy hearing him say that, so I walked over to Duren and asked, "Permission to hug you, sir?"

He nodded, and then stood up and grabbed me as if I were a man, hitting me on the back.

Then my phone rang, and I saw who it is. Oh my God, it was Zur. I stumbled to get it, forgetting Duren entirely.

"Hey, baby, how are you?" Zur answered when I picked up.

I was so anxious to speak to him, but also relieved that he hadn't forgotten me.

"Hi, Zur, how's it going?"

I looked up and saw Duren staring at me. I cleared my throat and wiped my smile away, trying to look more professional in my boss' office. It was as difficult as removing waves from the angry sea during hurricane season.

"I wanted you to know that I'll be there later in the week, and we can chat in person. Sound good?"

Good? Honey, he made me quiver and shiver.

"Sure, talk to you soon?" I asked.

"Yes. And, baby, I want you to know that I ..."

"Yes?"

"I love you."

I was stunned and shocked and so, so, so happy! I hung up, staring at my phone.

"Zur?" Duren asked.

"In time, I'll tell you all about him."

"Okay, so now, just open your check."

I held the brown envelope in my hands, and wondered why everyone was using brown these days: boxes, envelopes, etc. I tore it open and took out my very first Wall Street check.

"One hundred thousand. Is this correct?" I asked, shocked.

"Yes. You opened twenty-five accounts in two and a half weeks. You've raised over five million dollars."

"How amazing! Thank you for this incredible, um, job."

I couldn't even think straight, as thoughts of Zur had taken the place of the joy that money once brought me.

I walked over to my desk, and stared at Tanner.

"All good, Miss Becks?"

"Yes, Tanner. Please get me a Starbucks grande decaf latte with skim milk and Truvia." I pointed to the right of the hallway.

I looked over and saw Duren on a conference call. Jaxwe was beside him, glaring at me as he spun in his chair.

Then I heard over the intercom, "Would everyone meet me in my office, right now."

With that, all the brokers dropped their phones, books, leads, Starbucks coffee, and bimbos and walked to his office, which was big enough to fit the whole firm, so bloody wicked!

"Good morning, boys. Today, I'd like to announce that

Sophie Becks, a newbie broker in our firm, is our new top producer. Now some of you may ask yourselves, 'How the *hell* did she do it?' She will tell you. Becks, please stand over here, and give the a.m. meeting."

Oh my Gucci heels and handbag! Me, give a meeting? I slowly walked up to the front of the room, wishing I could open the glass door and run down the staircase.

"Good morning, everyone. As some of you know, I'm Sophie Becks, and I'm not going to give you the same speeches you've heard a hundred times before…" I held up the check Duren had given me. "Here's my first check, one hundred thousand dollars, after taxes. Not bad, but it signals the beginning for me and the end of the road for a few of you."

They all stared at me, not as if I was a piece of meat, but the bait.

"So here's the deal," I continued. "I've opened twenty-five accounts in two and a half weeks, and I plan to open forty accounts next month, which will make all of you," I pointed from one end of the room to the other, "fucking little sissies."

Oh, I was ruthless! I couldn't believe I said *fucking*.

Duren stepped in, and said, "Whoever opens forty accounts first will get my Aston Martin. Incentive enough?"

I loved boys in Maseratis and Bentleys, but I sure loved the idea of me in an Aston. I smiled, thinking of the magic I made in that car with Zur, and I was motivated as hell to get it. I smiled, staring at the room filled with hot, sweaty, expensive cologne. I was about to do the unthinkable, and somebody, anybody, better help me, pronto. I walked out of there still smiling, and as I looked at Tanner, I realized I was now both ruthless and hot, and an up-and-comer on Wall Street.

I spent all morning on the phone, pitching like a cricket player in the Caribbean. I had two decaf coffees, and Tanner was working his ass off helping me with trades, paperwork, phone calls, and follow-ups. His first day was hectic, and glancing over at his Chippendale-ness helped.

Around noon, he asked, "Miss Becks, I was thinking, shall I get us lunch?"

"Yes, it's midday, and I don't eat lunch later than 12:45 p.m. most days. I'll have a salad, no croutons, grilled organic chicken, toasted walnuts, cranberries, and a light raspberry vinaigrette, plus a sparkling water with lemon on the side, not in."

He looked at me as if I was mad.

"What?" I asked. "Did you think I was going to eat fries and a fancy beef burger?"

"No, I ... I just didn't think you would be that specific." He looked at me with his ocean-blue eyes. His freckles were painted on in the perfect places.

"Well, one thing is for sure, if you're to be my assistant, you'll get the specifics. I'm going to let you know what I like and what I don't like. I don't like beef burgers or fried potatoes or anything with gluten."

"Yes, ma'am," Tanner replied respectfully, and then walked away to fetch me lunch.

In the meantime, Jaxwe stared at me as if he was about to come over and kick my ass out of the leather chair I'd upgraded myself to. So, being the polite well-brought-up woman that I am, I walked over to him, and asked, "What's your problem?"

He ignored me at first, and then closed his Apple laptop. He looked up at me with his pristine suit and yellow silk tie, and then stood up to his full six feet. His hair was shaped with Sebastian, and his teeth were whiter than cotton.

"With all due respect," he said, "you're a woman, and this is a *man's* world. I'm fucking all male, and you," he pointed at me with his long, perfect-looking finger, "are not going to be top producer next month."

"Are you done?" I asked. "Yes, I'm a woman in a man's world, but, darling, I'll beat you to forty accounts next month, and probably every month after that." I stared into his eyes without any frailty. "And, Jaxwe, get yourself a bloody shrink. You're going to need it," I said, touching his tie. Then I walked away.

One of the firm's other top producers, Tom, looked at me. "What's the beef?" he asked.

"Whatever, I can't seem to please anyone lately."

"Yes, nothing is ever enough," he replied.

Tom was cool enough, not a big hotshot, but he made a good living, was still dating his high school sweetheart, and lived in Long Island with a well-behaved dog. He was just about the only broker I knew that was normal, and not floating up on cloud nine with drugs or other vices.

"Oh, say hello to Rain for me," he said. "I saw pictures on his blog of his new girl, not bad!"

"What new girl? What are you talking about?"

He pulled up Rain's blog, and I saw my brother with a girl, a girlfriend, publicly. Now that was news! I immediately lost my appetite, even though Tanner had gone out to get my lunch.

When Tanner returned, I told him to, "Get Rain, my brother, on the phone." He immediately dropped his lunch and dialed Rain, but to no avail.

I checked my email and found an evite from Thomas for

dinner tomorrow. I smiled, but I also knew that I was not too thrilled to jump into his bed anymore. I called Thomas on his cell.

"Hi, Thomas, it's Sophie."

"Hi, what's going on?"

"I just saw your evite. What's the occasion?"

"I'm getting engaged," he said seriously.

I laughed, but maybe I shouldn't have.

"What's funny?" he asked.

"You're getting engaged? I kissed you less than two weeks ago. Shouldn't you have mentioned that at the time?"

He laughed, "Sophie, I'm joking! Gotta lighten up, Soph."

On a crazy note, why was I even bothered? I liked him, but I wasn't crazy about him. I was crazy about Zur.

"So will you be able to make it?" he asked.

I didn't really know if Zur was playing me or really coming back to New York. I didn't think that deep into anything.

"Yes, Friday, I'll be there," I said.

"Seven o'clock."

"Yes."

I didn't usually overthink dates and men. I liked to think of men as watches; you needed different watches for different occasions.

"And, Sophie, please come alone."

I smiled and laughed, "Will do."

At four o'clock, when the market had closed, I had Duren sign off on my trades.

"Can I do anything else for you before I leave?" Tanner asked.

"I'm having dinner with my girlfriend this evening in the city."

"You have a girlfriend? Damn, there goes my shot," I said

sarcastically. Tanner laughed. "Yes, sit down right there," I said, typing very quickly as I gestured to a chair with my head. Then I leaned over to him. "So tell me, how was your first day?"

"It was, you know, different and there was lots to do."

"No, you say, 'It was wonderful!' Why? Because enthusiasm sells!" I told him.

Tanner looked at me like I was the Mad Hatter from *Alice in Wonderland*, and I laughed as I watched my poor, innocent Abercrombie guy assistant make his exit.

At 4:15 p.m., my driver arrived, and I walked out of the office.

"Miss Becks, how are you? I hope pleasant," he said.

"Yes, very much so, thank you, Mr. Wheathly."

"Ready to get back to Long Island?"

Was I? I smiled, and on the way back home, I looked out the window thinking of everything that had happened recently, especially Zur. I didn't really know what I was getting myself into, but I trotted ahead regardless. I didn't want to be like most women, counting the stars before you saw them in the sky.

23

THE STARS WEREN'T ALIGNED

By Thursday, I was exhausted, and after a quick dinner, I was soaking in my bath. Typically, Rain stayed in Manhattan for the entire week, making his millions for his new high-maintenance girlfriend, maybe soon-to-be wife. Apparently she'd come over while I was away. Lovely. I hoped I didn't bump into her anytime soon.

"Sophie, can I come in?" asked Robin.

"Oh, no problem, I'm only naked in the tub, under a carpet of bubbles."

Robin came in and pulled up a chair beside me in the tub. "What are you going to do?" he demanded.

"About?"

"Your love life, well more like your sex life now."

He was clearly annoyed. What business was it of his?

"I just don't think too much about Zur and I as being in a relationship. For Pete's sake, he's in Dubai probably with a harem of naked women."

"Are you kidding me? I saw you two, and you have a thing for this guy."

"I also kissed Thomas before leaving. Your point?"

"My point… Well, what the hell is going on?" he yelled.

"Whoa, what's up, dude?" I exclaimed. "Like hold your horses. I'm not going to hurt myself, okay?" I looked away, as I didn't want to break my own heart. Again. "Thomas invited me to dinner on Friday, and I called him back."

Robin was livid. Why? I didn't know.

"That's crazy!" he said.

"No, it's not. I can't do this baloney long distance thing."

"Then play everyone, that's better. Sleep around."

"What is wrong with you?" I asked.

"What is wrong with me? You're my sister, okay? Not some whore. Make a decision. And don't break people's hearts," Robin said belligerently.

"I'll try to not hurt anyone's feelings, okay? Really, Robin."

He left, and I got out of the tub. I was so angry, not because I was far away from someone I really wanted, but because I was being judged for dating more than one guy. Hello? Didn't men do that all the time without being judged?

It was 8:45 p.m. when I went out onto my balcony. I looked overhead into the dark skies and listened to the waves from far away. It seemed impossible for me to think of having it all and enjoying it. Making a hundred thousand in a month using my natural talents was enormous, but could I really have it all without having someone there to ground and love me for who I was, underneath all the designer trimmings and glitz?

Zur had touched me somewhere that most men couldn't. But I also knew that men were vicious creatures that would wine and dine you and show you the clouds, just to drop you to the greatest depths, where you couldn't recover. I didn't want to be like Juliet or Anna Karenina. So from here on in, I was going to be like one of the boys. Not Jaxwe, though. He was just an imbecile. I would never be like him.

I yawned as I sat on the swing on my balcony, pushing my legs back and forth like I used to do as a child. But, I was no longer a child, was I? I stepped back into my bedroom and walked to my wooden antique dresser with gold-leaf edges. I put Zur's ring in its box. It had only been days, but it felt like forever. At least I'd gotten one call and an "I love you." What was love anyway? I took the box and threw it to one side of the room. I spent the next hour looking for gated homes on Long Island. I needed a great escape from everyone: a penthouse in the city, like Rain, or a house in the Hamptons, like my mother.

Around midnight, I could barely sleep, tossing and turning, thinking thoughts that should have ceased hours ago. I checked my email on my iPhone. I was so tired but I just couldn't sleep. I silently tiptoed down to the kitchen, hoping I didn't wake anyone, especially my mom. I didn't have the energy for her right now.

When I turned on the kitchen light, I saw Hannah crying. "Hannah, what's the matter?"

She turned away from me, wiping her eyes. "Oh, it's nothing," she said through her sniffles.

"Nothing doesn't come with tears. Tell me, I want to know," I said.

"It's complicated, Miss Sophie. I wouldn't even know where to begin."

I brewed a pot of tea as she cried and cried. Robin had broken off their illicit affair. I guess he had gotten tired of being a cliché and screwing the housekeeper, and had now started seeing one of Rain's coworkers, or so Hannah said. Somehow, I knew it must be something more. This was exactly why I hadn't wanted Robin to get involved with her in the first place. Hannah was inconsolable, and I couldn't do anything to help. She'd worked for my family for ten years. Bosses shouldn't do their employees and vice versa. It never ended well.

"Go on to bed, Hannah. Rest it out. I'll handle it."

"Please don't speak of it, I beg you, Miss Sophie. It was my mistake, not Mr. Robin's."

I walked upstairs with a cup of very hot tea, the way my palette liked it. But this time, I wanted to throw it all over Robin. I opened his door, and what do you know? He was on the phone.

"Let's talk. Now," I said firmly.

"Goddammit, Soph, I'm on the phone. What is it?"

"Are you yelling at *me*? You shouldn't be. What exactly did you do to Hannah?" I yelled.

"I'll call you back," Robin said into the phone and hung up. He then turned to me and said, "It's none of your business. We're adults."

"So you just sleep with her and leave her?"

Robin turned pale. In all honesty, he did look as if he really cared about her, but … and there was always a *but*!

"Listen, it was an error, okay? A big one," he said. "I didn't use her. I really liked her."

"Do tell me what happened, Robin, because she was a good person to us." I was annoyed, and honestly, Rain was higher up in my book now than Robin was.

"I'm going back to Rome to see Dana…" He trailed off.

I placed the cup of tea down on his dresser.

"You're leaving again?"

"Yes, right after your birthday."

Well, there went my anger. I was still furious about Hannah, but now I was also saddened by him leaving.

"So you're getting back with that stupid idiot that broke your heart?" I was quiet for a short moment.

"She's the only one I've ever loved. The rest was just sex."

Well, in my head I understood the difference between sex and love. For God's sake, it wasn't like wine and cheese. Sex and love didn't always pair together so easily. If you were sleeping with someone, it was a hint of passion with the possibility of love. But love and sex were very rare together, and trust me, I would know.

"I'm tired," I said. "Good luck with that. Hannah will surely be quitting, and I'm sure Rain will get married, and I'll move out. See you tomorrow, dude."

I closed the door behind me and headed back to bed. As I leaned over to place my phone on the night table, it rang. It was 12:35 a.m.

"Hello?" I answered. It was an unknown number.

"Hey, baby, are you asleep?"

"Zur?"

"Yes, Zur. How many men call you 'baby'?"

"Whatever," I responded.

"Whatever, huh? What's wrong?"

"What's going on?" I asked.

He exhaled deeply. "I'm not going to make it this week. It's been more difficult than I expected to move my business plans around here in Dubai."

I couldn't say exactly how I felt, but it would be somewhere in the range of disappointed to psychotic.

"Sophie, are you there?"

"Yes, I'm here," I said with composure, but honestly we'd see how long that lasted.

"Baby, I am not good with these things, but I meant what I said before."

I cleared my throat. When I did that, it usually meant things weren't good.

"Listen carefully, Zur. I'm not one of those women that needs a lot from any man, but for a minute in time, I felt really strong emotions for you. But, I can't do this…"

"Baby, don't do this," he pleaded.

"No, I have to. Don't bother with this thing between us anymore. Don't tell me that you love me. That's bull. You are just like every other man."

He paused and then sighed. "Baby, I'm very sorry…"

"Good night and good luck." I hung up.

I couldn't possibly feel okay. The harsh reality was that I didn't care for excuses. My father used them often when we were children, and I was both wary and immune to them.

I decided that men weren't like watches, after all. Watches could at least tell time; men couldn't even tell a good thing when it hit them in the head. I was sad, and I couldn't bear to hurt myself anymore. *Screw Zur*, I thought.

I sat on the floor of my balcony, thinking about the Hamptons and hoping that I wasn't deceiving myself. I wanted a relationship with him, even though we were cultures and oceans apart. I looked up at the stars shining in the sky. Zur's call had been a huge disruption for me. I was right back to square one.

As morning dawned, I was awakened by my alarm and Hannah vigorously knocking on my bedroom door.

"Miss Sophie, I knocked for about thirty minutes!" she said.

"I'm sorry, Hannah. I fell asleep on the balcony, and my back is aching."

"Well, here's your tea."

I sipped my tea all the way to the bathroom. I turned on the shower and stripped my clothing off, one piece at a time. I bathed hurriedly, and put on a collared silk shirt with ruffles, my pin-striped suit, and my Dior Mary Janes.

I grabbed my brown briefcase and ran down the stairs. My mother, in a bright silk shirt and trousers with a golden belt, stood at the bottom.

"Darling, do you have a moment?" she asked.

"Yes, Mother, surely, but just a moment," I said, glancing at my Patek.

I stepped into the library and saw my father looking like the lawyer he was.

"You missed dinner the other night, and well, we have news for you," said my father.

I stood there in silence, but it was hard as I saw how harmonious they both seemed.

"What news?"

"Your mother and I have decided to give our marriage another shot, for us and this family."

I looked over at my mother, and the truth was, I didn't care. She was one of those women that had always cared more about aesthetics than happiness.

"Congratulations, that's great," I said flatly. *Yes, sure, until the next flare-up*, I thought.

On my way out of the library, I looked back at them, and said, "Did you hear Robin's news yet?"

"No, what is it?" asked Dad.

"Robin is moving back to Rome."

My parents looked at each other in disbelief. My work there was done. I got in my limo and was off to another day of anger management.

Work was a marvel. I pitched as if I were hepped up on caffeine pills.

"Good morning, Becks, can we have a word?" asked Duren.

"Yes, I'll be right there," I replied, and joined him in his office.

"How's it going?" he asked.

"Uh, hectic actually," I smiled, though I know I looked tired. He looked at me as if he understood.

"Well, you are sure taking it out on work. Either that or you are just every man's desire."

I was flattered, but what the hell?

"What do you mean?" I asked him.

"Helene called… My neighbor's bodyguard, Syed, was asking for your address," he said, looking at me carefully. I didn't smile. "You're an amazing woman, Becks, and when you're up for it, you'll find an amazing man. But, Zur, he's a very private, very complicated, successful guy who has a son, and he never truly gives anything a real shot."

"A son?"

"Yes, it's a long story. He usually seems so reserved, so I'm surprised he was looking for you."

"Well, no need to worry, Duren, it's all behind me now." At this point I didn't know what was behind or forward, but I knew that I wanted that bastard as much as I wanted sparkling water with lemon – only all the time. Okay, maybe not quite that much. "I'm going to go back to what I do best now, work and money," I said.

God knows I'd probably be a lonely woman when I was ninety. I looked at Duren and smiled, but honestly I was a mess. Oh well, I was sure I'd recover sometime.

Around noon, Tanner asked, "Lunch, Miss Becks?"

"No thanks, I'm having dinner tonight with a very handsome man who cooks like a professional chef."

I felt stupid when Tanner walked away. I was very hurt, and when I was hurt, I said and did stupid things. I needed to get out from behind my desk and away from the phone.

I passed by Jaxwe's desk, and asked, "Hey, how's it going?"

He looked at me, confused. "What's up, Becks?"

"Nothing, I'm cool. Hanging in there."

"Good. I can't wait to drive the Aston," he said.

"No worries, I'll lend it to you sometime."

I smiled as I walked away. I looked back and saw him smiling too. What the heck, if you couldn't beat them, join them!

After a quick coffee break and a stretch, I was back at my desk. In no time, I got five qualified leads, and then I got a guy from London. I loved the Brits, so cordial and polite. He was so pleasant that I forgot it was a business call.

"So, Mr. Riggers, I hope to do business with you shortly."

"Yes, I'll wire the money over in the a.m."

And with that, I'd gotten five more accounts in two days. Not bad.

I grabbed my things and was headed out the door, when I remembered that I was having dinner with Thomas later. I went to the executive bathroom at work and took a quick shower. By the time I was finished, my driver was outside waiting for me, and we started the long drive back to Long Island. I was exhausted.

My phone rang. It was Hannah.

"All okay?" I asked.

"Yes, Mr. Rain wanted to know if you were free for dinner tonight."

"I'm headed to Thomas's. I'll be in late."

"Okay, I'll let him know. He and his new girlfriend were dining near the house and asked about you."

"Yes, do tell him."

I hung up. I was eager to see Thomas. I'd had more than enough family news in one week. Maybe I was just pissed off that my desire for Zur was nothing more than an empty locket.

In about an hour and a half, I arrived at the vineyards. I turned my phone on vibrate and walked to the front door, where a man in a tux led me to the wine cellar.

"Thomas?" I called out.

"Hi," he said from behind me. We hugged politely.

"How was your trip?" he asked, his blue eyes staring at me.

"It was fine."

"Just fine or exceptional?"

"I don't want to answer that. A lot happened."

"That's fair," he said.

We went up to a balcony made of dark wood with coffered ceilings and ancient lighting. Beautiful vines grew on the outer wall, and the balcony overlooked the vineyards, very Tuscan.

He pulled out a bistro chair for me. A white linen cloth covered the table, and there was only simple candlelight. Thank God. I didn't want him to try to romance me. I wasn't in the mood.

He sat there gazing at me, as he sipped on a glass of wine.

"Work is okay?" he asked.

"Yes, it's fine, really fine."

We ate our first course of mesclun greens with cranberries and some sort of horrid cheese. I drank a sip of red wine, which calmed me a bit and even more effectively got rid of the stinky cheese aftertaste. Now I finally understood what Zur had said about the wine.

"It's very strong but tasteful," I said, mesmerized by Thomas's eyes. Were they passionate, or was I just tipsy? Okay, I was tipsy in a few sips as I did *not* drink much.

Thomas touched my hands slowly, all the while looking at me. But, all I could think of was Zur. I moved my hands away, looking at my sad salad.

"Thomas, you're an amazing man. I just don't know what's wrong with me," I said calmly and with regret, but heck, that didn't seem to work.

"I'm not asking for your hand in matrimony," he replied.

I started coughing. "Why even mention that? Do you want me to run away?" I laughed.

He laughed too. "I know you're petrified of commitment, but gosh, that's horrible."

I didn't have the words to describe what I was feeling. I stared at him, wishing I wasn't so complicated. He was the epitome of faithful, a polo guy, a woman's dream. But I wasn't like other women. I didn't like simple. I loved complex individuals, the kind who couldn't be reached and didn't even know what loyal was.

The vineyards were beautiful in the moonlight, and after dinner, Thomas handed me a box wrapped in purple silk bows.

"For you," he said, as he sat next to me and kissed my cheek.

"Thomas, you never have to…"

"Yes, I know, of course. But when I met you, it did something to me."

We were so close that I could smell his cologne. Opening the package was difficult as his lips were now brushing my neck. I felt a renewed attraction to him, but I also had a desire to run. It was like waves hitting the sand in a powerful rush, and then receding forcefully back to the sea. I finally opened the package and, inside, found a pen.

"Thank you for this, it's sweet, but I just can't be with you like this. I have so many things that need to be sorted out in my life."

He pushed his chair back in a rage and walked to the balcony.

"Who is he? And don't you tell me it's work," he shouted.

Words left me for a moment, and then I yelled back, "I am NOT going to do this with you!"

I placed the pen down on the table and walked out of the vineyard, wanting to run, weep, and get away from it all, especially him. Why should he yell at me for being honest? I bolted through the front doors, but I had no one to take me home, as I had sent the driver away. I stood there, and Thomas came after me.

"Why don't you answer me?" Thomas asked.

"I don't want to answer you. I can't," I said truthfully.

He grabbed my hands and pulled me to him in such a rage. I was shaking.

"Look at me. You lied to me!" he said, grasping me harshly.

"Don't grab me like that. Get off me! Please, Thomas."

"You're seeing someone else? Just tell me." There was so much anger in his eyes.

"Get your hands off me, Thomas Laslay! You're a lunatic!" Yes, I meant *lunatic*.

Out of nowhere, a black Bentley pulled up. Zur jumped out, pulled me away from Thomas, and slammed Thomas against the car.

"Don't you ever touch her again," he said, as he punched Thomas squarely in the face.

"Get the hell away from me!" yelled Thomas. "I'm sure you're touching her, though. She has no emotions and no heart."

Zur held my hand as he led me to his car and drove off quickly. It was a scene that I would never have imagined could happen.

At the end of the driveway, he looked into my eyes and said, "Doesn't that name seem familiar? Laslay? As in the wine from the yacht?"

I looked away, with tears falling one drop at a time. I wiped my face, hoping he didn't see my pain. "What are you even doing here?" I asked.

"Why ask? The point is that I made it in time, after all." He looked out the window, livid and breathing heavily. "Did you go there to sleep with him?"

I didn't respond.

"Look at me. Did you sleep with him?"

"I don't want to talk about this, and it's not your business anyway, is it?"

"OK, let's not talk about it. I only flew fourteen hours, from the other side of the world, just to see you in another man's hands."

"That's not fair," I blurted softly.

He stopped the car and turned on the interior lights. My wrists were red from where Thomas had grabbed me. Zur stared at the marks.

"I should have killed the fucking bastard," he said, running his hands through his hair.

I turned the interior lights off, and he started driving again. It was dark, and I was sitting beside the man that I was made for. Never could I have predicted that I would feel so at peace sitting next to him.

"Can you spare a night of your life for me, baby? I want to take you somewhere special." He smiled at me, holding my hands tightly.

"I can, for you, Zur," I said. He pulled my face to his, and we kissed.

I felt my phone vibrate, and I saw ten texts from Thomas. I couldn't dare forgive him, at least not yet. They said that love could make you crazy. Well, Exhibit 101: Thomas. That was just an excuse for not being able to control your bloody anger.

As Zur and I neared Oheka castle, we clasped each other's hands tightly, and our eyes spoke many words to each other. I hoped that tonight would change our destiny. Love couldn't be that selfish, could it? I hoped that in the unwritten pages of our lives, we were somewhere in love together. I'd fallen in love, and I was terrified of how it would change my life.

24

OHEKA CASTLE

At the castle gates, I felt as if this could be a great new beginning for Zur and me. He looked at me and held my hand, slowly caressing it.

"I can't wait to get you alone, baby," he whispered to me. I was beyond tired, but I shared his passion, and my body ached to be naked with his.

Driving along the gravel path, we saw the bricked castle, now a hotel, which whispered history and elegance together in harmony.

"One day, our house is going to look like this," he said smiling. "The only condition is that you have many, many children."

"Your children, how many?" I asked. I smiled, but I felt that these children were only mere possibilities, not certainties. I'd often thought about children, but never about my own. I liked it best if I could just borrow them and then return them later to their parents. I noticed that Zur never mentioned his son, the one that Duren told me about.

Zur parked the car, and standing outside the front door to Oheka was Syed, his main bodyguard.

"Miss Becks, so good to see you again," Syed said.

"Yes," I said, as I stared at Zur, who spoke briefly with Syed in Arabic. Syed handed him the key to our room.

"The stars in the sky have nothing on you, my baby," Zur said.

Laughing, I walked away and to the bottom of the formal staircase. Zur lifted me in his arms, kissed me, and carried me up the staircase.

"Zur?"

"Yes, baby?" he asked, staring into my eyes as he stepped carefully on each marble step. Our world was closed around us; there was only him and me, surrounded by oil portraits and large palatial crystals hanging from thirty feet high.

"I love you more than my designer shoes, or Bentleys, or diamonds," I blurted out.

The beauty of all of the diamonds and rubies in the world could never come close to his laughter, as he opened the door to the bedroom and laid me on a bed of yellow rose petals.

"You are crazy, baby, just crazy, but the truth is, I'm so mad about you I can't even think." He stepped to the window, running his hands through his long, curly, brown hair. "I was in Dubai and I couldn't sleep. I went to Monaco to see my brother, who is in a coma, and all I wanted was you, no one else but you."

That moment was every woman's dream, to have a man like him want you more than all his notes in a bank in Dubai.

I jumped off the bed and put my arms around his waist, and we stood there as the wind blew the silk curtains across the white stone rails on the balcony. He placed his strong masculine hands on my face, slowly touching my lips. Our eyes danced wildly together. Minutes felt like eternity, as he and I kissed passionately.

"I love you forever, baby," he said, as he kissed my neck and unbuttoned my silk shantung shirt. The buttons were difficult, as they were made of fabric. He struggled with them, and I placed his hands at his sides, undid the buttons in front of him, and walked him to the bed.

He lifted me up and kissed me. I was held prisoner in his arms as he teased me, breathing softly into my ear. My body was shivering as the breeze from the balcony blew in cold, so Zur lay me softly onto the bed, walked to the door, and closed it. He took his shirt off and unbuttoned his pants. His stomach was well defined, and his arms were built to perfection. He was a sure a sight for sore eyes. I wanted a piece of him. No, I wanted every piece of him. He undressed me with his heart and soul. I couldn't have imagined that I would want someone like this, without boundaries.

"I need to know something," he asked.

"Anything," I replied.

He was lying on me with his arms over me and his bare Chippendale chest on mine. It was hot, like being in a heavenly sauna, and I didn't even like saunas.

"Tell me that you're mine," he said. "Tell me."

I sat up in such panic, looking into his green eyes. Was I in a movie? Romance, petals, candlelight, soft music, and now the idea of being his. The only thing missing was a white horse named Forever and a philharmonic orchestra.

"What did I say?" Zur asked, alarmed.

I held the white sheet around me, covering my bosom, and doing that breathing technique that a nun from Tibet had taught me in a meditation center.

"I'm sorry that I am such a Dumbo with this love thing," I replied. "I just have been so anti-love my whole life."

"Sophie, I've been around the world. I've had many women, and I've even had a child. But I had never really lived until I saw you walking on that beach," Zur said. Tears rolled from my eyes like the rolling lawns that graced my parents' home in Brookville. "I want to be there when you come home each day, and when you wake up in the morning. And when you decide to have a baby, I want it to be mine," Zur said.

Wow, too much, just TOO MUCH. But I felt one thing, I loved him more than anything else in my life. The money, the million-dollar career, the cars, even my walk-in Dolce & Gabbana shoe closet had nothing over Zur. I felt like I was becoming undone. My rational mind faded from being sensible to *what the hell*.

"I do know one thing, Zur, I love you." I stared closely into his eyes, holding his hand as he held me.

His lips caressed me from head to toe, from Monte Carlo to Egypt and back again. Passion made us one being, when I was in his bed. Background music played softly, as I lay on his chest and he kissed my forehead. Silence was our gentle companion, and making love was our sacred ritual.

I was getting beyond sleepy; it had been a long day. I closed my eyes, not feeling that I needed to run from him as I had felt in the past. The idea of sleeping with someone and then staying over at their place was something I normally had a panic attack about. But the lights were out, and I fell fast asleep as the next day snuck in.

Moments, maybe hours, passed as I tossed and turned in bed. A loud sound shook me from sleep, and I stood up frantically, finding Zur out on the balcony on his phone.

Dusting the feathers of the fluffy down cover off of me,

I wrapped the sheet around me and crept behind the silk embroidered curtain, listening to Zur and wondering impatiently who he would need to speak with in the middle of the night.

"I know, but I simply can't for a while. I am tied up here until I figure out business," Zur said. He sounded as if he was holding back anger. He hung up and looked behind him, and the look of displeasure vanished from his face, as he saw me standing at the door watching him.

"Did I wake you, baby?"

"I wasn't asleep. I'm tired, but I'm glad you're here," I whispered as he pulled me to him. He smelled my neck as if I were wearing something that smelled of roses or sunflowers.

"It's good to smell you," he whispered. He touched my lips with his fingers, teasing me. "And taste you," he said. He kissed my lips with his strong arms around my waist, holding me tightly as the moonlight dimmed in the sky.

Out on the balcony, it was charmingly rustic. The sight of the gardens at night reminded me of a chateau in the French countryside.

Zur took the white satin sheet down from around my shoulders, kissed my neck, and then pulled the sheet even lower. Our lips devoured each other, and his hands meandered below my waist.

"Baby, I need to have you right now," he said.

"What if someone sees us?"

I was naked from the back, but my breasts and thighs were covered with his body.

"They can look, but they can't have," he whispered in my ear.

I laughed aloud, with the happiest grin on my face I'd ever

had. It was ecstasy, passion, romance, and sinful lust; a full-course meal of only the finest for your sexual palette.

He lifted me and carried me to bed where we made passionate love. Our moist lips locked together, our bodies entwined, completely naked.

"Give me more," I begged. "More of you."

He smiled, his lips caressing my stomach, slowly trailing down to my legs. I'd never felt like a woman until the first time he'd placed all of him into all of me. I held his hands to my lips and gently put his fingers into my mouth. He got as steamy as a sauna, saying all sorts of things that didn't make sense to me.

"I don't speak Arabic! Say it in English!" I exclaimed.

"Oh sorry, baby, but I can't think as clearly as you can in these moments."

"Typical guy," I said with a smile, as he held my hands down on the bed, as serious as a lion intent on catching a mouse.

Our love was raw intensity. I didn't think I could ever feel this way, not in this lifetime.

Around three in the morning, we found silence after our workout. I pulled the covers up to my shoulders, and closed my eyes; I was out of service for the rest of the night.

As morning dawned, my phone would not stop ringing. I was bloody tired and needed more rest, but the phone just rang and rang. I finally picked it up in a rage.

"Hello?" I said.

"Sophie, don't hang up on me," a male voice pleaded.

"Who is it?"

"It's Thomas," he replied. I stood up from bed and walked outside, as Zur lay asleep. "I just need to know. What do you want from me?" he asked.

"I want nothing from you, okay?" I yelled into the phone.

"Don't you think we have to talk about this, about last night?" he asked.

"No, there isn't anything to talk about. Our little dilemma is over."

I hung up, thinking to myself, *Am I being cruel?* No, I wasn't being cruel. I was just in love with Zur.

I walked back into the bedroom, slipped under the covers, and looked at Zur. I shut my eyes and fell asleep beside the man that I couldn't dare to ever be without again.

8:00 a.m. came, and there was no buzzer, no Robin, no Hannah, no limo driver. And no Zur? My phone rang, and I answered it.

"Baby, are you getting showered?" Zur asked.

"No I, um, just got up from bed," I said, trying hard to talk, as I was still waking up.

"I left you a bath."

"OK, I'll go have a bath, since you insist."

I walked into the bathroom with my eyes barely open, and stumbled over my clothes on the floor. The bath was lit with candles and already filled with lavender bubbles. If a man ever wanted to keep me, he needed to be able to prepare two things well: a bubble bath with the finest bubbles and a cup of hot tea, well-brewed to distinction. Millions of dollars couldn't buy that.

There was a box next to the Egyptian bath towels. I opened it and found a long pink silk Versace dress with ruffles and sleeves. An American size 8, the perfect fit. I smiled, but I really couldn't comprehend all of Zur. He was like an angel from Dubai. American men weren't at all like this.

I held up the most beautiful dress that I'd ever been given, or even seen, and peeked in the mirror. I knew it was an iconic dress, as I had seen it in the golden pages of *Vogue* months ago. I couldn't believe Zur already knew what I liked.

I soaked for forty-five minutes in the hand-painted Victorian tub with gold feet, replenishing the warm water periodically as it began to chill. I had a grin on my face, contentment in my heart, and tears in my eyes. I loved him with every fiber of my being, but should I run away and not look back? Or should I run forward, even if I could end up broken to pieces? Love was never my forte. Wall Street was.

As I leisurely stepped out of the tub, and padded naked over to the bed, I looked for my phone. I couldn't find it anywhere, so I yanked all the sheets off the bed. My phone, and a bottle of pills that must have been Zur's, dropped to the floor. I couldn't even pronounce the name on the bottle's label.

I placed it on the night stand, and began scrolling through my emails, when suddenly, Zur wrapped his arms around me from behind. I hadn't even heard him come in. He moved my wet hair to the side.

"Hello, baby," he purred.

I covered myself with the white sheet as I handed him his pills. "What are these for?" I asked.

He looked somewhat disturbed that I'd found them. "Nothing, baby, nothing." He took them and walked out of the room, taking his telephone out of his pocket. I never felt that I needed to comfort anyone. I didn't really know how or why.

"Can't we talk about this?" I asked, following him. "What are these for?"

He clearly didn't want to talk about it. As I approached him, there was a knock on the door. I looked to Zur to get it.

"You should go finish getting yourself together," he said, motioning to the bathroom.

I walked back into the bathroom and closed the door, pretending not to care, but I felt that something might be wrong with him. Maybe I was unconsciously looking for an exit. I had already crossed the bridge to the unknown.

I looked through the crack of the door, as Zur stepped outside of the room. I was being way too paranoid. I guess this was what love did to you. I didn't know how to get a handle on myself or my emotions. I was in love. And being in love was very frightening.

I dried off and slipped into the silk goddess of a dress, sans panties. I quickly dried my hair with the loud hair dryer. You'd think by now they would have created a quieter dryer, right? I powdered my face, curled my lashes with Dior Black Out mascara, colored my lips with nude Dior lipstick, and put peach blush on my cheeks. I was an elegant beauty. Okay, maybe I was exaggerating a little. Just a tad bit.

Zur sat on the bed, waiting for me to come out.

"It's like magic, isn't it?" I asked, turning around so he could see my Cinderella-like transformation.

"Baby, you are the most beautiful woman I have ever seen."

I was never happier than now, seeing him smile at me with such contentment.

"Thank you," I said, putting my arms around him. I had so much love pouring from me. This was all new to me, but I didn't care. You only lived once, so you should experience love like this when it was on offer.

"Let's go to breakfast," he said. He held my hand and led me down a hallway with the most exceptionally elegant oil portraits

I'd ever seen. He kissed my hands as we walked down the long, stone-paved path behind the castle with the morning green grass in all its glory.

I remember playing hopscotch as a child, on the stone tiles behind our home. My mother had been livid. I think the idea of children being children drove her to Thailand and back.

Zur and I walked to the middle of the formal gardens, where roses of all colors bloomed like spring. I felt like Alice in my own version of Wonderland. We stopped at the most beautiful table dressed in white linens. There were roses in a tall, clear crystal vase with little pink crystals hanging from the edges, and teacups with pink saucers and gold trimmings. It looked like a tea party. God knows I'd been to many of those.

"You are simply the best," I said to Zur. "Thank you for being so gentle and kind." Then I thought to myself, *Well, not in bed.* I smiled.

He smiled, but he looked pale and nervous. I must have scared him south somehow. Could it have been my question about the pills, or his life in wherever he was last?

Breakfast was as fine as it could be, with English china in a formal rose garden with birds chirping and fountains made by Michelangelo himself. I ate toasted blueberry muffins with butter sent from heaven, and a butler brought us a bottle of champagne.

Zur handed me a glass of champagne.

"Isn't it a bit early to become an alcoholic?" I pronounced.

"Please, for me, baby."

"I'll try, for you."

Then I stared at the teapot, so lavish and delicately painted. I took a sip of the champagne, and then my eyes were lost in the bottom of the crystal glass. Script had been written all around the glass.

I turned it slowly around, reading the words: "Will you marry me...?"

"Oh God," I said, shocked. "This is why I don't drink."

Zur smiled and got down on one knee. He grabbed a pink velvet box from his pocket. It was so beautiful and little.

"Baby, will you be my wife, my friend, my everything, for the rest of my life?" he asked.

"Will I?" I asked. My heart raced like the White Rabbit, except he probably could have escaped. I couldn't, could I? I had been petrified of that question all my life. Oh God, I needed a Xanax. Like right *now*! I began shaking, and tears rolled down my cheeks, washing away all my carefully crafted Dior makeup. Zur looked like a deer on the highway about to get run over. Why did men propose like that?

"Sophie, baby..." He stared at me, as my single life flashed before my eyes.

"Zur, the moment I met you, I loved you from the very start," I began, as I stood quietly. I was terribly overwhelmed. I was scared, but I thought of him not being there beside me, and I felt I simply couldn't live without this man. "So, I, Sophie Becks, will. I will marry you," I said, tears streaming down my cheeks.

He opened the box to reveal a princess-cut pink diamond with intricately placed white diamonds all around it. He placed it on my finger, and I was blown far, far away.

"I live for you, Sophie, and I never want to be away from you, ever," he said, with tears in his eyes.

This led to more tears and confessions of love. I still had many things to learn about him, but regardless of who he was and where he'd been, our lives had surely led us to each other. I never thought I would feel this way about anyone. My life felt so complete in this moment, as I lay on the grass on top of him in the formal gardens at Oheka. For a second, I wondered at how one place could have such on impact on me.

"Baby, let's get married here?" whispered Zur.

"Sure," I replied. "When I was little and love was what I dreamed of, I thought that my prince would propose to me here and that a horse and carriage would carry us through the gates and down the paved driveway, and voilà, I'd be a princess."

We both laughed. We were so in love.

"Baby, I'll get you a hundred horses and carriages, just say the word."

"A hundred carriages!" I exclaimed, just to be silenced by his lips on mine.

Walking out of the garden with his hand in mind, I couldn't believe that I was about to be married. Life was suddenly so meaningful and in full color.

But before I could really process everything that was happening, my phone rang. It was my mother. I was hesitant, but I had to answer.

"Hello, Mother."

"Darling, when are you going to be home? You've been gone since yesterday."

"I'll be home by the evening, most likely."

"Well, we will be up waiting for you, dear."

"See you then," I replied. After I hung up, I said out loud, "Yes, see you with a ring on my finger." I turned to Zur. "That's not going to go well."

"What's not, baby?"

"The ring on my finger and my parents not knowing you."

"I'm not looking forward to it either," he said, as another couple passed us by.

Upstairs in our bedroom, Syed was waiting for Zur. I was surprised, but I figured that before I walked down the aisle, it might be appropriate to at least know what Zur did for a living. Zur spoke to Syed for a few minutes on the balcony, and I wondered what could possibly be so important. But, I'd definitely learned not to pry, just look at Thomas.

I spent the afternoon on the internet, checking prices and surfing the web, until Zur took my iPad away and undressed me with his eyes.

Kissing my neck, he played with my hair as it covered my eyes. He tucked it behind my ears, and I giggled.

"Let's take a trip to Monte Carlo, Italy, wherever, just to be with each other," Zur said.

Zur handed me a glass of champagne, and I sipped on the bubbly, smiling. But in reality, I was a Wall Street broker, no? I had work to do. I was where I had wanted to be, and doing what I had wanted to do, my whole life. Surrounded by men with custom suits, cigar breath, and Maseratis, and I was going to be more successful than they were.

"I just don't know if I can take more time off, at this point," I said. "I'm a brand new broker working at a top brokerage firm with a boss that people would die to get the chance to work with."

"And I am a billionaire, from all the way across the globe, who has just proposed to you," he replied, getting out of bed and running his hands through his hair. He paced to the end of the bed, and looked at me with eyes that said, "How could you even think of rejecting my offer?"

"Okay, and I suppose it displeases you that I'm independent and love what I do." I was annoyed.

"No, that's not what I said!" he said angrily, his voice rising.

I looked away from him with an ache in my heart, not knowing why I was slipping away so fast. I wanted to please him in every way, but gosh, I'd seen the Lifetime movies. And those love stories never really ended well, did they?

"Listen, baby, I mean well, you know that?" he said, holding my hands and looking into my soul with an aching that no man had ever had for me. I reciprocated the same feeling.

"Well, I did just bring in lots of money for the company. I could also still work from Europe with my phone and laptop. Maybe Duren will understand..."

He lifted me up and embraced me. "And you'll meet my family," he said, holding my hands.

"What have I done to you?" I laughed.

"I'm a man in love, with the most amazing woman I have ever laid my eyes on. That's all."

I held him in my arms, wondering how I'd gotten so lucky, and when I'd become so open to love and marriage. I guess, as they say, love happens when you're not looking for it, even when you'd taken it completely off your "to do" list.

As I stood enveloped in Zur's arms, I held his shoulders and stared at the walls graced with portraits of beautiful things.

"I live for you, Sophie. I live for you, my baby," he whispered in my ear.

How could I not be in love with this man?

25

VIVERE: DARE TO LIVE

After breakfast, and a few hours spent mostly in bed, Zur and I headed toward my home in Brookville. Though the drive wasn't that long, it was filled with a sweet silence. The touch of our hands spoke a whole library of words without the need for sound. Music played softly in the background, as I looked out the window to the trees and green hedges ringing golf courses and large estates. I couldn't have imagined that my life's path would be going in such a different direction than I'd planned.

The ring on my finger shone, as the sun glistening through the windows of his Bentley hit the stones.

"I've never been to Brookville, and I've visited Long Island on many occasions," Zur said, breaking the silence.

"You're here often?" I asked, surprised.

"Now I certainly will be, and I do have a penthouse in the city."

"I guess we still have a lot to learn about each other."

"Yes, baby, we will learn that and many other things about each other," he replied, running his fingers along my cheek.

He leaned over at a stop sign and kissed my forehead. The feeling of belonging to this man was indescribable. It was beautiful on so many levels, but I guessed it could be frightening as well, depending on who it was.

"So, your parents," I asked Zur, "are they, you know, normal?" That didn't sound right. It figures I'd get it wrong, as wrong as a compulsive shopper asking if a Prada bag was on sale. Ugh!

"Baby, is that a real question?" he said smiling, but his smile soon disappeared. "I'm going to be honest with you. My family is Turkish Muslim, and my mother is overbearing and protective, and my father is laid-back, but very religious."

I thought about the fact that I wasn't Muslim. Zur was, as most Arabs were. I didn't think that would sit very well with my family.

Driving through the gates to my home, he looked over at me, and smiled, "Not bad. Now I don't have to worry that you were the typical girl who only wanted me for my money."

"So, could you be a bit more specific?" I teased. "You know Wall Street stockbrokers make a decent living themselves."

"Yes, I'm sure, but after we marry, I don't think you'll need to work anymore. I make more than enough to support ten families, you know. I'm not trying to be cocky, but it's the truth."

Money wasn't my issue with this new arrangement; it was my career. Work was my life, and I loved what I did. I had hoped that marriage wouldn't mean I'd be sitting at home bored all day, like all those Wall Street wives I knew.

"You know I'll need some time to adapt to that culture thing, as I'm as independent a woman as they come." I climbed out of the car, and leaned back in through the window. "I'll see you soon?"

He leaned over to me and kissed me softly and slowly. I

didn't want to let him go, but I saw Robin standing at the door, pretending to act busy. Was he really trying to dust the leaves off the topiary?

"I have to go," I said, nodding at Robin.

"Yes, call me later, okay? And let me know what happens when you share the news with your family."

"Yes, it's probably not going to go well, even if they are having shots of scotch when I tell them." I would have invited him in, but my family was finally in recovery mode from the drama of the summer months. I was afraid to throw them over the edge with meeting Zur, quite yet.

Zur kissed my fingers, and then my forehead. He held my hands tighter, as if begging me to not leave.

I looked over at Robin, and I knew this wasn't going to be okay. I expected a bad reaction to my very quick decision to run off and get married, but to an Arabian man? They wouldn't quite share my view of this as an exotic romance story. Jeez.

Zur waved to Robin, and I watched until the black Bentley had disappeared down the driveway completely.

"What's going on with your Arab?" Robin asked judgmentally.

"His name is Zur," I exclaimed.

Robin's attitude had been annoying me, not to mention the fact that he slept with Hannah. If I lost Hannah, I lost everything. I needed her, and she took care of me.

"Listen, what's this guy got on you?" Robin asked. "Yes, he's obviously loaded, but he's an Arab, from God knows where."

"That's quite enough, you racist freak," I yelled at him. "Well, you're going to have to get used to him because he's going to be your brother-in-law." He stood there, stunned into silence.

"Really, I'm a racist? We're Becks, we are who we are. We marry our own, Sophie."

"Look around us, Robin, the marry-your-own nonsense doesn't seem to be working so well." And there it was, like a scene out of a movie, one I wished I could erase from my DVR.

I held my left hand up, and showed him my ring. Sure, it was probably worth half of the value of all of my parents' homes, but it was nothing, simply nothing, compared to being in love.

"What the hell?" he yelled.

"So inappropriate, Robin! That's not very becoming of a Becks. Our mother would be so, so upset," I said sarcastically. I felt good as I quietly stepped into my parents' home.

"Darling, where have you been?" my mother inquired, as soon as she saw me.

"I was with my fiancé."

"Your what?" she said, stunned.

I let out a dramatic sigh, "Since when do you care, Mommy dearest?"

My dad looked at me, and reprimanded, "That's not very polite, Sophie."

I wasn't in the mood to have this meeting right now. This type of thing should have happened when I was sixteen, and throwing tantrums because my parents refused to take me to a friend's house. My father walked over to the bar and poured some scotch from his crystal tumbler. Robin walked in and sat down next to me. Surely he was beyond livid by now, and this was beginning to feel more like an intervention.

"Well, we are missing Rain, but he's in the process of getting engaged to a very amazing woman," my dad paused and then swallowed his scotch in one sip. He'd soon need to double up on that.

My mother sat there like the First Lady. Her appearance was always pristine. Her hair was in a delicate bouffant, and her pearls lay delicately on her neck. She looked like Jan, all prim and proper. Except Jan had affairs like my dad had scotch.

"Sorry, darling," my mother interrupted, "but before you give your grand speech, I need to address Sophie."

"Yes, dear," said my father.

I'd never seen them work as a team, but tonight they were aligned perfectly. Team Becks, huh!

"Darling, when did you become so unladylike and unmannerly?"

I looked at my mother, and exclaimed with utmost poise, "Am I really so unladylike, Mother?" I would certainly have made my etiquette teacher so proud. "Well, let's see, I must have become so unladylike when you stopped being a mother. I'm afraid I don't know the exact time that happened."

Hannah poured me some tea with a serious expression on her face. I picked up the teacup and my ring glistened like a diamond that had just been recovered from the Dead Sea.

"Is that an engagement ring?" asked my father.

"Yes, it is. I'm going to get married," I blurted out in an unemotional way. Even that sounded raw coming out of my mouth.

Robin placed his teacup down in a fury, "How dare you, Sophie! Do you even really know this Arab guy?"

"How terribly displeasing, Robin," I said, trying to maintain my calm. "How dare you call him an Arab again!"

"What is he then, Irish?"

I couldn't bear to hear any more. My eyes became wet from

emotions that were never well suited or accepted in my family. I thought, *Keep your poise and contain yourself. This isn't a shrink session.* To think that I actually worried about making less than $100,000 a month, as it would be disgraceful for my father's image. I had so many rules about things I did for my last name's sake, and not for myself.

"How dare you do this to us, after all we've done for you as parents!" My mother stood there and wept, as if I had burned down their house and robbed a convenience store.

"It's my life, and I'm in love with him. I'm an adult, and I'll do as I please."

I surely wasn't going to just do what others wanted me to. After all I deserved a little bit of happiness, and this family was anything but happy. It was a white-picket nightmare of codes and conduct. God forbid I fell in love with anyone they disapproved of; would they put me in a dungeon? Hopefully it was one equipped with a designer shoe closet and a personal chef. I stood up, gathered my thoughts about how much it sucked to be their daughter, and then headed out of the room. My father grasped my arm and pulled me back.

"You will not marry him," he commanded. "Do you understand? I forbid it. I don't know him, and I don't want to."

I pulled my hand away as tears began to flow from my heart. My mother began crying again, and I looked at her with such animosity. For all my life, she had never been there for me emotionally at all. Why should she cry now?

Robin looked at me, and said, "What should you do in a situation like this?"

"I don't want anything to do with you, Robin, ever, ever again." Sadly, I meant it.

I walked out of the room to the sounds of my mother weeping. Maybe her driver would take her out to her Hamptons house, as our family's reality wasn't ever in her life's plan.

Walking up the long, marbled staircase, I looked around and remembered how I had felt as a child. Sure, I had all the material things I needed, but I didn't have my parents. They were overachievers, and as much as I had the private schools, drivers, housekeepers, and Hannah, it would have been wonderful if they had been there, just a tad bit.

Hannah stood at the top of the staircase with more empathy for me than my mother.

"Miss Sophie, I'm so sorry that your parents are not understanding you right now," she said with tears in her eyes. I held her hands and then hugged her.

"They've never understood me, but it's okay, Hannah."

Tears rolled down my cheeks, and I held her as if she were my mother. Then I continued down the hallway toward my room. The truth was always there, wasn't it, staring you dead in the face when you least expected it? Such an undignified moment.

Closing the door behind me, I was disheartened, as it felt as if no one in my family cared to be happy for me. I was alone. But then I remembered my very best friend, Jan. How could I have forgotten her? She was always my strength and my brain, when both failed me.

As I dialed her number, Rain opened my door, standing there in all of his successful glory.

"How are you?" he asked.

"I'm not so well, but thanks for asking."

He walked over and hugged me, which was unexpected.

"Thank you. I needed this," I said, as I released my tears and my emotional wreckage in the safety of his arms.

He was my big brother, after all. Sure, he was sometimes an ass, but he had good reason to be - he was a Becks! The golden one.

He sat on the edge of my bed as I sat down slowly next to him. He looked at my finger as if he'd seen a ghost.

"Sophie, are you...?"

"Am I what?"

"You know, pregnant?"

"No, Rain. No, I'm not. I'm just in love. I've never felt this way before."

I stood up and walked around my room, looking out the balcony to the ocean view. It reminded me of Zur, and I hoped that I would never have to be without him ever again. Now I felt entwined with him, and in him. It all began when our eyes met that first time.

"Soph, they are just, you know, shocked. That's all."

"I get it, but it doesn't matter to me. I'll be leaving soon."

Rain tried to speak, but I wouldn't let him. My tears were as rare as a golden egg. So when I did cry, it was like the flood of the century.

"Rain, don't try to argue their point," I said. "I have to make this decision on my own."

"You're my sister, and whatever you do, I hope that it is right and will pan out well for you."

He held me close to his heart, and I cried an ocean. For everyone, there comes a time that love finds you, and you can't run from it or deny it. You had to embrace it, for better or worse, no matter the outcome.

Looking up at Rain, it warmed my heart to know that he understood where I was on the map of life.

"This is Anna," he said, showing me her picture. I entertained the idea that Rain could be in love. She was a light-haired, blue-eyed girl, very model-like. Rain was happy, and I'd finally realized the importance of happiness.

"So when do I get to meet this famous Arab?" he asked, smiling.

"Please don't call him that," I replied, smiling back. "And, I don't know, soon, perhaps."

"Well, I have to be in Muttontown in half an hour, so I have to get back to consoling our dear parents. They're not very happy right now." Rain hugged me and headed out of the room.

"Oh, Rain, if you are going to Muttontown, could you drop me off at Jan's?"

"Yes, sure. Hurry, though," he said. I wiped up my face and powdered everything under the sun, and then I called Jan.

"My gosh, darling, I thought you'd eloped to somewhere exotic, like Marrakech," Jan said.

"My God, really? It's Dubai, enough already."

"Well, I have to learn these things. You can't expect I'd learn this stuff overnight," Jan said.

"I'm going to be over in fifteen minutes. Is that okay?"

"Yes, darling. Thank you for saving me from my dinner with Ker. It's pure matrimonial boredom."

"Oh no, not bloody dinner!" I replied, laughing.

Jan always knew how to make me laugh, but I was afraid that I wasn't going to be laughing for long. I hung up the phone, and met Rain outside. I admired his Bugatti again, it was the supermodel of cars.

"So how do you like the Bugatti, eh?" I smiled at Rain.

"It was the price of a fucking house!"

"I can imagine. So congrats on your engagement, as well. When is the wedding?"

He blushed. "We haven't set a date yet, but we're looking at homes in Muttontown. I haven't mentioned it to the family yet."

"Muttontown is beautiful. You know Jan lives there. It would be good for you to meet her."

"Yes, that would be great," he replied.

We stopped at a stop sign, and then took a right turn onto a most appealing, tree-lined street.

"At the gold gates, take a right, and slow down," I said.

"What the heck? This is your friend's house?"

"Yes."

The guard at the gates smiled. "Miss Sophie Becks, another boyfriend?"

"Nope, my brother."

"Thank goodness!" the guard said.

"They must think you're very popular, huh?" Rain said.

"Well, I am Sophie Becks!" I laughed.

At the grand front entrance, Jan waited for me in a long silk gown, chandelier earrings with pink and white diamonds, stiletto heels, and shades like Jackie O.

"Darling, this is not your Arabian Prince Charming. Who is this charmingly handsome lad?" Jan said.

I laughed as Rain got lost in the sticky web of Jan.

"Jan, this is Rain, you know, my brother."

He walked over to her and kissed her on both cheeks. I'm sure he wanted to kiss her in other places too. They had instant chemistry, oh my goodness gracious!

"Okay, I remember, so this is the Wall Street one with no manners," she said.

"Really, Jan! Edit." I said, laughing.

"So sorry," she said, holding his hand.

I turned around and saw Ker standing in the study, looking out the window. Sneaky was his middle name.

"Would you like to come in?" Jan asked Rain.

"No, thank you. I'm a bit busy right now, but I'm sure I'll see you around."

"Yes, I hope so," said Jan, as their eyes locked without any way to unlock them.

Rain returned to the car, and I entered the house, waving back at him.

"Darling, come on in," Ker said to Jan. "It's a bit cold out, and you're not wearing a sweater." Please, a sweater wasn't his main concern. His wife was a cow that needed to be milked by the hour, and he'd know that if he weren't so concerned with his portfolios.

I hugged Jan and held her hand as we walked inside.

"Well, you're not wearing a sweater, darling, but are you wearing knickers?" I whispered out of earshot of Ker, and in his British accent. "Please," I said, returning to my normal voice. "If I were married to you, Jan, I would hire a bodyguard for your vagina."

"You are so inappropriate, Sophie!"

"Yes, and *Fifty Shades of Grey* isn't?" I teased.

"Oh gosh, let's move on already, shall we?"

"Yes, Mom." I smiled.

We made our way to the back porch that overlooked the ocean. There were ceiling-to-floor glass windows, silk-covered armchairs in blue and white stripes, and a table made of an old boat from some shipwreck. Some magazines that Jan had once modeled for in her youth, lay on the table. Jan was a beauty now, but in her twenties, she had been a fashion model with a degree from Yale.

Her maid brought us tea, petite cucumber sandwiches, and scones with raisins and cranberries. I poured myself tea into a traditional English blue-painted teacup, and I added milk and Truvia. By the way, if you invited me to any fancy party without Truvia, I wasn't going. What would I to use to sweeten up those teas from around the bloody globe? Jan took her tea with a small silver teaspoon of manuka honey and a wedge of lemon.

"Thank you for the tea, and for always remembering the Truvia."

"Darling, what kind of friend would I be?" she replied.

I sipped on my tea, and Jan looked at me suspiciously, as she placed her tea down.

"Okay, spill the beans," she said.

"I'm—Well, Zur proposed to me, yesterday."

"No way! Are you banged up, Sophie?"

"Jeez, no. But I am going to marry him!"

"God, those Middle Eastern men sure know how to romance a lady. My next man has to be Arabian. Maybe, a billionaire oil sheikh."

"Really, Jan, be serious."

"And your parents? How are they taking this news?"

"They're furious, and not really speaking to me. But my story is simple: I'm very much in love, and for once, I'm going to plunge in."

Jan was shocked beyond words. "Darling, marrying and plunging are two very different topics. For instance," she said, pointing to her gown, "my neckline is plunging, and you are getting married."

"Yes, but before I plan anything, I'm going to the French Riviera with him. He has a place there. I know that I'm mad about him, but marriage and forever... I need to spend more time with him, and not just in his pants, you know."

"Yes, I can imagine. When I fell in love with Ker, our sex was better than caviar and wine. I mean better than anything. But now, it's like reading a bloody encyclopedia." I laughed. "That's a great idea," she said, squeezing my hand. "I support you, but you are an extremist. You know that, darling."

I loved her for being her, and for always being there whenever I needed her. We laughed together as I thought about my engagement. I felt less anguish than before, and more like I was finally ready to think about permanent. "Permanent" sounded better than "forever." It was bittersweet, but excitement had hit me like a sailboat hitting a buoy.

Jan and I kissed goodnight, and her limo driver took me home to my dysfunctional palace of great luxury. Luckily, no one was awaiting my return. The house was silent, but there were the faint sounds of opera echoing from my father's study. I took off my heels and quietly hopped up the back staircase.

I changed into my nightgown and got under the covers, listening to the crickets outside and the sound of Bocelli singing "*Vivere*" emanating from my father's study. God what was next, Pavarotti?

The next day wouldn't be easy. I lay in my bed trying to figure out the next move on my path. I was more conflicted now, because love had found me at such an important juncture in my life. To me, Wall Street was the epitome of financial success, but here I had this man that lived on the other side of the globe and wanted me to cruise by his side. I knew nothing about commitment or true relationships. This was indeed a defining chapter of my life, and I needed to act accordingly. It was as if high tide had rushed in so quickly on the beach, that all I could do was walk ahead into the water, without looking back.

So it turned out that "*Vivere*" was incredibly appropriate tonight. "Dare To Live." My father had an obsession with that song whenever he was feeling emotional, and I had no choice but to embrace the music.

26

Photographs Speak a Thousand Emotions

It was Sunday, and I had set a meeting with Duren to discuss my news. The stars seemed to have a new plan for my life. I'd never dreamed of falling in love, especially this quickly, but it had happened. Wish me well!

My limo arrived at six in the morning, and I was dressed to impress. Hopefully, I'd impress Duren enough for him to keep me at his billion-dollar company, despite my flitting off to Europe. I wore a pintuck, striped suit with a form-fitting pencil skirt, silk ruffled blue shirt, and my pink Manolos, which adorned my feet like the star on a Christmas tree. Yes, I was surely ready to meet with Duren.

"Miss Becks, you look like a million dollars," exclaimed Mr. Wheathly, as he opened my door.

"That's kind of you, Mr. Wheats! I have to look extra spiffy today, as there is a possibility it may rain."

Well not literally, but metaphorically. Mr. Wheathly looked at me, and then at the sky and nodded quizzically. It was as sunny as a summer's day in Newport.

As the limo made its way onto the Long Island Expressway, I thought about my groom-to-be, Zur. My groom? Heck, I'd never held a dust cloth in my life, done laundry, or washed the floors. Was I really ready to tie the knot? To be a wife? Those commercials with the housewife cleaning the dishes and mopping the floor was certainly not my idea of being someone's wife. That was a housekeeper's job. Truthfully, it probably wasn't Zur's idea of a dutiful wife, either. *What was his idea of a dutiful wife?* I felt flushed just thinking about it.

I opened my laptop and found a cold, brief email from Duren: "Looking forward to discussing this new development." Uh oh! Okay then, so this meeting could be a holy mess. I scrolled down a few more emails to the one from Zur. He'd sent me links to places to get married around the world. *Already!* I thought. *At least show this to me on the Riviera after you wine and dine me.* The list was filled with the most-stately places on five continents, the kind you needed millions to book. These next two weeks would prove to be the determining factor of whether I really could get married, or if this love thing would pass by like the clouds in the sky. "I love you" and "I can't live without you" were very different phrases. I needed to explore the difference between the two before I strolled down the aisle.

I was so nervous that I bit my nails. Love was the one thing they said to never choose over a successful career, and here I was feeling a bit dumb, and about to either get fired or embraced. Yes, you have a better shot at stealing a homeless person's lunch than receiving empathy from any man, especially on Wall Street.

The limo pulled up in front of my building, and I breathed deeply, like a monk meditating in the Tibetan mountains. Well, except for the fact that they sat in the same position for six whole hours without budging, and they practiced celibacy! I could *try* to sit still for a few hours, but celibacy? Hell, no. Not after Zur. He'd brought my body back to full, tingly awareness!

I stood in front of my glass, forty-floor story building, and felt as if I had somehow lost my way. See, when you came from a financial family like mine, with Rain becoming a Wall Street securities trader, my dad a Wall Street lawyer, and my grand-father a notorious Wall Street stockbroker, you never gave up a job like this. You got a divorce first. Yes, a divorce was deadly, because your family's name would be worse off than tarnished silver spoons in my mother's formal dining room, but leaving a ridiculously high-paying job on Wall Street was worse. Even Robin, as pristinely priest-like as he was, was getting blank checks from my dad, my mom, and Rain. So in my head, he was a Long Island con artist. Yes, the Becks were all in the financial business.

I entered the elevator, and pressed the button for the twenti-eth floor, practicing my breathing and wanting to smack myself. The secretary greeted me with a strange nod, as I walked into the office. She was probably not happy to be here on a Sunday. I went straight to Duren's office, and into the unexpected.

"Sophie, please close the door and sit," said Duren, with fire in his voice. He stood facing the wall, with his hands in his pockets.

My heart was beating fast, and my hands were sweating, as I placed my derriere on a chair, and my Hermes on top of a table; though, I think for $18,000 it deserved its own bloody chair. I twirled the ends of my hair. I think the last time I did that was when I was fifteen and my father had called me into his office. I'd been terrified then too, as I had fired my French tutor and pretended that I was too advanced for her. After my meeting with my father, I hadn't wanted to speak even one word of English.

I waited for Duren to speak. He was the Richard Gere of Wall Street, but today he looked like one of the older models from a European ad. He wore a pink, linen, collared shirt, black trousers, Hermès brown belt, and brown loafers. I noticed a bit of gray grew along his sideburns; it was just a bit sexy, I had to admit.

Well, of course he was sexy; he was so bloody smart, and power was his middle name. Any man with power was a turn-on to women. Yes, we didn't need big muscles, just a brain for intellectual stimulation and a bank account the size of Switzerland. Well, unless we fell in love with you; that seemed to be the one and only exception to the rule, sort of like winning the lottery.

After a few minutes, he turned around and looked at me as he never had before. The look was angrily seductive, and seemed to say, "How dare you?"

"I have given you a chance, Sophie, to do what most women can't accomplish, and yes you are talented, a star." His eyes pierced me in fury. "Why are you getting engaged?"

Why did he think?

"I'm in love with this man," I said, "and for the first time in my life I'm going to take the leap."

"And why do you think I should let you do this, risking your accounts, and burdening this firm?"

Confused, I paused and said, "I thought because I was brilliant and wanted it more than any of your other brokers. And brokers can get married, I wouldn't be the first."

He stood there like a statue, staring at me. His eyes did all the talking, as if I could understand his silent communication.

"I'm sorry that I have displeased you so greatly, Duren."

He was quiet for at least two minutes.

"Call me by my first name, Chance."

It felt awkward, but something in me softened at the sound of his business manner turning emotional.

"Chance, you're an amazing boss, but what exactly are you getting at? Please speak English, as I'm afraid that my intuitive senses aren't working right now."

He smiled, and something in him turned more human.

"When I first met you, I... I wanted to know you more than on a business basis, but that would mean cheating on my wife."

"Okay, that's all I can hear," I said, as I stood up. Did I need this right now? I was in love with Zur. I felt passion and fireworks with him. I picked up my laptop and my purse, and took a few steps toward the door. I wasn't sure of anything now, except the pink diamond I wore on the "I'm-taken" finger. "You're married to an exceptional woman, with, um, with very, very expensive taste," I continued, "and she needs you to either love her or, at least, be there for her lavishness."

He started laughing. "Love her?" he exclaimed. "Women don't know what they want; you know that."

Really? No words could help me now, so I glanced at him and left the room. A man of such power as Duren, should not be kneeling before me, verbally begging me for cheese. What was he talking about? I would never want to walk down the aisle with roses and thorns that cost a quarter million dollars and a Wall Street man, just to get divorced.

In my hurry to leave, I'd forgotten that I'd come to ask for some time off. Talk about an unexpected turn of events! I hurried into the elevator, and quickly pressed the button for the lobby. I tried hard to find that loving place I had with Zur—before the craziness of the last two days.

As I held my finger on the "close door" button, Duren put his hand in front of the sensor and held the doors. He stepped into the elevator, pressed the stop button, and glared into my daring eyes.

"Why are you running from me?" he asked. "You're in love with that billionaire asshole, aren't you?"

He blocked me against the wall, and I looked up to see his reflection in the glass ceiling. I could feel his breath on me, as we stood close, face-to-face and eye-to-eye.

The scene felt like it was out of a romance novel, where a fireman rescued a sexy woman from a fire, but I didn't need to be rescued, and this was no novel. I was almost twenty-five, and my hormones were raging. Zur was awakening me in an ungodly way.

"Tell me, if you are so in love with him, why do your eyes speak to me that way?"

And then his lips were on mine, like a rainstorm on a hot desert—soft, smooth, and intense with passion. My lips were like the sand, wet from the powerful raindrops soaking me. Remembering the ring on my finger, I pulled away, breathless.

"No, we can't," I said, looking away.

Oh God, my boss had just kissed me. And it was lovely, no, no, no! He smelled like Davidoff had run away with Klein. Zur had that exact scent too. "I'm gonna need therapy," I said aloud, as I pressed the button to the lobby, starting the elevator once more.

Looking into his eyes from a distance, I couldn't deny that that kiss was no simple mistake. I walked out of the elevator, and Duren followed.

Out front, Mr. Wheathly opened the door for me, and at the same time, Duren got into his black limo. He was staring at me, and I paused and looked at him. He was nothing like Thomas or Zur. Yes, he had the looks of Clooney and Gere and the success of Buffett, a combination that was pure ecstasy. But he was not Zur.

"I hope your man likes competition," he said, "as I'm not giving up and I'm not backing down." He fixed his collar and got into his limo, as I stood there dumbfounded.

"You were right," Mr. Wheathly said, knowingly. "It's raining."

"Yes, it is," I said, as the craziness of the last hour rained down on me. The storm in my heart had just started.

On my way home, I realized that my phone was turned off. Astonishingly, I had missed ten calls. Rain, then Jan, then Hannah, and then Zur had all called. Yes, Zur. I dialed him first, and he picked up in a panic.

"Baby, are you okay?"

I replayed the image of Duren massaging my lips, and I could barely speak.

"Yes, I guess."

"You guess? Baby, what's going on?" he inquired harshly.

"I'm sorry. I'm just so tired. It's been a long day."

"A long day? It's nine in the morning!" he exclaimed.

"I know. I'm just tired. I was up late last night trying to figure out what I was going to do about work."

"Okay, call me in a little while, okay?" He hung up.

Gosh, why couldn't I get this right? Why was I thinking about Duren's kiss, his urgency for me, his kindness, and the ever potent boss-and-employee fantasy? Why was I so screwed up?

"Miss Becks, that limo is trying to stop me. Shall I stop?" Mr. Wheathly interrupted my thoughts.

"What are you talking about?" I asked.

Wheathly rolled the window down, and from his limo, Duren asked, "Why don't we have breakfast and talk about things?"

"What things? Things like your lips on mine? Your sudden feelings for me right before I commit myself completely to another man?"

"I don't want to lose you," Duren said. "Either at the brokerage, or personally."

There was desperation in his voice I'd never heard before. Well, that's what feelings could do to you. I never thought that he had feelings for me, but then there was the beach house in the Hamptons, the housekeeper he hired, as clearly there was nothing domestic about me, and the account leads he sent my way so I could make my own money.

"Let's do breakfast, please. Let's not act like the kiss in the elevator didn't happen," he pled.

And like the charming lady I was, I said, "Yes."

We went to Cipriani and shared everything but our lips. Apart from being starved, I couldn't bear to think that he was trying so hard to get a moment of my time. I ordered the Eggs Benedict and sparkling water, with lemon of course.

"So, are you getting married?" he asked.

"Are you asking my mind or my heart?" I replied.

"Then what do you want to do?"

"Do about what?" I took a sip of my water.

"The firm?"

"I don't know. I don't have it all figured out yet."

He had exceptional etiquette at the table. It was hard not to notice as he ate his poached eggs with a knife and fork.

"I'm going to the Riviera for a week," I said.

"It's beautiful there. Elizabeth Taylor and one of her husbands used to live there."

"If I were that beautiful, I would probably have a few husbands too." I was being sarcastic, and he indulged me.

"You are so beautiful, Sophie," he said.

Placing my silver fork down, I had a déjà vu moment as we stared at each other. It was hard to see him pouring out his emotions. He was a polo playboy. Was I really that beautiful?

"Thank you," I replied. "And so are you, Chance Duren." I guess there was some mutual attraction between us.

My phone rang, and I picked it up to see Zur's number.

"Would you mind if I answered this?" I asked.

"No, please do," he replied.

"Hi, Zur," I said.

"Hi, baby, I'm sorry I hung up earlier."

"It's fine, though I'm busy right now. Can I call you when I get in?"

"Where are you?"

"I'm having breakfast."

"Breakfast, with whom?"

I stared at Duren, and said. "With a friend."

Duren started laughing.

"Where are you?" Zur asked again.

Yes, this was why I'd never had a relationship before. I excused myself from the table and took the call outside.

"I'm on a business breakfast."

"With whom?"

"My boss."

"Okay, the same boss whose Hamptons house you lived in?"

"Yes."

Zur paused, and I could almost hear his anger smoking through the phone line.

"I have to get back in," I said. "We can talk later?"

"Yes, I'll see you at five."

Hanging up, I turned to find Duren standing behind me.

"He has every reason to be insecure. You are such a beauty, a talent, and any man's dream."

He stood close enough to put his hands on my face, and I blushed. I wouldn't need Nars blusher if I had him; that's how rosy cheeked I was. I fixed his collar and gazed into his eyes. He leaned over to kiss me, and I stopped him.

"Don't. This isn't right. I can't. We need to forget about what happened this morning."

I turned away and didn't dare try to understand my feelings, whatever they were. They were wrong, and I needed to suppress them completely. I walked back inside the restaurant.

Back at the table, I sat and sipped on chamomile tea, praying that it really had calming capabilities, as I was as wired up as if I'd taken a shot of caffeine. Duren, Chance, whatever he wanted to be called, drank cappuccino with a bit of fluffy white cream whipped to perfection.

Looking at my Patek, I told Duren I needed to leave. I had some things to discuss with my parents before they left for their trip. They were going on a marriage-fixing trip somewhere. Well, my father probably realized that my mother's Hamptons house was way too close to our home, and a bit of distance could quite possibly fix their marriage. They say the Krazy Glue of any marriage is distance. I say, *bon voyage.*

"Thank you for breakfast, Chance," I said.

"Thank you for dropping the formality." He grinned like a high-school boy.

"Surely I'll see you before I leave?"

He held my right hand, and said, "Yes, I will see you again." He kissed my hand.

Before he could kiss anything else, I walked away, left the restaurant, and stepped into my limo. I looked around to see Chance standing at Cipriani's golden doors. The look we shared defied definition.

"To Long Island, Mr. Wheathly."

"Yes, Miss Becks."

We started off home through the Midtown Tunnel. I had maybe an hour to myself to think, and I didn't even know where to begin. My family's issues weighed on me heavily. My birthday was coming, Robin was flying to Rome soon to maybe rekindle love for his past fluff, and I was headed to the French Riviera to find my purpose in love and in life with another human being.

I didn't know what to do about Chance, or how I could possibly forget his kindness, genuineness, and belief in me. And now he shared his vulnerability with me, a quality that was rarely found in anyone inside my family circle. My family wasn't perfect, but one thing was crystal clear at the end of the day: I belonged in that circle.

I thought about the kiss in the elevator, and Chance's outpouring of emotion. I couldn't lie, that kiss had moved me, and I'd never been the type to deny what my eyes and heart told me was true. But why now? Why awaken to the possibility of a kind and distinguished man at the same time that I'd finally found passionate, out of this world love with an incredible man from the other side of the world?

I refused to let this sink me. This was destiny knocking at the door that I had locked long ago and buried the key. I hoped I would know what the way forward was. I was certainly ready to become the best female stockbroker Wall Street had ever known, but was I willing to jeopardize love? Wish me well, will you?

27

CAUTION

When I arrived home, my parents announced that we were having a formal dinner to discuss life as a Becks. They were convinced that I was marrying for the wrong reasons. Well, show me a right reason, as most married people wished they could run away to a desolate island with some hot, younger model. So, what was the point? They apparently didn't realize that all of their kids were highly dysfunctional, but very successful, which sounded an awful lot like mom and dad, themselves.

I took a bubble bath and thought of Zur. I thought of the time I spent in the heat of his body and listening to the melody of his accent, under the satin covers. We were madly in love, true. But I vowed to think about things logically, with my head not my heart, before I went off to settle down in another country with him. This was a serious commitment, not just a new pair of Manolos. I loved Manolos, but marriage? Even Jan was highly miserable about the way that road had swerved. Marriage was complex and could be lonely, frightening, and as bitter cold as Antarctica. What frightened me the most was the part about being with only one man, forever.

It was almost dinnertime when Zur called me.

"Hey, where are you?" I asked.

"I'm headed over to your home; we have a lot to discuss."

He sounded angry, as if I had committed adultery, or something. Well, I almost had.

"What's going on?" I asked.

"A lot's on my mind, and I'm not going to sugar coat anything tonight. See you soon." And he hung up.

Talk about blunt! I hung up and headed downstairs, where my parents were eager to give me a good share of their own verbal whipping. My parents, Rain, and Robin were all in the dining room already, and it was unlikely they were gathered to have Thanksgiving dinner. It was only the beginning of September.

"It's so lovely to have all of you here together," my mother said. "Your dad and I want to calmly address you all. Robin is moving to Rome for Dana. Rain may marry Anna, and Sophie may marry some man that we don't know, from some Arab country. I mean, have you seen the news about the people from those countries?"

"I am sorry, Mother, but that's so sad," I said laughing at her. For Pete's sake, leave the leaves where they'd fallen, but not my mother; she couldn't help herself.

"Sophie, don't be rude! Your mother has feelings," interrupted my father.

"Well it's about time she had some sort of emotional reaction! She's been mostly cold and absent my whole life."

"Stop, Sophie, you're being cruel," said Rain.

"I like to think it's honesty. She was never pleased with me, ever," I responded harshly.

Hannah served dinner, but I couldn't eat at all. During dinner, my father had a seemingly bottomless glass of wine. I knew something else was not right. At about seven-thirty, he stood up and clinked his fork against his glass to announce his own big news. It had better be good, as dinner at that table already felt like the last supper.

"Your mother and I are going to live in Ireland for the next year," he said. In my opinion, my father seemed greatly discontented with his life; this was more than a mid-life crisis. He had cars and houses to prove to everyone that he had money, but this felt like he was running away from something.

"Dad, are you okay?" I asked. I was worried. Maybe he was either too drunk, or too unhappy, to simply be my mother's toy Ferrari anymore.

In the middle of this chaos, the doorbell rang, and in walked Zur, right into the lion's den. When I saw him standing there, I knew that this probably wouldn't end well. My entire family turned around to look at him. As gorgeous as Zur was, I knew that's not what they would see; they saw trouble, a man too outside my normal life. My mother stood up, shook his hand, and left the room.

"You're the one that stole my daughter's heart," my father said sternly. He was completely drunk. "Well, I don't approve of you marrying her. She's from a very proud family, with the utmost decency and class that most people can't match. And who are you from?"

"Nice to meet you, sir," Zur said, carefully maintaining respect for my drunken belligerent father.

My father picked up his drink, took a big gulp, and walked out of the room. Robin then stood up, shook Zur's hand, and left the room. He had clearly joined my parents' side.

Zur looked over to Rain, who politely and decently shook his hand, smiled at both of us, and said, "They'll come around."

Zur had no words. If his family hated me like mine hated him, this relationship was over before it could begin.

"Sophie, shall we?" he asked, motioning outside. I could tell he was angry.

We walked out of the house and got into a black Ferrari. Zur drove to the end of the driveway and stopped, without a touch or any words, dismissing me whenever I looked at him. He just sat there in a silent rage. Apparently, first came romance, then insanity. Zur then took out a few photos and threw them at me.

"What is this?" he demanded coldly.

I looked at the photos. They were of Duren and I at breakfast; I was fixing his collar and smiling. I looked happy. Zur had obviously gotten the wrong impression; tears flowed from my eyes.

I picked the photographs up one by one. There were images of everything from Duren staring at me outside his limo, to us sitting across from each other, to me fixing his collar. Where should I begin? Things did look a bit filthier in pictures. Pictures added words where they didn't belong. How did he even get these?

"So?" Zur asked, with tears in his eyes.

"I didn't cheat on you, I swear."

"No, you were just looking at him, touching him, and staring into his eyes."

"This is my boss. We're friends, and I told you we were having a business breakfast. I didn't lie to you."

"*That*...does *not* look like friends!" he growled ominously.

My emotions went from shock and uncertainty to anger. What was wrong with him? I wanted him to stop this nonsense, but he didn't; he went on and on about it as if he had caught me in bed with Duren.

"What do you do for a living?" I interrupted his rant. "To have all of these personal pictures of me? Is this why you have bodyguards all the time? To spy for you?"

He went quiet, and the truth was that I wanted to get out of his car and never look back.

"Don't ask me what I do for a living; it's not your business, okay?" he yelled at me. He tried to regain his composure, but he couldn't; his anger was out of control. "You are the only woman that has ever gotten this close to me. I will go back to what I was before you came; you are not worth it," said the once love of my life.

I turned my face away from him, hiding my tears as they streamed down my face. I also vowed I would never allow myself to bare my soul to anyone again, but I didn't really want to leave. How could there be more moments in my life without him? My heart sank as he pulled himself away from me, closing me out with each word. Looking at my finger, I slowly pulled his ring off and handed it to him.

"Give this to the next woman you fall in love with, as it's clearly no longer me."

He grabbed me by the wrist and looked into my eyes.

"I will not be with you anymore. You can go back to your boss and your life as if I didn't exist. You understand? It'll be as if that day on the beach never happened," he said coldly.

It felt as if my heart had been ripped out through my chest.

"Who are you?" I asked. "You're not the man I fell in love with. How can you tear me to pieces just when I had started to believe in love?" I said quietly.

I opened the door to his car and stepped out without looking back. I wanted to drown in my tears. How could I have let this happen? I was so very in love with him, and I let my guard down, and now I seemed to be dragged all the way down to the bottom of the deep, blue sea.

I walked down the driveway, crying all the way, and into the garden at the side of the house, where I often went to think about life. I thought back to the last time I was there. It was about four years ago, and I was graduating from college. My mother hadn't bothered to show up, and the cold reality of my family hit me hard. My family was obsessed with the way things appeared to the world from a distance. I always had to be a certain way, no matter what I wanted. It wasn't good enough to just be happy and lead a simple goose-chase of a life.

I lay down on the grass, watching the trees sway in the September breeze. I had lost him, and I was alone. What should I do now? If you hurt me once, you never got another chance, especially if you hurt me as deeply as this. Of course, he was the greatest love that my heart had ever known—the only cloud in my sky, the only fish in my sea, and the only breath that I wanted to breathe. I was shivering, tears forming in my eyes every time I thought of him.

"Miss Sophie, please forgive me, but I know you must be cold," Hannah said, carrying a warm throw blanket. She had either heard me from all the way down the driveway or saw me from the kitchen window.

"I am. Thank you," I said, wrapping myself in the blanket.

My tears would not stop. I was bitter and enraged, because I was in love with an ass. I wanted to punish him for what he had done to me.

Hannah sat beside me, with her own tears in her eyes.

"What is it?" I asked, concerned.

"It's the best thing happening at the worst time with the

absolute wrong person," she replied. As complex as that sounded, I got it. I felt her sadness.

"What is it? I need to know," I said.

Hannah's tears spilled onto her cheeks, as she said, "I'm pregnant with your brother's baby." *What?*

"Oh my God!" I said. I hugged her, and just when I had stopped crying, tears again welled up in my eyes. "Did you tell Robin?"

"No, I don't want him to know."

"That child shouldn't be as screwed up as we are. He needs to know."

"He's leaving in a couple of days to go see the woman he loves," cried Hannah.

"Oh please, the idiot isn't in love with that whore," I replied. At least it made Hannah smile.

A cool wind swept the fallen leaves over us, and I said, "Let's go in. You'll catch a cold, and you need to take care of yourself, especially now that you're expecting a child." I smiled, cautioning myself not to say the normal sarcastic things that naturally flowed out of my mouth.

Walking into the house, the silence was broken by Rain and Robin arguing in the kitchen.

"Where are my parents?" I asked Hannah.

"They went out for a drive. I don't know where."

I grabbed my phone, which I'd left on the entrance table, and saw two missed calls from Duren. The message he'd left was very unclear: "Sophie, please don't make plans for tomorrow. I'd like you to dine with me."

Why did he want to see me on my birthday? Did he know that Zur and I had broken up? How could he?

I walked into the kitchen and asked Rain and Robin, the two great comics of the Becks family, "What are you two fighting about?"

"Why do you care?" asked Robin. "And why do you look like you've been crying for hours?"

I sat at the table and made myself a cup of tea. "Well, it looks like I'm not getting married or anything."

Robin sighed in relief. "No offense, but you are not the marriage type—at all."

"What am I then, the sleep-with-a-woman-and-bang-her-up type?" Maybe I'd said too much …

"What are you saying, Sophie?" he asked.

"Nothing, Robin. Rain, where's your wine? I need something to drink, like now."

He poured me something red. I took the wineglass and started to leave the kitchen.

"Sophie, what happened with Zur?" asked Rain.

"Do you really want to know?"

"Yes," he said, looking at me as if he were trying to figure out how to comfort me.

"He thought I was having an affair with Duren. Zur hired someone to follow me when I met Duren for a business meal, and then slammed me with pictures of us in close proximity to each other."

"How close?" he asked.

"Close enough to suspect we were doing it. So I handed him his pink diamond back, and walked away," I replied. Robin stood there silently.

"If you want to talk things through, let me know. I know how much you loved him," said Rain.

I nodded and left the room. I went to the back balcony where I could listen to the waves and feel the chill of fall sweeping in, one orange leaf at a time.

Sipping on wine and watching the sunset, I called Duren. He picked up right away.

"Are you okay?" he asked.

"Yes, why?"

He paused, and said with great concern, "I got a call from your boyfriend."

"You what? Why?"

"He told me he could have killed us if he was up to it, but he wasn't. He said I could have you, that he is done and is going back to where he came from. Then he called me a son of a bitch." My tears flowed again. "I'm sorry for it all. Apparently yesterday's breakfast made him believe that we were intimate. Did he hurt you?"

"Not physically, but he broke my heart," I replied. I couldn't stop crying. All this wine wasn't helping either.

"I'm coming over. I'll get you through this. You hear me?"

"Yes, but I don't need you or anyone. I'll talk to you tomorrow when I'm more together."

I was far from getting it together, and not all that sure that tomorrow, my twenty-fifth birthday, would be any better. I leaned on the balcony door, and slid down to the floor in a fetal position, crying and crying. I couldn't deal with it, and I didn't want to either. I was at the edge of a cliff and didn't know my way back.

I finally got to the point where I was all cried out, so I stood up and walked toward the steps that led down to the ocean. It was cold and breezy, but I was heartbroken. When you hurt so much inside, it was hard to feel the cold. Step by step, down I went, looking ahead as it got darker and colder and not really knowing what I was doing. Maybe I didn't care, as all the things I cared about had left me.

He had a secret life, and I wondered a million things, like if he had ever really loved me. Had I just fallen in love with him for the mystery of it all? Or was it just that I was a woman that men simply wanted, and I had let my guard down?

It had begun by me simply walking on the beach, meeting his eyes, and falling madly in love with him. In the passion of it all, love had been instant. It wasn't about his bank account, or his last name, which he still hadn't cared to divulge to me, and it wasn't just about the love we'd made. It was about his ability to fulfill my need to be loved more than anything in the world. He gave me the love that most would never dare to find. Screw chasing pink Bentleys in diamonds and Dolce pumps. I wanted love like his forever, even though I didn't really believe in marriage, as much. A big old contradiction, wasn't it? I was still head over mountain cliffs in love with him, and I hoped that somehow the wind would one day blow him back to me.

I shivered as the waves rushed over my toes. And as I looked back toward the house, I saw a light flashing.

"Have you lost your mind?" Rain shouted to me, as he caught up to where I was walking.

I smiled. "I think so," I said, as he wrapped me with a blanket, and guided me back to the steps. "What are you doing?" I asked.

"Saving you from yourself," he said, as we walked up the steps.

At the top, a tall, dark man in black was waiting on the balcony.

"Who is that?" I asked Rain.

"He works for your boyfriend," he replied.

I recognized the man as Syed. I looked like a mess: no makeup, no fancy clothes or silks, no Dior shimmer, and no shoes. Lovely.

"Sophie, how are you?" he asked.

"Hi, Syed, what are you doing here?" I stood far away from him, no longer trusting anyone that much.

"I need you to know that I'm off duty, and I bring you news."

"What is it? Did he pay you to kill me now that he's done with me?"

He smiled. "No, it's never like that. He's in bad shape, and I have never seen him in love like this."

"Why do you care?"

"Because I have been at his side forever, and it's my duty to protect him, even from himself," Syed replied.

"Isn't that lovely," I said. "Then you shouldn't have let me meet him then. Sort of late, aren't you?"

"The man is in love with you, and it kills me to say, he can't—I repeat *cannot*—live without you."

I went blank. Looking away, I murmured, "What do you want from me?"

"I don't know, but he's locked himself away and won't speak to anyone." He took a deep breath as if he didn't want to tell me what was coming next. "He's leaving to go back to Dubai."

I wasn't shocked. "Well, there isn't anything I can do to stop him. I wish I could, but it pains me to see him be so cold to me when I did nothing wrong."

"I don't think he really believes that you did something wrong. It's about where he comes from, his family, and the duty and loyalty he has to them. It's not that he doesn't love you; he just doesn't want anything or anyone to hurt you."

I couldn't believe that Zur had turned out to be like every other man.

"I've loved him from the moment I met him. I can't deny that. But he's locked me out now, so you need to take care of him. Thank you for risking so much to speak with me, but the only one who's hurt me is Zur." My words faded, as I smiled and stepped away.

In the scheme of things, the man that I had loved wasn't at all who I thought he was. Money, power, sex, and important last names seemed to go hand in hand with pain and unfulfilled desires. I had fallen into the trap and I needed to climb out.

Syed walked away, and I went to my room, closed the doors, and locked the world out. I needed a therapist to help me sort through my frail emotions, preferably one that had a soft velvet sofa and sparkling water to cleanse my palette from the disdain that I now felt for Zur and all men.

Just another day, and another useless emotion.

28

QUE SERA, SERA

I woke up early in the morning and felt the after effects of both the heartbreak, the wine, and of being in the cold for such a long time. I realized that Zur was the source of all of those things. Love and all its accompanying fairy tales had left me without a horse or a saddle.

Looking at my Jaeger watch, I felt older and surely a few weeks wiser. *Happy birthday to me!* I thought. I didn't know what to expect today, but something had to give. Grabbing my laptop and turning it on, I realized that I was now single and needed to throw myself a party, something to ease the aches and pains. Really, someone else should have planned me a blast of the century.

Never had I thought I would know the experience of falling madly in love and then watching it make a U-turn out of my life so quickly. Ironically, that was what life was all about: there were many highs and then great drops to the bottom. Not only were the drops hard on your derriere, you could seriously injure yourself in the process. Obviously, I was now officially done with commitment and holy matrimony.

Shutting down the laptop, I got out of bed, opened the

French doors, and stretched my arms. I looked forward with a grin on my face.

"Let's see, what do I want for my twenty-fifth birthday?" I asked myself. Well, I needed another toy, something to snap me out of post-breakup funk. Not another pair of Manolos, or Vuittons, or diamond earrings from David Yurman, though his collection could always make me smile on a hopeless day. I needed something that money couldn't buy. I couldn't believe I had just said that!

I didn't know what it would be, so I closed the French doors, and sneezed. Allergies; my eyes felt puffy and itchy. Maybe I shouldn't have cried like I was on the *Titanic. Whatever...* Men were almost never emotional, and that was a good thing. Could you imagine if they went around crying like they were having PMS all the time? Not a pretty sight ...

In the midst of all my mental fierceness, I forced myself down to the kitchen, where Rain was reading the newspaper. As I put my tea leaves into the teapot, he came up behind me and dangled keys next to my ear.

"Happy birthday!" He kissed both my cheeks, smiling.

"You didn't have to...What is it for?"

"It's a penthouse in Gramercy!"

"What? No, no, no, really, that's so kind, but why?"

"You need to get away from here and find yourself an older man with money and a heart, not a playboy with an accent." He smiled.

"Thank you, Rain. That's an awesome gift," I said, walking to the table with my teacup and laughing. "I'm fine. I've never felt so much inner peace and tranquility. It's amazing."

He looked at me, bewildered. "Peace of mind and tranquility, my bare bottom. Really, Sophie, after your meltdown on the beach last night and the balcony?"

"Yes, I have a gift; it's called moving on, okay?"

"You are so like me, Soph, it's scary."

"I know, I'll be okay."

"And one more thing, since I love you so much." He threw another set of keys on my lap.

What the heck? "Are you lending me your Bugatti for the day?"

"No, happy birthday, kid."

"What, what, what?" I shouted.

"Yes, the Bugatti is yours, but please drive a little slower."

I ran to him and hugged him. Holy Moly! I was glad that Rain was beginning to have a heart. I really appreciated him. Maybe it was maturity, or my recent heartbreak; you almost had to have your heart broken to become more mature, and vice versa.

"Rain, I love you, even without the Bugatti and penthouse."

He looked around and blew me a kiss.

"Where's Robin?" I asked.

Talk about the devil, he walked into the kitchen right then, looking like a hot mess.

"Guys, I have a problem, a big problem," he said. "Hannah is pregnant."

I went over to him and gave him a hug. I felt for him, but I knew that Hannah was better than Miss Rome. "Congratulations," I said.

"Happy birthday, Soph," he replied like a lost sheep.

"Thank you. I feel smart and old and broken, just like it's supposed to feel."

I left him there to feel the sting of his actions, as I certainly wasn't going to be his mama. I could be many things, but that wasn't one of them. I sipped on my tea as I strolled through the many formal rooms in our home. I walked to the piano room and put my teacup down. I got my fingers in place and began "Scarborough Fair." It was amazing how time flew, and how the sounds of sadness resonated with you more as you got older. You weren't always sad, but whatever you went through surfaced time and time again, reminding you of its little scrapes and whimpers.

As I played the keys, my phone rang, and no it wasn't Zur. If we were still together, he would have sent me a thousand roses already. One for every tear I cried last night. Instead, it was Duren. I wasn't expecting Zur to call, but I'd hoped he would. I probably had a better chance of winning the lottery than him calling. After all, according to him, I was having an affair with Duren. Hmm ... maybe I should actually do it ...

"Hey, birthday lady, how does it feel to be in your mid-twenties?"

Smiling, I felt like yelling, "Yay!" Instead I asked, "How does it feel to know that you have kept some very important information from me?"

He was as silent as a bird trying to steal a worm from someone's nest. "What do you mean?" he finally asked.

"I need to know what you haven't told me about Zur."

"It's not for me to tell, Sophie, but for you to find out," he said. "So what do you have planned for the evening?"

"Nothing at all."

"Well, how about I send you a limo, and we'll have just a friendly dinner?"

"Sure, do frogs fly?" I asked.

"No, but I could make you fly," he quipped seductively.

I smiled cheek to cheek. "Where and what time, Mr. Chance Duren?"

"Seven o'clock, your home."

"You are too kind."

"And you are too deserving of my kindness. Oh, and Sophie?"

"Yes?" I asked.

"Wear pink!"

"I'm not of fan of pink lately," I replied.

Hanging up the phone, I couldn't have smiled more. I needed friendships like this, with no romance attached. Maybe I was kidding myself, but I wasn't about to become a nun or a hermit anytime soon.

I stared out the window for a few seconds until my phone rang; it was an unknown call. I answered it and heard a very familiar voice.

"Sophie, happy birthday! How are you?" Thomas asked.

Great, this was what my life had turned into, Thomas on my birthday. "I'm okay," I said.

"I'm so sorry about our last meeting. You have this power to drive a man mad."

"No, I simply think men are naturally crazy. I'm not that talented."

He laughed.

"Well, thanks for, you know, thinking of me," I said.

He said his farewell and politely hung up.

I was moving on ... simple as that. I would find my way. If I was to be with Zur or Thomas or Duren, it would all flow au naturel. And right now, nothing was flowing at all, and I couldn't be bothered.

As time flew, and minutes passed into longer hours, I did

my normal routine and then hurried downstairs to test-drive my Bugatti. Wall Street stockbrokers had many types of things they regularly indulged in; for a woman like myself, it was cars that people didn't often get to drive. Having a list of high-powered men at my beck and call was tempting, but I'd rather drive a Bugatti. A Bugatti was beyond typical; it was fast, extravagant, and seductively exclusive. It fit me like a pair of Prada Mary Janes.

As I headed out of the house, the doorbell rang. It was a delivery from the mailman. I felt like a housewife, one of those who gets the mail in four-inch heels and a bouffant with red lips, smiling as she racks up a $10,000 bill to give to her husband. Dreadful and pitiful, all at once.

Holding the box, I shook it slightly, as I wondered what it was and who had sent it. Then the doorbell chimed again, and I placed the box down on the ground, promptly forgetting about it. I opened the door to Jan.

"Happy birthday, my darling!" Jan exclaimed, as she handed me a blue Tiffany box with blue ribbons. "What's happened to you?" She held my jaw, examining me.

"I have had many rough days lately, and last night was one of them. You know, men and heartaches. God, Jan, what the hell am I doing?"

"What's wrong with you and Mr. Hot and Sexy?" She was studying me like I was a frog about to get dissected.

"We broke up, as apparently I'm cheating on him."

Jan gave me a wicked smirk and led herself into the foyer. "I wonder why he would insinuate that. Darling, look, you are too beautiful to sit around moping over one man. Let's get you cleaned up. I'm taking you to lunch. Somewhere swank. Hurry, let's go. Get ready, or I will dress you myself."

"I'm fine. I look great," I said, placing the blue box down. But looking at myself in the mirror, she was so right; I was not my normal fabulous self.

"Please go upstairs and put on something cute. You look like you've lost a loved one."

It was true. I was buried in my internal loss of a man that seemed to have lost his soul.

I walked up to my room, slow and saddened. For royals' sake, I was moping as if I'd lost my job. Yes, my million-dollar job.

I peeked into my luxurious closet, and then looked at myself in the oval gold-brushed mirror that my dear mother had bought for me at Christie's. I thought the mirror was better looking than me, and I was very good looking.

Jan joined me and stared at my outfits. "It would be good for you to get over that prick. I mean, who walks out on you? You are like a rare version of Cleopatra." She smiled at me.

"Blah, blah. Please, I can't even keep a man, like hello."

I was sulking, sitting on my closet floor. I was ready to drink myself fun with something, anything but wine from Thomas's vineyard. I'd rather sip unbrewed tea than that. Jan stooped down next to me as I sat on the floor looking like I needed a makeover.

"Sophie, you are gorgeous and at the prime of your life. Don't take this so hard."

Blah Bolshevik, I wasn't listening. I stood up and picked out a vintage dress that was more on the informal side and tried it on.

"Can you imagine that this still fits me after five years?" It was an old, graceful, and very French, little dress.

"Darling, when we were in the Hamptons, I should have led you somewhere else," Jan said. "You're in a messy situation, very, very messy."

Looking at myself in the mirror, I looked dreadful. "This isn't messy, it's bloody sad."

There was a knock on the door, and I called out, "What is it?"

"A box came with a limo driver," Rain said.

"Come in!"

"Oh my, it's your hot brother," whispered a very happy Jan.

A very buff Rain entered in his workout sweats and tight muscle shirt. He was my brother, and it grossed me out to see the way that women looked at him.

"Hello again, it's Jan." She shook his hand, and the way he blushed was very sinful.

Rain handed me the box that was wrapped in a pink bow. Great, pink! Ever since that incident with Zur, I truly hated pink. Pink Dior gowns, pink Chanel shoes, pink diamonds. I didn't ever even want to wear a pink thong.

I opened the box, and wrapped in pink tissue paper was a long silk gown in, yes, pink. The dress looked vintage with a black silk bow wrapped around the waist. On a sour note, it was the kind of dress that Zur would have bought. Enough of him already.

"My God, that's such a beauty," Jan said. "Who sent it?" She grabbed the note and read it aloud: "Sophie, my dear, I am going to give you the best birthday you've ever had, and I hope that you sparkle in this dress tonight. Love, Chance. P.S. – Bring your passport." Jan looked at me. "Oh my gosh, darling, you move on quickly!"

"That was a quick turnover, but isn't Chance your boss?" Rain asked.

"Yes, he is, and he's simply a charming man," I said, holding the gown up against me as I looked in the mirror.

"Yes, who happens to be up there with Buffett, making millions of dollars, and trying to woo you!" said Jan.

"Well Buffett makes billions, and I highly doubt anyone could be another Buffett," I said.

"Oh, well what a hand-me-down Duren is then, but his millions will do," Jan said facetiously.

"No, I don't want love or romance. I'm done," I said firmly.

"Yes, you are, but apparently love and romance are not done with you. This is going to be an amazing high-profile rebound," she said, holding my shoulders as I was lost in what she was saying. I'd never thought that Duren would want a chance to woo me.

"It's not what I want," I said.

She stood calm and quiet as she looked into my eyes. "What happened between you two?"

Rain said, "This is getting complicated, ladies. I'm leaving." He hugged Jan and walked out of the room, laughing.

"Your brother could be a good way for me to meditate on the things that I take for granted," Jan said.

"Eww, that's so gross!"

"Okay, tell me what happened," Jan said.

"Well, it's simple: Zur hired someone to see what I was up to one morning, and I was having breakfast with Duren."

I wished I'd known I was being followed. I would have left Duren there at Cipriani, alone. I got up and walked away from Jan. Never had I lied to her, and one look at my eyes and she would know—not just how I felt, but also what I did with Duren.

"Okay, I'm waiting—so what happened?"

"Duren kissed me in the elevator." I cleared my throat.

"You kissed him back?"

"No, he kissed me, and I pulled away."

"Thank heavens! You were about to get married and go away to the Riviera and such."

"Yes, I remember feeling confused as to what I felt for Zur. And who gets married when they're unsure?"

"Love alone isn't enough to commit, ever," Jan said. "You have to have all the right emotions, textures, layers, you know."

"No I don't. I don't think I'll ever know," I murmured.

"So the truth is—and I mean this well—even though Zur hired someone to follow you, you can't be appalled that he dumped you. In the end, you sort of cheated."

"I don't cheat, ever. It was a mistake."

At this point, I tossed the dress onto the silk covers of my bed.

"Maybe not with your body, but in your heart, you were in heat for that Wall Street fling," Jan said. "He must have seen that kiss or known that something had happened," Jan said. "Trust me."

As Jan put the pieces together, I thought maybe I was wrong to have been there, breath-to-breath with Duren. But like they say, *que sera, sera*; what will be, will be. I knew this was it for Zur and I, but I wasn't going to be lost in what was. This was as messy as love got, and I was going to delve in again, without him and his pink diamond.

"Well, I've got to get back to Ker," Jan said. "He's driving me nuts about stupid things, typical man. Consider yourself lucky you broke it off before the 'I dos.'"

"Why, aren't you nuts too?" I asked. I was finally smiling.

"My darling Sophie, marriage makes you nuts. I love you. I'll call later?"

"OK, I'll walk you out," I said.

We went down the stairs, and I opened the door to see her limo waiting.

"So where are you off to with D?" she asked.

"It's a surprise, I guess. But, he did say passport..." Hmm...

"Right, I'm sure he'll blow your mind." She kissed me on both cheeks and smiled. She was my fairy godmother.

Closing the door behind her, I felt empty. I was conflicted about opening her Tiffany's box, but I finally did. "My God, diamond earrings! She is nuts."

As I put them in my ears, I looked at myself in the mirror, and smiled.

❧

At exactly 7:00 p.m., the bell rang, and I walked down my staircase in the couture pink gown he'd sent, with my Chanel shoes and my hair blown out to perfect style. My lips were in Dior's best pink, and I held my Hermès like the man I longed for.

I opened the door to see Duren in dark-washed jeans, pinstriped pink shirt, and a blue bow tie—as preppy as any man in my dreams, handsome, sexy, and soft. What the hell was he ever doing on Wall Street?

"You look like a million dollars," he said.

"That's very cheesy, but thank you," I replied.

He smiled as if I'd just kissed him, and held my hand to help me down the stairs. As we walked to his limo, I put on my Cavalli shades and admired my ruby nail polish sparkling on my perfectly manicured nails.

Duren barely took his eyes off me. My God, you'd think he couldn't focus on anything else. I realized then and there that

311

he'd hired me, not because I was a talent, but because I was a hazard to his health.

"Do you know that it's not polite to stare?" I asked.

"Yes, I do. I can't wait to make you happy," he said, grinning.

"About that, I'm unavailable," I said. He blushed as I stared into his deep eyes and dimpled cheeks.

As we arrived at a private airport in Long Island, I asked, "Where are we going?"

He walked with his hand in mine to a private Boeing, placed his arms around my waist, and whispered, "Paris."

"Paris! Are you kidding me?"

"Well, after that ordeal with Zur, I want you to know that I'm not ever going to lose my chance with you again."

Though I believed him, I knew Wall Street men and their rebuttals all too well. How could I believe this smooth-talking, salesman? Not even to mention the fact that he was married. This evening would be a lot to take in.

We took our seats on the jet, and he put his arm around me. Then he handed me a glass of sparkling water and smiled, as he said softly, *"Allons-y!"*

29
BONJOUR, PARIS!

After only a few hours on the plane, my ass was tired of being in a pretty gown, and I would have given anything for sweatpants. I didn't know if Duren had planned a day trip or a week or what. All I knew is that I would be naked with Chanel on my feet. I had no fancy luggage, no clothing, no other shoes, nothing. Nevertheless, according to *Vogue*, I could shop my way to fancy. After all, Paris was where fine clothiers were discovered and where the finest fashionistas flew to watch supermodels strut the latest fur and fancy! At least my Birkin was filled with Dior lip gloss and Chanel face powder. Yes, that should count for something. A girl without a Birkin or Dior lip gloss was in dire need of a kick in the rear end.

Duren glanced at me every once in a while, but he was mostly on his iPad, working. I wish I had brought my iPad or laptop, I could have gotten some work done too. Going to Paris was dreamy. It was *très romantique!* The only thing troubling me, was that the thought of Zur and the yearning to hear his voice and have him hold me was heart wrenching. I didn't know if I was moving too fast, but my life was now taking me in a completely different direction. I'd be stupid to just sit and wait for a lost love to scoop me up and take me to where perfect may be. The enormity of love that I held for Zur needed to be thrown in a chest and dropped into the ocean, as it weighed on me like an anchor on a yacht. We had hours to Paris, perhaps I should get a little sleep.

Upon landing, Duren handed me a champagne glass filled with sparkling water and lemon, and said, "Here, I know you need sparkly all day long."

"True, but really, all day long?" I asked.

"Anything you want, all day long. I can accommodate you."

Hmm…sensually awkward. I was tired, but excited to be there. When I took French classes as a little girl, I remember hoping to someday traipse across the famous limestone with my long pink frilly frock and big floral hat, screaming, *"Bonjour, Paris!"*

Funny, I was as odd now as I was then. My life never seemed to follow a flat, formal plan. I stood up and smoothed my now slightly wrinkled dress, and took Duren's hand as he led me to the top of the steps. As I greeted the morning sun, I placed my shades on and sighed in relief. I looked like a movie star with my Hermès silk scarf tied in a French knot on my neck. A black Mercedes waited for us outside. Duren was a complete gentleman. I couldn't have asked for more.

"Are you okay? Was the flight okay?" he asked.

"Yes, it was, thank you."

He held my hand as he greeted the driver in French. *"Bonjour, Bernhard."*

I smiled as I remembered the Hamptons and Helene's French. It was like boot camp for Paris. Sitting back in the Mercedes, I looked into Duren's eyes as our attraction developed a baby step at a time.

"You must have taken this trip a million times with your wife," I said, without thinking.

He looked at me, and then gazed out the window, lost in thought. I must have said something wrong.

"I'm sorry. That was wrong of me to bring up," I quickly added.

"No, it isn't. I'm just content being with you, here and now," he said quietly.

I held his hand and kissed it. I did feel something for him, but I couldn't elaborate on it yet. I had no luck with men. They come in with all their feathers puffed up, and I somehow found a way to push them right out again. Yes, high as my standards were, it was always like a fairy tale in the beginning and a nightmare at the end. So why should I put myself out there again? No answer? I thought so ...

"To the Ritz!" Duren told the driver.

"*Oui, monsieur!*" said the driver.

I wished I'd brushed up on my French. I felt five steps behind, and I imagined I would need to know how to meet and greet in French.

I lay back in the Mercedes, listening to the sound of French intoxication on the radio. If you didn't know you were in Paris by the little French *patisseries* and *boulangeries* on the side streets, just turn on the radio. You'd feel like firing that American tutor that you had to teach you French. The French were passionate about their language, and every now and then you had to sound like you had a sore throat to get it right.

Duren was busy checking his stocks, I'm sure. A man in his business rarely made time to play. More or less with *moi*. Hopefully this didn't turn out to be like a game of cat and mouse.

"What do you say we stay at the Ritz tonight and then go to Auteuil to visit my brother tomorrow?" Duren asked.

I wondered about his motives. Paris was the city of love, and love usually came with hanky-panky, non? What had I agreed to? I was unsure of this trip, our relationship, and my future—all in one serving!

"*Oui*, whatever you like. I didn't know your brother was in Paris."

"Yes, he's married to a very lovely girl, and they live in a French mansion house, with all those gardens and statues women like."

"Very funny. But really, gardens and statues, I do love that sort of thing." I tried not to sound like a kid, but I'd never been to France. I'd read books on it, but this! Holy moly, I was in heaven. I hoped Duren didn't feel like hell when he realized how hard it was to be with me.

I liked to think of this trip as a trial. How much could he tolerate me? See, if married people did a trial time of living together, there would be fewer divorces. The man would know right away about her cost of maintenance, and the woman would know he wasn't making enough. Most women divorced men because they have to live on a certain budget. Like hello, me and a budget were not in harmony. And FYI, put the toilet seat down.

"I do have a request," I said. "Please, I beg, take me to the Louvre. I need to see the *Mona Lisa* and the *Venus de Milo*."

He smiled. "Is that all you want?"

"Oh, and I have no clothes to wear."

"No clothes, hmm, I could get used to that."

I nudged him with my bag, and he behaved.

"I'm taking you shopping," he said.

"I'm fine. I can afford clothing. You know that better than anyone else."

"I do, but my job now is taking care of you."

Aww, that was sweet, but I also felt the urge to run. I wanted to hold him and thank him for being kind, but instead I scooted away and looked out the window. Really, I wanted to accidentally fall out the window. I was never good at emotions, and whenever I did become emotionally entwined, it was difficult for me to not be negative about the outcome; after all, I've seen everyone in my life struggle with love.

I saw the Eiffel Tower through the dark windows. I'd dreamed of this since I was a little girl. I smiled at Duren.

"Arrêter ici, Bernhard, *s'il vous plait."*

"You're not stopping are you?" I asked, with a happy grin plastered all over my face.

"Of course I am," Duren said, smiling.

The car stopped, and I got out, as excited as if I were the first person in the world to see the Eiffel Tower. I walked a few minutes in my Chanels, which were surely a masterpiece of leather and velvet with Swarovski in all pastel colors, but, darling, walking a great distance in them was not only impractical but painful.

Standing at the Eiffel, lit up against the night sky, I screamed a million words on the inside. My smile probably spoke volumes and volumes. My grandmother once brought me back a petite golden Eiffel Tower statue that still sat on my writing desk in my room. Now I was actually in Paris! *Magnifique!*

Duren stared at me, smiling. It was a beautiful moment, and his smile and the content in his eyes said it all.

"I never imagined anyone being this happy with the Eiffel Tower. If it were a man, I'd be jealous," he said.

"You could never be jealous, could you?" I asked softly.

Walking closer to me, he brushed my brown locks back and put his soft hands on my cheeks. He slowly moved toward me.

"*Tu me faites fou,*" he whispered.

"It sounds beautiful, but what are you saying?" I laughed, certainly disturbing the romantics around us.

"You make me crazy," he said, with eyes full of affection.

How could I not respond to that? I didn't know he spoke French so perfectly, sort of like a freshly baked baguette with freshly churned sweet butter.

I moved my face to his, and we shared a kiss with the Eiffel Tower behind us, surely helping me to let go of all that I had held in. In this moment, I was sure, and I vowed to silence my crazy emotions that wanted to drown me.

"To the Ritz!" he said.

In the Mercedes, I spent a few moments contemplating that kiss near the Eiffel, and washed Zur out of my mind.

We pulled up to the Ritz; it was a Parisian masterpiece. Vividly, I remembered reading Hemingway's famous quote: "When I dream of an afterlife in heaven, the action always takes place at the Ritz, Paris." He was such a mastermind with words, they flowed as well as the river did into the sea. Did Monet or Renoir ever make errors with their paintbrushes, and if they did, could you tell? Probably not. Art was art whether it was with words or oil paints.

Two doormen opened the doors for us, and I walked with Duren to the front desk. I thought, I must have someone bathe me in a warm lavender bath while I sipped on the finest red wine, eating *chèvre* with brioche. I must be starving.

Down the crimson carpet was a grand entrance into the place where Princess Diana once dined. I couldn't have imagined the flair of elegance, from the ceiling lit in paintings, to the damask drapery that hung like pearls from Jackie O.'s neck. The place smelled like pure Parisian bliss.

I walked hand in hand with my boss, feeling sketchy and so very *méchant*. But it felt right, as our porter took us to our suite. I wasn't in love with Duren, but I was greatly taken by his manners, principles, and the fierce name behind the man that held my hand with such gentleness. I started to think of him as an excellent rebound.

We were staying in the Coco Chanel Suite, need I say more? From pearls with her interlocking black "C"s to gowns that would make you cry, she was iconic and classic. Not everyone wanted a Bugatti, but every woman of class wanted a piece of that legacy, a part of Coco Chanel! The white door opened, and all I saw was the marbled floor with the black "C"s. I wanted to bawl. It was as if Coco had invited me to tea.

I hugged Duren. Every woman in this situation would have dropped her panties happily. But, as we all have realized by now, I'm far from every woman.

The porter spent some time going over the history of the suite. But honey, if you didn't know the story of who she was, you shouldn't stay there. The porter left the room to us, and I felt overwhelmed with emotion.

I placed my Hermès down on the gold-brushed table, with legs like Tina Turner, and Duren took off his Givenchy black jacket. I could feel the intensity between us, and I knew that this thing of ours was going to lock us together like the "C"s in Chanel. Was I ready? Was the queen ready to rule England from the moment she was born, or should I first find a warm robe to throw on before I went any further? The robe won.

"I'm going to have a bath," I said. "And then we think about it all?"

He smiled, but as I left the room, the fire in his eyes lit a spark in me somewhere. I'd gladly take the robe off after a lavender bath and lay with him, but this wasn't the right timing.

I took my clothing off, grabbed a warm, fluffy, complimentary robe, and threw it over my naked body. I gazed around me at all the beautiful pictures around the room. It was hard to be in Paris, and in that suite, and not feel emotion.

Turning the gold swan faucet on, I splashed my face with water. I poured bubbles into the tub and got in. About twenty minutes later, I almost didn't hear the knock at the door, as I was playing Vivaldi on my phone. A woman came into the bathroom carrying a silver tray with the most gorgeous royal teacup and little French pastries.

"Helene, what are you doing here?" I asked. Yes, it was Helene from the Hamptons!

"*Bonjour, Mademoiselle Sophie.* Mr. Duren sent me a plane, and here I am, at your service."

I wondered who else he sent for? At least she was mostly speaking English, quite a relief.

"Tea, the way I like, with milk and Truvia. You are so perfect," I said.

She smiled as I stepped out of the bath, and put the robe on. Sipping my tea as I looked for Duren. What else could I need? Yes, clothing!

"Chance?" I called out.

I found him on the balcony, which reminded me of *Romeo and Juliet*. He was smoking a cigar and looking at Place Vendôme.

"I see that you flew Helene here," I said. "Did you really need her?"

He didn't respond at first, but I'd learned that when he did that, I needed to pause, compose, and reassert. The man was complex, but as fine as jewels from London that had been hidden like a treasure trove deep in a cave.

"My divorce is final today," he said.

Uh-oh! I hoped he wouldn't drown me with emotion. "Sorry that you're feeling so…much," I said awkwardly, as I put my hand on his shoulder. This all stirred up more emotions than I'd had on the beach.

He turned around and held my hand, leading me to the grand living room. It seemed like the kind of place where you truly got to the bottom of how you felt. A photo of Coco Chanel standing at the balcony hung above the fireplace. I couldn't help but wonder if she had her own issues with men or if she had meetings discussing matters of the heart right here in this very room. Or maybe she ran from men, as beautiful and poised as she seemed. Men could drive you far away.

"I am to blame for your love affair with Zur," Duren said.

My perfectly brewed tea suddenly felt cold and uninviting. I placed my royal rose garden of a cup on a golden coaster on the table, trying hard to not tear up. "My love affair with him was not your fault. Who would have thought that I'd have fallen for him?"

He cleared his throat in a manner that told me the worst was still to come. "I should have warned you about him," he said, staring at me.

"Warn me? Why? Is he some sort of criminal or something?

What is he?" There went my poise. I wondered how tea would look all over his Givenchy shirt, pink and all.

"Well he isn't from a family that sells stocks and bonds."

"I'm aware of that. The night we broke up, his bodyguard came to me and told me that Zur couldn't live without me. I got the impression that there was much more to the story than I could even imagine."

Helene walked in and poured me a fresh cup of tea. Tea time was as important to me as high tea at the Ritz was to women in Paris. I sipped my tea, trying to calm myself and keep from yelling. I didn't care to delve any deeper into who Zur was.

Zur's family, they would hate me either way, when all I did was truly, madly love their son. Perhaps I loved him more than they did, not for his glittering elite status, his last name that I still didn't know, or his Bentley, but for his love. Yes, love. The love that would always be the most priceless thing I'd ever gotten in my life. God, did I say that? Hell, I meant pearls.

A bit of advice: don't fall in love with someone you can't have. It was like walking into Christie's in Paris and bidding on an auction for a Le Brun painting that you simply couldn't afford. Zur stole my heart and part of my soul, and I might never get them back.

"I was going to have high tea here at the Ritz later, but I'm all tea-d out. Can I use Bernhard to take me shopping. Is that okay?"

Duren was speechless. I made my way back to the grand bath, to a tub that may have cost more than a normal person's savings. I didn't care. I needed more time to soak and relax.

"Sophie, I'm so sorry," he said with the worst look in his beautiful green eyes.

I called out behind me, *"À la fin." Not bad for a woman that's heartbroken*, I thought. After my bath, I'd wash out the idea of Zur—for good.

I was sure that Duren was burning inside for more than that. His divorce from his supermodel wife had to hurt. After all, his money was worth far more than his love for her. What did he expect, for her to wait for him?

If I were on the balcony of this suite waiting and waiting for my true love, and he didn't come, I'd somehow find my way down. I'd walk down the road to Le Castiglione and have a meal, like butter and baguettes. I was trying to simplify my meals, as the men in my life were very complicated.

30

RITZ AND HEMINGWAY

It grew late as I soaked in the tub, looking out the great doors and listening to Paris. It was magical and mystical and so lovely that I stayed in the bath for two long bubbling hours with no disturbances. I did hear Helene speaking in French. She was wonderful. She was my new Hannah.

Helene knocked, and called, "*Mademoiselle Sophie*, a gift!"

"Come on in."

Behind her was Duren, in jeans and a t-shirt with French words on it and bare feet. His hair was brushed back and his face neatly groomed. He had pink roses, champagne, a tray of fancy French bonbons and petite cream-filled brioche, and tiny balloons tied to the tray. I was happy, as I was starving. Duren placed the tray on a vanity stool decked in velvet with gold legs and pulled the stool over to me. He then gave me the champagne and the roses.

He made himself at home on the floor next to my tub. I wondered who had picked it all out, he or Helene or Bernhard. Smiling, I ate my bonbons. I let the balloons sail into the molded ceiling as I picked the petals off the roses and put them in the tub. The bubbles covered my naked body, and lit candles surrounded me.

"Happy birthday to you," he sang.

"Thank you," I smiled. "Though it's technically not my birthday anymore."

"As long as we are in Paris, it's still your birthday."

Supposedly the dust of Zur had settled. Duren's serenade warmed my heart like the French pastries that I literally gulped down, forgetting any sort of diet.

"Are you drunk?" I asked, laughing.

"No, I'm just not used to this," he replied.

"Used to what?" I teased, biting my lip.

"Chasing after a woman, wanting a woman, and having her driving me so crazy."

I blushed, and I felt like slipping into the bubbles to hide my face. "You are alive and divorced!" I said.

He dipped his hand into the tub and threw some bubbles at me. I threw bubbles back at him as he poured water from a vase over my head. I felt like a kid again, running in the bath naked as my brothers chased me around our bedroom-sized tub with a sitting room. Here we were, Duren in his forties and me twenty-five, laughing as if we weren't at all responsible adults with our inappropriate use of bubbles.

I got out of the tub and ran from him, forgetting I was naked. He playfully grabbed me from behind, and held my waist, and as the bubbles went flat, our eyes caressed each other.

"Here, your robe," he said, as he handed it to me.

I covered myself, but he couldn't take his eyes off me. We both looked the other way, and I tried hard to figure out what had just happened. You could say it was fate, unwinding our uptight asses, or our lonely selves craving more of each other without titles.

"Your bubbles are all over your pastries," he laughed.

"Good thing I'm no longer hungry. I seem to have lost my appetite, could be the extra carbs."

More likely it was Duren's sexy blue-green eyes that complemented his blue-washed denim. He wore his jeans like a new Gucci handbag.

I smiled as I dried my hair, looking in the royal oval mirror that Coco once looked into. "Can you imagine that this was Coco Chanel's place?" I asked, trying to kick the pink elephant out of the room. "Where will you take me next, the White House?"

"Wherever my money can take you. Just tell me where you want to go," he replied.

Turning the hair dryer off, I placed it gently on the vanity. I looked at him, wondering how screwed up his life and marriage must have been.

"Thank you for doing this, but if I'm ever with you, as in, you know—"

"Yes, I know," he sighed.

"I won't be with you for diamonds or luxury. It will be for you, the you that you are."

He was blown away, like *Gone with the Wind*, *The Notebook*, etc.

"No woman's ever told me that before," he said.

"Go figure! If you took them all here, they'd not want you, dodo; they'd want your wallet and where you can sign."

We both laughed. His dimples were like Le Brun's paintings, priceless and out-of-this-world gorgeous!

"Get ready for some shopping and wandering. Whatever you want to do today," he said.

"Yes, I do need to go to the Champs-Élysées."

"Okay," he said. He paused at the door to the bedroom, and our eyes met in the mirror.

I didn't think he could be this way. I'd only seen his devotion to a company he'd created and that had brought him great success. Today, I was seeing a very different side to him.

The only clothing I had to walk around in was the dress from last night and the robe I was now wearing, but soon I would get my Parisian fashion on. The French had a flair for fashion that was couture without any pressure. At last I was done with my hair and glossy lips. Those were intact, for now at least.

I followed the light sound of opera to yet another living room, with antiques and gold-lacquered boxes, but no Duren.

"Chance, where are you?" I called.

"In here!"

I walked into a room filled with racks of clothing. Displayed on a velvet shelf was a Chanel opera-length pearl necklace.

"Unbelievable!" I said.

Duren came up from behind me, and moving my hair to the side, placed the pearls around my neck. The scent of him was intoxicating. The touch of his fingers on my neck made me want to go Katy Perry on him. You know, *roar!*

"It's perfect, and so are you," I said.

Our eyes were lost in each other's, as our lips greeted each other in ecstasy. He kissed me like a lion who had been hunting its prey for weeks. Passion oozed from both of us as he wrapped a hand around the back of my neck and kissed it softly.

In seconds, he lifted me up and walked into the living room, placing me on the sofa.

Pulling away from him, I untwined our hands and our lips, and asked, "Wait. What are we doing?"

He let out a huff of air. "That's not a question to ask right now. Let's just follow this where it leads us."

"You're rebounding, and so am I," I said.

My brain couldn't stop thinking. Work, relationship, sex, intensity … What if I screwed up my career? Yes, and what if I lay in bed with him and got a good gift for it? Yes, yes, yes!

"Sophie, please come here," he said. "I want you." He sat there with tousled hair and a bulge in his dungeon. The Champs-Élysées would have to wait until later!

Just then, someone knocked on the door, and I looked to the sky and thanked God. At the door was a man that bore a strong resemblance to Duren, and the way they hugged made it seem as if they were family.

"Sophie, this is Rafael, my brother. Rafael, this is Sophie Becks."

Yes, perfect, a family member. "Hello, nice to meet you," I said.

He was tall with tanned skin, dark hair, and light eyes. Hey, the more the merrier. Duren insisted we all go to l'Espadon when I was ready.

"I'm going to be down at the Hemingway with Rafael, if you need me," Duren said.

I shook Rafael's hand. Then Duren took me to the room where he had my new stylish clothing.

Holding my face gently, he whispered, "I will wait until you are okay with moving forward, *oui?*" He kissed me softly and left the suite.

I held the pearls and blushed as I walked through the racks of clothing sent for me to try. The dresses and gowns were intricate with crystals and lace, black and pink and beige, all from Chanel. I'd seen this documentary of ateliers that worked on sewing all sorts of things.

I tried on a black gown with a petite bow at the front. It looked so stunning with the pearls that I couldn't put a price on it. The shoes I chose were velvety soft with pink bottoms. I was head over heels in love with a simple dress by Chanel. It was delicately styled and one of a kind, a classic, a work of art. It didn't scream, "I'm yours;" it screamed, "Work for it, Monsieur!" As I stood there in that dress, I got lost in today and how quickly things had changed.

Two or three hours later, Duren came back, and I was waiting in my black Chanel gown and opera pearls. It was so *Vogue*. He put his key on the golden Victorian table.

"Do you like?" I asked, as I spun around with the biggest smile I'd ever had. It was better than my first check as a broker, and that was big.

"I love it. It's astounding," he said.

"How can I thank you for such an amazing birthday trip?"

"It's not over yet." He kissed the palms of my hands. "I'm going to shower, and then we'll have dinner with Rafael."

I watched him walk toward the bathroom and thought things I probably shouldn't have.

As I turned, I saw Rafael at the door. I invited him in and tried to entertain him, but I was quite uncomfortable. It wasn't anything to do with Duren. It was just awkward. Rafael sat in the living room completely gaga over Chanel's photo and exquisite style.

"So how's my brother coping with the news?" he asked.

"Good, I suppose," I said, thinking he meant the divorce.

"That's good. He was in a bad place a few months ago. That's hard for any man." Now I was lost. What was he saying? Was he talking about his marriage?

"Yes, I imagine so," I replied.

Rafael took his merry time looking around. From time to time he smiled, clearly quite content in the surroundings. One minute trailed to the next, and we were both silent. I was trying to figure out this thing that affected Duren while pretending I already knew.

"So are you guys dating?" Rafael asked.

That was awkward. I mean, I didn't even know what the heck I was doing, except trying to move really slow.

"Not sure what we are at the moment. I'm on a very different path in life," I said.

"So is he. I'm sure that one day he'll get the chance to be a dad to someone."

What the hell? "A dad to someone, what are you talking about?" I asked.

Surely he'd had a lot to drink at Hemingway's. Talk about spilling it all out in the first meeting!

"Cooper wasn't his son. Ivania cheated on him," he said.

"Are you serious?"

"Yes, what part don't you get?"

Duren was really broken, and I thought I was in a bad place. As I poured myself sparkling water into a teacup, I was beyond stunned and beyond sad for him.

Duren appeared at the door as I sipped the sparkling water like mini-shots. Laughing, he took the cup from me.

"What's wrong?" he asked. "Rafael making you nervous?"

"No, no, I'm just, uh, having a great time here. It's so relaxing," I said.

"Did someone spike your tea and sparkling water?"

"Stop being silly. I'm wonderful."

"Okay, let's go," he said to both Rafael and me.

At the elevator stood our very competent porter, who followed us around, making sure everything was to our liking. I waved to the porter as I walked down the blue Savonnerie carpet on my way to the greatest restaurant in Paris, l'Espadon.

Duren held my hand, and we noticed a male celebrity making his way by the presence of the blinking paparazzi on the red carpet. It couldn't have mattered which billionaire was prowling down the corridors. The beauty and lavish opulence of the Ritz couldn't be stolen.

Gold leaf brushed the walls amid a harmony of drapery, and a floral scent permeated the opulent setting. Belle Époque statues held candelabras. There were baroque-styled flowers by the famous Varda, and smiles from the plethora of kindness floated around. The staff made sure everyone's fancies were met.

L'Espadon's entrance was stunningly Gatsby. The restaurant was filled with the glittering elite from Paris and all over the world. There were women in long gowns and painted pouts that read, "Kiss me now or never." There were men of all classes and net worths, aged like France's tasteful wine and cheese.

Here was heaven on earth. The many courses were sinfully delicious, and the sparkling wine made my French even better.

"Sophie, you are such a beauty," Rafael said. "My brother is very lucky."

Blushing and looking into Duren's eyes, I felt a wave of heat pass through me.

Our eight courses were petite and full of different layers. Rafael was in love with his palette and had an overpowering desire for cheese and wine. The sommelier came with a cart, pairing him the finest of both. Duren's meal was a museum of gastronomy's finest. I couldn't wait for dessert, though with my cinched waist, I could barely eat one course, let alone eight.

As dinner and our many courses fled, my phone rang off the hook. As I turned the ringer down, Duren caught my eyes. "All okay?" he asked.

"Yes, I need to be excused for a moment, thank you."

Walking across the room and out to the side, I answered, "Hello?"

"Sophie, how are you?" No, it couldn't be him. I didn't hear right.

"Who is this?" I asked, covering my other ear to hear better.

"It's Zur."

Time stopped, and stood as still as the crystal chandeliers that seemed to be in every corner of the restaurant. I didn't know quite how to respond. The sounds of the pianist in the tearoom echoed out to where I stood.

"Hello." I cleared my throat.

"No response to me?"

"*Non.*"

"Happy birthday. I'm sorry I didn't get to tell you so yesterday. And I miss you … Like more than anything." His voice was shaky, and I was in such a different place.

"I'm in the middle of dinner in Paris, so nice of you to call."

"Did you get my gift, my note, anything?"

"What are you talking about?"

"I had it delivered to you."

Behind me, Duren wrapped his arms around me, kissing my neck, heavily breathing, and exuding his sexual energy. The last thing I needed was trouble in Paris, especially after all that Duren had done for me.

"I must go now. Be well." I hung up.

Where and when did I ever get the courage to sweep him back to where he'd come from? I couldn't look back and self-destruct anymore.

"I'm going to go up to the suite. Is that okay?" I asked.

Duren held me to him, and I placed my head on his shoulder. Something about him gave me peace. I felt safe with him, not like I was reckless or running wild.

"Should I bring your dessert to the suite?"

I nodded and started to walk away, letting his hand slip from mine.

"What's the matter?" he asked.

"Nothing. I'm tired, I ate too much, and my head hurts."

Finally, he let me go, and I walked around the Ritz, losing myself to it all … The history, the ambience, the idea that some of the greatest writers and royalty had once walked where I did.

Something about my time with Zur felt too unreal. I had to let him go. Hearing his crackled voice made me realize that it was not to be. It was never to be.

Back in the suite, I poured myself some sparkling water and stood where Coco once did. I looked out at Place Vendôme and watched as people walked by below. I held my pearls and leaned over the rail.

Several minutes later, the door opened, and Duren called, "Sophie?"

"I'm in here," I answered.

He followed the sound of my voice and took off his Prada jacket, revealing his Burberry cashmere sweater. He wore a black alligator Fendi belt with black pants and Yves Saint Laurent loafers. God, I wanted him, right here and now.

He walked through the formal room with the most exquisite vitrines everywhere, and out to the balcony. Duren came closer to me, putting his hand on the famously black rails of the balcony. He put his mouth on mine, and I reciprocated like a woman craving raw sugar.

I unbuttoned his shirt as he tried to unclasp me from my dress. He carried me through the corridor and into the bedroom, laying me on the satin sheets that probably cost the same as my gown. The bed was unlike anything I'd ever slept in. "*Si les murs pouvaient parler …*" I murmured.

Duren took his sweater off and then his belt, slowly looking at me lying there in my gown, bare feet on the bed, my soul aching for his touch. Finally, a man that had everything!

"Sophie," he said, breathing on me as he rubbed my cheek. "Is this a one-night thing?"

"Oh my goodness, you're crazy to ask that," I smiled and studied his features up close. I couldn't get why he suddenly looked like David Hasselhoff in his way younger athletic days. Teeth never looked so perfect as his. Well, Thomas had great teeth, but he turned out a bit psycho.

"I want to have you, but not with you still in love with Zur," Duren said.

As his hands touched me, I realized that he was being like the emotional woman and I, the man.

"I'm not in love with him anymore." I sat up at the end of the bed. This moment was so déjà vu. The lights dimmed, music played in the background; there were even lit candles. Holy goodness, was he going to propose to me? He might as well ...

He held me close to him, and his kisses were as sweet as crème brûlée. He slipped my gown down to my knees. "Delilah" played in the background from his phone. My silk undergarments remained on, but everything else I wore fell to the floor.

Body to body, we kissed and touched as if it was our last moment on Earth. Duren's stomach was chiseled, and his arms were way better than Popeye's. He had me.

By 1:30 a.m., we lay in bed, tired as two stockbrokers on Wall Street could be after markets, except right now we weren't discussing stocks and commissions. We had crossed lines and boundaries. Smiling, I lay on his chest, listening to his heartbeat and not wanting to run. Yes, I said it: I didn't want to run. I wanted to stay there and sleep in his arms until the sun came up.

31

Venus de Milo

Venus, the goddess of love, had touched me many times in one year. I hoped that by standing next to her, I could change that love spell. Duren had arranged for me to walk through the Louvre so I could see the *Venus de Milo* without the hustle of the tourists who wanted the bang for their buck.

Was it love? Was it the power of being me? My charm, charismatic ways, and devotion to humanity—*not!* But I had you for a minute. I could be those things, but I first needed to do serious yoga and raise my kundalini to get there. Since being in Paris, I felt as if I had been here forever, but really it had been a mere day and a half. My life had changed, though, or maybe it wasn't so much my life but me. The call from Zur, and then Duren's love all through the night, was refueling me and my view of things.

I walked through the museum. It would have been easy to get lost there. I visited Venus and her other Louvre friends. It was very moving, but also frightening to be surrounded by all the classical French and Roman art.

I texted Duren, and he headed out to pick me up. I couldn't really imagine him relaxing, but I guess he was having a morning of relaxation today.

Helene was with me, and she had surely been staring at *Venus de Milo* for centuries. Well, minutes upon minutes at least.

"Are you loving the *Venus de Milo*?" I asked.

"*Non*, I am wondering what she did to lose her arms."

This was where I should have laughed. Helene whispered some phrases in French to me and walked off. I couldn't understand her at all. I was really just beginning to brush up on my French.

The Louvre was a real experience for those who lived for the classical and baroque. Next, I went to sit and stare at the *Mona Lisa*. I was completely alone, and I wondered about what emotions I had inside. The presence of the *Mona Lisa* was chilling, her in that dreadful frock with a smile that had no end or beginning. Was her husband in Florence so mad at her, that she stood there to be painted without laughter? Questions flooded my mind like *The Phantom of the Opera* without pause.

A man wrapped his arms around my waist, and I turned to see Duren.

"You scared me!" I said, taking his hands away from me and wishing I were alone. I tried to figure out why I was emotionally built half-man and half-woman.

"What's wrong?" he asked, his innocent deep eyes prying into me.

"Nothing at all. I think we should leave today," I replied.

"Why not in the early morning, huh?" Duren's voice deepened.

Helene came up behind us as we made our way out to the limo. She got in the front with the driver to give us space. Duren and I sat in the back alone.

"Something happened. What is it?" he asked.

I stared into his eyes and outward to the dark shadows of Paris. The clouds grew bigger and darker until finally they burst with drops of drizzle.

"It's nothing at all: work, stocks, clients," I said, lying my ass off.

Usually a man and woman passionately fell in love, and then months later the man called her out of the blue, saying, "It's not you; it's me," with the man wanting space. That was me. I felt love as if it was the last blast of heat on a winter's day, and then I moved out of it quicker than a flash in a storm. A day or two with a man was enough for me. I didn't need a year or two, or even months.

"Work, stocks, clients, is that the best you can do?" he asked.

The silence between us grew as I felt aggravated toward him, at his wanting me.

"It's an excuse for wanting me to back down, isn't it?" he said.

I pretended to compose myself in silence, but I was boiling like a pot of tea that had been brewed way too long.

"What is it that you want from me?" I yelled, realizing how rude I was. He looked at me with great fury.

The limo stopped at the Ritz, and the doormen opened the doors with umbrellas and all the bells and whistles. The Paris norm. Whatever. I'd lost my appreciation for the magic of Paris in two short days; I needed out now. And sure as hell, I needed to be shielded from all of Duren.

Walking down the red crimson carpet, with Duren behind me like one of Zur's bodyguards, I felt as if he owned me. He clearly wasn't loving the fact that it took a hell of a lot more to woo me than most women. But I wasn't most women, and the sad thing was that even Criss Angel couldn't keep me wowed for long.

Walking into our room, I walked to the bedroom, to pack my new clothing and things. I placed my pink chemise and bralettes into my new Louis Vuitton suitcase, and I heard a slam behind me.

"What the hell is this, Sophie?" Duren asked.

It wasn't his fault. He hadn't done anything to hurt me. I was already damaged when I walked into this short-term, stronger-than-life, current-riding-downstream-into-a-waterfall relationship!

"What is it with you and your coldness?" he asked. "All I tried to do was make you happy."

What did he want, applause? An Oscar would have been appropriate, as he had definitely acted well.

"Happy, you want me happy. Well, let's see," I exclaimed, pacing around the expensive French carpet with patterns hand-sewn by some wealthy somebody in Dubai, hopefully not related to Zur. "Happiness is for people who don't have much, who are okay with living on a tree-lined street with homes so close you can see your neighbors pick up their newspapers every bloody morning. It's for women who marry men that can't afford es-tates in Brookville and for wives who don't need much but their husbands' hands at the dinner table each flipping night. That's happiness, and honestly I don't need it." What a speech that was. You would have thought I was a true Rockefeller. "Okay? So don't try to make me happy, please."

I looked out the window that gave life to the room, and Duren smiled with sarcasm, looking at me with guilt in his eyes, guilt for things I didn't even know of. He should have thought twice before indulging in my Agent Provocateur. Turning away from him, I knew that earlier he wasn't just relaxing; no, rumor had it he was out with one of Zur's bodyguards. What on Earth was going on?

He grabbed my hands and pulled me to him, drawing my face to his. If there was a moment in my life that I needed to run away from all chains of honesty, it was now. He put his soft, masculine hands on mine. He had eyes like an angel, but desire like the devil. He looked into my eyes, breathing as heavily as he would have making love to me.

"I asked Zur to follow you in the Hamptons." Duren walked to the opposite side of the room and back. "So I felt guilty seeing you so torn up." What?

When Zur told me we were over, it felt as bad as losing all your life savings and maybe your wife to a more wealthy man. That was supposedly rock bottom. There was a reason they said don't ever mix business with pleasure, because here I was, stuck in deep. And I had to admit, I was still wounded by the charm of a man whose profession was probably sketchier that Mozart's first concerto.

I stumbled for the words to say. I was blown away by Duren's true dirty desire for me. "So, what? You paid Zur to woo me in the Hamptons, to fall in love with me?" I stared at Duren as if I was about to go ballistic on him. My eyes alone must have given him more grief than he'd had in a while. I hated Duren at that moment. Angry tears fell from my eyes. I felt so betrayed from all angles. I stood at the window and cried as silently as I could.

"No, we were friends, and I asked him to watch you closely, not to fall in love with you."

I was fuming with anger.

"What did you do to make him leave me like that?" I demanded.

Duren looked the other way, pretending as if my question didn't exist. "You couldn't live one day by his side, not really, and nor would I let you. I would rather lose all my fucking money," he declared.

What a raw, broken moment. He was sitting in a wing chair with his head in his hands. His eyes looked as if he'd had too many shots at Hemingway. I was stunned by his confession. One word for that brave, man-of-the-year confession: sad.

"That's very kind of you," I said. "But your money has been your flag, your purpose, your worship, your whole life. I'm going to pack my things and catch a flight out. Maybe I'll see you Monday; maybe I won't."

Pretending he didn't exist, I packed my bag and called a cab, not Bernhard. As I zipped up my bag, Duren had a breakdown. I didn't understand men in such power. They fell in love and then went crazy, mentally and physically.

"Sophie, don't leave," he said. "I did it because I wanted you, because I fell in love with you. I was never even in love with my wife this way."

Romeo was dead, but fear not, his brother was alive, and his name was Duren.

"Well, you should have told me that before you let me go to your stupid mansion."

With my bag and my Hermès, I walked down the stairs. I put my new Bvlgaris on and paused on the interlocking marbled black "C"s on the floor. I thought about the black Chanel gown and the priceless pearls. I took them out of my case and placed them on the gold table with golden legs so divine. I looked back at the balcony that made history, smiled with a broken heart, and closed the door behind me.

Ever heard the phrase: "Love don't live here anymore"? It was my new anthem.

At the foyer, I didn't have to worry about a $30,000 bill. Nope, the bastard deserved it, for lying to me and, even worse, for letting me drown in lust with someone that was asked to watch me closely. Zur did more than Duren had bargained for. I hoped watching me was worth the friendship. And my night of hot steamy pleasures with Duren? Well, I'd look at it as a gift to him. After all, my heart wasn't really there. Or was it?

I stood there on that crimson carpet for well over ten minutes waiting for my cab. If this was Wall Street, it would have been one second. Then, to my dismay, a black well-tinted Rolls-Royce pulled up. I looked away. I was tired of seeing dollar signs flash like the lights of paparazzi! The window rolled down, and there was Zur's Syed.

"Sophie, can we talk?" asked the well-dressed bodyguard.

"What are you doing here? What do you want from me?" I disdainfully asked the bastard.

"Zur needs you, more than ever."

"Go away please."

"It's gotten to a point where I can't save him."

"Let me guess: I can?"

He looked away, as sketchy as a sketchbook.

"She's not interested—at all. Let him know that," Duren said, as he walked up beside me, as if he'd scooped me away to a private island all to himself.

Syed looked shocked. Duren and I clearly looked like an

item, or at least it looked like something had actually happened between us this time. Syed looked wounded in his attempt to scoop me back to his boss.

At this moment in time, I might have gone to Zur, but after Duren's confession, I couldn't possibly entertain another heartbreak, despite the natural human instinct of attraction that catapulted Zur and I toward each other. It hurt me that the attraction that was so fierce and piercing was the subject of a whopping financial deal or a friendship between a Wall Street businessman and a crazy, sexy Arabian playboy, a badass in a Bentley.

I was no longer caught in the middle, as Syed drove down the road that led to the heart of Paris.

"Where are you headed?" Duren asked me.

"Long Island. I'll see you around!"

There were many things I had enjoyed about Paris. I'd have to visit again, especially the Ritz and the Coco Chanel Suite.

My chauffeur pulled up, and I waved to Duren as I headed off to the Charles de Gaulle Airport. Was I running from the entirety of Duren and his passion for me? *Oui*. Getting onto the commercial flight, I felt human and normal. I wondered if I retired from Wall Street if I'd be able to live like a normal human being. Probably not. So I was going to do my very best to live this thing called life, even if I was alone. Maybe after I got therapy I could be somewhat normal.

32

THE BROWN BOX

I arrived at JFK, and it was nothing like Paris … At least when the French cursed at you it somehow still felt romantic. As I waited for Mr. Wheathly, I couldn't stand the incompetent drivers that stood there in their dreadfully black attire and snooty attitudes, as if uniforms and limos were the new "in." For America's sake, how was I to know what Mr. Wheathly was driving?

"God, lady, I'm not your driver!" one of them yelled at me. Attitude, I tell ya.

"Yes, and if God were a lady, you'd be in a dungeon, idiot," I screamed.

As Mr. Wheathly pulled up in my Bugatti, everyone's jaws dropped. Bugattis were rough and noisy, but they were far sexier than that shirtless guy from that prison show. And he was super gorgeous, right up there with the Veyron. Mr. Wheathly put my luggage neatly into the handsome trunk, and I looked around and flipped off all the other limo drivers with both hands.

Then I remembered how much my finger missed that outrageously priced pink diamond. Back to sweet reality, wasn't it? My trip to Paris was over, and maybe my glitzy, short-term office flirt fest was too. Certainly my life was more operatic than Pavarotti in *Rigoletto*. I felt like Julia Roberts in *Pretty Woman*, except no man was ever going to tolerate me as much as Gere did Julia.

I opened the built-in backseat laptop and checked my emails, wanting to scream. I had my work cut out for me, especially with finding a new housekeeper now that Hannah had left, and a new assistant, as well. Tanner had moved on to a more "stable" boss, poached with more money by another broker in the firm; I guess one who didn't run off to Europe at a moment's notice. He had only been with me for a week. How's that for loyalty! I'd decided not to hire a young, attractive hottie of a man this time, you know, lawsuits and such. I'm sure I was now considered a high-risk factor and a threat to most men. I needed to protect my soon-to-be millions. After all, I had more brains, beauty, and talent than any man in a $4,000 suit, Patek watch, and crocodile shoes in *Boiler Room*.

Ha, I was going to play hardball with the pros—*if* Duren wanted me in. Call me *genius* or *jobless*, or *crazy*, but as they say, "The sky is the limit!" Accounts, commissions, and hotshots.

When the Bugatti pulled up to my parents' lovely home, the driveway was empty. I reminisced about Hannah and how much this house was just an expensive luxury with frills from Kashmir and paintings from Christie's. Nevertheless, if I were to ever settle down, I wouldn't mind something like this house, a good starter. Starters started at $4.5 million, not bad; that was considered Long Island reasonable.

"Mr. Wheatly, you are always a gentleman," I said. "I hope you stay that way."

I politely smiled as he opened the ancient mahogany front door. He put my luggage into the marbled foyer and smiled.

"Can I help you with anything else, Miss Becks?"

"No, I will be fine, I hope."

He left in a jiffy, and there I was alone. If I were to drop one of my pearl earrings, it would probably echo. In the kitchen, I brewed myself tea and then sat staring at all four walls, wondering when and how my life had gotten so exciting and then suddenly quiet.

Then the front door slammed open and closed, and I almost choked on my tea. I heard loud steps that sounded very Robin. He stomped when he was mad, as if he were still ten years old. He wasn't nurtured by my parents either, and was a mess growing up. Maybe that was why he sought love in very wrong places, and lusted after women that needed more help than even *moi*. Well, emotional help. Otherwise, wouldn't you say I turned out quite a masterpiece?

Robin came into the kitchen, looking as if he needed a live-in therapist.

"Hey, Sophie, back from your back-to-back fling with your second billionaire?" he asked.

"Ouch, talk about direct and unpolished. Yes, I'm back."

"Good. There are two packages for you." He placed a blue Tiffany's box, from Jan, and another big brown box on the counter. I thought the brown box probably came from some of my online shopping, Barneys or Saks—marry them together and you'd have a problem!

I put my warm, delicious, ginger-pear tea aside and ripped the tape from the brown box, stripping away every bit of peace of mind that had taken me weeks to conjure up. There was another box inside, a maze of brown imperfection. Stripping that box open, I found another box, like those Russian dolls, one inside the other, a whole family.

"Who would do this?" I asked.

"Only the weird men you date," scoffed Robin.

"Talking about weird, what's your situation with Hannah?"

"If we had a situation, I missed it," he said, nonchalantly. Stopping my unwrapping, I looked at him and wondered how he had ever gotten worse than Rain.

I said, "She's having your baby, moron!"

"If she is, why the flick did she leave me and run back to Barcelona? She could be anywhere for all I know. I'm not chasing her, okay? Let her have a taste of single parenting, OK?"

He wasn't making any sense to me, but I had my own problems right now and didn't want to get involved. I walked upstairs to my room, with the smallest box in my hand. I put it on my bed and tried hard to not think of everyone's issues. I thought I was bad with commitment, but here you had my genius of a brother with even more issues, and my father with his twenty-six-year-old mistress with breast implants and lips like Angelina. Horrid.

I needed to relax, so I started a bath. I undressed and slipped into the blissful bubbles. I washed my face with warm water and then opened the box. It was big enough to fit a box of cookies or something like that. Inside I found yet another box. I was in awe as I pulled out a pink velvet box, like the one I once would have died to have forever—Zur's box.

As I opened it, my eyes filled with tears and my heart with sadness, the kind that I flew miles and miles away to get over. I even slept with my boss to get over him. That was beyond deep. The deep blue sea had nothing over the love that Zur and I once shared.

The pink diamond was even better than I remembered. It was magic and glitter and beauty that didn't exist until we had

347

each other. What was I saying? This crap was over. I put the ring on the ledge and put on some Bocelli. I needed a man to sing to me loudly. Not Pavarotti, or I'd beat Zur silly.

A few minutes of tears later, I got out of the bath and put my robe on. I searched through the box and found a letter. Sitting on my bed, I knew I had to face my fear. Honestly, I had already failed at this short-lived, passionate relationship and had moved on in an inappropriate way. The letter was written in English with ink spills here and there.

> Sophie,
>
> I thought I'd die without you, already. I can't even think that I had you, and now I don't. If I were the better man, you would have been with me, not your new billionaire boyfriend who hired me.
>
> I imagine you're happy with him, perfect picture of new love rebounded, right? I'm sure he told you the story and you slept with him right after. He's a salesperson. It's as if he wanted me to see you and steal you away. Let's not kill your potential marriage with him, as you will probably marry him and have your first child in perfect order. My life isn't in order. How could a man like me ever have a woman like you? I suppose he can't.
>
> I've loved you from the moment I saw you. I'll never forget the day I kissed you, the way you felt and the way your hands melted into me.

I lived for you then, and I can't forget you, baby.
I've tried.

I am missing you, missing you, missing you. May
you always keep my ring, as my heart still beats
for you.

Zur

How was it that love could be so wrong and cold? My heart was
filled with what-ifs and how real our love still felt, a short moment in my life that would forever remain with me. I know that
I couldn't forget Zur. Even if Duren was perfect, he could never
be Zur. Sure, I started out as a favor he was doing for a neighbor,
but now I was a part of his heart; as he was part of mine.

Tears poured from my eyes, as I let the letter fall to the floor
next to my bed. Unsure of how best to approach the situation,
I was now lost in an unfamiliar zone. It was frightening and
surreal. I thought of Duren and what I had done to him. Was
he in love with me, and could I really love him back? I brushed
my hands through my hair as I cried tears that belonged to a
river somewhere. I didn't know what to do.

In the midst of my distress, there was a knock on the door.
Wiping my tears, and hiding my emotions like they were illegal,
I called, "Come in."

My mother, as fine as China, walked into the room. "Sophie
darling, when did you get back?"

Clearing my throat, I grabbed my reading glasses from the
night table to cover my puffy eyes. "Today," I said.

"Can we talk, please?" she asked, strolling into my room as
if it were a garden party.

"Yes, I guess we can."

Scooting away from her, I expected to receive the brunt of it all, you know the bad boyfriend from Dubai, then my trip to Paris with the wealthy Wall Street perfection with money, looks, great family, etc.—the kind of lecture that would make you wish you drank like a housewife.

"How was Paris with your boss?" she began.

How should I respond? Great sex and wine overlooking the Chanel balcony?

"It was, um, quite interesting. I saw so many things and ate amazing butter and pastries. And I even pranced near the Eiffel Tower, hoping it would make me feel—" I stopped speaking, as I couldn't possibly tell her about thinking of another man while with another.

"Yes, I remember the Eiffel Tower with your father, so young and romantic and very stupid I was."

"Why stupid?" I pried.

She stood up in her knee-length tweed dress and matching jacket with black Yves Saint Laurent pumps. "Well, darling, love is indeed blind, and once you feel it so greatly, you forget your senses, completely."

Sighing heavily, she sat next to me and lifted my chin so I was looking at her. "I'm sorry that I was never there for you. I was so caught up in my own unhappiness."

My mother unhappy with my dad? *That was mind blowing,* I thought sarcastically. And their relationship looked so robotic.

"What unhappiness are you talking about exactly?" I asked.

She walked to the French doors, twirling her pearl necklace and staring out toward the horizon. "Do you think your father was the love of my life, Sophie?"

I could not bear to think further; I had my own small crisis …
Where could I find Zur? I didn't know how far I would go to be
with him until right here and now. I still loved him, whether I was
in Paris at the most mind-blowing place with Duren or with any
other man who was as perfect as James Bond. I was still madly,
and undyingly, in love with him. If I could, I would take him back.

"Your father was the better man, my dear, but he wasn't my
shining knight or Redford. He was Yale educated and came
from an exceptional background of elite lawyers." She smiled
with the deepest look I've ever seen her give me. "Sophie, life
isn't just about your heart fluttering and magic in silk sheets; it's
about morals and character and mostly about knowing that you
can live your decision through."

Had I ever been lost in the woods, I would have found my
way better than I could have understood this heart-to-heart
with my mother. In other words, the thrill, the romance under
the moon and on the sand, and the Bocelli serenades didn't last
long. *Sad and exhausting*, I thought, *and all for nothing*.

My mom holding my hand felt so odd. All my life I'd never
had a moment like this with my perfect mother.

"I do want you happy and not running through life like you
seem to need to," my mom said. "But at the same time, Paris or
not, darling, you love Zur."

"I do, but I don't know where to begin with him."

"Start with your heart, and then find the right time, and
it'll happen." She kissed my forehead and walked toward my
vanity. "One more thing, about your father: he only had that
affair because I went away and, um, did what my heart pleased."

This was a very shocking confession! She pleased her heart?
Yikes …

"Which was?" I asked.

"Be with the man I've loved my whole life, the man that couldn't give me all of this and all of you."

Putting that together, I was shocked and confused. Thank God my mother wasn't a therapist, or else all women would cheat on their husbands and feel okay about it.

"I get it, Mother, and I wouldn't want to ever cheat on my husband. Of course, right now it's looking like I may not ever have one."

"Well, then you shouldn't marry just for money and last names."

"Yes, I don't know how I could marry a man if I didn't love him. I rarely love, and when I do, it's more complicated than anything."

"That's life, darling. It's your charm that men are drawn to. I see it." She gave me a kiss and walked out of my room, as she did when I was twelve and having a tea party.

I had a lot to think about, and a lot of work to do. While I was lost in my thoughts, my phone rang. I couldn't find it for the life of me, and finally found it buried in my Hermès, under my makeup.

"Hey, Soph, are you okay?" Duren asked.

"Yes, why?"

"I'll be over in a few minutes, okay?"

"Um, okay ..." I said, wondering what the hell had come over him, wondering why he was always there even when I never asked him to be. He must have flown back right after I did. Why was it that the pull between us was more than passion and deeper than attraction?

I hurriedly glossed my lips with Dior, which was mandatory if anyone came over—well, one of my male companions at least.

I went downstairs into the foyer, and saw that, luckily, my mother had left. One pep talk per ten years was all I could handle. I sat down on the paisley English chair that graced the cathedral foyer, and then I stood again, bouncing up and down a bit. I was suddenly nervous and afraid, and butterflies flew in my stomach like it was a summer parade.

Then I heard footsteps leading to the door knocker, which no one ever used. Most everyone loved the button that echoed through the house like church bells in Barcelona. I opened the door, and Duren stood there in his finest clothing and Prada loafers, stunning and not a bit happy. Tension and anger pierced his eyes.

"What is it?" I asked.

"Nothing, just wondering why you hadn't called," he said.

"I was trying to get my thoughts together. That's all."

"Yes, I'm sure. Where's Zur?" He acted like a crazy man newly out of jail.

"Zur? Why do you think he's here?"

"You're wearing his ring."

"Oh, this," I said, looking at it as if Zur were hiding in my bedroom or something.

Duren invited himself in, mad as heck.

"What's wrong with you?" I asked. "Tell me."

"Where the hell is he?"

"I don't know, I swear to you."

He tried to pull himself together, and I had a moment in which I wanted to comfort him. Me comforting anyone was always a moment to remember. I placed my arms around him, feeling a sense of love. Yes, love. Everyone had flaws, right?

"I'm sorry that I left like that, and I'm sorry that I'm all screwed up inside. I can't bear to go through that heartbreak again."

This was the moment that defined the past and the present. I could wish that my love for Zur was nothing, but as much as it was something, he wasn't a Redford or a knight. He was not the better man.

"I don't want you perfect, but I want you in my life, and not with another man," Duren said. "A man that buys love, for whatever it's sold."

I was filled with emotion, and tears began welling up in my eyes. He wiped them and held me closer to him, as his arms armored me like a shield.

"I love you, Sophie."

I didn't respond. If I did, where would this love lead me? Not a clue.

I cried as he held me so close to his chest and kissed my forehead and hands.

"I am sorry for what I did," he said.

"It's fine," I said, wiping my tears and feeling quite embarrassed that I wasn't that tough Wall Street egotistic, money-crazed human being he thought I was. My eyes were red and my nose looked like Rudolph's.

I barely noticed Rain's limo pulling up. Rain opened the door, confused as to what the hell type of circus my life was.

"Hey, Soph, last I heard, you ran off to Paris, and here you are," he said.

"Hello to you too, Rain," I said.

He hugged me, holding my hands. "The ring, the ring, I would hate to be you."

"This is Duren, my boss," I said.

"Yup, hate to be you, but you will someday grow out of this phase of men." He turned to Duren. "Nice to meet you. I saw you in *Forbes* a few years back. You were a little bit younger," he said teasingly.

"I was in my late thirties," Duren replied.

"Wow, you are my idol. In *Forbes* in your thirties; I can barely be on any good list with my new fiancée," Rain said laughing.

I was so tense, just standing there. Nothing made it through me. I was deeply saddened by my life, as good as it was.

"Well, we should all have dinner sometime," Duren said. "I would love to meet your charming family."

"Well, they would love to meet you too, if you were in my life romantically," I said, probably a little too cruelly.

Rain looked at me, and paused awkwardly. "We'll chat later," he said, walking away.

"Yes." Duren smiled. "What's it going to be?"

"I can't move forward without closing this door?"

"Yes and giving that ring back! My check to him must have paid for that."

"Really, was that necessary?" I said.

"No, but do what you have to do to give it back. I'll wait for you." He stared into my eyes, with sex on his mind, I'm sure.

"Can you do me a favor, please?" I asked.

"What is it?"

"Take me to Zur."

He looked away and then made a call on his cell. After a

short conversation, he looked at me and said, "Get ready. I'll take you to him."

"You'd do that for me?"

"I'd do anything for you, anything."

The passion between us was fueled by all the things he could do for me; it filled me up little by little. His lips reached out to me, and a wave of heat came over me; it was more than a sexual urgency to be there beside him. He was beginning to fill me again with pieces of love that I thought I'd lost.

He took my hand and led me to his limo. I was taken by his power to please me, with not just one thing, but everything. Men could learn the way to a woman's heart from him, as he was doing everything right. Maybe it was his knowledge of *The Art of War*, his great sales pitches, or just his dangerous arousal for a woman he wanted. After all, his life was mostly money, money, and more money.

"I want you right now, Sophie," he whispered.

"Please, not here. There are cameras all around this house." I smiled, as I entered the backseat of his limo. He closed the door.

33

LOVE ON WALL STREET

Wall Street had many material things you could fall for: the stocks that drained your life, the men in their prim and proper suits and ties from designers whose names you couldn't pronounce, and your big-shot boss that rocked your world in Louboutins or Pradas ... in Paris. Then, eventually, you find out that it's all unnecessary bullcrap, a realization that pisses you off.

My world was still upside down, but I was bouncing back after the pink-diamond effect with lots of sparkling water and sex in places that I don't even recall. It was blissfully the most pivotal point in my life. I had made my first million in no time, and now I was falling in love with a man that could buy me the moon and customize the sky for me. What more could I have asked for?

Yes, one more night with Zur would be wonderful; one where I could get all the answers my heart needed, but surely that was the one thing that Duren would never allow. In fact, we never met with Zur that night, several months ago. Duren had distracted me with dinner in a beautiful restaurant on the ocean and a night of glorious sex. Go figure. Maybe Duren should customize a rocket ship to send Zur away. That way Duren would never have to worry about me falling in love with Zur again! Love was a funny thing, and I no longer dwelled on it.

"Good morning, everyone," Duren said. "This morning, I have a brief announcement to make." Yes, Duren was giving his morning speech.

I was so tired that I wore my new fake nerd glasses to hide the fact that I hadn't slept well since Paris. Duren had officially won me back, and I was officially a lunatic that could sell words to the dictionary, all while wearing a Chanel tweed suit and pink Prada Mary Janes.

Looking at the floor, I thought of a million things, knowing that Duren's speech wouldn't last too long.

"Sophie Becks is going to be promoted to a partner of this firm."

WTF! My God, a partner? No, no, no, this was supposed to be a fun, romantic, screw-me fling while I made millions, not a partnership of his company! I knew I was stupid, but the truth was that I'd worked my ass off to be his secret lover. I half smiled as everyone drowned in their self-pity.

"Becks, you are the one and only woman I know that could do what you did in such a short time."

I thought, *Yes, I know, sleeping with you and making you so crazy that you have no idea what you're saying.* My gosh, this was exhausting. I was barely here, and when I was, I opened accounts while fixing my nails and texting.

All of the color drained out of Jaxwe's face.

"Jaxwe, darling, what happened to you?" I asked. "You were the best I'd ever heard of, but it looks like I've taken your place and office, yay. But honestly, thank you, Mr. Duren, for giving me more than I expected," I added with a wink.

Everyone stared at Duren. It was clear we were more than doing the dirty; we were losing our minds together! I was in awe of what ecstasy felt like. Well, I was happy to be of service to him. I liked to consider it my calling in this world. I shook my head at him, left the conference room, and walked into his executive office. I smiled as he followed and closed his blinds.

"Everyone thinks I screwed my way here. I should be offended," I said to him.

He kissed my hands as I leaned over to him. He wrapped his arms around my waist and kissed my neck, and then sat in his European leather armchair on wheels. I hoped I'd get to put my derriere on it someday. When I started on Wall Street, I was blown away by his success and the charisma he wore about him like his suspenders, so well and so naturally.

"You shouldn't be offended by what anyone thinks. Come over here. I need your opinion on something. I can't decide." He was looking at a catalog.

"Wow, is that Tiffany's?" I asked, wondering why he'd need my advice.

"Yes, do you like this one?"

"That's an engagement ring!"

I walked away from his dark-cherry desk, maybe not quite realizing what he was trying hard to get at.

"No, it's a friendship ring; don't panic," he said laughing. "Before I make you a partner here, I need you to be my partner."

I had a moment of great clarity. I said, "Let's not rush this, please. I know you mean well, but I don't want a partnership here. Don't you think I'm nuts enough?"

Laughing, he swept his hands through my hair.

"I don't want to crash and burn again," I said. "I did that once already, without blinking."

"You're not, because I'm not getting younger, even though you look like you are, and I want you for the rest of my life."

We stared at each other, and I was surprised at how our relationship had changed. I was moved and, with no sarcasm, I wanted him for the man I saw every day when we were alone, not the savvy Wall Street overachiever. He was soft, caring, and so delicately moving with his emotions. For the first time in my life, I wasn't confused. I wasn't in lustful bliss; our intimacy went beyond silk sheets. We had meaningful conversations filled with emotions.

"I think I may love you in a very natural way, Chance. Yes, I do love you," I said.

I kissed his cheek and placed my hands around his head. I leaned on his desk, staring into his eyes. With his lips on my neck and my hands in his hair, I suddenly felt sick to my stomach. Our lips met, and our passion rose to such a height that I felt I was at the top of the Empire State Building. One touch led to another, and the next thing I knew, he lifted me on his desk and was unbuttoning my shirt. He was kissing me like our lips were the ticker on the New York Stock Exchange.

"Stop, please, I'm sorry," I said.

"What's wrong?" he asked.

"Nothing, I just feel nauseous. I need to use the bathroom."

I buttoned my shirt and ran to the bathroom, which was a few rooms from his office in his private corridor. I closed the door, knelt on the floor, and threw up.

A knock on the door followed.

"What's the matter?" Duren asked.

"Not now, I need like twenty minutes and Annie."

"I'll get her."

Annie was the front office manager, a woman in her mid-thirties. Jeez, she was the *only* woman I knew there, and right now I needed a woman. Looking at my Jaeger, it was 9:50 a.m. I hadn't eaten anything all day, but I was still sick to my stomach ... No, I couldn't think ...

Annie knocked on the door and came in with all sorts of things: ginger ale, toothbrush, wet cloths ... She would have made a great air stewardess.

"Sophie, this is odd to ask, and I don't know how to..." Annie said.

"Just ask, please," I said.

"Are you pregnant?"

"Pregnant?" Hmm, let's see, having a little too much passion as if I were English and sex was tea. Contraception, what was that again? Oh my God, I did try to use protection at times. When did I last have my period? I couldn't remember. I was fuming. After an hour of bathroom downtime, I walked out polished as ever and sicker than ever.

"Can you call my driver, and get him here right away?" I said to Annie.

"Yes, will do."

Duren was standing at the door, alarmed. "Are you okay?"

"Yes, everything is wonderful and under control."

As I was about to walk out of his office, he grabbed my hands, staring into my deep seductive eyes in panic. "What is it? Tell me," he pleaded.

"It's nothing. Don't hold me like that please. I have a stomach bug, and I'm leaving. Is that okay?"

Let's hope this stomach bug doesn't have two legs and wear a diaper, I thought.

In panic, I grabbed my things from my shabby square desk. I was picking up my Hermès when Jaxwe came up behind me.

"So what makes you think you're better than me, Becks?"

I looked at him in bewilderment, thinking, *Not now, dude.* But of course a broker without a rebuttal was a dead broker.

"Well for starters, my attire costs more than your mortgage. But more importantly, I've got the numbers to prove it. In the short time I've been here, I've made more than you have, by far, so please don't insult yourself by asking such a stupid question. Kindly move away from me, and don't you ever think it's okay to bloody question me." I pushed him to the side and left the office.

"Didn't you just come in?" Jaxwe asked. "It's not even ten, and you're leaving. It's amazing Duren gives you that much privilege. I wonder why ..."

If I weren't so sick, I'd consider knocking the bastard out with my Hermès bag. I thought, *Sophie Becks, composure and silence.* But no, that was not possible coming from me with all this stuff that was going on.

"Don't you wonder what I do with my spare time with Duren. Just know one thing: very soon, I'll be your boss."

He looked as if I'd stripped him of his custom suit and given it to a homeless man. I left him to stand alone in his Jockeys. There's a view for you. That would be nothing like a penthouse overlooking Manhattan; it would very like opening your window and seeing your neighbors—dreadful, distressing, and very unbecoming. Yes, that was how I'd sum Jaxwe up.

"Sophie," called Duren, walking across the room to me.

The entire office paused, just like when I walked in to get

this job. Duren held my hand and walked me through the front office and to the hallway. We should have just invited the office to listen. I'm sure they were convinced we were having an indecent affair.

Men like Duren should never sleep with their employees. Think of this word … *consequences*. For example, with the litigious society we live in, the woman could turn desperate and sue your ass broke. But worry not, I was that one out of two billion that didn't care about having anyone else's money. Right now, I needed a place where I could get some peace of mind. If I could buy that, it would fill my walk-in closet like my extensive designer-shoe collection.

"Are you pregnant?" Duren asked.

Leaning against the wall, gazing into his eyes, I wondered how I had gotten here so quickly. Was it really as they say? Faith knocks, and destiny walks right in, sometimes without invitation?

"I don't know. I'm just nauseous," I said, fixing his collar. I had a tear in my eye that he couldn't see. It was very, very tiny. Maybe I was still stuck in my emotional cave waiting for a breakthrough.

"If you are, is it my child?"

I laughed but I was angry at the question. "I've been with you alone for the time we've been together. If it's any comfort, I sleep with only one man at a time. I know I can be notorious, but for God's sake, I come from a mother who only cared about me having proper etiquette and morals. Hell, I could be as stupid as Jaxwe, and she wouldn't care as long as I had proper decorum."

"I'm sorry. I just needed to know." He kissed my head.

"Yes, well, after your ex-wife, you probably need that in writing, right?"

Apparently, my judgment on jokes was as bad as a First Lady's decision to wear jeans to a State dinner.

"Let's go to my place in the city," Duren said. "I need you to rest."

"I really just want to go home, please."

We got into the elevator, and he said, "My home is your home." He smiled, holding my hands.

In his limo, with my head on his shoulder, I remembered that day in the conference room when I told him I was going away with Zur. And now, I was in all areas of Duren's life instead. It was unimaginable.

In minutes, we were across from Central Park and on an elevator heading up to what felt like the sky. He opened the white door to his penthouse with views of the park. It was very formal and decorated like a room from Oheka. I placed my Hermès on his foyer table.

"I'll draw you a bath, okay?" he asked.

I nodded and smiled as he held me close to him. He was so compassionate. I'd been taken care of my whole life. Hannah used to set me baths with bubbles and rose water, and now it was Duren.

On an antique mirrored table, I looked at a picture of Duren holding Cooper as a baby. Duren looked happier than when his screen went green at work. I couldn't imagine any woman would cheat on a man like him, so considerate and kind, not to mention what he looked like with his shirt off and his lips like an angel.

"It's almost ready," he said. "Can I make you tea?"

"I do need tea, thank you."

Staring at me, he bit his lip in great seriousness.

I sat on his velvety sofa, admiring how pristine his loft was. The art was very simplistic, the kind from a nobody artist that somehow sold at an auction for $200,000 anyway. I could never understand if it was an error, or if this was really art. Every book written about Wall Street lined the shelves of his built-in library, like a museum.

My goodness, this man's mind was so sexy. If this didn't work out, I was going to date a scientist. God, men's brains were now a turn-on, one of the long-term effects of working with brainless stockbrokers. Male stockbrokers wanted anything with plastic boobs and short skirts, and female brokers wanted men with intelligence.

I know, it's like hearing Hugh Hefner say, "I love this one. I want to spend my life with her." Yes, okay, wait until another pair of boobs stick out, tell me how you feel then.

Women are very much like men, except with better manners and high standards. At least, that's how I was. I didn't know if most women just wanted anyone that wanted them.

"Your tea," Duren said, handing me a white teacup and saucer. "Milk?"

"Milk is fine, thank you."

He smiled at me.

"Why are you smiling?" I asked.

"Nothing at all, I just like having you here."

"Give it a few hours, and I bet you'll be calling Mr. Wheathly to come get me."

"No, I won't." He glanced at his Philippe. "I have a conference call with one of my big clients. Your bath is probably ready by now."

He kissed my forehead and walked out of the room. That was the Duren I saw from time to time: business, money, no time for jack squat else.

I sat there by myself with tea that was nothing like Hannah's. Making myself at home—looking at Manhattan, as silence filled the penthouse from the ceiling to floor—was sickening. I was such a Long Island girl.

I closed the blinds and headed to his room. I wondered how quickly he had taken the pictures of his ex-wife down. She was nowhere to be seen. The apartment was pristine and cleaned of her image to perfection.

Waltzing into the bath, I saw the tub with bubbles and a lit candle. He'd laid out a robe next to the vanity with a toothbrush and Tom's for my breath. How lovely. Did he customize underwear for me too? Thank God not. That would freak me out and send me running out of the building in a white robe.

I turned off the lights, shut the door, and slipped into the tub. I played Chopin on my phone. I soaked in the tub, thinking of everything one could possibly think of. For example, if I was pregnant, was my life over? I'd seen babies, and sure they were precious, but would I ever be ready to settle down with anyone?

The fear of loving and losing was way too much for me. I didn't want a relationship built on just last names, money, and notoriety. As much as I was cloaked in expensive things, I was still human and terrified of commitment and making decisions that I couldn't live with. And what about Zur? How was I to completely let go of him?

Half an hour into my bath, I heard the door chime and chime. Where was Duren? Maybe lost in his office somewhere.

I got out of the bath, barely wiped myself off, and threw the robe on. I walked into the foyer and then the kitchen, no Duren.

"Duren? Duren!" I called.

Turning down a hallway, I realized how huge this place actually was. It wasn't a loft; it was gigantic. I went and opened the door. Never in a million years would I have imagined ever seeing him again, but there was Zur.

"Sophie?"

"Oh my God, Zur?"

We stood there lost for words, my heart pounding and my eyes glued to his.

"Um, you're here for Duren, aren't you?"

"Yes, he requested that I meet him alone."

"Well, you're here, so come in," I said, pretending we hadn't shared a bit of heaven together.

"I don't know where he went. Maybe I should text him." I looked down at the floor and then up at ceiling.

"Sophie, about us, I … I don't know where to begin."

"To begin, you lied to me. You made love to me and proposed, and then you left me. As if that wasn't enough, you were friends with Duren and were hired to watch me. And I didn't know any of this."

I thought about trying deep breathing. He deserved the worst. Tears fell from my eyes as I looked away. I had wanted closure, and here it was, so cold and dark and impossible.

"I know what I did, okay? You don't have to tell me. I'm paying for it now," Zur said. "As for my love for you—"

Duren walked in, and said, "Don't bother about your love; you don't have any. You knew how I felt about her, and you pursued her. Is that a fucking friendship?"

As Zur looked at me, I could see past the bad playboy speech and behavior. He had to have loved me. Zur turned stone cold and looked away, but I could feel his heart beat underneath it all. I could feel his unshed tears.

"Tell me, Zur: Was this love all a payback to our friendship?" Duren yelled.

Zur ignored Duren and looked at me. I was so cold on the outside, but inside, my emotions ran high.

"Sophie, do you want me to tell you I don't love you anymore? Tell you to be with him?" Zur asked.

I was shaken. I knew right then that my life had changed. I was in deep with Duren. I couldn't get involved with someone else, even if he was staring me in the face.

"Do you want to move on with him and forget me? Answer me; tell me that," Zur said, staring into my eyes.

Duren could barely contain himself. "Leave now, and don't ever come back."

I needed closure with this. I couldn't pretend that he ever loved me. "I have your ring. I'll give it to Duren to give to you," I said.

I walked away from both of them and lay in Duren's bed, crying one tear after the other. This was it. It was over, done, closed—"Con Tè Partirò," according to Bocelli. I'd closed the door to Duren's bedroom and my heart.

Within minutes, Duren came into the bedroom. Looking at him, I felt hopeless. "Were you testing me?" I asked.

He stood silent with eyes so red. I looked away from him, my hair dripping of water. He placed a towel over me. "Go get dried up," he said. "We'll talk when you're warm." I walked to the bathroom, and truth was, I was scared. What if I was pregnant?

In the bathroom vanity, I found a pair a Juicy Couture sweatpants and hoodie that were so not me. But I was cold and thankful to have something to wear apart from my glitzy silks and Chanel tweeds.

I touched my stomach and wondered what it would be like to be a mother with Duren beside me, the better man, not the playboy who made me wail.

In the living room, Duren was having a glass of wine, sitting as calm as the ocean before a storm. I didn't know why he'd need to test me. I wasn't a whore.

"Sophie, sit, will you?"

As I made my way to the living room sofa, I said, "Thank you for the sweats and especially for Zur. It was very thoughtful of you to send him to your place while you and I were both here. You didn't trust me with him alone, did you?"

"No, I didn't, because he would have taken you away from me. Don't think I don't know that."

I couldn't look at him at all. My eyes were glued to the floor; the carpet was better than the art surely. I was trying to not yell at him for being so insecure.

Duren stood up and placed his empty glass down. He paced by the window.

"I don't want to hurt you," I said. "I do love you."

He looked at me. "I wouldn't mind having you at least fake how you feel about him."

"He's always going to be an issue, isn't he? I don't love him like I did. Yes, I was in love with him, but don't question my love for you. This is not a bloody competition," I yelled, and I hoped he caught it all.

I was furious as I sat there on the sofa, angry and crying like a child. All my emotions came tumbling down like the train of a gown. We were both silent. The hurt I saw in his eyes overwhelmed me. I wanted him now more than ever.

"Can you do me a favor?" Duren asked. "I bought you a test. Can you take it? If you're having my child, I want to know."

Not saying a word, I took the test and walked into the bathroom. I was in no way ready to have a child. What would I teach the child? How to sell stocks and bonds?

I couldn't pee, so I drank two bottles of Pellegrino. I read the instructions while I waited. What was I supposed to dip it in? My gosh, wasn't it stressful enough taking it?

I took the test and waited for the result: negative. I sighed in relief. I wasn't ready for a child, nor was I ready to take a pill that screwed me up.

I walked back to Duren. From a distance he looked lost and pale. Did he want a child of his own, or did he have second-wife syndrome?

I stepped close to him. "Hey," I said, placing my arms around him.

Grasping my hands, he looked at me. "Are you?" he asked.

"No, so you don't have to worry about me having your child."

The look in his eyes was pure disappointment. In some stages in men's lives, they feared a pregnant woman. Some didn't return calls, while others had their million-dollar portfolios threatened. Duren looked like he wanted a few pregnancies.

I turned away, pretending to look at the things on the side table.

"I didn't worry about that. If it was my baby in there, I would be ecstatic," he said.

"You are too much, I mean too much."

I smiled with relief that this all was going to be behind me sooner rather than later, both Zur and a pregnancy that I wasn't ready for.

"Why were you so sick this morning?" asked Duren with his arms around me, kissing my neck soft and slow.

"It must have been the birth control pill I took today. It made me feel so ill that I'm not doing that again."

"Why are you taking it? What are you afraid of?" He turned me to face him. We were so close together that our eyes and breath met.

"I can't be pregnant. I don't want to be pregnant and alone, or pregnant and not married." Well, if there was one thing I could do, it was summarize my emotions.

"I love you, and I want you to have all the things that you desire. Why don't we—"

"Duren, one step at a time, please."

"Yes, that's one thing about me. I skip steps."

Our bodies moved closer to each other, and with his arms all around me, we kissed.

"I love you, know that. I want you to always be mine," he said.

I reciprocated the emotion with a deep kiss and my hands buried in his hair. "I do love you, Duren, more than I expected."

Our kiss, our love, our new lives: it was everything to me now. But who would have thought that change could be so 360, so quickly?

Later that night, I opted for a simple dinner in and early bed, as our romancing was exhausting. Helene made dinner, and we both sat there weary. After dinner, I sat on the balcony looking at the city, busy lights, and skyscrapers. Duren read the news in his English leather chair with his plaid robe and Oliver reading glasses.

I had missed the closing bell, so my few hours before bed were work and no play. My playtime in my life was my time with Duren. One of my stocks had gone up 20 percent the first half of the day and down 8 percent the second half, very similar to the pros and cons of my world.

I fell asleep around nine-thirty with my glasses still on, wearing Duren's plaid pajama shirt and argyle socks. I woke up slightly as Duren lifted me up and carried me to bed, placing his goose down cover over me and dimming the lights.

I awoke around two in the morning with Duren sitting next to me.

"Why aren't you in bed?" I asked.

"I couldn't sleep. I have a lot on my mind."

Who thinks at 2:00 a.m.? I thought. *Yes, Duren.* I was so tired. I wanted to cover my head with his covers and pillows.

"Sophie, stay here," he said. "I'll have my assistant help you move your things, sound good?"

"No, I'm not a city person. I need trees and acres of land where I can't see my neighbors."

"That's crazy, don't you think?" he said with a laugh.

Maybe I was the crazy one.

"So will you move in?" he asked.

"I can for a few days a week, but not seven days. That's just insane."

He dimmed the lights, and we lay in bed, lost in each other's bodies. Lips to lips, chest to chest, and heart to heart. We became one, and beside him, I found my place.

34

COMMITMENT OR COMPLEXITY?

The next morning I was awakened by Helene opening the blinds.

"Mademoiselle Sophie, are you all right?" she asked.

Rolling out of the most exquisite bed I'd ever slept on, I looked at the time on my Jaeger. I couldn't believe it was so bloody late. "Where's the boss?" I asked Helene.

She smiled. "Waiting in the breakfast room for you."

I hurriedly washed up and gargled with Tom's. Then I applied L'Occitane. I loved the lotion even more after my trip to Paris. Smiling, I wondered about my new love for all things French.

I waltzed into the beautiful, quaint breakfast room. Murals of the countryside in France covered the walls. There was one famous piece I couldn't remember the name of, a man on a horse chasing a dog. The breakfast table was whitewashed, and the English armchairs were blue and white.

"Good morning," Duren said.

Breakfast was oats with fruit, yogurt, and buttered toast. I sat next to Duren. He looked serious, biting his lip as if someone had committed a crime.

"What's the matter?" I asked.

"Did you sleep well?"

"Like a child. I was tired."

"Yes, I saw." He smiled.

I started eating the dreary oats, which I hated. I poured water into a teacup from the white teapot, only to realize that the water was cold. Holding the teacup up, I noticed something at the bottom.

"My God, there's something in there! Chance, please tell me this is a mistake."

The look in his eyes said it all. "Sophie, I love you more every day. Will you marry me?" He was on his knees on the hardwood floor, like an ad from Anthropologie. "Shall I say the first time was a mistake, and may the second be forever?"

"Chance Duren, you must love me. I know you do. I just never want to let you down."

I teared up a bit. I felt lucky to have found love again after Zur. My thoughts flashed back to the castle when Zur proposed, the most special thing that had ever happened to me. It made me sad to remember how madly in love with Zur I'd been. What was the point of loving someone that in the end chose his world, with his things, over me? What was love, anyway?

As I sat with the ring, I thought, *Oh my God, not again.* Would I ever take a proposal serious after Zur's?

"Let's try being together without the strings tied to choke, as I think marriage is beyond me." Surely, it was a bad thing to say, but I'd rather sound bad than lie to this man. "I'm sorry, Chance."

"What exactly is 'let's try being together?'" he asked.

"A suggestion, as I clearly don't know anything about

marriage, and I don't want to act as if being proposed to is the new Prada handbag."

"You're comparing this to a new Prada handbag?" he shouted.

"Stop being so sensitive," I coldheartedly responded.

"Sensitive? I had a day planned to find homes for us possibly, and then this ... suggestion. I'm going to catch up on work. My driver will take you home."

He left the room in a tizzy ... Wow, whatever.

Was I supposed to say yes to his proposal and find us a home overlooking the ocean somewhere with perfect views of Long Island? And yes to a butler, housekeeper, driver, pool guy, and so on. Maybe yes to the pool guy if he looked like James Bond. But no, I can't say yes to the life and not Duren. It looked like I was never going to get past where I was.

As I changed in his bedroom, and sifted through my Hermès trying to find my phone, I was suddenly stricken by the book on his nightstand: *How to Keep a Woman*. How ridiculous. He couldn't keep me entertained for a few hours, let alone forever.

I was fully aware I had issues. That was why I made an appointment to see the psychologist Frederic Bergius, the next best thing to Botox on Long Island. Therapy was necessary, but expensive. Who charged $250 for forty-five minutes? I mean, he had better have a concierge, a butler, and a manicurist. Fine, I'd just settle for a comfortable chair in velvet.

As I left Duren's place, he was nowhere to be seen, and maybe it was best that way.

Helene opened the door and said, *"Au revoir."*

"See you, Helene."

Instead of using Duren's driver, I chose to take a cab, which was dreadfully horrific. It stunk and was dirty. I felt as if I needed to bathe in sanitizer.

Duren didn't even call, which made me realize something empowering: I wasn't madly in love with him. I didn't want marriage. I wanted unrealistic flings that gave me a temporary emotional high. When the high was over, I needed something else.

Right now I felt a great lack of fulfillment. My emotional troubles had all started up again after Zur came in and left. Maybe I was simply too torn on the inside. Maybe Duren couldn't fill the hole inside me, and I couldn't use his love to replenish the emptiness.

An hour and forty-five minutes later, I arrived at my home, and I had another realization: I needed to move out and into my new bachelorette pad in Gramercy. It had just been sitting there empty for months. Thanks to Rain, I wouldn't need to touch any of my shillings. I had worked hard to earn the large amounts, and I couldn't ever go back to $200,000 a year; that sounded like madness after being a Wall Street broker.

In my room, I made appointments to find another new assistant for me and someone to help at my new home. I needed my own everything. Rain and Robin were gone, and so were my parents. I wondered where they all were and what had happened.

The Gramercy keys that Rain had given me for my birthday were on my desk, but I still had no idea where the apartment was, so the keys were useless for now.

As night came, I felt like a lost mess—alone in a boat, without Pi. All for the best, I supposed; a man like a lion could eat you alive.

I lay on my bed, looking at my coffered ceiling, and wondering why everything was the way it was. I especially needed to sort through the winds of my changing emotions. Almost a year had passed so quickly, and I realized that I was not only bored with Wall Street, but I also didn't need or want anything else. Except maybe the French Riviera?

At 10:45 p.m., Duren called, but I declined his call. Thank God, Apple was smart enough to have a decline feature. Why complicate everything with a bloody chat? I declined Duren because I was now ready to let us go too. I had nothing to lose and had only my own strength to gain.

I was tired out of my wits, and threw the down cover over me and closed the blinds with the remote. I was alone, and the house was quiet. If a pin had dropped, it would have echoed.

But the silence was soon killed by the alarm going off, the blast echoing in my ear. I got out of bed, not knowing who I should call. I went downstairs, way too emotionally exhausted to panic. For crack's sake, if it was burglars, I would kindly send them off with my Bugatti and Hermès—not my Van Cleef, though; kill me in those.

I heard a pounding at the back door and saw a group of guys. Luckily, I had my robe on. I opened the French door and yelled to the morons fixing one of the outdoor alarms, "What the hell are you doing?"

"Sophie Becks, we meet again, and I see not a lot has changed."

Oh good frickings, it was the one and not my only, thank God, Thomas. Well let's measure up, Thomas to Duren. I was getting better at finding them and worse at keeping them.

"Hello, Thomas."

He came over and pulled off his gloves to hold my hands,

kissing them. Today he looked like a hunky, muscled contractor guy that needed a towel to wipe off the rain that had dampened his hair. But when his big hands touched mine, I felt so weird. Nothing—not a buzz or a hair-standing-on-end moment. I did feel the drizzle of the slushy rain, though.

"Sophie, get out of the rain," Thomas said.

"Yes, I need to. Good seeing you," I said, getting back into the warm house.

"Yes, I heard you're getting married soon?" he asked.

"No, some things don't change. I can't seem to commit to anything but work. I have so many issues with this word *commitment*."

He smiled. "Yes, I see your Bentley didn't work out."

"Yes, that and Paris and you."

I was more screwed up emotionally than Hugh Hefner. Though he was surrounded by all those attractive women, he thought two Bunnies were a commitment.

"It's simple," Thomas said. "You're just not ready, and you haven't found the one yet."

Laughing, I shrugged it off. I wasn't settling for anything, though me settling was equivalent to any other woman finding the man of her dreams, who also happened to have a massive bank account.

"Night-night, Thomas."

He nodded and couldn't take his eyes off me. But luckily I could take mine off, like a switch. I went back to bed.

❧

The next days were rightfully insanely busy. I found a house-keeper, Juliana. She had a weird accent, but it worked. Then there was my new assistant, my third, who was very poised and organized, and as hot as the tropics. His hair was better than any woman in a commercial. He could probably teach me a thing or two about being feminine.

I saw Duren, but I barely spoke to him. At conferences he'd sit at the head of his perfect everything and try hard to get my attention. I was happy where I worked, and my poise was like poison. I didn't care about anything but work and making my own Swiss bank account; and that I did better than anything else. Sure I had a list of men to choose from, but their desperation for me made the list very short.

Next Saturday, I was moving out of Long Island to Gramercy. I'd discovered a thing or two about myself, and I was okay with being alone and making more money than people my age ever do. Becoming that broker was killer, and my personality on the phone closing accounts and such was lethal. I was a born salesperson.

About two weeks later, on a Friday at exactly 10:30 a.m. Duren held a conference with the best brokers.

"As you all know," Duren said, "I'm opening another branch office and I'm recruiting new brokers for that office."

In my mind, I was doing numbers and creating a long list of things to do with Jan.

"We are moving to Paris," Duren said, looking at me.

I knew things had been rough between us, but Paris? Was he too desperate for me, or was I stupid to think love would *ever* be enough?

After a half hour of discussions about the new office, all his other top brokers had left, and I was gathering my Christian Lacroix notebook and my Montblanc pen.

"Don't you think you've punished me enough, Sophie?" Duren asked.

Looking at him, I tried to think of something great to say, maybe a big word in a stupid sentence. Anything?

"Punish you?" I said. "I wasn't trying to."

"Well, if I can, let me say that I'd hate it if you chose Paris, because then I couldn't see you every day."

I was lucky to have someone find me and scoop me off my ass, while showing me love. I longed for him, but I was finally successfully practicing celibacy!

"My apartment is very nice. I spend quiet days and long nights alone there," I said. Duren stood there looking lost.

"I'm sorry I never apologized about it all," I shyly admitted.

"I knew you needed time to think and not feel rushed, but whatever I did, I did it because I wanted you by my side."

I'm sure he meant it, but I was no longer buying it. "Thank you for all that you've done."

I walked out of the conference room, hurting as if I'd lost my only true love. I was on the phones from eleven-thirty to seven-thirty. I got hung up on at least thirty times, but the other fifty times, I got real leads. I didn't care if I had to sell my bloody story. Where could I begin ... I was beginning to become a real Wall Street storyteller.

When I had finished working, I noticed Duren had his blinds up. He was on the phone and lost in his computer. It was a good day in terms of volatility. Staring at him in his blue pin-striped suit, black-band Cartier, and black reading glasses, I put my earphones down. I wondered why I ran so far from him. A man like that was a lottery win. Maybe I cared too much for my singleness.

Leaving the office at 8:30 p.m., I was exhausted. Truth was, I was thankful to be alone and to have a city place. I waited for a cab, as Mr. Wheathly was now very busy with Rain. I checked my text messages. Jan was in dire need of some celibacy of her own. Ridiculous! She was married and committing yet another sin. With whom? No idea! I was so terribly tired that I couldn't spare one extra emotion for anything.

A dark-blue, two-door Bentley pulled up to the curb. I really gave it no thought, as the men that worked here had all kinds of toys. Some were precious, some were fake, most were bought, and few stayed long. I had a feeling this Bentley was Duren's new car—you know, trying to kill me with a good impression.

I texted away, and when I next looked up, I realized it was Syed.

"Sophie Becks, do you have a moment to spare?" he asked.

"What is it, Syed?" I replied. He looked pale and overworked.

"Yes?" I asked.

"Zur would like to see you, whenever you're ready."

There was a second Bentley behind Syed. Zur was in the driver's seat. Good to know he could still drive, after driving me out of his life. The windows of Zur's Bentley came down, and so did my walls, one block at a time.

I sighed. It was the sight I had hoped for. Oh, the beautiful complexity of a woman's desire! I didn't know what to say. I had no control over the desire of my heart. It sounded like a page from a lost love story, but men on Wall Street always said that love was bullshit. Yes, right on. Bullish was good, but love wasn't bullish; it was just bull.

35

My Past and the Present

My past had followed me to my present, and I was in awe of how, though I thought I was finally over him, I still really longed for Zur.

"Sophie, how have you been?" asked Zur.

Rome wasn't built in a day, but it burned in one. It was the exact same with all those majestic walls around my heart. As Zur's eyes pierced deep into my soul, the walls fell altogether.

"I'm fine, I guess."

"You guess? You look way fine in your business suit," he replied.

I smiled and gazed into his eyes, thinking of how heavenly he still seemed. I couldn't imagine how a person could have this effect on my senses.

"Well, it was good seeing you. My car is here," I said, walking toward my car, trying hard to shut him out.

"Good seeing you? That's all?" he asked.

I wanted so desperately to smack him for being so sexy and persistent. "What did you think? You'd show up, and I'd run through the willows into your arms?" I sighed.

"No, but maybe a new start for us?"

"A new start? It never works that way. You walked out and then back in, and you think I want to remind myself of where we once were?"

He got out of his navy Bentley, which somehow brought out the green fierceness in his eyes. "I am sorry for the way we met, and I want nothing more than you beside me in my life. It doesn't matter what ties I had before."

I had no way of beginning to figure this out. Even though my heart ached for him, I couldn't drop it all again for the stupid possibility of "us." The love wasn't stupid: the mountain of emotions that I felt with him just a few steps away made everything I once felt so alive. But *us?* Yes, very stupid.

Looking away from him as he held my hand, I couldn't forget the way he felt—his hands, his love, his change from highly complicated to needing only me.

"Please get back in your car and leave," I said. "Please, I beg you." Me begging was similar to Vuitton merging with Prada, a great impossibility.

"No, I'll never leave again. You can tell that to Duren. I'm back now."

It was funny how late he was. In the conference room, I had decided on moving to Paris. And Duren? We weren't an item anymore. A new start, my new beginning, with *moi* alone. So wrong I was ...

"Get in. I'll take you where you need to go," he said, opening the door to his Bentley.

At first, I hesitated, but his dear eyes hypnotized me. I sat in the front seat, wondering what the heck I had stepped into. Wasn't it enough that Duren thought I was the one for him? I couldn't get a hold of where my life was going or what it was turning into, something very theatrical with *complicated* written in gold calligraphy.

"So tell me what's going on with you," Zur said.

Zur was a crazy driver even with his hands on the steering wheel. He made my eyes wander. The scent of him was so deliciously masculine that I was beginning to forget the walls I'd built so high, guarding my heart with my dear life.

"Not married I see?" he said.

"No," I said. "It's been only eight months since we walked our separate ways, too early for me to run off and wed, don't you think?"

"I'm surprised Duren hasn't proposed to you yet."

I was silent. I really didn't want to add anything to his lost friendship with Duren.

"I didn't know you two were once friends. If I did, I wouldn't have gotten involved with you."

"It's not your fault," Zur said.

But I meant it. If I had known that Zur was supposed to simply keep an eye on me, I would have walked past him on the beach with, at most, a wave.

"But what if you fell in love with a person, and no matter what the circumstances, you couldn't forget her?" He slowed down as he glanced my way.

"Complicated," I said.

"Very. I wasn't man enough for anything then, but now I am."

"Lovely."

He drove even slower as I looked over to him. I remembered how we were, lust finding love and becoming one.

"Make a left here," I said. "I live in Gramercy. Well, not for long—I'm moving to Paris."

"Are you?" he asked, stopping the Bentley in the middle of the road ignoring the other crazy New York drivers who loved to honk. Who did that sort of crazy crap?

"Are you trying to kill us both?" I screamed.

He had no words, but his eyes were telling me things I didn't want to rediscover.

"Please, please pull over," I said.

Pulling down a side street on a block that I'd never been down, he parked with a vengeance. Well, it was a very upsetting moment for him for sure: being too late for the one thing he discovered he wanted. I wanted to cry then and there, as he was the only thing I had ever wanted, but now I was afraid to ever go back to where we once were.

"Sophie, I've loved you since I first saw you. I lost you once and now again."

I simply had no words. No matter what, I always loved him— so much that I'd already walked out on Duren even though he was the perfect man.

I looked at a young couple passing us by, hand in hand and madly in love. Simple but true; they were in the full bloom of love. Looking at them, I thought about how I really could have just been Zur's.

"I loved you through all of it, my trip to Paris, my lonely nights, my opening accounts," I said. "I mean, how could I have been so good at it all if I weren't heartbroken?"

He looked into my eyes, and if there was one person I got, it was him. I understood him without words.

"Don't go to Paris," he said. "Stay here with me."

I wished that I could stay, but somehow I couldn't. Too much had happened, and a possible commitment with Duren had made me want to run miles and miles away. How stupid I was to think pleasure and business could rock to any rhythm. I had my high at the Ritz and my low here and now. I knew one thing: I wasn't going to break Duren's heart again; I cared for him too much. For crying out loud, he had always been there for me.

"When did you move here, baby?" Zur asked.

Baby. I hadn't heard that in ages. "Not that long, still trying to move my things in. With my back and forths, I decided that I needed a change."

"Looks like I'm late again," Zur said. "I am going to miss you as I never have anyone else." He looked at me with his hands cradling mine.

I believed him. But love was life putting you to bed, the firewood that burned into flame, and the thing that would test you till you were broken.

I said, "Well, I'm really exhausted, and it's past my bedtime. It was ...well, you know, good seeing you."

He turned to me and did the unthinkable: he kissed me, soft and passionate. His lips were his words. Did I respond? I wanted to run with his lustful masculine scent, plunging myself into my ruthless desire to feel him, body to body, breath to breath, and maybe heart to heart.

But I couldn't. I pulled away and got out of the Bentley. Looking back, I paused, knowing I would never forget him, and wishing that somewhere in me it was different.

"Sophie," he called.

I looked back again from the steps to my apartment.

"Have I lost you?" he asked.

Though I had no tears in my eyes, I had them in my heart.

I was more confused than when I'd started. "I don't know. I really don't know."

I blew him a kiss as the doorman opened the door. Not looking back again, I stepped into the elevator. I was as blank as a canvas in an art studio. Walking into my apartment, I dropped my things on the floor.

I'd just ordered all my fine fabric furniture custom-made from God knew who, so my place was currently unfurnished. I'd also just bought my first oil painting done by a famous English someone. Custom drapery hung like that in my mother's home. My apartment was lavishly beautiful, and the windows were large enough that I could breathe the fresh Manhattan air. I was definitely conflicted about my path in life and my lack of desire to ever marry or become domesticated. But the good news was, I seemed to have many options.

I walked through the hallway filled with artistic photographs of France, including one of the Eiffel Tower. I remembered standing in front of the Eiffel Tower as Duren tried so hard to fill the hole inside of me. Continuing into my very formal sitting room, I was startled. Duren was there, stealing my moment of peace and tranquility.

"What are you doing here?" I asked. I was stunned and appalled, him standing with his hands in his perfectly pressed suit pockets, staring at me as if I'd cheated on him a thousand times. But Duren was composed, so I didn't feel threatened.

"Were you with him?" he asked with jealousy.

I didn't know where to begin. I didn't even want to begin.

"No, I wasn't with him, nor am I with you. You know I can't go on like this." He was in love with me, and I thought love was nothing short of baloney. "I'm leaving to Paris, with your permission, on Sunday."

He was stunned. "My permission, why?"

"Because it's your firm. I work for you, technically, and to not complicate this ... whatever this is ... We had an incredible relationship in Paris."

"Yes, we did, until I proposed and ruined my chance with you. Had I known you think marriage is like Prada bags, I would have just bought you a Prada bag."

I smiled and walked over to him. "It's not that bad. What's bad is my love for Zur. I will love him forever. I don't want to hurt you, but I can't pretend it doesn't exist. It does."

I felt so stupid. Duren was the kind of man you had to be crazy to not be in love with. But I had to be bloody real and truthful, even if it meant being alone in my sixties with no diamond on my left hand.

Clearing his throat, he said, "You have my permission to leave. Jaxwe will be the branch manger as he has more experience than you."

Jaxwe and I were always having it out, but apparently that was the torture I'd have to deal with.

"Really, Jaxwe?" I said. "I opened my first twenty-five accounts in a month. It's insane for you to make Jaxwe manager over me, don't you think?"

He was as silent as a mouse trying to sneak the cheese out of a trap. "Sophie, let's forget that anything ever happened between us." He grabbed his Givenchy jacket and walked to the door. He stopped before leaving to look at me one last time. "You know he must love you to keep coming back to you. I want you happy, Sophie, even if it's not here."

"Chance …"

He stopped me. "Don't. The rest is history between us. FYI, Jaxwe can make decisions based on trends and loyalty, you?"

He left, closing the door behind him. Maybe closing the door for good, as Duren was the kind of man who kept his word; and he certainly didn't consider me loyal. Leaning on the window in the empty formal living room, I watched him get into his limo. I felt saddened by Venus's love spell. Had I screwed my life up because I wanted to be so blunt? Was I wrong? After all, in Paris, Duren was the rebound I needed. He saved my soul from drowning.

I sat on the floor made with faded oak and cherry wood and began crying and crying. I don't know if this was the beginning or the end. It was like a scene from a Broadway play about a wretched woman.

At least I had a Victorian tub to soak in and a teapot of chamomile to sip on while I drowned in my sorrow. I got into the tub, and the warmth and scent of lavender gave me some clarity and calm.

As I sipped on my chamomile and played with the bubbles, I heard my phone ring. Turning the brass swan tap off, I hopped out of the tub, dripping water on my dark wooden floor. I then realized the sound was the door. I put my robe on and answered the door. It was the one and only, Zur.

"It must be luck that nearly every time I see you, you're in a robe and wet." He smiled.

"Come on in," I said, wondering if that was the right thing to do.

He was wearing linen pants and a button-up shirt with a blue blazer. He handed me a rose that I knew was from the table in the foyer of the building.

"For you, baby," he said.

I smiled, smelling it.

"It's real all right," he said. "I know how to pick them."

I laughed and placed the single pink rose in my Versace vase with other flowers that had withered away. I grabbed a towel and dried my hair as I led him to the kitchen for a drink.

"Can I get you anything?" I asked, looking into the almost-empty refrigerator. I had sparkling water and organic milk.

"No, looks empty. Should I have someone bring you some things?"

"So kind of you, but I have an assistant."

"That long-haired girl?" he asked.

"No, he's a very pretty boy," I said with a smile.

"Pretty is precise."

"There's nothing to sit on, but I do have a bed. Oh God, I didn't mean it like that. I'm sorry." I was sorry for saying that. I didn't need any more strings to choke myself with!

"That's great, Soph, but that's a bit fast, even for you," Zur teased.

"You can sit in the living room. I'll bring you chai."

All people from the Middle East could relate to chai; apparently that was all they related to. I put chai and some scones from a boulangerie in Tribeca on a gold-brushed tray and sat on the floor next to Zur. I poured him tea as he stared into my soul. I was nervous and heated on the inside.

"You are so domestic, Soph," he said. "When did this happen?"

I giggled like I was a teenager, running wild and away from all the right things, like my senses at this moment.

"I have always been like this. I just didn't know it," I said, sipping on my tea.

"So this Paris thing, is it for good?"

"I'm not sure. I'm going to have my people find me a place. It's not all fully sorted yet."

"That's lucky. I did business in the Auteuil area, months back."

I felt as if fate had our names wrapped in a coil and sewn together. "Auteuil is so lovely," I said.

"Yes, it is, like you are, baby."

The sexual air between us had found its way in somehow; maybe it had seeped in through a crack in the window. It was magic sitting beside him, magic having him twirl my hair at the ends, and magic looking into his green eyes. His hands were so soft and lips so divine.

He moved closer to me, and I wanted to fight it but couldn't. As the distance closed, our attraction became stronger and more magical. His lips reached me, and his eyes filled me. Kissing me softly and putting an unruly stray hair behind my ear, he touched my face, putting his fingers on my lips.

"I love you, Sophie Becks," he said. "I will love you for the rest of my life."

I exhaled in delight. Zur was finally here, and as complication made its way out, he made his way back in, and into me. On the floor, I lay beside him with my head on his chest. I pulled a blanket over me as moonlight shone through the windows. We were silent, but our love filled the room.

"It's funny how much we fit, even when we were away for so long," he said, running his fingers through my hair.

"A lot happened between Duren and I," I said. "You need to know that."

"Yes, I know. If I wasn't back in your life, he could have been the one here. And madly enough, he would have fit too."

Was he right? No way. I said, "It was a crazy time with you, and the way it ended, I was done, but I'm—"

"Shh, it's fine. I'm here now, and I hope I don't have to leave."

I hugged him, wondering where we went from here.

He took a deep breath and looked into my eyes, almost in tears. "I left for a few reasons," he said. "One, you have a more normal life than I do. I have bodyguards; you have housekeepers."

I smiled, but he couldn't.

"Two, I was sick a few years back. I didn't want to marry you if there was a chance I'd not be around."

That line made my eyes wet and my heart sad. "Not around, where were you going?" My bearings were all screwed up.

"Baby, I was *very* sick. I thought I might die."

He stood up and looked out the French windows with his hands in his pockets.

How did I get here? I was sitting on the floor with tears streaming down my face, not knowing what he would say next. I was almost heartbroken again, and I felt stupid for not trying to find him when he had walked away from me last fall.

"But are you okay now?" I asked.

He knelt to me with tears in his eyes. "I am. And this is where I want to be, here with you. Regardless of what my life gives to me in the future, I don't want to ever not be there for you."

I thought back to my pregnancy scare. If I were pregnant with Duren's child, this conversation could have killed me. I loved Zur more than my own life. Now I was not selling or buying. I was living.

As he held me in his arms, I knew I'd finally found what I had needed. Life wasn't about the millions I made with my eyes closed; it was being beside him with my eyes open and my heart engulfed in the flame of love that killed Romeo and Juliet.

But I was still going to Paris, with no one beside me. As strong as love was, I was equally determined to never give up on my killer independence and ruthless abilities as a stockbroker.

I got off the hardwood floor, and in my bare feet, led him to the bedroom. Closing the door behind me, I dimmed the lights. Zur put his hands on my neck and his lips on mine.

"Baby, I am sorry," he said.

Smiling, I unbuttoned his shirt as I looked deep into his deep-river eyes. I kissed him back as he lifted me onto the pillow-top mattress with lots of throw pillows and sheets with florals everywhere. My robe fell to the floor.

"I love you, Zur," I whispered in his ear, as my iPhone played Andrea Bocelli.

"Oh God, baby, are you really listening to that music?"

"I fell in love with him at some point," I said laughing. I grabbed my phone and turned the music off, as Zur covered me with my down comforter.

The room filled with the scent of nudity and our desire to do nothing but please each other. Our love was not just lustful; it was powerful, seductive, caring, undying.

"Baby, I love you more than anything," he whispered softly to me.

I had again found that thing that women would surrender their walk-in closets, weekday Maseratis, and weekend Bugattis for. What the hell was I thinking and doing? I was moving to France! But the softness of his hands and the warmth of his lips were mine, all mine, for this moment.

I was sure reality would hit eventually ...

36

FOR THE RECORD

Zur and I spent the night in ecstasy, but I was still moving to Paris. Zur had my company for a day, and as much as I'd love his hand in mine and getting lost in each other's eyes, Paris was on my mind.

Early morning on Saturday, I found great happiness packing my things in my Vuitton cases. It was funny how, only yesterday I was still thinking about decorating this place, and now my life was changing so drastically. Looking polished in my tweed Chanel suit, I sipped my morning breakfast tea in my English china as I gazed out the silk-draped window and then to the finest man I'd ever had in my bed. I'd had a few men by now, but there was something about my Arab. Yes, I called him an Arab, but I meant it in a hot and sexy way. May God forgive me a glimpse of bodily confection.

"Sophie, I'm going to miss you," said Zur. He kissed my neck as I threw my Dolce pumps into a suitcase. I was smiling, but was lost nevertheless, looking at his perfect-featured face and facial hair with dark brown locks, so dreadfully sexy. His sexiness was that of a god.

"I'll write you, and certainly we'll speak," I said. Yes, okay, and my mother was really from a convent. Seriously, after we'd had this sexual lust under the covers, in the Victorian tub, and even on the wood floors, I would write him?

"Write me, baby? When does writing make up for anything? I do get to France often…" he trailed off, hoping for me to say that I wanted him to visit me. I didn't.

He stared out the window with his bare back facing me and his manly hands in his linen trousers. My things were packed, and I'd had the most remarkable night any woman could desire. As my dear assistant took my things out of the bedroom, I sat on the edge of the bed in my suit and dangling pearls.

"I wish you'd just wish me well, as I have always had bad timing with love my entire life." And like words form a sentence, my emotions formed tears, ones that I couldn't show.

"Baby, I wish you everything your heart desires, though it seems like I'm not there, where you are," he said, kissing my forehead.

I put my hand upon his and my head upon his chest, hearing every beat of his heart, hoping never to forget the sound and what love once meant. Though I felt so much for him, it wasn't enough to keep me there.

"Your Wheathly is waiting and your assistants, and I'm sure the list goes on and on," Zur said.

As he held me, I teared up silently. I wiped the tear away with a polished finger, hoping he didn't see me.

"I better be going," I said, and kissed his lips, suppressing all my desires to lie there bare, in his arms. "Take care of yourself. Well, have Syed take care of you, and I will see you again if it's meant to be."

We stared at each other with emotions that couldn't be

spelled or written out, a love that would never survive our reality. Our love was a disappearing act.

Picking up my black alligator Hermès from the bed, I looked into his warm lion eyes, knowing that this moment could be it, the moment of final farewell.

"You can lock up and leave the keys with Hunter, downstairs," I said. As I opened the door, I look around one more time. We stared at each other in silence from here to Dubai. "For the record, you were the one that I wanted, Zur."

As I walked out, it felt like a bad scene from the Diana story, except she was royal and I was just stupid to ever believe that love stories were supposed to make you as giddy as a ride on a roller coaster and happy as making your first million.

Mr. Wheathly stood outside, polished like a stolen diamond. It felt bitter without the sweet as I was leaving everything behind for a life I knew nothing about.

"Miss Becks, you look ready for Paris," Mr. Wheathly said.

"Not yet; Wall Street first, then Brookville."

Smiling, I stepped into the Bugatti. What a life I had. I rolled the dark window down and looked up to see Zur staring down at me from the balcony. I waved as the Bugatti made its way to my new path, whatever the hell that was.

My assistant was sitting in the front seat with boxes on top of him and my Vuitton luggage beside him. He was cramped, but that luggage was classic, very shiny with a quietly complex rainbow of colors. One client's commission alone had bought me the collection that was worth thousands.

My flight to Paris would leave the next morning at 9:39 a.m. via Duren's private jet. Now it seemed like pleasure first and then the pain. I was going to miss Zur more than my walk-in closets at my parents', my tub, and my views of the Long Island Sound.

"I forgot Jan! She's going to kill me," I murmured to myself. Never mind Rain or Robin; I was certain they would have their girlfriends to entertain them with mere madness. *First stop, Wall Street*, I said to myself. *It's going to be short and so not sweet.*

I checked my phone. Zur had sent me a picture of us lying next to each other. It was beautiful and a moment to never forget. I wanted him in my future, but only if we were to be paired naturally like wine and cheese. From where I was looking, it wasn't going to ever happen. That was why it was called love's dream: it started from your heart, and then your head had to deal with the realities of what may never be. If we weren't a complement for each other, it simply couldn't be. I was so done with forcing things that weren't au naturel!

Wheathly dropped me off at my office building. Walking along marbled black-and-white floors, I stopped in the corridor to fix my tweed jacket and powder my face. I was drenched in nerve-racking emotions. I had now officially done the sensually wrong with Zur, and that put me back in the running for bitch of the year.

Duren wasn't going to be happy with me no matter what, so going to Paris was officially both a lovely comeback and a drawback.

"Good morning, Duren," I said, popping my head into his office, not surprised to see him here on a Saturday with everything that was happening in the company. What I was surprised to see, was the entire company sitting in the adjoining conference room as I walked by. Did I miss an email?

"Sophie Becks, so kind of you to join us," he said with a forced smile.

"Well, thank you, Duren, but I'm not here to work. I'm cleaning out my desk. Excuse me."

"Please stay for a few minutes, I'm making some important announcements."

"Everyone, Sophie and Jaxwe will be starting our branch office in Paris," Duren said.

There was applause, and Jaxwe and I glared at each other. How the hell would I work closely with him? But then there was the good news: at least we wouldn't sleep with each other; that was written in stone, the only guarantee in my life. We did have a thing for each other, we both hated the other.

"Jaxwe will be the principal, and Becks, yes, um, Becks, well a broker regardless."

Broker regardless? Oh, really? Well, I slept with him regardless of his behavior or his … No, I had nothing on him; he was perfect. But wow, that was a bit cruel and insensitive. Wasn't I a partner now? Or was that now undone, just as our relationship was undone? I couldn't really expect more from him, though. He looked distant and hurt. It was funny how I felt staring into his eyes, as if I had completely messed up but was okay with that.

At my desk, my old assistant Tanner came over to say good-bye. "Thank you for the opportunity that you gave me," he said.

He turned back around and walked back to his desk quicker than Duren could call in a trade. As I watched him walk away, I smiled and went back to clearing out my desk. I put my letter opener into the dreadful brown box and then a photograph of me in front of the stock exchange with Ker.

"God, I must call Jan. She's going to kill me if I leave without a good-bye," I said to myself as Duren touched my arm. I jumped. "You freaked me out, Duren."

He smiled, and then his face went back to that serious look of his. "I came to speak with you. I'm going to miss you, and I do still want to be with you, somehow," he said.

Well, such was life … You couldn't have it all. I was so against love, but then Zur stole my heart and a part of my soul. Duren was smoking hot, but too late. He was the epitome of perfection with a splash of humanity and a soul that shone through his way-too-successful demeanor.

I put my expensive stationary, a leafy plant, and my fountain pens into the box. I looked at Duren as I listened to the background music by the Neighborhood: "It's too cold for you here and now, so let me hold …" What a song.

Duren's face turned pale. He looked heartbroken. I didn't know how I ever could have loved him. My heart sung and beat completely for Zur. My body ached for him. But it was over between me and every man I had ever dated. I was leaving the country and hopefully this charade behind me. Though the most perfect man professed his love for me, I couldn't reciprocate in that way.

Duren bit his lip as he watched me empty my desk. Everyone pretended to be busy but stared in our direction. Was I being heartless? Yes, I was, and maybe, just maybe, I would regret this someday.

"Tell me, Sophie, are you back with him?" Duren asked.

My face was serious as I didn't want to add more fire to the flame. "Not really. I don't know where we will end up. Duren, please don't do this."

"In my office, please. Everyone is staring at us."

This was the moment I had been dreading. As we walked to his office, he shouted, "It's Saturday, everyone go home." Duren closed the door behind us. At one time I thought I'd stay here on Wall Street forever with Duren. After all, he had been the only person who believed in me.

Closing the automatic blinds, Duren looked at me and said, "Now, tell me that you're with him." Silence had barged into us, like a little stone cracking your windshield, with a shatter.

"With him? Meaning Zur?" I asked angrily.

"Heck, are there more men in your life I'm not aware of?"

Yes, I was the Wall Street harlot. "Wow, is that how you insult me, Duren? I'm not one of your little puppets. Don't you ever ask me that question again." I pointed my finger in his face. Yes, I just yelled at my boss.

"You don't get it, do you?" he shouted, walking to the far end of the glass room.

"No, I don't get anything about men. Isn't that obvious?"

"You made me fall in love with you, and now you're just walking out on me? How does that happen to me?"

It was pure anguish from his heart to mine. I stood there, calm on the outside and like a raging lion on the inside. "What do you want, Duren? A bloody prize for that? I'm in love with someone else, and that's your fault."

"You still work for my company," he screamed. "How am I supposed to see you and talk to you and not be with you?"

He grabbed a photo from his desk and threw it across the room. Pieces of glass shattered everywhere. I wasn't scared, though my heart was beating as fast as a horse galloping in the wilderness. He took all his accomplishments and qualifications in gold-leaf frames off the wall, and slammed them one by one onto the cherry floor. Bits of glass shattered all around me.

He stopped himself as his assistant opened the door to see the mess.

The assistant hesitated, and then asked, "Sir, are you okay? Shall I clean this up?"

"No, stay out," he said.

Yes, bitch, you stay out while I get my ass hammered.

"If I had known what your visit today would turn into, I would have been okay with just a call. You shouldn't have come," he said.

The look in his eyes led me to tears. How could words fix this, or how could emotions justify all this assholery?

"I'm sorry you feel that I did this to you," I said. "I know now that this is it."

His face, the face of perfection, was now a face of great destruction, and I wasn't going to be a psychiatrist. I looked into my Hermès and took out my Christian Lacroix notebook worth millions. It was fancy, but it was so pricey because it was my client book, which meant my entire career. I placed it on his desk, and said, "Thank you for the opportunity. I resign."

Duren cringed. This was my payoff for everything, though he didn't need my clients. He made his first billion, probably, by my age. I left his office. The firm looked at me silently, pretending they hadn't just lived through that moment, the one in which my life crumbled because my principles were more important than silk sheets in Paris with Chanel pearls.

In embarrassment, I held my brown box and got in the elevator. Jaxwe walked in behind me. In the elevator with my greatest enemy, fantastic. I hated him, but now he was first in line.

"What now?" Jaxwe asked.

I stared at the box in my arms, thinking of my black book.

God, that was hard. And bloody stupid. Stupid, stupid! I could kick myself. Not with these shoes, though.

I walked outside on Wall Street, right where I would have died to be over a year ago. Now I stood by my Bugatti Veyron with my brown box. I looked into Jaxwe's dark-green eyes for a moment and then stuck my hand out to him.

"You won, and I wish you well in Paris," I said.

"What? You aren't going to Paris?" He was stunned.

"Not with this firm, I just resigned." I got into the Bugatti and rolled the window down. "From Wall Street to France sounds good, though." I smiled at him, though I was heartbroken, and then Wheathly drove away.

I remembered the first time I stepped onto Wall Street—the men in their custom suits with Pateks glistening on their wrists, as the nobodies polished their Italian-leather shoes. And let's never forget the money clip with the Montblanc to sign your first million away.

And just like that, I had messed my whole life up, but I was still better than most men. You see, they usually messed it up for greed and women. I messed it up for *love*. Yes, love, love, love. The funny part was I didn't know who I really loved: Zur or Duren. Now that was being lost too.

Either way, I was going to Paris. And yes, at the age of twenty-five, I'd made my first $4.5 million dollars. Not bad for a bloody woman.

37

A ROYAL BETRAYAL

Wall Street was everything they portray it to be in the movies, and truth be told, even when you retire from it, you still reek of wealth and sickening ambition.

After leaving the office, I went to have breakfast with my mother, the First Lady of fancy. To her, my net worth was worth more than my bloody ass in love and happy. Jeez!

"Darling, it's been a wonder seeing you around lately. You look so very grown up," she said.

Hello, I wasn't even twenty-six and ready to have a proper midlife crisis. I said, "Yes, I feel very old already, old and clueless about love and such."

I kissed her on both cheeks in the very refined European way. Home was quiet, yet busy with preparations for Rain's engagement party, with caterers and flower arrangements arriving one table at a time, with maids here and there. For my last night here, it was far from serene. Peonies and pink roses were the new Maseratis and Bentleys, at least for tonight.

My parents were obviously happy that someone was settling down with a somewhat-normal person. My mother, paying the highest regard to sophistication, had hired Hilda, her new chef;

Rosa, her new housekeeper; and Benny, the pool guy who was not to my taste, eww. Like hello, pool guys in Long Island were supposed to look like Calvin Klein models in boxers, not this guy who was drenched in ugliness: tall, disproportioned, with arms like Shrek and dreadful hair.

My father was absent, like my desire to plead peace with Duren; though this festival of beautiful sophistication made me reminisce about Paris. Sure, it had been a brief run of romance, but still I didn't know what exactly I had felt for him, especially after he ruined me publicly. My new pretty boy assistant had disappeared after this morning's visit to the office, so I assumed he must have quit, as well.

"Darling, can you check in on security?" my mother asked. "The last thing I need is for a dinner like this to have poor security."

My mother was persistent and very to the point. Honestly, how long would this marriage last? For God's sake, this was Rain, a Wall Street player; I gave it two years.

"I'll go make sure that your security is on point," I said, laughing to myself. My mom had a way of turning any emotion into some business proposition. No wonder love and business seemed like biscotti and tea to me.

Walking up the driveway, I couldn't be surprised that my parents were highly particular about this dinner. Whatever happened to opting for a castle or a haunted palace for an engagement party? Let's call a spade a spade-with marriages, first came the honeymoon with champagne and caviar and then the lack of fulfillment and restlessness, with of course the whining husband. The driveway was busier than a plastic surgeon's office on a bloody Monday morning.

"Please drive slower," I pleaded with the driver from Main Street Florist, who was the Prada of flowers on Long Island.

As I watched the caterers from La Bonne Boulangerie take out trays of lavish petite desserts, I remembered how my mom would have these posh tea parties when I was growing up. It looked like not a lot had changed, except she was also thrilled that she was getting a somewhat-decent new daughter-in-law. Decent, I must speak now or forever never have peace. Rain's fiancée was stunning, but most women were with extensions and makeup; without makeup and early in the morning, every woman would scare you.

My father's yellow Panamera was parked at the end of the driveway near the gate. He was talking on his cell phone in a high-pitched voice. I couldn't take my eyes off of him and his pin-striped suit and dark-brown hair starting to turn gray. Business was the blood in his veins. I never could understand why my overachiever parents ever questioned my need to be so successful.

"Sophie, darling, it's been forever," he said.

"Hi, Father, good to see you."

I stood poised, remembering my obligation to success and my family's name. Parting with my client book was worse than Zur leaving me in Duren's lap with a pink diamond. Forget love; well bravo, I'd have to take shots in my mother's fine-china teacups. Yes, I must be a lady, but hell, I may as well be a bloody drunk one.

"Don't you look sophisticated at your age," I said to my dad. I smiled as he pulled me close for a friendly father-daughter embrace, which was as rare as my Bugatti, which Robin had stolen somehow.

"So how is Wall Street and my portfolio?" he asked.

His portfolio was now with my idiotic ex-lover/ex-boss.

Gosh, where should I run and hide? "Uh, we can discuss that later. Today we celebrate the hypocrisy of love," I sighed. "What is it?" my father asked. "I know when something isn't right. Is it my portfolio?"

How dare he bother me about his quarter million dollars in a portfolio that I was not busy looking at? How could I say, "Daddy, I'm sorry. I was too caught up screwing my boss in Paris." Oops!

"Father, don't over think things," I said. "Duren is handling your account. Better the boss than the daughter." I tried to brush things off, but this was a Wall Street defense lawyer I was talking to.

"Soph, dear, please don't screw around with my money. It's nothing to you Wall Street salespeople, but to us lawyers, it's a new watch."

My dad was smiling. He shouldn't have trusted me with his bloody money, as I clearly was too busy finding love. As I walked away, I noticed him staring at me. Damn, I'd gone from great success to great unhappiness in no time.

Trying to get the security detail's attention was equivalent to talking to a concrete statue. "Hello, I'm speaking to you. No, don't shh me!" I yelled.

"Sorry, miss, I'm in the middle of a call, regarding nothing that concerns you," the ass of a gentleman said, turning away from me, and cooing at his "babe."

"Listen, get off the bloody phone, and do your job," I responded. Let's just say that I was a little annoyed. When I was opening accounts, I always focused. So why couldn't this idiot focus on his job? No time for play when you were working, unless of course you were a preschool teacher or a mother.

"Miss, who do you think you are?"

"You idiot, I'm Sophie Becks. Page your boss right away." I was pissed that this guy was busy making love on the phone while on my parents' checkbook. And I was pissed about Duren and his asshole attitude.

"Miss Becks, I'm so, so—"

"You are so gone, okay? This is juvenile. Where's your boss?"

"Sophie," a male voice said behind me.

I looked around to see the one and only, Thomas.

"Hello, Thomas, we meet again."

He gave me a half smile and shook my hand.

"What kind of employees do you have representing your company?" I asked.

"What was he doing that aggravated you so much?" he said in an annoying sort of condescending manner.

"Oh, that's the best you can do?" I asked.

He looked around with flushed cheeks. I mean, this was number three. If he had played his cards right, he would have been my number one. But no, he had to suck at romancing a woman like myself. Forget the moonlight and red wine with serenades from a violinist in a vineyard. He was dreadful and sad. Why? I didn't know. I pondered on the stupid idea that it was my fault. Again, nothing was my fault. I was perfect, never arrogant, never self-centered or too demanding. Gosh, I was humble, always. Right, and I was really related to a saint.

"What is it with you and your need for over-the-top perfection?" Thomas asked. "Everything always has to be over this line of your stupid high standard or nothing. He was doing his job, okay? It was you misunderstanding his duties, not him."

I was over-the-top annoyed and good gracious, did I really

go out with him? He was worse than … Yes, worse than Zur and his pathetic desire to hurt me and then pull me back in with eyes that told me stories of romance and sex.

"The hell with you, Thomas. You really know how to make a woman feel good—not."

He tossed his gloves to the side of a brittle bush and said, "I don't have to make you feel good. It's your Bentley guy's job, not mine—remember that."

He stormed away from me with the greatest indignant huff anyone could have displayed, and I stood there alone, feeling like such a screw-up. My gosh, now I could one-tenth comprehend why Wall Street men were always high and in denial. I went back inside and took a bath.

Around six-thirty in the evening, I was cold and shivering from my long, exhausting bath. My mind must have run a million marathons, written a thousand chapters, and confused my heart, all at once. I was torn between my instant attraction and passionate love for Zur, and my desire to forever stand devoted and true at Duren's side. He was the only man that could have brought me to my highest peak in life, and that had to count for more than I was ever ready to face.

My pink silk sheath dress lay on my bed. I slipped my robe off and stepped into the custom silhouette. I straightened my hair in a Japanese fashion, silky with a gloss that spelled supermodel. I opted to wear pink diamond earrings and a Van Cleef all-around necklace I'd given to myself. Then, there it was, the most exquisite ring I'd ever seen, the pink diamond from Zur I'd never returned. God alone knew what he had done to fetch me such a gem. It was so dazzling, that as I placed in on my finger, I thought of it as my Elizabeth Taylor collection, bigger than the moon and glitzier than a runway model in diamonds.

I put it on my ring finger, wondering how it would feel to be ordinary, with only one man to love. It sounded whorish and indecent, but I was lucky to have two incredible, screwed-up men love me so darn much. I put the ring back in the box and pretended that it didn't exist.

The only thing I knew for sure was that my Dior pumps with the green alligator bows on the heel were a pristine match for my outfit. No kidding, I looked exceptionally stunning, with glistening locks and pink lips and eyelashes you'd hunt down Mac for. No, it wasn't Mac; it was from a beautician in Paris.

"Sophie, darling, what's the matter? You're so late for your brother's shindig in all its rapturous elegance," said a voice next to me.

I turned around to see Jan, Long Island's most notoriously dressed, in diamonds no man could ponder affording.

"Jan, it's the best feeling to have you here," I said, kissing both her cheeks and looking at her in pearls with rare yellow diamonds and silk like a Parisian goddess.

She sat beside me on my pink velvet settee, literally looking at every part of me. "You look like a million and one dollars," she said. "How is your sex life?"

Yup, leave it to Jan to heap you up and shovel you out in five seconds.

"It's rather, well, complicated, of course."

She held my right hand and smiled. "No ring?"

"*Non*, I am officially single and leaving for Paris tomorrow."

"Talk about living it up! You are too much, but I've missed you."

"I've missed you too, and I'll miss you even more now."
Hugging her tightly, I realized that she was the only person I
felt really close to. "Let's go down to this formal dinner to meet
the newly engaged."

Speaking to Jan, I realized that there was more to life than
marrying a Wall Street tycoon with golden dust from here to
Mars.

"So are you taking the boss and boyfriend along?" Jan sipped
on sparkling water from a crystal glass.

I didn't know how to really answer that. "Hmm, let's just say
that when one leads the way, the others follow."

Smiling, I walked into a room filled with soon to be in-laws.
It was beautiful and frightening—beautiful because the decor
looked like a garden palace in the south of France and frightening because all the women were adorned in custom gowns and
the men looked very good-looking in their suits and spit-shined
shoes. The pink peonies and pink roses were the hue of the night.
There were crystal settings with roses mixed in with greens and
peonies, pink linens, with gold settings. I hoped that when I
was to really marry someone, my mother would do this for me.

I saw Rain's fiancée. I totally forgot her name. *Was it Anna?*
Well, whatever her name was, she wore a lilac Lanvin gown
with a pink silk belt tied in the back. Her hair was dark-blondish
with highlights, and her teeth looked as if someone had painted
them with Wite-Out. Yes, she was perfect, a living, breathing
plastic Barbie doll.

"Sophie, so glad you could make it," said Barbie Anna.

Make it? Darling, I live here! Well, at times.

Rain walked over before I could speak. I guess he knew I
was feeling coldhearted tonight.

"Hey, brother of mine, how are you?" I asked.

"I'm good, as you can see. You've met Anna."

"Yes, I have." I grabbed a glass of wine from the waiter passing by in his godforsaken black suit with the ugliest bow tie on the market. I gulped the wine as if it was the last drink on earth, smiled, and moved away.

I turned to Jan, and said, "I don't know where to begin. I've got issues, and I can't think clearly."

Thomas was in my line of vision now, wearing a light-blue suit with a pink shirt and hair that looked better than any woman's there.

"You and I both," Jan said, grabbing another glass of vino and sipping it as if she was dying of thirst.

"What's your issue?" I asked.

She paused. Her eyes were locked in the opposite direction.

Just then, a text from Zur buzzed in, pleading with me to have dinner with him tonight before I left.

"No, sorry," I texted.

Sure he made me scream things that weren't even in Madonna's *Erotica*, but that was then, and also yesterday. I couldn't ruin myself any further until I knew where I stood. At least with myself …

"I'd like to make a toast," said my mom, quite poised. "My darling Rain, you look just as handsome as your father did forty years ago, and I'm so proud of all of your accomplishments."

I couldn't bear to hear it all, and trust me, there was a lot to be said. I imagined Rain in diapers reading the beta screen, with a cigar in his mouth. No, not a lit cigar. Jeez, he'd have only half a brain by now. And if there was one thing that was outstanding about him, it was his brain and high level of success. But love, too, was now beginning to define itself in his life.

As I sipped red wine and tried very hard to fight the urge to text Zur, Rain started his own speech, the one he'd perhaps dreamt of when he made his first million and moved into that penthouse overlooking all his colleagues. His eyes were distant, as if he was lost in the moment. His speech didn't match the desire in his eyes, which were lost somewhere behind me. I turned and saw Jan, with her blue eyes sinking into the poor boy's soul. Uh oh!

I sipped a little more on the red wine. Oh, it was addictive! But there was Jan staring at Rain as if she hadn't eaten in months. Unsure of how I felt about that, I turned away and looked at everyone else. Rain's speech was not poignant; it was empty and vague, and his eyes were locked on Jan's like a secret locked away in a mansion somewhere blissfully exclusive. I couldn't be thinking clearly.

"Love is such a mockery," Jan said. "Let's go get some fresh air before I die of hearing all that bullcrap."

I felt as if I was having hot flashes. I could use the fresh air.

"What's wrong with you tonight?" I asked Jan.

She didn't respond with words, but her eyes tried so hard to tell me. I tried to follow her outside, but my dad grabbed my hand and pulled me to the front of our mansion-sized room. Me standing in front of 125 people that were more polished than my great-grandmother's silver spoons.

Oh God, not tonight, please! I screamed in my head.

"Sophie, will you give a speech, dear?" asked my stupid dad. Yes, stupid. He was so smart, but so dumb at the same time. How was that even possible?

I'd had two glasses of wine in twenty minutes, and my eyes gazed longingly out the back and to the ocean, which was practically in the backyard. I briefly contemplated making a run for it.

"Th-thank you, Father. Um, well, good evening, everyone. I'm Sophie, Rain's sister, and to be honest, I'm so conflicted about Rain wanting to marry. I mean, have you seen the divorce rates in this country?" Yes, I really said that. WTF. "Not to drown Rain in his own milk, but I personally don't believe in marriage, simply because it just doesn't last."

I looked at the lawyers from my dad's firm, the women from my mom's million-dollar divorce settlement club, and the new in-laws, who were Jehovah's Witnesses. Oh hell. The only people smiling now were the men. But this wasn't stand-up comedy; this was me being tipsy enough to speak my truth, which was always very blunt and sarcastic.

"And on a better note…" my dad whispered to me, as if he was about to kill me right after I finished speaking.

"But now I see that Rain has found someone wonderful to share his life with," I continued. "So I'm not going to be too judgmental." Everyone laughed. My dad handed me a crystal champagne glass, and I lifted it up, and said, "Here's to hoping it lasts at least a year!"

I smiled, and the crowd thought I was joking … But really, this wasn't going to last long. We toasted the Wall Street way: sarcastic, smooth, and cruel. Yes, I didn't believe in happy ever after. Not anymore.

My dad smiled, held my hand politely, and walked me out of the room.

"What was that?" he yelled at me.

If he knew the mess my life was in, he'd have more pity for me.

"Well, you know how I feel about love, Father. Why put me up there to say something that I don't even believe in?"

Was I really having this conversation with him? I shouldn't drink so much wine. It either gave me courage, or numbed my ass, so I could say any bloody thing and feel good and neutral about it.

"Only a few months ago, you were in love and getting engaged no matter what the rest of us said, and now you're trying to ruin Rain's engagement," my dad said.

"I'm not trying to ruin this dinner. I have a lot going on. Please don't upset me, okay."

Then Robin walked into the room, and oh my, he wasn't alone. A very pregnant Hannah was beside him, looking ready to pop.

"Hannah!" I ran to her, wrapping my arms around her.

"Miss Sophie, I've missed you."

She was nine months' pregnant and glowing like a firefly, except way bigger, in a good way.

"Dad, Hannah and I are having a baby. I'm sorry I never mentioned it," Robin said nonchalantly. He was now officially the biggest loser in my family according to my parents, how lovely.

I bet my dad was wishing he hadn't wasted money on Yale and had instead sent Robin on a far, far away vacation, as if to say, "Don't come back, you're such a screw-up." Gosh, there were a few of those in this room. After all, in my family, net worth equaled, "Darling, we are so proud of you." Of course it was bullcrap. But fear not, bullcrap would get you anywhere in a private jet, with maids and such. Hello, I lived it.

"And on a better note," I whispered to my father, who was more uptight than a thong in Barbie's derriere.

"Robin, I'm so happy for you. Hannah was always more like family the whole time she worked here," I said as loud as I can.

"Sophie, this isn't a reunion and is surely horrible timing for such," my father responded. I grabbed Hannah's hand. My dear father looked how he probably did when he got caught with his busty, brainless assistant. He turned to Robin and said in a bitter, cold tone, "Dear God, Robin, what were you thinking? I just..."

"Yes, Father, and here you were acting as if *I* screwed up this engagement dinner," I said, smiling.

"Sophie, Robin, we shall discuss this tomorrow," he said dismissively.

"I can't. I'm leaving for Paris in the a.m." I patted my dad on the shoulder. It was perfect ... And for the first time, I walked away from him.

"All okay, Soph?" Jan asked, when I returned to her side.

"Yes, my brother impregnated our housekeeper, and now he is doing the right thing. So good that my brothers are finally owning up to their dastardly deeds."

By 11 p.m., I was just about tired of the formality, and the truth was, that everyone was either stoned or gossiping. Jan got a call and told me she had to take it. She walked outside in a rush, as if her husband had just found out that she'd been cheating on his perfectly filled Swiss bank account with the pool guy, gardener, and personal mechanic for Ker's eight-car collection. That was why marriage wasn't like a Prada handbag. At least you got what you paid for at Prada; when you got married, there was just no telling what you were going to get.

I was alone in a room with Long Island's most wealthy, who

were all enormously full of themselves. I was bored, and sipping on sparkling water, when this tall, dark male with deep brown eyes walked my way, looking at me. Hello, I *had* to look. He was right in front of me.

"Hi Sophie, I'm Channing."

Channing, darn, he was charming. And I liked charming. Charming Channing! *Ha!*

"Hello, nice to meet you," I said. "You work for my father?"

"Yes, we're colleagues."

"Colleagues? No way you are colleagues with my dad. You're too young and good looking."

His smile was authentic and gave him immaculate dimples.

"That's funny," he said.

I sipped more of my water. I needed to think clearly and be ladylike, and not be a drunk.

"Want to catch some fresh ocean air on the balcony?" he asked.

I hesitated. "Only if it's free and friendly." I thought about what this conversation was going to do to me; at least I mentioned friendly. Besides, he worked for my dad.

"So you're a Wall Street broker, huh?" he asked.

"Was. I'm moving to Paris tomorrow."

I sipped on more and more water. As we stood on the balcony looking at the view I grew up with, the winter cold brushed my face, and I felt change coming. I decided to go with it. My life was never going to be what it was.

"I heard you were engaged," he said, "but I don't see a ring." He looked at me as the moon shone, and the white frost on the windows, along with everything outside, froze.

"I could have been, but the truth is—"

He finished my sentence, saying like a sensitive interrogator, "You don't believe in love, right?"

He was over six feet tall and super gorgeous, but I had been through the gallery of successful, gorgeous men in suits with ties that were only appropriate for tying my wrists together at playtime. He was like a fish trying to get into a pond with a waiting list and lots of requirements, like a country club in the Hamptons. After all, I was a bloody Becks who had a list that wasn't easy to fill.

"Love, marriage, and all that stuff, I need a break from it," I said.

"Well, whoever broke your heart must surely regret it, as I think you are quite captivating," Channing said.

Thomas walked up, and said, "Sounds like you're trying hard to impress Sophie, but I'll help you with a little FYI."

"Oh God, are you serious, Thomas? Tell us, shall you?" I said, annoyed.

"Sophie can't love another; she is too in love with herself," Thomas said bluntly.

"Hmm, a woman with her own agenda, I like it," said Channing.

"I'm not in the mood for rookies," I said. "So, gentlemen, have a good night." Seeing them both stare at me was creepy, but I had a private jet to catch in the a.m. "Au revoir, boys, you look good together."

Channing pulled a business card out of his alligator wallet and handed it to me.

"Oh, how precious, another interested man, Sophie," Thomas said.

"I have enough of those. Truth is, Channing, I may never call," I said.

WALL STREET TO FRANCE

"Well, at least I know I tried," said Channing, as he held my hand and kissed it.

I felt a tinge of the emotions that I thought I'd already moved past. Thomas stared at me with such anguish; it was cute but deadly.

"Thank you, Channing."

Like a woman who couldn't care one tiny bit, I walked away, searching for Jan, to no avail. Somehow, in a room filled with people, I felt empty, alone, and sad. It wasn't that I was leaving for France. I felt as if I'd lost parts of myself, pieces of my heart.

My phone rang with an unlisted number. Unlisted always meant trouble, temptation, and accusation. "Jesus save me," I whispered.

People filled the entire house, and Thomas's wine had made its way into everyone's hands. However, my parents were nowhere to be seen. And I supposed that Jan, too, had left without a good-night kiss, not that I needed one. She was my best friend and companion in climbing a ladder to all my great successes. I wouldn't have become a broker if she hadn't invited me to broker parties, in mansions with boys driving Maseratis in polished John Lobbs, all so polished and crisp, and spoken to her wonderful Ker for me.

The phone continued to ring. Well, I supposed it was time I grew up and answered the phone already.

"Hello?" No answer. "Hello?"

Gracious, it was an accidental dial.. I could hear sounds of pleasure and groaning over the line. Holy gumballs, that was Jan's voice!

"Faster, darling, I love when you do that to me," Jan could be heard saying.

I held the phone away from my ear, as clearly this was no funny business with a man she'd been married to for thirty years. It was safe to say she was getting a fast, bumpy ride on someone's you know. I tried to hang up, but since she had called me, it wouldn't disconnect us.

I put the phone back to my ear and screamed, trying to get Jan to hang up. I pressed the pound sign to bring attention to my hearing her get pounded. God forbid she dialed her husband! I pressed the pound sign for at least three minutes—nothing. She was in a lustful, erotic place that I didn't need to be witness to. But I couldn't seem to hang up.

"Rain, darling, I want you in me forever."

"For—? What—? *Who?*" I screamed. No, not tonight, please. I couldn't believe my ears. I threw my phone deep into my Hermes bag, as I had been through enough affairs, indecency, and betrayal for a lifetime.

Even if I had tried, I could not just sleep this one out. I looked for Robin, and tried to find Barbie Anna, as Barbie without her Ken was nothing less than a disaster. For minutes, I paced the room in panic. I dug out my phone from my purse, and saw that we had finally been disconnected. I dialed Jan's phone, and she didn't pick up, but I found my way over to Robin.

"Have you seen, Rain?" I asked him. "Where's his Barbie doll lady?"

"What's wrong with you?"

"This is serious. Where is he?" I said.

"I think he went for a drive."

I'd never run to the six-car garage that fast before, but I needed to see if they were there. I looked in to see the Panamera, nothing. The Mercedes, nothing. The Lincoln. My mother's Jag, nope, nothing. The old Hyundai, what was this thing doing in here? But no, nothing. I slowly walked behind the Bugatti. It was apparent, that my brother was a chiseler for another man's woman, all while Jan, bemoaned for her life. And that was a lot! Jan was in the front seat of my car, riding Rain like a horse in the derby, except this wasn't the derby, it was more like the *Titanic*, where they rocked each other's worlds only to sink the ship forever. Let's not forget it was Rain's engagement night, and my mother's grand effort to reform a cheating son. This was lovely, with a hint of tragic.

FYI, don't get engaged to anyone if your guy can't get a hold of himself. I knocked on the window urgently. Once they both saw me, I left. My presence should be enough. I wasn't a therapist, and I couldn't fix this. Thankfully, I was leaving in the morning, getting far away from this madness.

38

ALL THAT GLISTENS ISN'T GOLD

Night was dark, and apparently so was Rain. My mom was sitting in the kitchen nook in her robe, with a cup of tea in hand. Being the First Lady, she was ordering everyone around—well, her staff, which consisted of a group of house attendants, a butler, and her driver. Let's be real, she was good at that.

I sat next to her, without words. Hell, I felt like *crap* was the very unpleasant word that fit my situation: the loss of my million-dollar career and my Christian Lacroix book that was worth more than twenty alligator Kelly Birkins. Do the math. And yes, I forgot one very important detail—the loss of my sanity.

"Dear, what's the matter? Here, let me fetch you tea. Sugar and milk?" she asked so politely. I didn't know if I could ever be as refined or happy as she was, or pretended to be. But maybe if I were to marry into money I would be happy having that much help around the house to yell at and belittle at times. Wait, I didn't really know what her happy was.

She brewed the tea to hot perfection, and as I sipped on it,

I clearly looked disturbed, as my mother said to me, "Whatever it is, you can share it, dear."

That really meant, "Whatever it is, don't mess it up, Sophie."

"Tomorrow is bittersweet, Mother. I've just ruined so many things in my life that I need this time to breathe, think, feel, you know?"

"What exactly did you do?" she asked, sipping her tea and looking at me. She placed her tea down, and I still didn't respond. I was already in deep. "Well, it can't be that bad," she said. "You already have a bright, terribly successful career."

About that ... I didn't. But I couldn't let her know yet. So much for work and romance too.

"So where in Paris will you be?" she asked.

I paused, remembering Duren and his true feelings for me. I wondered if it was supposed to be him and me, or Zur and me. Though I loved Zur like crazy, I couldn't deny that when he left, Duren filled a big part of me. To say the least, I was terribly conflicted.

The door opened, and in came the star of the night, Rain. My mom's face lit up as he walked into the room. I couldn't bare to look at the champion of a double life.

"Good evening, folks," he said.

"Folks, are you serious?" I commented.

"Sophie, it's my night, and you're not going to ruin it, so keep your opinions to yourself!"

"Sure, as you are such a gentleman. Wait until your Barbie doll finds out who you really are."

"Children, please get a grip and show some of the refinement I raised you to have. Now."

Right, let me look into my panties and find my refinement.

I laughed at my mom placing her English trellis hand-painted teacup and saucer in the hands of her maid.

"Good night," she said. "We will see you in the morning, Sophie? Before you leave, we shall have breakfast?"

"I'm flying out at ten," I said.

"Great, I'll have time to attend to the plants in the arboretum."

"Right, you do that, Mother," I said sarcastically.

I looked at Rain in great disgust. Not only did he cheat on the night of his engagement party, but he did it with my best friend! As I stopped myself from pushing him off his chair in the hopes of him breaking a leg, I had even crazier things floating through my thoughts.

"Why did you do it?" I asked him.

He poured some red wine into a champagne glass and drank it like most miserable men would. As we stared at each other, I couldn't understand his look of discontent.

"Sophie, you're old enough to know that love is fucking bull-shit. The only time it makes any sense is if money is involved."

I didn't expect him to be so cold and blunt about it, but it was what it was.

"What the hell are you saying? You're getting married to What's Her Name!" I screamed as Rosa, the housekeeper, stared. She was probably wondering where my mother picked us up. She had obviously picked me up from Neiman, and Rain was surely related to Hef. We were refined only at formal dinners and garden parties; outside of that, we were an outrage to the country club—arrogant, loud, and maybe a little anti-commitment, more than a little. Blame it on my parents. They did a great job in hiring nannies and drivers to drive us to school meetings and the best private schools on Long Island. Yes, I felt proud to say that money did get you everywhere!

"I'll tell you, but don't say a word, promise?" Rain asked.

"Promise, moron? What is it?"

"Our father, the businessman, promised me a percentage of his law firm if I were to marry within the year, and as my bonus, I'll get all the money out of trust from our dear grandfather. I'll be richer than your lover boss."

I suddenly felt high on tea leaves. Was that even possible?

Rain smiled at me as he had yet another glass of red. "And in case you're wondering, Jan is *amazing.*"

Yes, she was amazing; even her "holy grail" apparently had a net worth.

"I'm sure she was, is, but I am very disappointed in you and her, and in this family."

Not really, but it sounded liked the right thing to say. For Pete's sake, Rain was worse than Jordan Belfort. At least Belfort wrote a book and set new goals for men.

"I can't wait to pack and leave in the morning in search of my new life and career," I said. Surely, I meant it.

"And what the hell are you going to Paris for? Didn't you quit?"

"What? How did you know?"

"Let's just cheers," he said, handing me a teacup filled with wine from that imbecile Thomas's winery. "Here's to secrets, and not just secrets, but to the ones that we die with."

OMG, he had not changed. He was the same ass he was when he first started on Wall Street.

"Good night, Rain, and good luck with your very stupid, secret, and pathetic life."

He was a lost soul in a screwed-up, immoral family system. But I wasn't that far behind, as I was his sister.

"But you've forgotten the most important part, dear," Rain murmured in a slightly sarcastic tone, just like my mother.

"What is that?"

"I'm worth more than all your ex-boyfriends, bosses, friends' husbands … etcetera."

Yes, I should have been worth even more than that soon enough, but let's not be so harsh on ourselves. I had memories of things and places that most people didn't get a front-row ticket to—love and lust in the front seats of Bentleys and the Ritz's very own Coco Chanel Suite. Darling, that was priceless.

Stepping through the dark corridors, I paused near my father's office. Brilliant art that could have been in the Louvre hung along the walls. I couldn't bare to walk past it. Some clear realizations were slowing crawling in. Though my family had more concern over their net worth than human morals, they always stuck it out, even through the bull.

Robin was probably too normal for all of us. He was so down to earth that if he ever went to Manhattan and took the subways, he'd stop to talk to the homeless man with the cup in hand and the stupid note of something dramatically eye catching, like "My wife left me with nothing. She even took the dog. I need money for beer!" Yes, it was brutally honest. But Rain and I couldn't bear to be like Robin.

"Sophie, you're still up?" my father asked.

"Yes, heading to bed now, I suppose."

"Well, before bed let's have some alone time, so I can better understand where you're headed."

My father was very to the point. In fact, he did archery in

his office; that's how precise he really was. I sat with extreme caution as I looked around at everything on his walls. My father was decked out in his suit, hands in his pockets, with black, square Versace glasses. His seriousness had seriously kicked in without an invite.

"So, tomorrow you're going to Paris?" he asked.

I nodded my head, wondering why I'd had to pause near his office, and get dragged in for this "chat."

"And your firm, is it in Paris as well, or will it be just you and your boss?"

"Me and my boss? What's that supposed to mean?"

He took up a crystal bottle of golden brandy and poured a glass with his eyes glued to me.

"Father, it's all business," I said. Yup, business ... I was sticking to my story. Yup, and the Ritz was business too.

"I wasn't born yesterday. First it was the Arabian playboy, now the Wall Street tycoon."

I felt like an ant about to get eaten by an anteater in a bad children's story. "Okay, so what are you getting at?"

"It's very simple: you go to France and find your path. Forget the part of you that wants to live free and wild with the Arab."

"'Live free and wild with the Arab,' how colorful of you!" I rolled my eyes at him.

"No, you will not make a mockery of all my hard work here."

My father didn't know what I was made of, but he was about to find out. "What do you call a man who was paid, or shall I say bribed, to marry a woman for a mere advancement in life and access to a trust fund? And what do you call the man who gave the bribe?"

You should have seen the look in his eyes. It was as if I'd just said, "Screw you, Father," but with such poise and respect.

He smirked and then gulped that killer of a stinker drink down. "Sounds like you're the female version of the Becks men. Regardless, I can't let what happened with Thomas ever repeat itself."

"That's fair. I should have never been curious about where wines were made."

"Please, it was more than where wine comes from. Your curiosity for men is simply inappropriate and must stop."

Well gold shillings! Did he have to insult me like I was a teenager offering my wares up to any man I came across. I couldn't possibly answer that eloquently.

"If you're proposing that I marry some okay business graduate from Yale that comes from a country-club sort of family, perhaps I should desire that. But at the present moment, I will not marry for advancement or for love."

"Well, what can I do to speed the process up?" asked my father.

"I don't imagine such an opportunity will ever present itself."

He smiled, and now I knew why my mother had everything money could buy. She was married to a man who only cared about proper timing and appropriate business manners with ample net worth, and such. This family was so emotionally taxing.

"Fortunately for me, I work among men who would eat your prestigious law firm alive. FYI, I made over four million dollars this year. I don't need money from a trust or a percentage of anything," I said. "And for the record, I won't be settling down anytime soon. My love life is a disaster." I stood up from his comfortable, yet expensive seating with a sigh.

"My jet will take you to Provence tomorrow," my father said. "Be ready. You'll meet your cousin there. You need to know where you belong in life."

"Thank you for the opportunity to ruin my life, Father, but I'm going to Paris."

"It's not ruining your life; it's called finding yourself. You are my only daughter. Before you ruin your life any further, go to Provence, and from there, you'll know where you belong. And good night," my father said, as he closed the door behind me.

Now it was as clear as the big blue sky. I felt as if I was in an insane asylum of expectations. Should I have thanked him? Or left screaming? What did he expect from me? It was true, though; things were messy, and my life was overly complex. So that night it was no longer Paris, but Provence!

39

PROVENCE

When morning came, my new assistant, Heather, appeared at my door, dressed to New York perfection, brilliant. My father had made some calls to help me clean up my life, and had hired me an assistant and made my travel arrangements. Yes, I was now worse off than Robin. Forget the millions I'd made; what mattered was the apparent mockery I was making of my last name. Whatever.

My limo had arrived, and I was ready; all dressed in my pink collared shirt tucked into my skinny trousers with a Hermès belt and big black Bvlgari shades. With a scarf tied around my neck and holding my pink Hermès purse, I looked dashing.

My luggage was at the door, and I realized that I wasn't that important to anyone. My leaving for France was designed for me to find myself. Hell, couldn't I do that at Barneys? Getting into the limo, I glanced at the front door. There was no one there, and surely, I felt it. So much for getting this far, overachieving, and bending the rules so I could be happy.

"Well *au revoir* to you, Long Island," I whispered, and then turned to Mr. Wheathly. "Here we are, packed and ready for my new life."

"You do look ready, and if I may say, the only thing missing is a smile?"

"A Beck doesn't really smile much, but one can try."

I felt empty and alone, with just Mr. Wheathly and Heather by my side. Where was my therapist? Perhaps my father forgot one.

After a dreadful forty-five minutes, we arrived at MacArthur Airport. I would be taking my father's very own Boeing, and to top it off, I had my very own flight attendant. I felt like a celebrity, except I hadn't acted in any movies, discovered a country, or saved anybody.

As I stepped onto the white iron steps leading to the plane, I heard the screeching of a cat-gone-mad driver. A navy Bentley, followed by another car, pulled up so close to the jet you'd think the bastard was drunk. Zur, it was Zur. I wanted to bawl as if I were on the *Titanic*, but luckily I kept my composure.

"Baby, please don't leave," a very conflicted and torn-up Zur begged. Still, he was hot, and his attire for a man emotionally worn out was incomparable. Two men with big muscles and suits came out of the car behind him, and by the looks of it, they weren't his people. "What the hell, can I just have a moment with her?" he asked them.

One of the men, who looked a bit like Bruce Lee, glanced at me and then nodded and said, "Thirty seconds."

"I must go," I said. "I hope you find everything in life that you need, especially a woman who's not a threat to your last name, whoever you are."

Silence fell over us like a pair of pumps that were no longer in fashion. His eyes had the look of a sick, tired dog, and I had an ache in my heart that money couldn't remedy.

"My family, is that it—my name? Yes, that's it. You're leaving me because of that?"

Zur took a step closer to the plane, causing Bruce Lee to grab his arm and say, "You need to leave now."

Then, like clockwork, Syed stepped out of the car and held Zur back from knocking out Bruce Lee.

"You don't know what I'm going to do to you, you son of a bitch," Zur said, pushing away the airport security guard, who was here to provide security for people with names like mine.

It was the worst sight ever. I knew that no matter where I went, no matter how desolate, he'd find me. That was the way it was, but fortunately, I had some sense left. I looked at him in all his remorse and pain for who he was, and I knew it was my out.

"I love you, Sophie, and I don't care what I have to do to find you. I will," he wailed.

Tears rolled down from my eyes as I looked away, walked onto the jet, and shut everyone out. The flight attendant brought me a bottle of sparkling water with lemon, a pillow, and a book. Ironically it was *The Wolf of Wall Street*. Well, if Belfort caused so much grief and survived, then I'd come out of this in Chanel and Louboutins. My mind played the scene with Zur over and over. I didn't know how to let it go, but I knew I had to.

Hours later, we arrived in France. It was certainly some of the most beautiful countryside I'd ever seen, the kind you found in magazines. I'd seen many pictures of my father's upbringing in Provence. His father was a Frenchman with exquisite taste for ladies in the land of love and excess. That was supposedly the story of how my great-grandpa immigrated to America. My mother came from a wealthy family whose last name resonated like *Kennedy*. And years later, I was born—the first granddaughter to add some conflict to the Becks legacy. It wasn't so bad being born into a family that was emotionally challenged, if you also came from a legacy. See, no matter how screwed up you were, if you came from a family whose last name would get you anything, darling, it was always your glory days, and my glory days were getting into all sorts of trouble with men.

It was evening when we landed, and I was picked up by a Frenchman who looked as if he was running away from a James Bond movie in a black Mercedes S550. I felt as if I'd walked into the plotline of a movie where I'd been kidnapped by a sexy man who longed to ravage me. Except the truth was that no one longed for me, especially after they saw my true colors.

"My God, I'm so jet-lagged. How far away are we?" I asked the driver. Though he was as hot as the Bahamas in June, he was poised and very businesslike. I was impressed by his efficiency, and his ability to stay focused and not bore you with his French. Don't misunderstand me, but I'm sure anyone who spoke fluent French didn't like to speak English.

"We will be at the chateau in twenty minutes, give or take a few minutes, Mademoiselle Becks," he replied.

His English was right on. I was so happy that I wouldn't have to translate what he was saying. I knew that I needed a French tutor, pronto, as I was going to get ripped off if I didn't brush up on my French. I smiled at my assistant, Heather. She had been respectfully quiet during the majority of our trip.

The roads in France were not like Long Island's rows and rows of roadways. Here in the country, the roads were long and winding, flanked by the fresh blossoms of the olive trees that were loved greatly by L'Occitane, which was an important factor in my skin's beauty. Thank God the skincare angels had dropped me in Provence. I was hoping my next best skin-care secret would have something to do with rejuvenation.

I smiled at the driver, as he blushed and tried to focus on the roads. I was bored and afraid, and felt like Mary from *The Secret Garden*, except that Mrs. Medlock was replaced by a handsome young man with manners. Though I was off to a new, unknown place somewhere in the French countryside, I tried to console myself that I was going to be okay. The scene of Zur at the airport played in my mind like a dying flower in fall.

So love again had failed me. What was the point of a prince in a story if he can't save anyone, including himself? Exactly.

In my life, my standards and the code I lived by took first place, regardless of how it felt or how much I'd loved and failed. I didn't want to be a married woman, having flings and dalliances with every man who suited my fancy, like Jan. That was the reason I didn't accept Duren's proposal. I cared for him, but I was in love with Zur, a love that no pink diamond could resolve.

"Mademoiselle Becks, *nous etes ici*," the driver announced. "We are here."

We were in a village with harbors and fields of lavender, in a town fit for *Town & Country*. The beauty met my heartache head on. We drove down into gated fields of blossoms, leading to a chateau with more rooms than a castle.

"Do you have the correct address?" I asked, sure I was in the wrong place.

"Yes, Mademoiselle Becks."

As he stopped in front of Chateau Becks, I was lost in the ambience of old country charm. Though the place was far from old, it felt as such. I could only hope the cousin I'd never known was warm and kind, but I knew to not get my hopes too high. I'd always thought the best of the worst.

I knocked with an old rusted iron lion's mouth knocker on a grand door, and a woman in a maid's outfit answered. "*Bonsoir!* Mademoiselle Sophie, I presume," she said in a French accent. She kissed me on both cheeks. "*Je m'appelle Eloise.*"

I tipped the French driver as he brought in my faithful friend, Louis Vuitton. My assistant stood beside me, smiling as if she'd won the lottery.

"This is going to be the best trip/job I have ever had! Thank you, Miss Becks."

From another room, I heard a lady screaming in French. I couldn't tell if she was happy or sad or mad. Looking around, I saw paintings of people and animals, and to the right of the corridor, the man on the horse.

"My God, that man is everywhere."

"A man?" asked Heather.

It was exactly like my father's except ten times bigger, with a light on the very top to illuminate it.

"*Je suis désolée*," a very attractive young lady, the one who had been screaming, said. "You must be *the* Sophie Becks?" She stared at me as if my name was someone's bag I'd stolen.

"Oui, Mademoiselle, it is I."

She kissed me on both cheeks. "I'm Chloe Becks."

Yes, my father's brother's daughter. I'd never met her, which was yet another family tradition; we didn't know much of our extended family.

Chloe said, "I've heard so much about you from my mother, who, sadly, isn't going to be joining us, as she's away all the time."

I smiled and wondered how far the Ritz was. Jeez, how did I get here?

"It's fine, apparently the mothers in our families are not what they used to be," I said, trying to be funny, but to no avail. I didn't think she had a funny bone in her body. "This is my assistant, Heather Morris," I introduced them politely.

"*Enchante.* Well, help yourselves to any room. We have many on the east side with pool views, and on the west there's the bar for those days you need some companionship. I've got a class to get to, but if you need something, call Eloise. She's here nearly 24-7. So, so good to meet a family member. I'll see you soon," she said, grasping my hand and quickly shrugging it off, as if I was a germ. Her mother was probably a germ; that was probably why Chloe had turned out so like a Becks.

Again, how far was the Ritz? If this was punishment for playing with too many hearts at once, I deserved it. Dear Chloe left, and I wanted to sit in a tub and cry my heart out.

"Okay, I take that back," Heather said. "This could be a very, very, very big learning experience."

Walking up twenty-nine steps (yes, I counted) with my Hermès and a bottle of sparkling water, I was exhausted—exhausted from the plane ride, the car drive, and now Chloe.

I picked a suite grand enough for a princess—and her assistant, that is. The opulence tickled my sadness. The room had a twenty-foot ceiling with a dull, rusty chandelier. The draperies matched the blue striped wallpaper. The bed comforters were white and tucked over sheets of yellow and blue. There was a blue Versace vase with the Versace face done in gold. It was quite a design, looking as if it was inspired by Halloween at Oheka.

The suite had two rooms, and mine overlooked fields of something. I hoped it wasn't grapes. I associated grapes with Thomas, and right now men were like carbs. I couldn't eat any, at all. Just feed me Pule cheese with Château Le Pin wine. I needed fancy and right now. I lay down on layers of French down comforters, as my assistant hung up my gowns and such.

"Should I have brought a tutu?" she asked. "No, really, I think I might need one." She laughed.

Eloise entered the suite, and asked in English, "Shall I get you anything?"

"Oui, cheese and wine, merci." It looked like I was born to be taken care of. Eloise made certain I was taken care of, as did Heather, my new and promising assistant.

The chateau was built like a set of a foreign movie, with its fields of olive trees and lavender. But mostly, I was happy to have this time to reflect on my path in life and let bygones be in the damn ditches.

"Mademoiselle Sophie, here's your tray," Eloise said.

"Kindly place it on the bistro table next to the doors, thank you." I smiled, as I tossed the covers from me and placed my feet on the hand-painted ceramic flooring.

"Very soon we would have you join us for dinner," Eloise said sternly, but with a smile. "You'll see your dear cousin, Pierre."

"I look forward to meeting him. What business is he in?" I politely asked.

"He's the finest, youngest real-estate tycoon in Provence."

"Isn't that lovely, another Becks with brains and ambition."

"Well, if I may say so, I have never yet met a stupid or understated Becks," Eloise said with a smile.

"Then you haven't met my brothers," I said with a laugh,

though I meant it. The stupid part was that they were like a vacuous ad from Ralph Lauren. My brothers' IQs were high, but their common sense was severely lacking.

I sat at the bistro table outside on the graceful balcony. This place was something my mother would have loved. The view into the gardens behind the chateau was something just shy of extraordinary.

My life was certainly more than ordinary; therefore, my lack of compassion for my love life was a challenge. I was in love within the threads of my soul, but outwardly, I was busy trying hard to deny it. What was the right answer for me? Yes, precisely, I was troubled about that. Then I thought about Duren, who wasn't at all a fling. In all honesty, sparks did fly there.

Then there was Jan and her great betrayal. Maybe it wasn't intentional; maybe they couldn't help themselves. I knew that love and attraction never planned its entrance. Like lightning, you only knew that it was there when you were struck by it.

My father's departure speech didn't put me in any great rush to find myself either. I was devastated by the list, and the good name that my soul mate—well, the man I was to marry—was supposed to come equipped with. Dear God, what if he had one and not the other?

I would be a single, hopefully still attractive woman, making at least a few millions. I'd have my driver take me around to my penthouse near Central Park, home to my little poodles and terrier. I'd sip tea while reading novels about life as we know it. I'd wear my great-grandmother's strand of pearls, the Monet of jewelry.

My assistant and I sat on the old iron Chelsea chairs, feeling the chilly evening wind that shook the tree leaves. An aromatic scent was in the air.

"So what exactly is your plan for your career now?" my assistant asked.

"Hmm, well first, I plan to be a sommelier and a cheese connoisseur. Then I'll spend my days visiting the many places in Provence. Please find me a French tutor as I'll be lost with only *bonjour, ça va bien*, and *bonne chance*. I'll need better conversation skills you know."

She wrote it all down in a pad with one of my Montblancs. She seemed nice. She was well put together and wasn't a loud, freshly graduated student from Cornell that needed an experienced someone from Wall Street. In return, she got someone that needed a lot of help to turn her life around. That was me, and I certainly loved helping people out.

Her nails were painted pink, and she wore a sheer Peter Pan shirt with ruffles, pink skinny jeans, and white pumps. As she helped herself to a glass of champagne, she asked, "I was thinking ... Is it possible that I could have some time to travel to Marseille? I studied there when I was in high school, and—"

"Of course, you may. Why do you act like this is a boot camp?"

She smiled. "No, I think you're amazing. I'm ever so thankful your father knows my dad."

I nodded, but I didn't want to hear another word about my father. I was disappointed about the way I'd left. You'd think that he could have learned empathy at Yale or Harvard. For crying out loud, I was his only daughter. And in regard to marriage and finding a husband, they'd better not invite me to a polo match, or I would inevitably make Becks into the next *Sopranos*.

"Anyway, you can ask Eloise who might be available to take

you to Marseille. I'm going to go for a walk around," I said, placing my phone down on the glass table that had a French-washed, dark wood bottom with arched legs. The French baked baguettes, churned butter, and made the best Bordeaux in all of the world, but there was nothing like the French wash. I walked down the oak stairs to the elaborate formal library.

The halls were like those of an ancient castle and were lined with photographs of Chloe and her mommy dearest, in what seemed to be better times. There was also a boy, dressed as if all ready for *GQ*. And then there was, who I guessed to be, my uncle on one end and my aunt on the other, so rough and cold looking. It seemed like they had a Becks marriage, like my parents—married to the name, not each other. Further down the back of the chateau were many other rooms, but frankly, I'd already seen enough of wealth and had dealt with the agony of having so much.

I exited the back of the old chateau, which was beautiful, but dreadfully full of excess odds and ends, like an old movie I watched growing up. The only thing missing was a witch in the tower. Well, I was sure that Chloe was a witch, at least at certain times.

I went down a few steps and pushed open an old rusty door that led to fields of trees in the distance. Though it was now dark out, soft lights lit up the gardens as if it were the setting of a Merchant and Ivory film. The trees were in bloom with white flowers, so beautiful and still. The aroma was strong but lovely, and I walked toward the trees along a neatly planted path, as the grass jutted out in spots. It was spring, and the air felt light and carefree as I took in the scent of Provence.

The only time I'd visited a winery before was with Thomas,

and the vines here reminded me of him, the way they lined up in such an order it would be impossible for them to ever be unruly. I walked a great distance into the olive trees. It seemed that the great beauty of the grounds of an estate never seems to match the hearts of those living on it.

Among the essence of the trees and all, I felt deeply, truly hurt. I didn't think it was any one thing; it was everything—my love for Duren, my misplaced emotions for Zur, Jan and my brother, and my father. It was enough to make me spend my days soaked in milk bubbles, sipping on Le Pin or Bordeaux, making my way to the twelve-step recovery program.

I exhaled as I made my way to the front of the chateau, and I saw a well-dressed man. He was on the phone, yelling at someone and smoking a thin, long, sophisticated something. I stood there amazed at how he was screaming at someone who must have seriously screwed up. Did it remind me of anyone? Yes, myself, when I was a stockbroker on Wall Street, hungry to rip someone apart like a wolf, and for what? Money didn't drive me anymore; it was about success that couldn't be matched by anyone, especially men. Yes, I admit I was more than a bit sexist.

"Oh bloody God, you scared me. You must be …?" the man asked.

"I'm Sophie. I take it you're the well-dressed boy in the photographs in the halls on the west side of the chateau."

"Hmm, I'm impressed. I'm Pierre. I believe we're cousins."

"Indeed we are, and our inclination to shoot everything that upsets us must be a genetic thing," indicating the phone in his hand.

He was very polished, wearing suspenders with orange

skinny pants, the original gold-buttoned blazer, and a blue-and-white pin-striped shirt that was as preppy as you could get.

He said, "Well, it looks like you have found the most notorious of all the Becks, and I'd be happy to show you around."

He made me smile and laugh, and if I were a mockery of men, then he was a forgery of all the men in this family.

It was almost 9:00 p.m. when Pierre and I got back to my suite with its dull country colors. If I were to jump off the balcony, I'd land on olive trees at least.

"So where will you be working?" Pierre asked.

"I haven't figured that out yet. Why?"

He paused, maybe hesitated, and then his response changed my destiny.

"Well, why don't you jump on board with me and be my partner in crime, at Becks and Spence?"

"I'm not a Spence, and you know it." I smiled. I was flattered, but the truth was, I was still in the gutter emotionally.

"So …" He paced with a hand in his pocket.

"What?" I asked.

"You seem to be thinking way too much."

I didn't respond, as my assistant came in with my phone in her hands.

"Is everything okay?" I asked.

"You have a big problem. Zur has called you a million times," she said.

And like magic, the phone started ringing again. I said, "So this is a million and one? I need to clear my head before I speak to anyone on that end."

"I have an agenda," Pierre said. "I see you're clearly a true workaholic."

"I was, but now I'm on vacation, and I have to clear my head. My situation is just ridiculous," I held up my phone as Exhibit A.

"Yes, yes, I see your boyfriend can't get enough of you, and you're gorgeous, just stunning." He was French but sounded like a Brit.

"Okay, what exactly do you need, dear boy?" I asked, laughing.

"I need a partner for three months, and then you can leave. I just can't replace my ex-partner with someone stupid."

"That's fine. I'll help out, but what exactly am I helping you with?"

"Miseries and murderous things. Get your game face on. I'll see you downstairs in the study in thirty minutes."

He left, and I looked at my phone to see yet another call from Zur. As much as my heart ached for him, I wasn't giving in. So I texted in a very polite manner, "Zur, please don't text or call me anymore. I need time, and when I come back, we can talk."

You'd think he'd say, "Anything for you, Sophie." But nope, my dear Zur was greatly annoyed and frustrated with me. "Sophie, f- off," he texted. Wow, talk about drama, and I wasn't even Julia Roberts. He was sweet when he was sweet, and when he was mad, he was crazy as hell.

"How should I respond to this?" I asked my assistant, showing her the text.

She grabbed the phone and smiled. "You should be polite, even though men can be so rude and mean."

Never did I ever listen to good advice, and indeed, I disregarded Heather's as well. Zur's and my texts went back and forth all night, but after that, we didn't speak for weeks. Rumor was he'd had it out with my father. So sorry I missed that! What a turn-off love could sometimes be.

Duren and I didn't speak either. It was as if the moon and the stars were no longer aligned. For that matter, my father had left me many voice messages about my choices as a woman not measuring up to the Becks family's pie-in-the-sky standards … blah, blah.

My dear friendship with Jan was now null and void, and as sad as it was, I learned to let it go, as well. Even the best of friends grew apart sometimes.

§

The next few months were quite busy. I did partner with Pierre. He had a hundred employees, and most were Americans.

He cursed in French and, when not angry, spoke the best English. But truly, he was my twin. We had an equally strong work ethic that couldn't be defined. His company was one of the most successful businesses in Provence, and *oui*, I was working on my French. Thank heavens.

Since I'd arrived at the chateau, I'd become very acquainted with Eloise. In fact, every day at seven in the evening I did yoga and meditated with her, while I drank some Le Pin out of a water bottle on the side. That explained why I'd laugh when she chanted OM, as she became one with herself. Though she was no replacement for Hannah, I took a liking to her. She wasn't a replacement for Jan either, but even if she had nothing in this world, she was good to me.

What more could I say? Life was beginning to look better,

and hats off to the men of my past. I, Sophie Becks, was finally
moving on. And by the looks of it, so were they.

In the evenings, I read in the library. The polo boys wanted
nothing to do with me, as Pierre had made it clear I was a Becks,
and my sense of self-worth had finally kicked in. Yes, yes, yes.
So France, in reality, was exactly what I needed.

I hoped to finally read *Fifty Shades of Grey*, as I needed at
least a few shades of gray in my life. For Provence's sake, my life
was one hundred shades of bloody blue—thanks to Pierre, who
had me wrapped up in his business, as if I needed more money.
Funny thing about money was when you lived liked this, it wasn't
a problem. I was drama-free, and my stress was under control.
I was feeling at peace, possibly because I spent a lot of time in
the chateau alone. I'd feng shui-ed myself.

I'd come to a conclusion: working long, cruel hours screaming at clients about the stock market was no longer my thing. I
needed to be free and enjoy life a little, so I was going to travel to
the Riviera, Nice, and Rome in search of new things, and maybe
men. No man should ever take you to a place like the Riviera.
Why? Well, everyone who was anyone not only banked there,
but also flew there to bask in the sunlight.

I was soon to go away on business with Pierre. Chloe had
many issues, and turned out to be an alcoholic, very sad. I
couldn't help her; I needed help myself, as I sipped wine as if it
were tea, even drinking it from my Aunt Vivian's teacups from
Barcelona.

My assistant left over a month ago. Her boyfriend had
threatened to leave her, and apparently she didn't have a back-
bone of any sorts.

God, what next?

Something in me wanted a man by my side, but the memories of both Zur and Duren were like the dregs of a lake turned upside down. I loved them both, and one was right for me while the other was sexy for me. Zur made me feel things I didn't know I could, and say words I didn't know I could pronounce. The good news was that his family was like oil and I was sparkling water, so we really didn't mix.

Money could buy you many material things, but it couldn't buy you the right man. And the right man was like the *Mona Lisa*, which was meant to be seen and left in the Louvre where it belonged. Love flies you up to cloud nine and then drops you at the peak of your high. And, darling, let's hope you have that emergency button you press to deploy a big old parachute to save your sad ass. If you make it, you'll need a few years, a few bottles of Le Pin or Bordeaux, a good therapist (a damn good-looking one sure helps), a million dollars for your excessive shopping, Prada bags and Louboutin shoes to help you catch the next Wall Street millionaire, and yes, a jar of La Prairie for those under-eye circles from all the crying and whining you'll be doing with your housekeeper! Yes, housekeepers were good; pool boys were bad! And when you see the hot, self-involved delivery guy, close the drapery and let him leave the package at the door, as a rebound with him is shameful. My rebound was something to write home about. He was a Wall Street tycoon with a heart, an impossible combination.

And now, I was *très bien*. As they say in this part of France, "*La vie est belle.*"

Printed in the United States
By Bookmasters